MATTHEW LYNN

The Watchmen

ARROW

First published in the United Kingdom in 1999 by
Arrow Books

1 3 5 7 9 10 8 6 4 2

Copyright © Matthew Lynn 1999

The right of Matthew Lynn to be identified as the author of this work
has been asserted by him in accordance with the Copyright, Designs
and Patents Act, 1988

First published in the United Kingdom in 1998 by William Heinemann

Arrow Books Limited
Random House UK Limited
20 Vauxhall Bridge Road, London, SW1V 2SA

Random House Australia (Pty) Limited
20 Alfred Street, Milsons Point,
Sydney, New South Wales 2061, Australia

Random House New Zealand Limited
18 Poland Road, Glenfield
Auckland 10, New Zealand

Random House South Africa (Pty) Limited
Endulini, 5a Jubilee Road, Parktown, 2193, South Africa

Random House UK Limited Reg. No. 954009

A CIP catalogue record for this book
is available from the British Library

Papers used by Random House UK Limited are natural, recyclable
products made from wood grown in sustainable forests. The
manufacturing processes conform to the environmental regulations of
the country of origin.

Typeset in Plantin by SX Composing DTP, Rayleigh, Essex
Printed and bound in Norway by AiT Trondheim

ISBN 0 7493 2328 0

The Watchmen

Matthew Lynn is an experienced business journalist. He was educated at Balliol College, Oxford, and works at the *Sunday Times*. He is the author of two best-selling business books, *The Billion-Dollar Battle* and *Birds of Prey*. His first novel, *Insecurity*, was published in 1997. He lives in west London.

Also by Matthew Lynn

Insecurity

To Angharad

Prologue

Sir Ian Strang looked up into the clear dark night, admiring the soft glow of the stars high above him. There were no clouds in the sky, and the pale half-light of the moon combined with the shimmering starlight to cast a warm reflection on the sea and on the grass on which he stood. For the first time in days he felt secure. Safe. And at peace.

They will never find me here, he decided.

The wind was blowing from the west, rippling around his shoulders, and whipping up the waves that were breaking at the foot of the cliff. White foam crashed up on to the rocks, creating a mist of spray. For a few moments Strang just looked into the dark waters below, allowing his mind to ruminate briefly on the endless mystery of the ocean. The Atlantic coast of the west of Ireland had always been his most treasured stretch of water. And right now there was nowhere he would rather be.

Turning up the collar of his long, black coat around his neck, he walked briskly along the cliff. His mind was in turmoil, and he needed the air and the sound of the waves to clear his thoughts. Nothing had turned out as he expected. And, for the first time in a career lasting almost half a century, he was unsure what to do next.

Strang glanced down once more, over the edge of the cliff and into the crashing waves below. He knew, now, what they were capable of, and why he had to prevent them amassing any more power. He knew also that he had been right to flee.

Strang turned and, with his back to the wind blowing strongly now from the west, walked across the field and back towards the cottage he had rented for a few days. A whiff of smoke was drifting from the chimney, lying still for just a few seconds before being caught up in the wind and disappearing into the night sky. This, at least, would give him a few days' peace in which to plan his retaliation. Everything had been organised using another name and there should be no way he could be traced to this location; the flights, the property, the rental car, all of it had been booked using an alias. The details had all been taken care of. Here he should be safe. For a few days at least.

Sir Ian pushed the heavy wooden door and stepped back inside the cottage. His daughter was sitting by the open log fire, her shoes by her side, a glass of brandy already prepared for him. He took the glass and sipped gently, glad to feel the warmth of the alcohol on his throat. Taking his pipe from the table, he reached for a match and began the slow but comforting ritual of igniting the tobacco.

'Have you made any decisions?' she asked.

'There's nothing I can do on the board,' Strang replied. 'The votes are tied up. But tomorrow I'll start contacting some of the biggest holders of the stock. Some of them have shares in Cable Media because of me and I think they will be on my side. If I call in sufficient chips I should have enough votes to force an emergency general meeting.'

'To ask for what, exactly?' she inquired.

Strang took a deep puff of his pipe, watching the smoke curl upwards to the low beams of the ceiling. 'There is only one thing I can ask for,' he replied at length. 'To vote him off the board.'

Kim Chung slipped the gear on the hired Ford into fifth and allowed himself a few minutes of relaxation as the car sped through the quiet, empty roads. There was no traffic at this time of the night and the houses he passed were already dark. The wind was bending the trees, but the night was clear and a half-moon bathed the open countryside in its pale reflection. Into the tape deck Chung had inserted a Mozart violin and piano sonata, and the slow beauty of the music soothed his nerves as he drew closer and closer to his destination.

He turned off the main road just after eleven and drove up the single lane twisting along the rugged coast-line. To one side he could see the open, dark ocean, its surface broken by white foam; to the other, rolling pastures, interrupted only by low stone walls, and flocks of sheep and cattle resting beneath trees. Chung could make out the cottage in the far distance and noted that lights were still shining from the ground floor. It was isolated, standing by itself close to the cliffs, with no other houses in sight. Perfect, he thought to himself.

A mile short of the cottage, he pulled the car to the side of the lane. He killed the engine and waited for two minutes, enjoying the dying chords of the movement on the tape deck. He needed to clear his mind before contemplating the task ahead. From the boot of the car he took out the jack and the largest spanner. Pulling up the collar of his coat and wrapping a patterned silk scarf around his neck, he started walking the mile up the lane towards the cottage.

'Good evening, Sir Ian,' said Chung, after Strang had opened the door.

The man in front of Strang was just under six foot; large for an oriental, with broad shoulders and thick legs. He appeared to be in his mid-thirties, with close-set eyes and cropped black hair. Japanese, perhaps, thought Strang, or Korean or Northern Chinese. It was hard to tell. His accent was clipped, close to being English without quite getting there; but the manner was precise and educated, with the tone of a man who was used to being in command. 'What is your business?' asked Sir Ian.

The force of the blow felled him to the ground. The car jack, held tightly beneath a black leather glove, crashed into Strang's stomach with aching power: twenty pounds of metal propelled by two hundred pounds of tensed muscle. The old man clutched his ribs. His eyes were closed and he was coughing violently. Chung pushed open the door, allowing a brisk draught of wind to rustle through the room. He knelt over Strang, grabbing his arm, twisting it behind his back, rolling the man over, and pushing his face into the hard wooden floorboards. Chung pulled a roll of copper wire from his pocket. Forcing Strang's hands together, he began coiling the wire round his wrists, tightening the strands, so that it started to cut into his flesh. Within seconds he was incapable of any movement.

The woman stood motionless, her back to the fire, her eyes rooted to the scene unfolding before her. A silence had fallen on the room; she could not be sure if Strang was alive or dead, conscious or unconscious. She moved to the side of the fire and slipped her fingers round the brass poker standing next to the grate. The metal felt cold on her skin and for a moment she was convinced she should strike.

Chung glanced up, his eyes meeting hers. She looked into the brown, slanted eyes, but could find nothing there. It was like staring into ice; there was nothing to see apart from a pallid reflection of the observer. Chung lifted the jack and held it at arm's length above Strang's head. 'This will crack open his skull,' he said, his tone polite and almost sorrowful. 'So disarm yourself.'

The woman let the poker fall to her side. Chung stood up, walking across the floor and moving close to her. He was just a few inches taller and she could see a trace of perspiration on his brow. 'What do you want?' she asked.

The back of his hand crashed against the side of her face, knocking her to the floor. She was surprised by the power of the blow and she could feel nothing; pain would come, she knew, but it had not arrived yet. A trickle of blood from the side of her mouth was already staining the whiteness of her blouse.

Chung knelt next to the woman. He ran a hand through her blonde hair, then rested the back of his wrist on her bloodied mouth. She turned her head away in disgust. 'Does it hurt?' he asked.

She started to sit up, the ache in her jaw growing worse as she did so. Chung could see that she was trying to hold back the tears welling up in her eyes and her shoulders were trembling 'What do you want?' she asked again.

Chung leant closer, bringing his lips to the edge of her face. 'Silence,' he replied softly.

'Nobody will say anything,' she spluttered.

Chung raised a single finger to his lips. 'Ssh,' he whispered. 'I said I wanted silence. Now turn over.' Reluctantly, the woman obeyed lying with her face to the floor. Kim knelt beside her, running his hands along her back, massaging her behind the neck, kneading his palms into her shoulder muscles. 'Relax,' he whispered. 'Close your eyes.'

The feel of his touch was repulsive, the mixture of sensuousness and violence both lurid and frightening,

5

and she could feel her stomach sickening as his hands ran over her. For the moment, however, she found she was strangely relieved. A rapist was better than a murderer and for now, she told herself, she should play along.

Silently, Chung picked up the poker. He held it in his fist, momentarily admiring the decorations on the brass. With his left hand he rubbed the small of her back, while with his right he lifted the poker high into the air. It crashed down on to the back of her neck, opening up a flesh wound, through which more blood started to seep. With his left hand he could feel the nerves in her back jump, before falling quiet. He moved it slowly down to her wrist, checking her pulse; it was faint, but still there. Lifting the poker once more, he crashed it back down on her neck. The flow of blood increased, seeping out on to the floor. This time, her pulse had stopped.

Chung stood up, leaving the poker lying on the floor. He walked across to Strang, prodding the man with his foot. Slowly he regained consciousness. Briefly he was confused, unsure where he was or what was happening. But when he saw his daughter bleeding before him he recollected instantly. 'Why her?' he asked, his voice croaked by the intense pain rippling through his whole body.

Chung shrugged. 'I think you know,' he replied, his tone flat. He collected the jack and knelt down close to Strang, holding his chin up in his hand. 'If you didn't want her hurt you shouldn't have brought her along,' he said. 'That was very selfish of you. You must have known we would find you within hours. There isn't anywhere in the world anyone can hide from us. Not any more. The technology is too powerful.'

6

1

Why did they sack me?

Harry gently unscrewed the cap on the whisky bottle and poured a large measure of the liquid over the ice packed into the tumbler. Lifting the glass to his lips, he could feel the cold alcohol touching the back of his throat. Immediately, he began to feel calmer; his nerve endings started to settle down and the soreness in his head to ease, and the questions, momentarily at least, to subside.

The day had started badly and moved towards the lower depths of awful as soon as he arrived in the office. The traffic along the Fulham Road had been even heavier than usual, the fumes clogging up his vision, and sheets of rain had been pouring over the Embankment. Harry arrived at the offices of Croxley, Palmer just after 7.15, with only minutes to spare before the morning meeting. Without time even to remove his jacket, he glanced briefly at the Reuters screen, checking the prices on the dozen leading media stocks he covered. Nothing much appeared to have happened overnight, apart from News Corp being marked down in Australia following some remarks by the Chinese leadership about restricting the ownership of satellite dishes in the country; that could dent the profits being made from News Corp's Star subsidiary in Hong Kong. Harry scrolled on through the Reuters reports to see if he could find more details. It might, he decided, make a theme for the briefing he would have to give the equity salesmen in about ninety seconds. Nothing appeared. 'Damnit,' Harry muttered to himself, collecting some research papers lying on the top of his desk and heading towards the conference room.

'About fucking time, Lamb,' barked Keith Trimble, his eyes rooted to the floor as he spoke. Harry could feel his fingers scald as the foul powdered coffee he had just extracted from the office machine spilled over his hand. Trimble was just thirty-two, two years younger than he was. He had been promoted to head of equity research at the stockbroking firm only six months earlier. It was the first time Harry had worked for someone younger than himself. He had felt irritated by the appointment at first, but took it as a sign of encroaching middle age; it was bound to happen sooner or later and, in the City, almost certainly sooner. He wouldn't have minded if Trimble had not been such a bonehead. 'Traffic,' he said coldly.

Trimble ran his lean fingers through his hair, rolling his eyes sideways in exaggerated despair. 'What should we be saying about media stocks today?' he asked languidly.

Harry looked down the length of the room. There were thirty salesmen, lounging on their chairs towards the back, the men already with their jackets off and their shirt-sleeves rolled up, the women dabbling with their lipstick, while checking themselves in their pocket mirrors. Towards the front sat eight of the traders, the market makers who decided the bid and offer prices the firm would be putting up throughout the day. Their expression hovered somewhere between exhaustion and curiosity.

With his notes lying in front of him, Harry cleared his throat and began to address his audience. 'I'm still recommending holds on Pearson and Carlton. No change there. I have a long-term buy on Reuters. This might be the time to start building up our position, since there should be some numbers available on their new trading system and all the indications are that it's going well. There was some selling of News Corp in the Far East overnight, on access to the Chinese market. I don't think we should worry about that too much. It's an old bear story and might even be a buying opportunity. I'll keep the desk posted on that through the day. Actually, longer term there is a much better bear run. I think we should be telling all our clients to go short on Cable Media. In fact . . .'

'Not that old chestnut,' interrupted Trimble, his eyes rolling upwards and the sneer in his voice deepening.

Harry cast a sharp, dark look in his direction and noticed, with pleasure, a brief flash of concern in the younger man's eyes. Back off, pip-squeak, Harry thought to himself. This is my territory.

'In fact,' he continued, 'I'm in the process of preparing a longer note on Cable Media, which will, I think, drive the price down several points. It should be finished by the end of the week, and we'll get it printed over the weekend, and out to our larger clients by first thing Monday morning. But it would be good to start preparing our own position, and perhaps begin to spread the word that there should be a movement in the price next week. I don't want to go into too many details just yet. There are still some more numbers to be crunched. But essentially it looks as if the financing of their new satellite system doesn't work out. They have been far too optimistic about the cost of putting their machines into orbit. And they are being too bullish about the revenue flows in the first few years. That, as I'm sure we all know, is a recipe for disaster.'

To his left, Harry noticed that Trimble was scribbling furiously in his notebook. He looked up and smiled at some of the traders at the back of the room. 'We've heard this story before, Lamb,' he said.

'Sure, I've been questioning the viability of the Argus project for some weeks,' replied Harry. 'But this will be the first time anyone has come up with any independent research on the financing of the system. Up until now, everyone in the market has been working from the company's numbers.'

'Meanwhile, the price keeps on going up.' Trimble started flicking back through the pages in his notebook. 'Indeed, when you first began to make bearish noises about Cable Media seven weeks ago, the price was 580p. What is it now? Around 620p? I haven't checked this morning.'

'I've said all along this was a medium-term play,' replied Harry firmly. 'The policy of this research department is to capture long-term trends, as you well know.'

Trimble hesitated, avoiding eye contact with Harry before continuing: 'We'll keep tabs on Cable Media through the week, okay? Now diversified industrials. What do you have to contribute this morning, Simon?'

Harry shut his eyes for a moment, blanking out the scene in front of him. It was unheard of for a head of research to question one of his analysts at a morning conference; in particular one who had made the top five in the annual Extel survey of the big fund managers for the past three years. Trimble was getting too big for his boots, perhaps, betraying his inexperience. Or else . . . Opening his eyes, Harry shut off the chatter about the prospects for industrial stocks over the rest of the week and looked closely at Trimble. He was running a hand through his hair again and his eyes were fixed on the notebook, his fingers scribbling rapidly. He looked up momentarily, noticing Harry staring straight at him and a thin, amused smile spread slowly across his lips.

Unless something else is going on here, thought Harry to himself.

'Thanks for that, Simon,' said Trimble, slipping his biro into his pocket and bringing the meeting to a close. 'Time to start trading. Let's make it a good one.'

Back at his desk, Harry had listened idly to the messages recorded on his voicemail; there were a dozen or so from clients looking for his views on trading strategies, one from the investor relations man at Cable Media and one from a journalist. He pressed store on each of them; those calls would wait. His mind was too distracted right now. Trimble was starting to rattle his nerves and something would have to be done about it. The man was irritating, always had been, but now there seemed to be an aggression to his manner that suggested something different: a lingering air of menace. By himself, Trimble was a character of relatively little consequence. Harry felt sure that he could handle him. Yet he seemed to have a special relationship with Arnold Webber, the chief executive of the broking firm, and Webber was a much more formidable man. Not somebody whom Harry would tussle with lightly. Or at all. Not if he could possibly help it.

Harry looked down at the spreadsheets he had printed out last night, hoping to get a clearer picture of the financing of the Argus project. His assistant, Katie, was away this week. He could have used her mathematical skills to help him sort through the numbers. But, more importantly, he needed further information. Analysis, Harry had always maintained, was no use without the raw data to work on. Without that it was just playing games

11

with figures. He still did not really have precise data on how much it was going to cost Cable Media to get its birds into orbit. It's Tuesday, he thought to himself. I've promised to get this research note out by the weekend. Is that enough time? To hammer something together, sure. But to write something fresh and original that would get to the root of the company's finances? There was no way of being sure it could be ready.

The phone rang. More fund managers, thought Harry ruefully. 'Lamb, here,' he said, picking up the receiver.

'I thought you might like to pop up and see me later.' It was Webber.

Croxley, Palmer was majority owned by Harrington, one of the largest high street banks in the country, and Webber, its chief executive, had been drafted in from head office to try to improve the performance of the broking subsidiary; everyone knew the firm had not made an adequate return on capital for its parent, largely because its costs were so extravagant. Webber was a fiercely ambitious man in his late forties, often spoken of as a candidate for the chairmanship of the whole bank. That, however, would be two or three years away. For now, he had to sort out Croxley, Palmer. And that meant cutting costs.

Webber was sitting at his desk when Harry entered the twenty-fifth-floor office. He always sat behind his desk. He was nicknamed the cripple, since there was some debate among the junior brokers about whether he had any legs, they were so rarely seen. Walking around the trading floor was not his style. A short man, with thinning grey hair and a sharp sarcastic manner, he liked to remain in his office, poring over the figures and ratios, and dictating angry memos to his staff.

'How long have you been with Croxley, Palmer, Mr Lamb?' he asked politely.

'Eight years,' replied Harry. Come to the point, he thought to himself.

'Then it is probably time for a change,' said Webber, removing his glasses as he spoke. 'City careers need to be very mobile.'

'I suppose so, yes,' answered Harry. 'How long have you been with Harringtons?'

'We are not here to talk about me.' A look of irritation flashed across Webber's face.

Bastard, thought Harry. Why don't you just get on with it. 'How much?' he asked.

'We will pay out a year's salary,' answered Webber, relieved to be moving on to the details. 'Plus your bonus for this year. We will, as usual, require six months' gardening leave. After that you are free to work for anyone else. I'm sure a man of your experience will have no trouble finding another job.'

Harry sat back in his chair. The usual terms, he decided. Nothing special. 'May I ask why?' he said.

'Costs have to be brought under control at this firm,' said Webber. 'You are a very expensive overhead.'

Harry looked directly into the eyes of the man opposite. I can outstare you until the weekend, he thought to himself. To the end of the month, if you won't give me a straight answer. 'You know that the broking fees we generate on the media desk more than cover our costs. If you were looking to weed out the under-performers there are other places you'd start. We both know that, so why pretend?'

Webber put his glasses back on and swivelled in his chair, glancing out at the view of the City below. For a moment, Harry even thought he might stand up. 'You are a loose cannon, Mr Lamb,' he said, his tone indifferent.

The walk back towards his desk was long and lonely. Eyes appeared to be bearing down on him from all sides of the trading floor; this was a scene Harry had witnessed a hundred times as a spectator and he knew well the ghoulish tangle of excitement that a sacking always prompted among the witnesses. Public hangings, he sometimes reflected, would have attracted a healthy turn-out from the Croxley, Palmer staff. But this was his first time as a victim. He was unsure how to react. Act cool and casual, he told himself. Preserve your dignity. It might be all you can take out of here.

People averted their eyes as he neared them, burying their heads in their screens, or picking up the phones ringing on their desks. Suddenly everyone seemed to be busy. Embarrassed, decided Harry. He had done the same thing himself on countless occasions and for a moment he regretted his past indifference to the fate of his colleagues. I should have said something, he realised. Even to the people I didn't really know.

The security guards were already standing next to his desk; three of them, dressed in the dark blue uniforms of their trade. 'Half an hour to clear your desk, Mr Lamb,' explained the chief goon, with deadpan weariness. Just personal items to be collected. Nothing that belonged to the firm could be removed from the office.

Simon Tate, his colleague from the industrials desk, patted him reassuringly on the shoulder. 'Bad luck, Harry,' he said. 'Another stupid decision from the top brass.'

'It's like we always said,' answered Harry. 'Getting canned in this place is a matter of when, not if.'

'Sure,' said Simon. 'What's the story?'

'Some rubbish about cutting costs.'

'Not very convincing,' replied Simon. 'They could have come up with something better.'

'They don't have the imagination,' said Harry. 'I reckon that's the reason over there.'

Both men could see Keith Trimble coming towards

14

them across the floor. His shirt-sleeves were rolled up and a smug look of quiet satisfaction was playing on his thin lips. He stopped by the desk, allowing his head to droop slightly as he watched the trio of security guards go about their familiar tasks. 'I'll be sorry to lose you, but I guess the top guys know what they are doing. And I notice Cable Media is up eight pence this morning. It's lucky we didn't take your advice.'

'Just fuck off,' said Harry. Turning back to his desk, he noticed the guards had already given him a couple of bin-liners. He opened the drawers and started rooting through the piles of papers there. Most of it, he supposed, was company property; diaries, old notes from rival broking firms, company reports, spreadsheets, post-it notes so old they had started to decompose, a few half-finished packets of Nurofen. It wasn't much to have collected in eight years. Not much at all. And none of it was anything he wanted to take with him.

On the top of his desk there was a picture of Cassandra, smiling, and looking her most angelic and innocent. It was taken just after her second birthday, and though it was only nine months since then, she had grown and changed; her manner was already becoming less babyish. With a sweeping sense of regret and remorse, Harry wished her mother were still alive. Amelia would have known exactly how to cope with a day like this. She always had the right response to every situation.

Harry picked up the framed photograph and wrapped it carefully in one of the bin-liners. He took his filofax, tucking it under his arm, and picked up the spreadsheets he'd been looking at that morning. Wandering around the research department, he shook a series of hands, some warmly, some indifferently, others with a professional coldness that acknowledged these were people he would never be friends with outside the office. He

15

waved in the direction of the floor and some of the traders, those who weren't jabbering into the phones, waved back.

Eight years, he now thought to himself. Bugger it.

Harry drained his whisky and left the empty glass, the ice melting, on the drinks cabinet. With the music still playing in the background, he walked upstairs towards Cassie's bedroom. Carefully he turned the handle on the door, anxious not to wake her if she had already drifted off to sleep. Her nanny, Lucy, always put her to bed, and had done so before Harry returned home from the office. He looked inside, walking quietly towards the bed. She was tucked up beneath her Buzz Lightyear duvet, her thumb placed in her mouth, her knees tucked up close to her body, and her blonde hair spread out over the pillow. Her teddy was tucked up next to her. Harry sat at the end of the bed and looked down at his daughter. It was something he did often and it was in these quiet moments he missed Amelia most. More than a year had passed since she had died in a car crash, and Harry knew that he had still not come to terms with her disappearance from his life; the wrench had been too great and the shock too sudden. Inwardly, he could feel his heart sighing; there was an empty space in the centre of his stomach he knew the alcohol would not fill. No wife. And now no job. Cassie was all he had left.

Sleepily, she stretched out a hand towards him. Harry could see her blue eyes starting to open and he reached out to hold on to her. 'Daddy,' she said, her voice drowsy and slow.

'Yes, princess,' replied Harry

'Hug me.'

Harry reached down the bed and bundled her up in his arms, holding her tight, his heart beating to the warmth of her tiny body next to his chest. 'Everything's going to be just fine, princess,' he said softly.

'Yes, Daddy,' she replied.

He could see her eyes closing gently and he gave her a tight squeeze, enjoying the smile on her face. Laying her back down on the pillow, he ran his hand through her hair and kissed her on the forehead. He could tell from the heaviness of her breathing she had already drifted back to sleep. He stood up and walked towards the door, shutting it carefully behind him.

Downstairs the music had stopped. He walked towards the kitchen and contemplated putting one of the M&S dishes from the freezer into the microwave. He told himself that he should eat but somehow he didn't feel hungry right now. Food could wait.

Harry poured himself another whisky; it was definitely a two or three drinks evening. The chill of the ice and the warmth of the liquid felt comforting, and within minutes he found he had started to relax.

Why did they sack me?

The question was still plaguing him, swirling around in his head, loosening the neurones and opening up the nerve endings. He could almost feel the static charge in his mind. It was not as if he minded leaving the firm. He had been there long enough. It was time for a change and he was confident that there would be no shortage of offers from other companies. And the six months on full pay before he would be allowed to take up another job in the City would give him plenty of time to spend with Cassie.

No, it was not losing the job, but the manner of his dismissal that rattled him. Something about the day did not quite make sense. There was no rational reason for sacking him; the performance of the media team had been good, generating plenty of profits for the firm; it was obvious that Trimble hated him, but hard to believe

17

that Webber was so in thrall to that jerk he would allow Harry to be pushed out; and he was by no means the most extravagantly paid analyst on the team.

It had to be something else.

A loose cannon, Webber had said. Well, thought Harry, perhaps it was time to start finding out just how loose a cannon he could be.

2

Julia Porter freshened her lipstick in the mirror, stepping back a pace to examine herself. Long, dark-brown hair, swept up and held in place by a simple comb; pale-brown eyes, the lashes darkened; a pale-blue jacket from Joseph, with matching skirt, cut three inches above the knee; a single string of pearls slipped round her neck; one gold bracelet dangling over her wrist. I'll do, she thought to herself. Retrieving her handbag and brief-case, she stepped out of the Ladies and into the third-floor corridor. Welcome to the *Nightmare on Elm Street*, she muttered to herself.

The Elm Street building, a modern, undistinguished office tower just off the Gray's Inn Road, had been an unfortunate choice for the headquarters of the Serious Fraud Office. The press had been quick to pick up on the connection with the slasher movies. As the SFO zig-zagged from one disaster to another, 'Nightmare on Elm Street' had been a regular headline over stories of prosecutorial incompetence and investigative inepti-tude. Through years of trials that ended in failure the SFO had come to be ridiculed in financial and legal circles for its inability to secure convictions even in the most blatant cases of fraud.

The theory, Julia knew, had been fine. Set up seven years earlier, the SFO had been designed to bring together detecting and financial skills to track down cases of major fraud. Skilled policemen would work alongside bright accountants, lawyers and bankers to uncover financial malpractice, and to put together the mountain of evidence needed to secure a conviction. In practice, however, it had not worked. The police did not rate financial crime as serious stuff; the best of them preferred to track serial killers and drug traffickers, and resisted being moved to Elm Street. The accountants, bankers and lawyers could not have been less interested in detective work; there was far too much money to be made in the City to tempt anyone into moving to the police. Working for the Crown did not pay; nor did it look good on the CV. Elm Street was a career cul-de-sac.

The review was meant to change all that. A high-level Whitehall committee had studied the problems and decided that the lack of skilled financial analysts was the main failing of the SFO. They knew they could not pay the hundreds of thousands a year needed to tempt any partners from the big London firms to cross the line; but the committee concluded they might be able to persuade those firms to surrender some of their brightest young people to join the SFO on a one- or two-year secondment. It was the public-spirited thing to do, part of their duty to put something back into society. Or, perhaps more convincingly, explain how they might be blackballed from lucrative government consulting contracts if they did not play ball.

Julia had been flabbergasted when she was chosen. The rumours had swept around the London offices of her consulting firm ever since the new policy had been announced. Everyone knew it would be participating; the firm was one of the largest consultants to the government and there were too many millions at stake for the partners to refuse. The only question was who would get the call?

The office grapevine suggested some of the slow-laners from the research department would take the fall; junior number-crunchers and bean-counters, the people who had the lowest fee-earning potential. Julia knew she was too good to fall into that category. Still only twenty-nine, in the four years since she had completed her Masters in Business Administration she had graduated to the mergers and acquisitions department. Her specialism was target investigation; working for a company contemplating a hostile bid, she would find out everything possible about the business in their sights. It was hard, detailed work, requiring cunning, guile and sometimes subterfuge; tough and often exhausting, but enjoyable when it went well. And very profitable. Billing at £200 an hour, sixty hours a week, forty-seven weeks a year, she calculated that she was bringing in £564,000 a year, much more than her salary of £90,000. She didn't mind about the profits they were making from her, she knew it would all be paid back when she made partner in the next three or four years. But she did feel it secured her from being turfed out on lame, career-stalling secondments.

'Why me?' she had protested to Terry Sutton, her managing partner, when the news was broken to her. 'Why not a researcher? That's what they need, isn't it?'

'Because we have to send over someone good,' he had replied. 'The firm is being leant on very hard to participate in this programme. So is everyone in the City. Putting up one of the slow-laners would be worse than not taking part at all.'

'So why not one of the better bean-counters?'

'We need someone with investigative skills,' Sutton replied. 'What they require at the SFO is really very similar to the work you are already doing. Investigating companies without their co-operation. It'll be perfect for you, and probably very educational. The firm will, of course, continue to pay your salary while you are over there, plus bonuses and all the benefits.'

Julia pulled a face. 'What's the carrot?' she asked.

'It's a one-year secondment. We won't let it interfere with your career path here. Indeed, to make it worth your while, we will consider putting you up for a partnership one year earlier.'

'And the stick?'

Sutton averted his eyes. 'You know how the senior partners feel about loyalty to the firm,' he replied.

Julia could recall how she had looked away when the point was made; she was not sure she was being told the truth but could not yet finger the deception. 'There are several other people who could prove their loyalty by taking this assignment,' she said. 'And there are probably several other firms that would take me on if I refused.'

Sutton sighed. 'It wouldn't make any difference,' he said. 'The SFO asked for you.'

'For me?' she asked with surprise.

'Personally,' answered Sutton. 'It seems they have been very impressed by some of your investigative work, as indeed we all have. I don't think anyone has any choice in the matter, and that includes you. It is just something we are all going to have to live with.'

The third-floor corridor, lit by strips of neon, ran into the distance; this was a place where the senior people still seemed to work cooped up in small offices behind plywood doors. There was probably a tea trolley that came along at 3.45 every afternoon, she thought as she walked along the corridor, checking the names on the doors. She had been told to report to a Mr John Mitchell. A deputy prosecutor, one of eight within the organisation, who would be her supervisor for the next year.

His name was displayed on the side of the door. Julia tapped and stepped inside. The office was bare and utilitarian: a small entrance lobby, with a row of filing cabinets, a desk and a window looking out on to the street outside. There was space for a secretary, but no one sitting there; too early, Julia imagined. Through the open doorway leading to the main office Julia could see a man, his back to her. He turned when she entered the room and began walking towards her. About forty, with hair starting to grey around the edges, he was wearing a dark-blue suit, with a striped shirt and a floral tie. His eyes were blue and his smile was mischievous. Quite attractive, thought Julia. Not bad, anyway. For a civil servant.

He stretched out a hand. 'You must be Julia Porter,' he said.

She nodded. 'I hope I'm not early.'

'This is the public sector,' he said. 'The secretaries, support staff I suppose you would call them, don't start as promptly as they do in private industry. In fact, I think you'll find this place is not as swish all round as your consulting firm.'

Julia smiled, unsure how to take the remark. 'I'm sure I'll adjust.'

'I hope so,' said Mitchell.

Julia took the chair facing his desk, placing her hand-bag and briefcase on the floor beside her. Mitchell shuffled round behind it. In front of him was a large stack of papers. One folder lay open, a sheaf of papers spread out before him. 'We hear great things about you,' he said. 'Cambridge graduate, good exam results, in the fast lane at your firm. A tenacious, intelligent worker, with a rare talent for financial investigations. At least, that's what your managing partner said.'

23

Julia tried to look modest, while enjoying the description. 'I suspect they are exaggerating,'

Mitchell shook his head. 'No. We told them to send us their best. This place has been failing for too long. We need a couple of hits, big ones preferably, or it's going to be wound up.'

'That close?'

'Afraid so,' said Mitchell. 'The Home Office can't waste money on an establishment like this, not when it doesn't get results and not when there are grannies being mugged on the high street.'

'Too bad.' Julia was conscious of the lack of sincerity in her voice.

Mitchell laughed. 'It really is. You see, London thrives on being a financial centre; the whole City depends on it. But a financial centre can only survive if it's clean. At least reasonably clean.'

'I hadn't thought of it like that.'

'But enough of the theory,' said Mitchell. 'We like to start secondees off with preparatory work.' Julia nodded. 'The work of the SFO is to detect and prosecute financial crime, you know that. Hundreds of suspicious-looking incidents come into this office. Some of them are evidence of fraud, some are not. If we think there is nothing there, or at least nothing sufficiently wrong to start building a case around, then we drop it. If there is something there we launch an official inquiry.'

'My job is to start the investigation?' asked Julia.

'Absolutely,' answered Mitchell.

She hesitated, unsure of the right response. 'You think I have enough experience to do that?'

'Not really,' Mitchell replied. 'But we are chronically understaffed and you have to start somewhere. It might as well be the deep end. And it does give you a chance to see how a case begins. Probably you'll find a few that don't merit any further investigation. When you do find one that needs to go further we'll put some more experienced people on to it. You'll be part of that team. That way you get to work on a case from beginning to end. It's a great way to learn about the process.'

Inwardly, Julia sighed. There was a limit to how much she wanted to know about the process. 'Where do I begin?'

Mitchell gathered up the bundle of papers from his desk, returning them to the empty folder. He handed it across. 'Here,' he said.

Julia opened the folder. Inside were around fifty sheets of paper. She glanced through them. Each contained details of a stock transaction: date, size of purchase, person placing the order, the broker dealing with it, the person or company placing the sale, followed by the subsequent sale of the stock. 'Could you explain what this means?' she asked.

'Certainly,' replied Mitchell. 'Insider dealing. Everyone knows that insider dealing is rife on the London market, and that it's illegal. But in the nine years since it became a criminal offence there has only been one successful prosecution and that was for some guy in London who had made about ten grand. Small fry. It's not a very impressive record, and not one we are particularly proud of.'

'You think this is evidence of insider dealing?' asked Julia.

'Could be. The system works like this. The computers at the Stock Exchange track all the trades made on the London market, which comes to about five million a day. The machines are programmed to look for anything blatantly suspicious. For example, on Thursday you see a big buy order on a stock. Then, on Friday, a bid is announced for that company at a thirty per cent premium to the market price. That is suspicious. The Stock Exchange churns out the details,

25

then passes them on to the Department of Trade and Industry. If the culprit is obvious they appoint inspectors to start an inquiry. Usually, the culprit isn't obvious and they hand the details over to us. Our job is to look at the stuff, to see if we can find any hard evidence.'

'And you are handing it on to me.'

'Right again. The best way to beat the market is to form an insider dealing ring. It's like that film, *Strangers on a Train*, the one where two guys meet and they both want someone bumped off. They agree to commit each other's murders. That way they will probably both get away with it. Neither has a motive for the crime, and motive is usually what scuppers you.'

Julia leant forward. 'The ring carries out each other's trade.'

'That's it,' replied Mitchell. 'Person A, call him Bob, knows something. He tells person B, say Keith, who makes the trade. When Keith knows something, he tells Bob. They split the profits, and it's almost impossible to build a case because there is no way Keith could have known the information unless you can prove that Bob told him, which usually you can't.'

'Getting lucky on the market is not a crime.'

'Right. If it were just Bob and Keith you could probably catch up with them eventually. But if it's Bob, Keith, Terry, Sam, John, Alan, Roger, Mark and Simon, then it's virtually impossible.'

'All the same, you'd like me to try.'

Mitchell smiled. 'I did warn you that most of your projects would lead nowhere,' he said, 'but we check things out. That folder is a list of suspicious-looking trades that may well be evidence of a ring. Take a look at it. See if you can work out a way of building a case against them.'

'Any hints?'

'Not really,' Mitchell replied. 'As I said, there has only been one successful prosecution, so I think it's fair to say there's no established methodology for cracking these cases. Just concentrate on it as a crime. Look for patterns, shapes. Anything that might provide a clue.'

Julia leafed through, casting her eyes over the rows of numbers printed across the slim pages. They meant little to her, and she sensed immediately it could take days to start making any sense of the information. Her eyes rose across the desk, meeting Mitchell's, wondering if he were looking at her with more than a purely professional interest. 'Why me?'

Mitchell appeared distracted by the question. 'You are one of my secondees,' he answered, with an attempt at a smile. 'You drew the short straw, I guess.'

A single thought shot through her mind: he's lying. 'No,' she said carefully. 'You asked for me personally. I'd like to know why.'

For a brief moment, Julia sensed, the terms of the conversation had changed. They had swapped places; she was now leading and he was trying to catch up. 'I think you have answered your own question,' he replied.

'How?' she asked, genuinely bewildered.

'Think about it. The last thing this organisation requires is brain-dead time-servers. We need people who can see round corners. You've already figured out that it's not merely by chance that you're here. It was organised. We checked out a lot of people, made some discreet inquiries, and selected you for your ability to ask awkward questions and your reluctance to get fobbed off with platitudes. You've just demonstrated that. That's why you're here.'

'Perhaps I should keep my mouth shut,' said Julia.

Mitchell laughed. 'Perhaps so. Certainly around here. You can't trust anyone. I think you'll find it even more of a snake-pit than your consultancy.'

Julia smiled, noting that he had already stood up and was starting to walk her away from the office; a trick she had noted that older men were skilled at using when the conversation had started to go further than they planned.

'I'll show you to your desk,' he said, leading her towards the door. 'Work on these numbers for a couple of days and let me know how you get on. Don't worry if you reach a dead end. I'm afraid failure is expected around here. We'll just give you something else to do.'

Julia followed him out into the corridor towards the lift. Her workspace was on the second floor, and for several minutes she walked alongside her new supervisor in total silence. Already she was missing the atmosphere of her familiar office and wondering once again what she was doing here. Well, she thought, only three hundred and sixty-four more days to go.

3

His legs were starting to ache and Harry could feel a bead of sweat dripping off his brow. Casually he watched a single drop fall on to the newspaper spread out on the handlebars of the bike machine. Reaching down for the towel hung beneath the crossbar, he wiped his forehead. The monitor recorded he had already completed twenty minutes and masochistically he turned the dial to a higher level. He could immediately feel the muscles in his thighs complaining at the effort required to push the pedals forward. It was one way of dealing with the anger.

His eyes returned to the paper. Harry had already read the item once but still he could not believe it. It was just a few small lines buried on the back page of the *Financial Times*, the report on trading on the market yesterday.

'Turnover in Cable Media was brisk, following a recommendation put out on the stock by Croxley, Palmer. The broker was making bullish noise about the potential for the company's new European satellite system, which, it argues, could be generating profits sooner than current forecasts predict. Croxley analysts are targeting a price of 700p for the stock in the near term and the shares rose 15p yesterday, closing at 635p.'

The lines were curt and simple but they took time to digest and, though Harry read the words slowly and carefully, he still had trouble believing them. It was only three days now since he had left the firm, and already they had started dusting his fingerprints from the place. Putting out a buy note on Cable Media, the stock he had been most bearish about, seemed the cruellest way of dramatising his departure to the market. They might as well have put a sign up in the street telling him to go fuck himself.

Harry wiped his brow once more; the sweat had been building up precipitously since he had taken it up a level and he could feel the moisture dripping down his back. He hardly noticed that he had knocked the paper to the floor. Whom, Harry wondered, would they have got to write the note? Surely they had not replaced him so soon. Not unless they already had another media analyst lined up before they sacked him. But even so, nobody could have had a new note ready in just three days. It took longer than that.

'I think you dropped this,' said Julia.

She was standing next to him, holding up the copy of the *FT*. Her long brown hair was tied up in a pony-tail and she was wearing a pink leotard and skin-tight grey shorts. Perspiration was outlined on her back. Her eyes took in the man in front of her; about six foot, she judged, with a square jaw, and black hair swept back over his forehead with just a hint of grey starting to show through. By lifting the corner of her lip she allowed the fraction of a smile to appear.

'Thanks,' replied Harry, taking the paper from her hand.

'No problem.'

She headed towards the rowing machines. Five more minutes' work, she told herself. Keep myself trim. Then a night at home in front of the TV and order in a pizza. Not the most fun a girl could have, perhaps, but relaxing. With the pressures of a new job to cope with, she decided, she needed some time to chill.

Three more minutes, thought Harry, looking back at the monitor. His eyes wandered up briefly to the televisions at the front of the gym, but there was nothing on either Eurosport, CNN or VH-1 to hold his attention. Perhaps, he wondered to himself, they had had the recommendation on Cable Media already lined up written and ready for the printers. Maybe that was why they sacked me.

'Work-out done,' announced the slim red electronic lettering on the monitor. Harry eased his feet out of the pedals, his muscles aching as he stepped on to the ground. Downstairs he slipped into the sauna, wiping his brow continually as the sweat eased from his pores. Two other men were there already; brokers, judging by their conversation about the markets. They were talking about a programme trade executed that morning and Harry could not restrain himself from listening. It was only three days, but he found that he missed that world already; the constant drama of market, its heady mixture of information and gossip, of analysis and action, its endless and unyielding sagas of greed and opportunity had always riveted his attention, and he realised he wanted to be part of it again. He was too young to bow out. And far too young to bow out gracefully.

The thought was still running through his mind when, dressed again in jeans, a polo shirt and a loose-fitting blue blazer, Harry headed out of the gym. He glanced up and down the Fulham Road; Lucy should have picked Cassie up from her nursery and be meeting him about now. He glanced down at his watch. Six thirty. She was hardly ever late. Only when she had a new boy-friend and, since Lucy always kept him updated on every exact detail of her love life, he was sure he would know about it if there were anyone new on the scene.

'You ditched your paper,' said Julia.

Harry turned to face her, a look of surprise evident on his face. It was, he realised, the girl in the gym. She looked different in what were obviously her work clothes; a short red skirt over black tights, with a black jacket with gold buttons. Instinctively he tried to place her, professional, obviously, but what kind of a job was hard to tell. She looked too brainy to be in PR or marketing; equity sales, perhaps, he figured. Or consulting, or advertising. Something where women could be both feminine and smart. 'Sorry, I didn't recognise you at first,' he said at length. 'You look different with your clothes on.' He paused, already feeling slightly embarrassed by the flirtatiousness of the remark, wondering if it was too corny. 'Your work clothes, I mean.'

She smiled. 'Better or worse?'

'Well, different,' replied Harry diffidently.

In the distance he could see Cassie and Lucy approaching down the street. He waved towards his daughter and as soon as she caught his eye she began running towards him. Harry knelt down, opening his arms, ready to catch her as she threw herself into his embrace. He picked her up and swung her through the air, feeling the intensely familiar surge of joy that ran through him every time they were reunited. 'Hello, princess,' he said.

'Hello, Daddy,' Cassie replied, her delicate, tiny face creasing up into a smile.

'Your daughter?' said Julia.

Harry nodded.

'It was nice to meet you,' said Julia softly, slinging her gym bag over her shoulder and starting to go up the street.

Harry watched her as she walked away. She did not turn back.

Darn it, thought Julia to herself. Another married man.

Sergei Lykanov looked down at the two rumpled hundred-rouble notes. He folded the slips of brightly coloured paper carefully into his wallet and placed them inside his jacket pocket. An insult, he thought to himself; a cold and callous insult, calculated, or so he could easily believe, to turn men such as himself into mercenaries.

If there had been any doubts, and there had been plenty in the last twenty-four hours, this was the moment when they disappeared. A man could not be expected to live on the miserable rations this money would buy. It was enough for just some pitiful loaves of bread, some dried fish, perhaps some coffee and sugar, and a bottle or two of vodka to drown away the hunger. No, he decided, a man could not be expected to live on this money, nor with this treatment.

He had seen enough.

The two hundred roubles were meant to keep him and his family going for a month. The director-general of the Pokrovsk station had been almost apologetic when he handed over the money earlier that day. There was nothing he could do, he explained, the embarrassment written clearly on his face. It was all that had been sent down from Moscow this month. There was no more.

Lykanov walked through the dim and now empty computer room. A bank of screens covered one wall, monitoring the progress around the globe of the satellites operated by the Russian Republic, satellites that had once been the property of the Union of Soviet Socialist Republics. The old CCCP lettering, and the faded hammers and sickles, were still etched in to the sides of the machines; nobody had the time or money to change them and, in truth, nobody had the inclination. There were too many other things to worry about. Like eating. Like supporting a family. Like finding a way out.

Beneath the screens there stretched a bank of computer terminals. By morning, there would at least be a spattering of people at the terminals, drawing down the data from the satellites, and starting the initial work of processing and analysing the vast quantities of information a spy satellite could collect on its daily circumnavigation of the earth. But now, at this time of night, the place was deserted.

There were times when Lykanov almost felt jealous of the machines he tended and of their fabulous orbits. It was, he knew, a fanciful, sentimental notion, and one he tried to control; they were, after all, nothing but a ton or so of brainless metal and silicon, hurtling mindlessly round the planet. But they had a freedom and a power he envied. The satellite could go anywhere. And it could look at anything it wanted to look at. They had more freedom than a man could ever contemplate.

Satellites had been his passion ever since he was a small boy. It had been the glory and drama of the first Sputnik mission, back in the fifties, that had first captured his imagination and his spirit. The satellites had seemed the agents of a new age, one where technology would deliver peace and prosperity. And it was an age when his country, the old Soviet Union, appeared to have a decisive lead. For a young, ambitious and clever scientist there could have been no more natural desire than to work on satellite systems.

Youthful dreams, he reflected bitterly. Youthful and

foolish. Through his early years of training at the university in Moscow they had been told of the transformation the satellites would bring: the information on weather patterns from the space stations would solve the permanent food shortages that afflicted the Soviet Union, and that on hostile troop and missile movements would lift the threat of destruction by the imperialist aggressors which constantly hung over his country. It was important and prestigious work. And, as one of the brightest young scientists of his generation, Lykanov had thought his career would be among the most important and well-rewarded available.

The posting to the Pokrovsk station, when he was still in his mid-twenties, had confirmed to Lykanov his importance and swelled his ambition. One of several secret military installations built on the orders of Stalin through the early 1950s, the station was the nerve centre of the Soviet satellite programme. While it was the technological showmanship of manned space stations and missions to Mars that captured the headlines, it was the intricate construction of a network of powerful spy satellites that consumed the resources of the finest scientists and engineers the Moscow academies could produce. And the best of them were all gathered here, deep beneath the frozen Siberian wasteland.

The engineers at Pokrovsk knew better than anyone else why their city never saw daylight. They had nothing but the greatest professional respect for their rivals on the other side of the ideological divide, and they were well aware that anything on open ground could be watched and analysed in minute detail from space. Indeed, though they believed they were ahead technologically, it had been on their advice that nuclear and satellite installations started to be built underground from the mid-fifties onwards. Their orbiting spies had already gathered plenty of information on Nato installations and knew their opponents would be able to do the same.

At first, Lykanov had not minded the isolation. His station was at the cutting edge of Soviet technology and every luxury imaginable had been lavished on the scientists who worked there. Their living quarters were spacious and comfortable. There was good food to eat and plenty to buy in the shops: the best of everything available in the Soviet Union, sometimes even items imported from the West. And the pay was much more than he would have earned anywhere else; enough to raise a family in comfort, and to save for eventual retirement in a dacha outside Moscow. For many years it had been a good and, he felt, honourable life.

Glumly, his eyes straining from the few strips of neon light that the station could still afford, Lykanov glanced down at one of the monitors. It displayed an image captured earlier that day of the hillside in Chechenia; he thought he could make out a mortar position, but only close analysis would reveal its exact situation and strength. That would wait until morning, he decided, when the team reassembled. But there would be little enthusiasm for the task; it was not for work such as this, helping to destroy his own people, that either he or his colleagues had devoted their lives to creating a satellite observation system.

Everything had changed in the last few years and most of it for the worse. He had long since abandoned his faith in the Party, yet he found it hard to believe that anything much better would replace it. All he knew was that he was on the wrong side of history. Resources devoted to the military had been sliced to extinction and, although his station had been one of the last outposts to feel the squeeze, in the last two years they too had suffered. There was no longer any money to buy new equipment, or to stock the underground city with rations, or to pay them the wages they were owed.

Another monitor caught his eye, displaying an image captured from one of the regular scans of Western Europe. He peered down at the image. The criss-cross of canals he recognised instantly as Amsterdam, photographed at night, from more than a hundred miles up in space, but frozen in time with the kind of clarity that would usually only be captured from across the street. He could just make out the bright, garish lights of the city, twinkling against the water, and he could see groups of people sitting around outside cafés and restaurants, eating and drinking and enjoying the night air. He had never been there, of course; Lykanov had never left Russia and it was many years now since he had been outside Pokrovsk. But after a lifetime of designing ever more sophisticated satellite cameras, after years of testing the equipment, of taking fantastically detailed images from around the world, he was intimately familiar with many more places than most people would visit in a lifetime.

That was the trouble, he reflected. From here, deep underneath the Siberian ground, you could watch the world. You could see what it was like out there. Yet you could never leave.

Well, he decided, now he had seen enough. He completed one last tour of the premises, checking the satellites were all functioning correctly and the images were being relayed down to the station, ready for storage and for analysis over the following few days; he was in charge of information gathering here at the station and no matter how disillusioned he had become, he still took a residual pride in making sure the work was done properly. If he made his escape, he would not leave any problems behind for others to solve.

Leaving the terminals behind him, Lykanov walked through the long thin tunnel that connected the control rooms to the living quarters for the several hundred people who lived and worked at the station. He glanced at his watch; it was just before midnight and no doubt the bar beside the apartment complex would still be full of his remaining colleagues, slowly rotting their minds on cheap vodka, and complaining drunkenly of their ragged and unrewarding lives. He would not join them tonight; he no longer had the energy to complain. No, this would be one night when he would make sure he got some rest. In preparation for the day ahead.

I have lived in the dark too long, Lykanov decided, wearily climbing the steps to the third-floor two-room apartment he shared with his wife. His mind was made up. Tomorrow, he would make the journey to see the man who wanted to meet him. And if the offer was right, he would make a deal.

The rolling beat of a Van Morrison track playing in the background had started to lift Harry's spirits. From the window of his study he peered briefly into the darkness, catching the ugly, familiar din of a police siren flashing its way down the Fulham Road. The noise hardly registered. In front of him, the desk was strewn with papers: press cuttings, annual reports, broker's notes, share-price charts, all lying in a jumble, threatening to fall over the edge at any moment.

Somewhere in here, he thought to himself.

His eye was caught by a cutting from the *Sunday Times*, more than eighteen months old now. 'Multimedia Marriage' screamed the headline. It was a long description of the merger creating Cable Media early last year and Harry could not recall having read it since the deal had been struck. Taking a sip from his coffee, he started to scan through the page. Begin at the beginning, he told himself. Work forwards from there.

Samuel Haverstone, chief executive of Cable International, Britain's second largest phone company and one of the fastest growing forces in the global telecoms industry, stunned the stockmarket two weeks ago by launching a raid that scooped up 15 per cent of United Media. In the few days afterwards, it appeared as though the venerable media conglomerate was about to fold under the pressure, but behind the scenes United was preparing a stout defence for its independence. For Cable International, and particularly for Haverstone, control of United was the one prize that really counted.

In the last decade Cable International had grown explosively from its origins as a telecoms operator in outposts of the former British colonies by skilfully exploiting the emerging opportunities in the telecoms market. It had won the licence to set up the first rival to British Telecom in the UK; become one of the first movers in setting up cellular systems to operate mobile phones; won licences to run mobiles in Germany, France and Scandinavia; and had acquired ECI, the third largest telecoms carrier in America. In the telecoms industry, dominated by national monopolies, it was one of the few genuinely global players. But with the convergence of the telecoms and entertainment industries, Haverstone realised it had to move into the media industry if it were to survive in the long term. United was the perfect target. Originally just a newspaper company, the publisher of the two *Courier* titles, it had merged with several other companies over the decades to become one of Europe's leading media conglomerates. As well as the British newspapers, its empire now included BTI, one of the four leading record companies in the world; the publishing house, Crossthwaite; two regional ITV companies in

Britain; newspapers and magazines in Holland and Germany; majority control of the Hollywood studio, TDM; and most recently, a controlling interest in SBS, the satellite broadcasting company that was now beaming down a series of sports and entertainment channels across Europe and Asia. It was one of the few media companies with the kind of global reach to tempt Cable International.

Sir Ian Strang, the chairman of United Media, is established as chairman, with Haverstone as chief executive and an equitable distribution of board seats between executives from Cable International and United Media. Strang will have the personal choice of successor as chairman.

Strang's main fear, insiders say, had been of his company being swallowed up by the larger telecoms company. With guarantees of his own continuing role at the company he was ready to start the negotiations.

When the merger of Cable International and United Media was announced three days later, the stockmarket was as surprised as it had been by the dawn raid two weeks earlier; most experts had been readying themselves for a long and bitter battle between the two sides. Structured as a straightforward share swap, with a special dividend for shareholders in both companies, the new company had an initial market value of £30 billion, making it Europe's largest communications company.

'This is a historic day in the history of the communications industry,' said Haverstone as the deal was announced. 'With the creation of Cable Media, Sir Ian Strang and I believe we have created the one company in the world capable of taking advantage of the new technologies revolutionising both the telecoms and media businesses. This will be one of the most important companies in the world.'

Harry raised his eyes from the paper, taking another sip from the coffee on his desk. He pondered changing the CD, before glancing through the rest of his papers. It was mostly territory he was familiar with, he reflected; he had followed the merger closely at the time and had put out an immediate buy recommendation on the stock; both men were certainly right, he had decided, that the convergence of media and telecoms would create tremendous opportunities for any company with expertise in both industries.

Still, he pondered, it was strange how small details somehow escaped you. He looked back at the clipping to make sure he was right, and saw the words set down in black and white. Unless the paper had got its facts wrong at the time there could be no doubt: Haverstone had promised Sir Ian Strang that he could choose his successor as chairman. That had been one of the factors that had clinched the deal.

But when Sir Ian had died six months ago it had been Samuel Haverstone who had succeeded him as both chairman and chief executive, taking for himself complete personal control of the empire created by the merger. From what Harry knew of the tensions within Cable Media in the months following the deal, that would never have been Sir Ian's wish. Was that significant? he wondered. More than a decade in the City analysing companies had taught him that everything was in the detail. And this was a detail that, so far, seemed to have escaped everyone who tracked the company.

4

The list seemed to go on for ever.

Julia stood up from her desk and walked towards the percolator to collect her third coffee of the morning; too much caffeine, she decided reluctantly, as she stirred some milk into the polystyrene cup. It was her second week in the Serious Fraud Office, and she was starting to get to know some of her new colleagues. Four other fresh secondees shared this floor of the building: three men, all in their mid-twenties, a lawyer, an investment banker and another consultant. The fourth was a woman, Sarah Turnbull, who until recently had been working in the back office of one of the stockbroking firms and was the one person Julia had really struck up an acquaintance with in the first week. Female solidarity, she decided.

The caffeine felt good, curling around her veins and sparking some life back into her mind. A couple of days' more work, she told herself. And if she still hadn't made any progress by then it would be time to go to Mitchell and tell him she was getting nowhere. You could only beat your head against a brick wall for so long.

Julia had spent her first two days acclimatising herself to her new surroundings. She swotted up on the law on insider dealing and read some of the case files on previous investigations. Everything Mitchell had told her was true. The SFO had a terrible record in bringing successful prosecutions. But, even so, she felt she might learn something from looking where they had gone astray in the past.

One thing soon became clear. They were starting in the wrong place. They started with a tip-off, or some other grounds for suspicion, then went to the financial records to see if they could find the hard evidence to build a case. That might be the right way to tackle other crimes, but it was not working here. The insiders had covered their tracks too carefully and though there might be plenty of circumstantial evidence there was nothing an intelligent barrister could not blow away in court. No, she realised if this kind of investigation were to work, you had to start with the documentary evidence and move backwards to the culprits.

She suspected Mitchell already knew that and had given her the financial records as a starting point for precisely that reason. He wanted to see if an investigation could be completed successfully from a different starting point.

Knowing the shape of the task doesn't make it any easier, she told herself. Her raw material had been the printouts Mitchell had given her on the first day; a dense series of stock-trading records that covered more than a hundred pages, each one listing the date, the size of the transaction and the company dealt in. Each had just two things in common. They were placed with the same stockbroking firm, Croxley, Palmer. And each one made a profit, often a vast one.

Look for patterns, Mitchell had said, and, though obvious, it seemed to Julia to be advice that made sense. It was the only rational way to move forward.

Historically, the first trade on her list was made nine

months ago, last summer. It was a buy order for ten million shares in Thorn EMI, just before the company announced its demerger. The price then was £8.22p, pricing the trade at just over eighty million; a big order even by the standards of the institutions that invested on the London market. It was placed in the name of Hajeeb Investments, a company, according to the records, registered in the Cayman Islands. No hope of getting any more information from there about the firm, she reflected. The shares were held for three months, enough time for the demerger and the speculation about the sale of the record company to push the price comfortably above £12. By the time they were sold Hajeeb had banked profits of more than forty million.

Carefully, Julia logged the information into her desktop computer and moved on. She tracked three other investments in Thorn, each netting profits of more than ten million pounds, and each run through Cayman Islands companies: St Petersburg Investments, Palmira Trading and Ipoh International Mining. She noted each one, logging the time of the purchase and subsequent sale. It could, of course, just be a group of well-informed or merely lucky investors. But it certainly appeared suspicious. Looking up the possible location of each one, she discovered Palmira was a town near Cali, in Colombia, so that could be cocaine money. And Ipoh was a city in northern Malaysia, the centre of that country's prosperous tin-mining industry. Doodling in her notebook, she figured the investments could have come respectively from Middle Eastern oil barons, from the Russian mafia, from the cocaine kings of South America and from the tin magnates of South-East Asia. All of them would certainly have the money to play the markets on that sort of scale. But would they have the knowledge of a British company to deal so presciently?

Not impossible, but unlikely.

Julia discarded some of the smaller trades on the list, and decided for now, at least, to concentrate on those four companies.

The next set of trades was in the Swiss drugs company Sandoz. All four had invested in the two weeks before it announced its merger with its rival, Ciba-Geigy, later that summer. The stock had been held in each case for about four weeks, enough time for the price to rise by more than thirty per cent. Collectively, the four investors she was tracking had put in about a hundred million pounds, selling out at profits of more than thirty million.

Whoever they were, they were not a bunch of London barrow-boy brokers playing about with titbits of information that happened to fall into their laps. They were people with serious money at their disposal – very serious money. And, judging by the hundred million pounds in profits she calculated the four companies involved had already racked up, getting more serious all the time.

How could such a disparate group of investors know that much about a secretive Swiss company? she wondered. Enough to move in just a couple of weeks before a merger was announced. British and American companies were notorious for their leaks, and some insider trading before a big announcement was almost routine. But not the Swiss. They played their cards very carefully, and the discretion of the executives and advisers was legendary.

The following month there was a setback. All four of the companies she was tracking had taken heavy positions in Guinness, buying shares worth three million pounds in the last week of August. The stock had been held for three weeks, then sold at a slight loss. Two possibilities, thought Julia. They might be deliberately taking the occasional small losing position, in case they were ever the subject of an investigation; that way they could masquerade as innocent speculators who sometimes won and sometimes lost. It would certainly help their case if it ever came to court. Or it might be an inside deal that went wrong. Julia checked the cuttings on Guinness in the library. It transpired, from some of the market reports in early September, a rival had been readying a bid for Guinness, but it had ducked at the last moment. That made sense. Her prey could have had information that a bid was being prepared and had taken its position to reap the inevitable profits. When it was scrapped, they dumped their holdings.

The trail went cold for another month. Then the action started again. By now, the pattern was familiar. All four companies moved into the market within a few days of one another. This time the buying was in TSB, only days before Lloyds Bank launched its bid. Shares worth two hundred million pounds were bought that week, and sold just ten days later for more than two hundred and twenty-five million. The next month the same thing; another round of heavy share buying, an announcement that prompted a sharp rise in the price and the shares were quickly sold. Each time, profits of between thirty and fifty per cent were being made in less than a fortnight, and the sums involved were growing larger and larger.

Julia kept churning the numbers, crunching her way through the lists of stock trades. It was slow and painful work, numbing her eyes at times and making her senses ache. Each time she had to track the original share order, work out the size of the deal, then look through the cuttings for information that was in the public domain at the time the deal was struck. Every time, the same four companies showed an incredible ability to forecast events, getting into the market just before the prices started to move. It was, she concluded, about as clear a case of insider dealing as could be imagined.

At the time she started tracking them, she calculated the four companies involved had around a hundred million pounds in capital to play with; that was their seed money, the cash they were prepared to put up to get the ball rolling. Tracking the trades, it soon became clear that as the profits were taken out of one deal, they were swiftly reinvested in the next one, like a roulette player who kept his chips on the table. Except in this case, the players always knew which number would come up. They won practically every time.

Feeding the numbers into a spreadsheet, Julia added up the profits. By December, only a little over six months since the game had started, she realised that the hundred million pounds had been turned into a cool five hundred million. It was a huge number and one which, she concluded, would cause ripples and rumours even in the City of London.

And still the list went on.

Harry laid the flowers carefully by the side of the headstone; a bunch of yellow tulips, Amelia's favourite and the same flowers he had brought to this spot every week in the year since she had died. He stood silently for a moment, looking down at the simple inscription, wiping away what he took to be a speck of dust from his eye. Or was that a tear? It was hard to tell any more.

He always came alone. Cassie had been there for the funeral, of course, but since then he had not brought her here. He was not quite sure why, except that it didn't feel right. She was too young really to understand what had happened to her mother. Harry had explained that she had gone and was not coming back, and she seemed to accept that, although there was no way of telling what she truly felt. Perhaps when she was older they would come here together.

He knelt, looking down at the soft grass now covering the grave. Part of him wanted to reach down and touch the soil, as if that would bring him closer to her memory. But he held himself back. It was important to have his act together, to keep the show on the road, for Cassie's sake, if not for his own. Amelia would have wanted him to cope. It was the one thing he could do for her now.

He turned and started walking back through the cemetery. Cassie would be finished at her playgroup soon and it would be time to pick her up; one of the few comforting pleasures of losing his job was that he could spend more time with her. They could go shopping together. Cassie seemed to enjoy that. A girl thing, I suppose, Harry told himself with a smile.

The cemetery was quiet and empty; not many people had the time to visit on a weekday afternoon, not in this part of central London. They were busy in their offices, as, he supposed, he should be as well. That could wait. Were it not for Cassie, he did not suppose he would trouble himself right now with finding another job. No, he decided, I might just be happy to find out what happened to the one I had.

As he strolled through the gardens, Harry could not help recollecting that Sir Ian Strang had been buried in the same place and found himself wondering where he was. It didn't take long to find him; there were only a few fresh tombstones in the cemetery, and they stood out from the massed ranks of weather-beaten granite that filled the few square acres. He glanced down at the slab of black rock, noting the bare dates and the name. The man had been seventy when he died, a decent age, when a man might be expected still to have all his wits about him.

If he had been so concerned that Haverstone should

not succeed him as chairman of Cable Media, would he not have put in place plans for a successor? Someone he could trust? The question, Harry realised, had been buried in his mind for a couple of days now, but had only just surfaced.

He turned and started walking back through the graveyard, towards his car. None of my business, he told himself. And whatever involvement I might have had with Cable Media it was history now. The past; something, like Amelia's death, he should try to put behind him.

It was, Julia decided, always so hard to decide which pasta sauce to choose. There was the question of what type: arrabbiata, arnatriciana, bolognese, carbonara, or just pesto. Then there was the issue of which brand: Dolmio, Ragu, Paul Newman's or just Sainsbury's own label, which was cheaper but still quite good. 'Decisions,' she muttered under her breath. Two girl-friends were coming over for supper, and she had ducked out of the office reasonably early, stopping at the Chelsea Harbour supermarket to collect some food. Arrabbiata, she decided. Which meant a white wine, perhaps a chardonnay, or a Chianti. More decisions, she could hear her mind telling her.

From the corner of her eye, Julia thought she could glimpse Harry wrestling with the same dilemma. She had been watching him casually for almost a minute now, her eyes flickering from the sauces to the man standing along the aisle. At first she was not sure it was the same guy she had seen in the gym a few days earlier; it was hard to recall his appearance exactly. He was standing next to a trolley, already half full, and examining the labels on the jars. It was the little girl who clinched it. Cassie was sitting in the back of the trolley, wearing a floral-print dress, her tiny red shoes dangling over the edge. Julia was sure she would recognise her anywhere and together they were unmissable.

Idly, Julia scanned the length of the aisle, wondering when his wife would appear to tell him which sauce to buy. That woman shouldn't let him out on his own so much, she thought. It isn't safe. And, still smiling at the predatory tone of the thought, she started pushing her trolley away from him. Less mischief, she told herself. There is shopping to be done.

'Didn't we meet in the gym?' asked Harry.

The question took Julia by surprise; she hadn't planned to speak to him again and certainly hadn't expected him to speak to her. She stopped, pausing briefly, flicking her hair above her forehead, wondering if she had refreshed her lipstick before leaving the office. 'I think so, yes,' she replied hesitantly. 'You and your little girl.'

'Cassie,' said Harry. 'Say hello, princess,' he added, rubbing his hand through her blonde hair.

Cassie glanced up, her eyes straining, before looking away shyly. Julia leant over, patting her on the head. 'Hello, Cassie, I'm Julia.' Cassie smiled briefly, but remained obstinately silent. 'She's very sweet,' added Julia, her eyes moving back up towards Harry.

'And I'm Harry,' he said, extending his hand.

'Good to meet you,' Julia replied, taking his hand. Her fingers, she noticed, lingered just slightly longer in his grip than was strictly necessary and she had to correct herself, putting her hands firmly back on the trolley. 'Which sauce are you getting?'

'I don't know, really,' said Harry, looking back at the shelves and grabbing the first jar that came to hand. 'Pesto, I suppose. Something simple. Her nanny is away this evening and I'm not much of a hand in the kitchen. I wouldn't want to risk anything too rich on Cassie. Spaghetti hoops would probably be the best choice.'

'Her mother hasn't left anything?' asked Julia.

'Her mother is dead,' answered Harry.

There was a pause, heavy and purposeful, while Julia looked first down at Cassie then back up at her father. There was something about the flatness of his answer that she knew masked an immensity of sorrow. She felt stupid for having mentioned it, and immediately wished she had kept quiet. 'I'm sorry.'

Harry nodded. 'It's okay. I always try to slip it into the conversation pretty early on. Saves that difficult moment when people ask.'

He smiled, but Julia noted it was not a real smile; his lips moved outwards and his teeth were exposed, but there was no joy there, only resolution.

Together they started pushing their trolleys along the aisle, Julia keeping a vague eye on the racks, wondering whether she should stop and start filling her basket, bringing the conversation to a close, or say something else. 'It must be very hard for you,' she said eventually.

'I don't know,' answered Harry, a lightness returning to his tone now. 'Women bring up children by themselves all the time. It shouldn't be so difficult for a man. I can afford a nanny so really it's no trouble at all.'

They were standing in the drinks section now and Julia absent-mindedly took a bottle of wine from the shelves, hardly even thinking about what she was buying. Harry grabbed some Jameson's and a Johnny Walker Black Label, plus two wine boxes, one red and one white, and a six-pack of Beck's. Alcohol for the man who drinks alone, Julia noted. 'What do you do?' she asked.

'Stockbroking,' answered Harry crisply. 'An analyst. Specialising in media stocks.'

Probably pretty well off then, Julia thought to herself. 'Which firm?'

'Croxley, Palmer for the last eight years,' said Harry. 'But actually I'm casting around for something else at

51

the moment. Things stopped working out there. And you?'

Julia paused, uncertain how much she wanted to reveal to a stranger in a supermarket; there was something about his eyes that made him appear trustworthy, but one could never be sure. 'A consultant,' she replied. 'Usually specialising in financial investigations. But right now I'm on secondment to the Serious Fraud Office. For a year.'

Harry smiled. 'Busted anyone yet?'

'No. I'm not likely to either,' answered Julia, suppressing a giggle. 'I don't think the SFO ever really busts anyone and I'm hardly going to break their duck. I hardly know what I'm doing and I don't think I'm really cut out to be a detective.'

'You don't know until you try.'

They had reached the check-out and Julia instinctively joined the queue behind Harry. It would be a shame to wander off to another desk, she decided. Queuing by yourself in a supermarket is not much fun. Harry told her to move in front of him. And a gentleman too, Julia smiled to herself.

'I'm hungry, Daddy,' announced Cassie from her seat in the trolley as Julia was unloading her stuff on to the conveyor. 'I want munchies.'

'In a few minutes, princess,' said Harry. 'We'll be home soon.'

'Teddy wants munchies, too,' insisted Cassie.

'Teddy will wait,' said Harry. 'Trust me.'

Julia signed for her food on her switch card and waited for Harry's bill to be calculated. 'You said you worked for Croxley, Palmer?' she said.

Harry nodded.

'Perhaps you could give me some background on the firm some time?' asked Julia. 'Completely off the record, naturally.'

Harry hesitated. 'What have they been up to?'

'Nothing probably,' replied Julia casually. 'Possibly being used by some third parties. But it might be useful for me to know some more about how a stockbroker works.'

'Sure,' said Harry. 'I'd be happy to.' Briefly he wondered if he should ask her back for a drink and a bite now, but decided it seemed too forward. It had been a long time, he realised, since he had dated any women. There had been nobody since Amelia died and he had quite forgotten how these things started, or how quickly they could move. And anyway, perhaps she did just want to talk about broking.

'Munchies, Daddy,' Cassie interrupted his thoughts.

'You'd better get her home,' said Julia.

'She'll start creating a scene if I don't.'

'I'll be in the gym on Monday, so perhaps I'll see you then,' Julia added. 'After work.'

'I'm usually there around that time.' Harry extended a hand and she shook it warmly. This time his fingers lingered a fraction of a second longer than was necessary.

5

From the look on his face it was clear he agreed with her conclusions.

The spreadsheet was laid out on John Mitchell's desk, next to four pages of explanatory notes. The notes were superfluous, Julia realised, but writing them had helped her organise her own thoughts. Here the numbers told their own story, needing neither exaggeration nor amplification.

With the careful deliberation she imagined was ingrained into lawyers and prosecutors at an early age, Mitchell studied the file closely, at first betraying no sign of any reaction. He might be thinking anything, Julia decided; that it's the best piece of detective work he has ever seen; or that I'm a complete fool.

It was only after he had read his way through to the end and started checking back on some of the details that Julia was aware he was impressed with the work. To her own surprise, though she hated the idea of the secondment, she found she was pleased to have suc-ceeded in some small way; no matter how irrelevant the task, she decided, one never wanted to be seen as a loser. And, in truth, the challenge of piecing together the jigsaw had started to entrap her interest.

'It's a staggering collection of information,' said Mitchell slowly, looking up at Julia for the first time. 'If your estimates of more than a billion pounds in profits are right this would be about the biggest and most serious case this office has ever looked at.'

The papers he had just been studying represented more than a week's solid work. The four companies she started tracking had clocked up tremendous profits over a period of about nine months, but Julia soon realised there was no reason to stop the investigation there. If the insider dealing ring was using those four firms, they could easily be using others as well. Mapping the series of deals, she had then gone back to each one, looking up on the Stock Exchange records which other companies had been trading in the same stocks on the same days. It soon became clear that her early work had only scratched the surface. In total, she found forty companies, all based offshore and all making fabulous profits in the same series of almost identical trades. 'Do you think there can be any doubt?' she asked.

Mitchell shook his head. 'None at all,' he replied. 'It's as clear a case of insider dealing as one could hope to find. We have all the dates of the trades, the size of the deals, the brokers they were placed with and the subsequent piece of information that was being dealt upon. If I were a prosecutor I'd have no trouble taking this to court. It is circumstantial, of course, but that needn't be an obstacle. Not when the circumstances are as overwhelmingly obvious as they are here. There is no way that this kind of share trading could be a coincidence. Nobody gets this lucky.'

'So where do we go next?' asked Julia.

Mitchell stood up from his desk and looked momentarily out of the window. His back was to her and she could see that his shoulders were tensed slightly, as though he were weighing a decision. 'There is one problem,' he said at length. 'We have the evidence. We just don't have the culprit.'

'We know the companies involved,' said Julia. 'All forty of them must be mixed up in the insider dealing ring. It's impossible that they could be moving into the market independently of one another. Not always within a few days. That would be too much of a coincidence.'

'True,' replied Mitchell thoughtfully. 'There can be no question that all forty of them are linked. But my guess is they are just a front. Offshore companies usually are.'

'And we can't find out who owns these companies?'

Almost as soon as she asked the question she knew it was naïve and the expression on Mitchell's face confirmed her suspicion; she felt she had let herself down by even raising the possibility.

'Not from the Cayman Islands, nor from any of these offshore centres,' he replied. 'The secrecy over there is total. That is their one asset and they never put it at risk by revealing anything. Anyway, if we were to start poking around it would only arouse suspicion. The last thing we want to do right now is alert them that they're being watched. Give them any hint of that and the ring will tighten up and the money disappear.'

Julia sighed. The research so far had been interesting and the jigsaw made a fascinating puzzle, but she felt they had reached the end of the road. 'If we can't find out the ownership of these companies, we haven't proved anything,' she said. 'I don't see what we can do.'

Mitchell turned from the window and sat on the edge of the desk. 'Detection is a careful game,' he said. 'It moves slowly, piece by piece, until you have the whole picture. Often, it's the very last piece that allows it all to fall into place. But one thing is generally true. So long as you have enough information, and the patience to figure it all out, the answer usually emerges.'

'Give me a practical example,' demanded Julia. 'I can buy the theory, but I don't see how it helps us here.'

'Look at what we have.'

'Nothing.'

'On the contrary,' said Mitchell. 'We have plenty of leads. It's just a matter of looking for them.'

Julia walked round the desk, looking back down at the spreadsheets. Perhaps he was right, she started to think to herself. Perhaps there are leads here. 'We can take it that these companies are working together,' she started. 'They are probably all a front for a single organisation.'

'That would be a workable hypothesis,' said Mitchell, looking directly at Julia as he spoke.

She paused, still looking at the documents, allowing the next thought to develop slowly. 'If it's just one organisation, or perhaps just one individual, then there also has to be a source. If they are trading on inside information they must be getting it from somewhere. But where? The range of companies they are trading is too diverse for it to be a single person. I don't see how that gives us any leads.'

'One thing is obvious,' said Mitchell.

Julia looked at the list once more, already worrying she might appear stupid if she couldn't pick up on the clues. 'The companies whose shares are being traded are all in Europe.'

'Right.'

'So whatever the source is, it must be restricted to Europe,' said Julia.

'Interesting, don't you think?'

'So we're looking for a person who would have access to information within Europe, but not outside,' said Julia.

'And what else?' asked Mitchell.

Julia looked down at the documents once more, her

mind churning through the options. There was a silence lasting several minutes, while Mitchell watched her. 'They placed about a quarter of the trades with just one broker,' she said at last.

'Exactly.'

'But surely there's no reason why they should have done that,' she continued. 'It would make more sense to spread the trades around a variety of brokers, perhaps a different one for each of the forty companies involved.'

'That would certainly make their tracks harder to follow.'

'So there must be some reason why they've done it that way,' mused Julia. 'And that must give us a clue.'

Mitchell hesitated. 'True.'

'But I can't imagine what it might be,' said Julia.

Mitchell leant forward, looking at her closely. 'Well, we have some facts to play with. We know their information comes just from Europe and we know they prefer to deal with Croxley. Start chipping away at those two facts and I should imagine others will begin to fall into place. It's a kick-off anyway.'

Julia turned away, feeling pleased at the amount she had accomplished, but daunted by what remained to be done. 'So I'm not off the case.'

Mitchell shook his head. 'On the contrary, Julia. 'Your work is only just beginning. It would be crazy to take you off it when you've made such a good start.'

Richard Gregson waved a hand across the dealing floor, standing tall and erect as he did so, his thick nostrils noisily sniffing the air in the windowless room. 'We deal in more shit here than practically anyone else in the world,' he said firmly. 'In London, anyway, which financially pretty much is the world, these days.'

Harry smiled at the remark. 'I'm not sure your clients would like the description, Mr Gregson.'

Gregson laughed heartily. 'The clients are all whores, my man,' he boomed. 'They love to be fucked.'

Gregson was one of those Americans who struck Europeans as too big. He was more than six foot five, with a jaw like a bulldog and shoulders that arched outwards from his thick, broad neck. His hair was black, with streaks of grey, looking as if it were dyed, although whether the black was artificial to make him look younger, or the grey to make him look more distinguished, it was impossible to say.

He slipped an arm round Harry's shoulder, leading him down on to the dealing floor. Strips of fluorescent light covered the ceiling, casting a hazy glow on the three thousand square feet of turbulent space. Along its length were rows of desks, each one cluttered with phone lines and trading screens, the green lights flashing prices up constantly and adding a luminous haze to the already dazzling light. The traders sat at the front end of the dealing room, bellowing into their phones, each one dressed in regulation white shirt, the sleeves rolled up, their ties loosened. Towards the back there was a more sedate group of men, each peering into a terminal, their desks covered with papers and calculations. The analysts, figured Harry, the men who crunch the numbers. Across the top of the room, running its full length, was a Reuters display, with the latest financial news stuttering across in red lettering.

'I call this place the mushroom farm,' said Gregson, nodding curtly to a couple of dealers as he strode across the floor. 'You know why?'

Harry shook his head.

'Because I keep 'em in the dark and throw shit at them,' Gregson continued, laughing like a jackal as he did so. 'Then I come along in the morning and harvest all these beautiful, valuable mushrooms.' He smacked his lips together in an exaggerated kissing noise. 'There is a lot we can learn from the natural world, my man.'

'That's why there are no windows?' asked Harry.

Gregson halted suddenly, taking his arm from Harry's shoulder and turning to face him. 'Ever been to Vegas?'

Harry shook his head again.

'Get out there now, my man,' said Gregson. 'Capitalism at its rawest. You'll learn more in a couple of nights in that hot sand-pit than you will in a decade or two at business school. It's in the middle of a fucking desert, my man. But no windows. You know why that is? So the jerks don't know what time it is. Sit at the slots and the tables all night. Never know when to go to bed. They just keep playing. I learnt that pretty quick. The financial markets are a casino. So no fucking windows. Is that clear?'

'I think so,' replied Harry. If his mind had not already been made up, it would have been by now. There was no way he wanted to work at Gregson & Heath.

The call had taken him by surprise yesterday morning. He had been preparing Cassie for her play-group when the phone rang. 'I hear you're on the market,' the voice had snapped. 'Come and see me tomorrow afternoon. We might have something for you.'

He had, of course, heard of Gregson & Heath. Most people in the City had. An American who had first made his fortune dealing in junk bonds during the late eighties, he had decamped to London five years ago after that market had collapsed. For five million pounds he had taken control of Heath & Co., a tiny niche stock-broker and fund manager on the fringes of the City, which specialised in small industrial and textile companies. It was a move that puzzled everyone at the time; why should one of the brashest and most abrasive New York financiers be interested in an insignificant London broker? The logic soon became clear. Gregson only wanted Heath as a base; it had the regulatory approvals to deal in the London market that Gregson might have found difficult to obtain on his own and permission to deal in London meant permission to deal in the whole of Europe. The firm had quickly been turned upside down. From dealing mostly in industrial stocks, it now handled only distressed debt, a market that made the New York junk trades look as secure as the local building society. And from running small pension funds, the firm now ran only vulture funds, picking over the carcasses of dead, or nearly dead, companies in the hope of a quick and lethal profit.

His timing, most people in the City had been reluctantly forced to concede, had been perfect. By the early nineties the borrowing boom of the late eighties had left many companies burdened down by huge debts. Some could meet their interest payments to the banks, but many could not. Their debt, in the strangely genteel terminology of the financial markets, was 'distressed'. Useless might have been a better word. Yet not entirely useless. In many companies there was probably no chance of the debt being repaid. In some, however, a proportion probably would be. How much, exactly, was something on which different traders could take different views. And so long as there were different views, there was a market to be made.

It was an opportunity that Gregson's firm exploited ruthlessly. It would take on board the debts of ailing companies from the banks, who just wanted to be shot of the problem to clean up their own bruised balance sheets. It would be sold at less than face value; thirty pence would be a typical price to pay for a pound of debt. If the company eventually paid back fifty pence of each pound of debt, the buyer would make a big profit. If it only paid back a few pence, the losses would be huge. The risks were enormous and, unlike the equity and bond markets, these trades were entirely unregulated. There were no controls on the size of the deals, or on the flow of information. It was a wild and scary place to make a living. Which was why Gregson thrived in it, Harry realised after a few minutes at his side. He was a wild and scary man.

His firm had become the biggest player in the distressed debt market, ready to take billions of the banks and place it with investors around the world with an appetite for risk that matched his own. For broking the deals between the banks and the investors, Gregson & Heath collected a commission like any other broker. At the same time, it made a market in the debt, holding it on its own books. If the price of the debt went up while the firm was holding it, then it reaped extra profits on top of its commissions. The firm was registered offshore, so no one knew exactly how much money it made. But the profits in the last few years were rumoured to have run into tens of millions.

Gregson & Heath, unlike any of its rivals in the market, did not just trade debt. It bought the stuff. The firm ran three offshore funds that specialised in buying distressed debt. They were called vulture funds, for a very simple reason; like vultures, they circled the financial markets, swooping when they saw dead carrion, picking the meat from the bones. Often the funds would buy debt from Gregson's own firm. In any other market there would have been rules to prevent that; the potential for abuse was too great for any regulator to tolerate. But the distressed debt markets were not regulated. Anything went.

Everything, Harry realised as soon as he put down the phone, depended on analysis. To make money in the market, and to run his funds profitably, Gregson had to be able to calculate a company's financial position with perfect precision. Whether it was going to pay back thirty or thirty-five per cent of its debts made the difference between huge profits and huge losses. And to make that calculation required analysis. It was different from the kind of work he was used to as an equity analyst; Gregson would not have been interested in earning growth or dividend payouts. He would just be interested in cashflow. But it was analysis all the same. Which was why, he supposed, he was standing there that afternoon.

'So why did those jerks over at Croxley can you?' boomed Gregson.

They were sitting in his office now, both holding tins of Coke he had pulled from the fridge. The room, the only enclosed space in the building, was perched on the second floor, with a strip of open glass looking down on the trading floor below, but the glass must have been sound-proofed, since not a whisper from the floor could be heard. Across one side there was a desk, flanked by two black leather sofas, and behind the desk there was a fishtank, through which could be glimpsed several gaping tropical fish. They provided the only colour; everything else was black or grey, even the signed picture of Gregson shaking hands with Ronald Reagan at a Republican fund-raising dinner that was displayed prominently on the desk.

'They said I was a loose cannon,' replied Harry.

There were no windows to the outside world here either, Harry noted. Another hermetically sealed environment, preserved from contamination by daylight and the glimpses of reality it might provide; it was as if the place were entombed, a zone of indifference to everything apart from the relentless hum of the computers, the ringing of the phones and the surging waves of the markets they hoped to control.

'Tight-arsed English fools,' said Gregson, his wide

jaw broadening out into a chuckle as he spoke. 'You have to be a loose cannon to make money in this business. No point in everyone firing in the same direction. Train your guns any place you god-damn please. That's the way we operate here. Every man for himself.'

Harry nodded, but remained silent for a few seconds. He was not sure how much he wanted to tell Gregson; not the truth, that much he knew, but perhaps a sculpted version of it. 'I think some of my work was perhaps too close to the bone.'

'No point writing bullshit. Too much of that around already,' said Gregson. 'I hear you were scratching away at Cable Media.'

Harry gripped his canned drink. 'Word gets around.' He hoped he'd maintain a neutral expression, but was aware that hiding his feelings had never been a skill he had mastered.

'Sure does,' agreed Gregson. 'One of the great features of the London market. Information swills about all over the place. What was your beef with that company? Why the itch?'

Harry shrugged; no point in revealing too much, he decided, although he would like to find out how much Gregson knew. 'Nothing much,' he answered casually. 'I was starting to get interested in the financing of the Argus project. Perhaps they were being a little too ambitious. But that is only of relevance to the shareholders. The bankers behind the project needn't worry about it.'

Gregson eyed him closely. 'If the company is fucked, then that would interest a debt trader.'

'True,' replied Harry cautiously.

'Is the company fucked, Mr Lamb?' His tone as he delivered the question was pure ice; sharp, clear and very cold.

Harry paused. 'That piece of research was never finished.'

'But what do you think?'

'I think you should keep an eye on them.'

Gregson took a swig on his Coke and laughed. 'Companies are like cocktail waitresses,' he said. 'You only keep an eye on them if you think they are going to be fucked. That's free advice, Mr Lamb.'

'I'll keep that in mind, Mr Gregson,' replied Harry.

'You do that, my man, you do that,' said Gregson, standing up. He slipped an arm round Harry's shoulder. 'Now, what do you say? You come and work here and we'll get that cocktail waitress to lie down for both of us. We'll fuck her together.'

'I'll certainly think about it.'

'You do that,' said Gregson, walking towards the door. 'But remember. A man doesn't always want to think about things too much. Sometimes he needs to act on instinct. He starts thinking too much, he turns around and finds some other guy is eating his honey.' He slapped Harry firmly on the back while opening the door. 'That's two pieces of free advice I've given you this afternoon, which is two more than I usually give my best friend. So you think about it, my man. And you get back to me.'

Kim Chung ran his eyes carefully over the row of bottles behind the bar. There were several different types of vodka, a bottle of Japanese brandy and some Mongolian rice spirits he had never seen before. You would think, he reflected, they would know how to make a decent dry martini. But no. The waitress had just looked baffled when he made the request and he had to settle for a glass of neat vodka.

The bar was one of several in the centre of Yakutsk, a dismal concrete town on the main rail line connecting

Moscow and Beijing, a staging post, consisting of a rail terminal, some warehouses, distribution centres, one canning plant and not much else. Chung had flown in the day before and was already starting to dislike the place; he would be relieved once he had settled into a first-class berth on the night train towards Vladivostock that evening.

He scanned the rows of tables and chairs. Lykanov was instantly recognisable from the picture Chung had memorised before he left London; a short, stocky man, with broad shoulders and arms, and greying clumps of hair, tumbling over his forehead in a haphazard fringe.

Taking a sip of his vodka, Chung decided to wait a few moments before making his approach; surveillance had decreased dramatically in Russia in the past few years, but military scientists could still be expected to be watched closely by the police. There were too many people around the world fishing for Soviet expertise for any members of the old defence establishment to be allowed unrestricted freedom.

'A drink, my friend?' asked Chung, standing next to the scientist's table, bowing slightly as he spoke.

Lykanov nodded and Chung signalled to the waitress to bring them two more glasses. He glanced up at his new companion, now sitting at the table next to him. An oriental. He had not expected that. But he didn't suppose it was important. When you put yourself on the market you sold to the highest bidder.

'You are looking for work, my friend,' said Chung, speaking the words slowly and clearly. He was aware that Lykanov, like most Russian scientists, would read English, would be familiar with the language, yet would rarely have heard it spoken. 'Work similar to what you have done before,' Chung continued.

Lykanov shrugged. 'This is what I know,' he answered. 'Satellite systems are my life's work. But here in Russia there is no money any more.' He paused, looking down at the table and the single measure of vodka in front of him. 'A man has to live.'

'I represent some people who would pay well for someone of your expertise.'

Lykanov eyed the man closely; he appeared to be in his late thirties or early forties, with firm muscles, and a strong jawline, and dark, impenetrable features. His manner was polite and courteous, but with an air of underlying violence, his bearing alert and watchful, as though he were constantly preparing for some kind of confrontation. 'Who are these people?' Lykanov asked.

'They will also pay well for someone who does not ask too many questions,' said Chung. 'It is not at this stage strictly necessary for you to know who they are. The task is quite simple, really. To install and operate a satellite intelligence system. The platforms are all in place and the equipment is all there. No expense is being spared and you will have everything you need at your disposal. Be honest with me. Do you think you can do this?'

Lykanov nodded. 'It is what I have been doing all my life,' he replied.

'That is why we approached you,' said Chung. 'We will pay you one million American dollars, deposited in an account of your choice. That is a signing-on fee for one year's work. If we need you to stay longer than a year, the salary will be five hundred thousand dollars a year. All your expenses will be paid and you will be given everything you need. But there are two conditions. One is that for the first year you work only for us. You must have no contact with anyone outside our organisation, not even socially. The second is that you must never speak to anyone about your work. Ever.'

'How do I know I can trust you?' asked Lykanov.

From his suitcase Chung retrieved a large brown envelope. He pushed it across the table to the scientist, indicating that he should look inside. Lykanov opened it, peering in. There was a bundle of dollar bills, stacked in wads of fifties. 'Twenty-five thousand American dollars,' said Chung. 'Take it as a token of our good faith.'

Lykanov took the envelope, slipping it inside his own briefcase; it was more money than he had ever seen before, a hard currency, and already he could feel its power; he wanted to hold it, touch it and to sense it was real. 'And where would I be working?' he asked.

'London,' replied Chung. 'We will arrange for you to leave Russia as soon as possible. All the travel details will be taken care of.'

Lykanov was surprised. London, he thought to himself; surely the British had access to all the American satellite technology and that was the best in the world. What would they need with him? For a moment he hesitated; this man clearly represented something far more mysterious than he had yet imagined. It was, however, too late. Once you started there was no going back. The orbit, to use a language he was familiar with, could not be altered. 'I will wait to hear from you,' he said calmly. 'And I will be ready.'

Julia was sitting with her back to the room, holding a glass of apple juice in one hand and turning the pages of the *Evening Standard* with the other. For a moment, Harry just stood and watched her. From a distance, she looked like a typical City yupette. Attractive, no doubt, Harry decided; he could feel a sense of anticipation just gazing at her across the bar. Yet City career women had never been his type; they were too cold and calculating, too wrapped up in their careers and too obsessed with money and status. Fine for a brief fling; there had been a few of those with girls around the office before he was married. But not the

68

type of woman you wanted to get involved with. Not seriously.

He had found her that evening on the bike machines, dressed in a purple leotard, traces of sweat streaked across her brow and with headphones strapped tight over her head; from the slight movement of her lips he guessed she was humming along to the Simply Red video playing on VH-1. He tapped her on the shoulder and, when she removed one earplug, said he would see her in the bar after he'd finished his work-out.

Harry sat down beside her, ordering a beer. 'What did you want to know about Croxley?' he asked.

Julia took another sip of her juice. She looked at him and realised her first instinct had been right; she was drawn to his broad, well-sculptured shoulders, his thick black hair and, most of all, to the playful, mischievous quality of his expression. She liked him, but she was uncertain if this meeting was a good idea; a fluttering in the pit of her stomach told her she was nervous. Her motives, she realised, were confused. She wanted to talk to him about the investigation, yet she wasn't sure if she could trust him. And she wanted just to talk, to relax, but was unsure if she could trust him with her company either. He was someone she had just met, and of whom she knew nothing. 'Why did you leave?' she asked carefully. 'If that's not too personal a question.'

Harry shrugged. 'I don't really know,' he replied. 'They canned me. Happens all the time, as you probably know. But with me there was no warning, no signs that it was on the horizon. Nor, as far as I can tell, was there any reason for it. But perhaps I'm being arrogant. It could be I just wasn't good enough.'

'I doubt that,' said Julia, lowering her head slightly as she spoke and averting her eyes.

'So do I, in truth,' said Harry. 'But it's a mystery. One that I wouldn't mind unravelling, although it won't do me any good now. A matter of satisfying personal curiosity, I suppose.'

It was the honesty and directness of his tone that impressed Julia; he was opening up to her, telling her what had happened frankly, with none of the spin men usually put on their affairs in the company of women. 'In the work I've been doing at the SFO, the name of the firm has come up,' she said.

Harry looked interested. 'In what context?'

'Can I take it this is just between us?' asked Julia. 'I know very little about broking and it would be useful for me to bounce some ideas off somebody who does. But I would have to be able to trust them. I wouldn't want anyone at Croxley to know we were investigating.'

'No worries there,' replied Harry. 'I'm unlikely to be doing them any favours right now.'

'It's an insider dealing investigation,' said Julia. She paused, scrutinising his face for a reaction, but could find little written there, just an easygoing nonchalance, as though this were the kind of conversation he had every day. 'I started by looking at a series of offshore companies and tracking their trades through the London market over a period of about eight months. It's clear that something strange is happening. The trades are always made just before an important announcement that pushes the share price up.'

Harry shrugged, taking another swig of his beer. He was too busy noticing the contrast between her bright-red lipstick and the delicate shade of her hair to pay much attention to what she was saying; in truth, he admitted to himself, he was more interested in looking at her lips than listening to her.

'What should I make of that?' Julia persisted.

'Insider dealing is very common in the City,' Harry answered. 'Everyone knows it's illegal but that hardly deters them. For one thing, you almost never get caught. For another, nobody really feels it's immoral. There isn't really any peer group sanction. And the money is easy. So it happens all the time, at least on a small scale. In fact, every time one of the guys buys a new house in the country there are lots of jokes around the office about how he's probably been doing some dealing on the side. In many cases it's most likely true.'

Julia leant forward. 'In this case, about a quarter of the trades have been channelled through one broker.'

'That's unusual,' said Harry. 'A little amateurish, even. It would be more normal to spread the action around all of the brokers. Sounds like your people don't really know what they're doing.'

'I think they definitely know what they're doing,' said Julia. 'There's too much money at stake for them to be amateurs.'

'How much?' asked Harry.

Julia ran a hand through her hair; part of her was still uncertain how much she should tell him. 'Over one billion pounds,' she answered calmly, as though she were used to discussing such sums. 'That's what I've tracked down so far.'

The look of surprise on his face startled her; perhaps, she realised, she had not been as aware as she should have been of the magnitude of what she was dealing with. But the incredulity written in his eyes told her this was something out of the ordinary. 'Are you sure?' he asked.

'Quite sure,' replied Julia. 'I've tracked all the trades.'

'With two hundred and fifty million put through Croxley, Palmer?'

Julia nodded. 'According to my calculations, yes.'

Harry raised a hand to his lips. For a moment he was lost in thought. 'If there had been a client dealing on that scale we should have known about it on the floor,' he said eventually. 'The traders and analysts gossip about clients all the time.'

Julia ran through the names of the key offshore companies she had been following, noting the look of fascination on his face as she gave brief details of some of the profits made. 'You've never heard of any of these companies?' she asked.

Harry shook his head. 'Not a word about any of them,' he replied. 'Which is proof enough that something strange is happening. If the trades were legitimate it would have been the talk of the trading floor. No. Somebody must have wanted to keep the trades very secret.'

'Could we find out who it is?' asked Julia.

'I'm sure the SFO has the power to demand records of which broker dealt with those clients,' answered Harry.

'We don't want them to know we are investigating.'

'Then you have a problem,' said Harry. 'But there might be one thing you could do.'

'Which is?'

Harry hesitated. 'Try tracking their trades. With the new electronic trading system the Stock Exchange should be able to give you details within hours of any trades made by the companies you are following. Then you place an order for the same stock. Through a dummy account, I suppose. I would imagine the SFO could set up such a thing.'

'What would that achieve, exactly?' inquired Julia.

'Hard to say, precisely,' replied Harry with a broad smile. 'But it would certainly shake the tree. No knowing what might fall out.'

6

Alan Broat did not look particularly impressed. He was
a large man, with a moustache and a round face that
sagged into his rumpled shirt and suit; his clothes were
slightly tight, as though he were putting on weight
rapidly and his wardrobe had not yet had time to catch
up. His desk was cluttered with brokers' notes, a few
from Croxley, Palmer, and his eyes darted nervously
from the Reuters screen on his desk to the man sitting in
front of him. Surprisingly, Harry reflected, for one of the
City's leading fund managers, he was no poker player;
his thoughts flickered over his face, as easy to read as the
letters scrolling across a word processor. I might just as
well say what happened, Harry decided. 'I think they
were unhappy about a line I was pushing on Cable
Media.'

In truth, Harry was not even sure he wanted to work
with Broat's firm. For the first few days after his sacking
he had not even wanted to think about getting a new
job; after all, his salary would still be paid for another six
months, so there was no hurry financially. He would
have plenty of money for at least a year, perhaps longer.
There was no need to rush. This, he had decided, was
an opportunity to take stock. To take a look around and

start giving some thought to what he wanted to do with the rest of his life.

Still, it was good to know you were wanted. The call from Richard Gregson had opened up one possibility, that from Broat another. His firm was among the more respected of the City's fund managers, and a life managing pension funds and unit trusts might well be more satisfying than churning out notes on companies; at least he could develop his ideas and push them through, rather than just engaging himself in endless conjecture. It was a possibility, no more, he decided. Something to consider.

Broat had steered the conversation carefully towards the reasons for his departure from Croxley, Palmer, and Harry had tried spinning a line about how the firm had been coming under a lot of pressure to contain costs and he had just been one of the casualties. It was the same line they had spun for him and it sounded no more convincing on his lips than it had on theirs. Harry could see it was not working. And whatever job he wanted he was going to have to come up with something better. Broat was clearly trying to find out if there was any hint of trouble surrounding Harry's departure. He decided he might as well tell him the truth.

'What was your line on Cable Media, exactly?' asked Broat.

'I was starting to push them as an obvious sell,' replied Harry. 'Because of the debt structure of their new satellite system. Somebody obviously didn't like that line.'

Broat shifted uneasily in his seat, his tight-fitting jacket bulging slightly as he did so. 'Strange company, that one,' he said uneasily. 'We have quite a few shares in our funds. Almost two per cent.'

'I'd wind that down while there are still some buyers,' said Harry.

Broat looked uncertain. 'Have you had many dealings with them?'

Harry shrugged. 'Some. One sees Haverstone at the company presentations and, before he died, Sir Ian Strang.'

'What did you make of him?' asked Broat.

'A very reliable old character,' answered Harry. 'Not particularly dynamic, but a safe pair of hands. You could be sure he wouldn't take any crazy risks, but Haverstone is different. There is an edge to him. He has more self-belief than is really wise for someone playing with other people's money. It was a shame Sir Ian died. He reassured a lot of people in the City.'

Broat's eyes flickered back from the Reuters screen. 'Ever heard about the last calls?'

Harry shook his head.

'It was really strange,' said Broat, lowering his voice slightly as he spoke and adopting a confidential tone. 'The night before he died he called me. Said he was planning to get rid of Haverstone and he wanted to speak to me about it. Seemed to think it would be quite a fight and he wanted to collect support from some of the big shareholders before he made his move.'

Harry leant forward; suddenly his mind was emptied of any thought of getting a job. 'Did he say why he wanted to get rid of Haverstone?' he asked.

Broat shook his head. 'He said he would talk about that when he came to see me. Too sensitive. But he must have been pretty serious because he called at least two other people, as far as I know, and asked them the same thing. The next we knew he was dead.'

'And Haverstone was made chairman as well as chief executive,' said Harry.

Broat nodded. 'So I guess he won that one.'

Harry looked at the man closely, but could tell he saw

nothing strange about the incident. 'And don't you think there's something suspicious about that?'

'Suspicious?' asked Broat, as if the thought had just occurred to him. 'What do you mean, exactly?'

'Strang is organising a revolt against Haverstone,' said Harry, aware he was allowing his thoughts to run away with him. 'Then he dies. Seems very convenient for Haverstone.'

Broat laughed. 'That kind of thing happens on TV,' he said. 'Sir Ian died in a house fire. With a woman, I understand, who was neither his wife nor the mother of his children. It was an accident. At least, I suppose so. He said something about a website as well, where everything would be revealed if anything happened to him. Must have been drunk. That's probably why he allowed the place to catch fire.'

'Where was the website?' asked Harry. He was trying to keep his voice calm and even, and yet he knew the urgency of the question was transparent.

'I can't remember if he said, and I don't think anyone has ever seen it,' said Broat. 'I wouldn't have known where to look myself. All that technical stuff baffles me. The phone is about as hi-tech as I get.' Broat heaved his heavy shoulders and laughed, not noticing that Harry had slumped back in his chair. 'Now, tell me about the strategies you would be adopting if you were running the media section of our funds right now.'

Harry started talking, telling Broat about the stakes he would be buying and those he would be winding down. He could hear himself outlining different types of analysis and how he would apply them. Yet he was hardly aware of the words pouring from his mouth. He was wondering where he could get a copy of the autopsy on Sir Ian Strang. Broat might not think his death was suspicious, but Harry had seldom felt so certain of anything in his life. Strang's demise was a stunning coincidence, and, Harry decided, he was starting to get a little tired of coincidences.

Julia hesitated before picking up the phone. She was not a good liar and she was worried the nervous inflection of her tone would betray the untruths she was about to tell. Her fingers moved carefully over the keypad, tapping the numbers into the phone. 'Keith Trimble, please,' she said. Busy, replied the voice on the other end of the phone. 'I'll hold,' Julia answered.

The information she needed had flashed up on her screen only half an hour earlier. The deal with the Stock Exchange had already been set up and the regulators there had agreed to notify her the moment one of the four companies she was tracking made a trade. There was not long to wait. Only three days after the arrangements had been made an e-mail had come through; one of her four prey had just placed a five-hundred-million buy order for Staunton Tobacco. The broker, inevitably, was Croxley, Palmer.

Mitchell had been suspicious of the idea at first. Julia had managed to convince him, however, that if they were to make any progress with this inquiry they had to start finding out how some of the pieces of the jigsaw fitted together. And the only way to do that was to try putting them in place.

She had written him a brief memo, setting out the plan. The SFO would establish a front company that would establish an account with Croxley, Palmer. There could be nothing suspicious about that. The firm would track the trading strategies of the insider dealing ring, just as Harry had suggested. That way they would soon discover whether the brokerage was an accomplice, or just a victim of the ring. And if it was an accomplice they would find out pretty soon who their contact was within the firm.

'It's hardly orthodox,' Mitchell had said, on reading the memo.

'Orthodoxy has come up with how many convictions, exactly?' said Julia sarcastically.

Mitchell smiled. He was starting to like her gumption. 'Fair point. It's time we took a different approach. But if this is to be done it needs to be done properly.' He stood up, leaning against the desk, his back to her, looking out of his window. 'There would be no way you could operate from this building. It would be too easy for the ring to trace the calls and find they came from the SFO. That would alert them that an investigation was under way.'

'Then I guess we get a dummy office,' said Julia. 'With a phone and a computer. That shouldn't be too difficult.'

'It can be arranged, certainly,' replied Mitchell. He turned, sitting on the edge of his desk, facing her directly. 'Something else bothers me,' he said slowly. 'We've no way of knowing who we're dealing with here. We just know they are well organised and have a lot of money at their disposal. By doing this you'll probably shake loose some information. But you could make yourself a target.'

'A target?' asked Julia. 'For what?'

Mitchell shrugged. 'That's the trouble. We don't know.'

Julia hadn't thought much about his words since then, but now, listening to soft muzak played to callers on hold at Croxley, Palmer, they started to nag at her memory. The office had taken no more than a couple of days to arrange, a simple two-room box in a new development just past Broadgate on the edge of the City. There was a desk and a computer and a phone, plus a receptionist she shared with a dozen other small outfits in the same building. That aside, the place was completely bare: no pictures, no ornaments, not much of a view and nobody there apart from herself. For the first time she started to have doubts about what she was doing. I'm just filling in a year here on secondment until I go back to the consultancy, she reminded herself. There was no need to become too deeply involved.

Her thoughts were interrupted by a voice on the line. 'Trimble here.'

Julia clutched the phone closer to her ear. 'This is Samantha Draper,' she began. 'From Lexington Investments.'

'What's up?' asked Trimble.

'I'm interested in making a large purchase of Staunton Tobacco,' said Julia, trying to make her tone both casual and professional. 'Who's your expert on that stock?'

'I know a fair bit about it. Been pretty quiet for the last month or so. Not much chance of action there.'

'Perhaps not,' said Julia. 'But I've heard a whisper that something could be up. Anything like that on the grapevine?'

'Not that I've heard,' answered Trimble cautiously.

Julia paused. 'Well, I'd like to back my instincts on this one. Put Lexington down for fifty million.'

'It's your money,' said Trimble nonchalantly. 'Consider it done.'

Julia put down the phone, glad it was over. She pressed a button to spool back the tape, keen to hear the conversation once again; she couldn't be sure she had picked up all the right nuances the first time around. But the pause was still there, as obvious as when she had heard it before. Trimble had hesitated just before saying he thought there was nothing happening at Staunton. Even though his firm had taken a two-hundred-million buy order just that afternoon. There could be no doubt, she decided.

Trimble, and perhaps his firm as well, were not just on the periphery of this inquiry.

The reports struck Harry as strangely incomplete, as though he were looking at just the broken fragments of a story, rather than the story itself.

He had returned home that evening after a brief and furious work-out in the gym; he had looked around the place for Julia, but had, with what struck him as a rather exaggerated sense of disappointment, seen no sign of her. Lucy had left early on a date and she had not had time to cook anything. He had flung an M&S lasagne into the microwave and eaten it hurriedly, without paying much attention to the food.

Reading a bedtime story to Cassie took no more than ten minutes; he chose one of her *Spot the Dog* books, partly because he quite enjoyed Spot himself and also because he knew it always sent her to sleep quickly. The trick, as usual, worked; within seven or eight minutes she was slumbering peacefully and Harry leant forward to kiss her on the forehead. 'Sweet dreams, princess,' he had murmured softly.

Alone at last, he took himself down to the study, pouring a large glass of whisky. He slipped an old Clash CD on to the hi-fi and tapped his feet to the opening bars of 'London Calling', before sitting down at his computer and checking the modem was plugged into the phone socket. Then, he started his search.

The files on the death of Sir Ian Strang were not particularly extensive. He had keyed into the *FT* Profile database, tapping in a command to retrieve the stories about Strang printed in the last year. Almost all of them appeared in the week or so surrounding his death. The *FT* price was typical. Under the headline 'Cable Media Chairman Dies in House Fire' it read:

Sir Ian Strang, the seventy-year-old chairman of the media and telecoms conglomerate Cable Media, died yesterday in a fire at a holiday cottage on the west coast of Ireland. Police officials in Cork said the fire had destroyed the house completely, but that two bodies had been found among the remains. Dental records, the police said, had established the identity of Sir Ian, but not of his companion.

The police said that there did not appear to be any suspicious circumstances surrounding the fire. A preliminary investigation indicated that both victims had been trapped by the flames while they were sleeping. It is understood that Sir Ian was taking a short holiday at the cottage, where he had arrived earlier that day.

A statement from Cable Media last night described the death of Sir Ian as a tragic loss for the company. Samuel Haverstone, chief executive of Cable Media, said: 'His wisdom and experience were invaluable to all his colleagues during the recent merger that created Cable Media as one of the strongest forces in the global communications industry. His vision helped to create a strong European competitor in one of the world's fastest growing markets. His death robs the industry of one of its finest leaders and will be felt particularly keenly by his colleagues within the company. For myself, in the six months we worked together since the merger I had come to regard Sir Ian as an essential ally and adviser. We will all miss him greatly.'

A spokesman for Cable Media said that Haverstone would be assuming the chairmanship of the company until a permanent replacement could be found.

Harry scrolled through the rest of the files, but they all

said much the same thing, apart from a barbed remark in the *Guardian* City column about how it was to be hoped that a suitably independent replacement as chairman would soon be found; investors needed to be sure that Haverstone was kept on a short lead, it reflected.

Harry stored the files on his hard disk and took another sip of his whisky. None of the stories had mentioned any kind of conflict between Haverstone and Strang; the phone calls he had made the night before he died had clearly not been reported to any of the papers. The statement from Haverstone about how much he relied on the old man's advice was clearly a lie; the two men must have had some kind of argument and for Strang to have started calling shareholders it would have had to have been pretty serious. But about what, exactly?

Turning away from the computer, Harry started leafing through the files he had taken from the office on his last afternoon at Croxley, Palmer. He had been meaning to complete his research on the satellite project, yet somehow, in the days since then, he had possessed neither the energy nor the inclination to crunch his way through a series of financial calculations. But the germ of the idea still fascinated him. Cable Media was spending billions on building a new satellite system, one which, he strongly suspected, the company could not afford.

The Argus project had been announced with great fanfare in the weeks following the merger. The plan was to launch a series of low-orbit geostationary satellites covering the whole of Europe, stretching from the Urals in the east to the Atlantic in the west, from Scandinavia in the north to the shores of North Africa in the south. The satellites would be multi-purpose; each one would have the capacity to beam down up to two thousand digital television channels, as well as providing a ready-made network for both mobile and fixed-line telecoms systems. The beauty of a low-orbit satellite, circling the earth on the near fringes of the atmosphere, would be that it was close enough to dispose of the cumbersome big dishes that restricted the market for satellite communications. For television broadcasting, the dish would only be a little larger than a conventional aerial. And for telecoms, a tiny dish on the outside of a house would provide a line as perfect as the wires beneath the ground the established European telecoms companies had spent decades building.

There was little doubt Argus was the most exciting and ambitious project being attempted by any communications company in the world; with one system, Cable Media had the opportunity to create a lock on both the European broadcasting and telecoms markets. Nobody would be able to operate in either business without using the Cable Media system. It was a wonderful piece of technology, one that would enable the corporation to steal a march on all its competitors. But it was also horrendously expensive. Literature from the company estimated that twenty-five satellites would be needed to cover the whole of Europe, with another five high-orbit satellites to provide the communications links between the machines closer to the earth. That made a total of thirty satellites to be built and launched before the system would be completed.

Cable Media had said little about how much it would all cost, or where it would find the money. In his notes Harry had already started sketching out some rough ideas on the cost of the system. The satellites themselves were being built by a consortium of companies led by Aerospatiale in France; they would provide the basic platform, while most of the software inside the birds would come from Cable Media itself. No figures had been published on how much the consortium was charging for the machines, but Rockwell, the American company that also made commercial satellites, was estimated to charge about a hundred million dollars a-piece for its machines. That would bring the total to three billion dollars just for the hardware. But a satellite on the ground was no use to anyone. Getting the machine into orbit was the expensive part of the process.

Fifteen of the satellites had already been put into space. Launching them had become an increasingly competitive business in the past few years; the Americans used their Space Shuttle, the Chinese the Long March rocket system and the Europeans the Arianne. By rooting around in some data published on the continent, Harry had estimated the cost of each Arianne launch at around two hundred million dollas. A total of six billion dollars to get the machines into orbit.

Staring down at the numbers, Harry could see little way of avoiding the obvious conclusion: Cable Media would have to spend in the region of nine billion dollars just to buy its machines and get them into space. And that was before it paid the cost of the software to control them, or the systems and stations to make them operational. As far as he could see there was no way the company could afford an investment on that scale.

Perhaps that had been the reason Strang had wanted to remove Haverstone from the board, reflected Harry. Perhaps the old man had realised building the Argus system, at least within such a short space of time, was an act of financial lunacy.

He turned back to his computer. He would have to start crunching his way through the Cable Media balance sheet. He needed to know if his instincts were right, or if there was any way the company could finance the project from within its existing resources. Wearily, he called the spreadsheet up on his screen, punching in some of the numbers from the notes on his desk.

The work was engrossing, capturing his attention and blocking out temporarily all the other thoughts clouding his mind over the past few days. Immersed in it, he hardly noticed the sound behind him. It was only when he saw the tiny bob of blonde hair reflected in his screen that Harry turned around.

Cassandra was standing in the doorway, her thumb in her mouth, her teddy bear tucked up under her arm. 'Not sleepy any more, Daddy,' she said.

Harry picked her up in his arms, cradling her tight, sitting her on his lap and punching up one of the educational programmes he had bought for her in the last year. A dinosaur appeared on the screen and briefly Cassandra was distracted by the image. 'Bad dreams, princess?' asked Harry, ruffling his hand through her hair.

Her thumb still in her mouth, Cassandra nodded.

'About what?' asked Harry.

'I thought I saw Mummy,' she replied, her eyes cast down and her head nuzzling into Harry's chest.

Harry leant forward and kissed her forehead. 'Sometimes I imagine that I see her as well,' he said. 'And we will see her again one day, I promise. But not for a long time. Until then, Daddy will look after you.'

Cassandra took her thumb out of her mouth. 'Sometimes I get frightened,' she said.

Harry hugged her closer to him. Not for the first time, he felt her need for a mother. 'That happens to grown-ups as well,' he said softly.

7

The row of red pixels glowed on her screen, capturing Julia's attention immediately. She put down the handbook on Cayman Islands banking law she had been leafing through and fixed her eyes on the monitor. The words were clear enough. Her instincts had been right and the target struck with pin-point accuracy.

'DAVIDSON CONSUMER CORP LAUNCHES BID FOR STAUNTON TOBACCO,' reported the Reuters newsflash, flickering across the screen in neat block letters.

Her mouse clicked on to the words, dragging the story up before her eyes. The bid had been launched soon after the market opened: an offer, by the American company, of just over three billion for the British tobacco business. Already the stock had jumped by thirty-five per cent, slightly above the offer price, and the talk in the market was that the price would go higher still. Her quarry was sitting on a massive profit on its investment. So were Samantha Draper and Lexington Investments.

She glanced briefly around the bare and empty office, wondering if the SFO budget would stretch to furnishing the place with a few pot plants; the stark white walls, low-rent furniture and the numbing silence of the place made her feel cold and uncomfortable. Probably not. She smiled ruefully.

Julia looked down at the phone. Not to call now would look suspicious, she decided. She punched in the numbers. 'Trimble here,' came the reply after just one ring.

The hesitation before answering was unavoidable; she was still uncomfortable introducing herself as another person. 'Looks like my whispers are better than yours,' she said lightly.

'Who is this?' asked Trimble, his tone irritable.

'Samantha Draper, from Lexington Investments. The person you advised not to buy Staunton.'

Trimble laughed and Julia looked down at the phone to check the tape was running. 'Looks like you got lucky,' he said.

The casualness with which he could shrug off what would usually be an important client, even for one of the larger London brokers, struck Julia as yet another confirmation of her suspicions; Mr Trimble, she concluded, had other and bigger fish to fry. She was glad everything was being captured on tape. 'I just wanted to tell you to hold the position,' she said. 'Looks like it's going higher.'

'Sure, probably the right call,' agreed Trimble. 'Anything else you want to buy?'

'Not right now,' answered Julia.

'Whatever you say,' said Trimble sharply. Julia could hear the click on the line. He had put down the phone.

Calling up a spreadsheet on her screen, Julia started punching in the numbers. The insider dealing ring had made a profit of one hundred and seventy-five million. The amount of money involved, she reflected, was fabulous. And dangerous.

The fish swam engagingly in front of his eyes; a swirling

mass of different colours, at times garish and bright, sometimes subdued and subtle, but always appearing perfectly content within their own tightly bordered world. Cassie would like them, Harry reflected. He had been thinking for some time of buying her a pet, but had been unable to decide between a kitten and a puppy. Perhaps fish?

Richard Gregson's office was still empty. His secretary had shown Harry through the door and told him Gregson would be along soon. There were some problems on the trading floor, she explained. Harry could well imagine. Through the glass window he could see the American, in his neatly pressed cotton trousers, green polo shirt and deck shoes, gesticulating wildly above one of his hapless employees. It was not an elegant slight and the words, no doubt, were not elegant either.

Harry sipped his coffee. It had already been a promising week and, if his instincts proved right, it could be about to get better soon. Broat had come through with the offer of a job; Harry would be in charge of media investments across the firm's funds and would take control of launching his own multimedia fund, investing in anything to do with communications around the world. Harry was tempted and suspected he would accept in the next few weeks. But the restrictions around his payoff from Croxley, Palmer meant he couldn't start there for six months. Until then, he was a free agent.

Broat was certainly worth keeping in close touch with. He might want to work for him; he might also want, at some stage, to find out more about the last calls Sir Ian Strang had made. If, he decided, he ever came close to tracking down what had really been going on at Cable Media.

Harry had checked his contract through carefully.

Though it explicitly prevented him from working for another firm dealing in equities for the next six months, it said nothing about debt trading. An oversight by the lawyers, he imagined; the debt market was still so new, the legal men had obviously not caught up with it yet. So far as he could see, if he wanted to take a freelance assignment with Gregson there was nothing to stop him. Particularly if it meant he could make a quick fortune.

'Useless cocksuckers,' spluttered Gregson. The American arrived loudly back in his office, his broad frame towering above Harry, his face swollen and red with anger. He took a diet Coke from the counter and started swilling it down his throat. 'The fish have more brains than some of those traders. That's why I keep them around, you know. So my staff can get a look at intelligent life occasionally.' His eyes narrowed, focusing intently on Harry. 'So what's up? Mr Lamb,' he continued. 'You wanted to see me this morning.'

'I have a proposition that might interest you.'

Gregson nodded, taking another swig from the can and sitting down opposite Harry, his legs sprawled out in front of him. 'A deal,' he snorted. 'Shoot.'

Below, through the internal glass window, the chaos on the floor was so intense that Harry could virtually feel it; but within the office there was only an eerie stillness and not a single ripple of noise seemed to seep through the sound-proofed windows. 'It should make you a lot of money,' Harry said.

Gregson laughed. 'If I had a dollar for every time someone said that to me, I really would be a rich man. And it should make you a lot of money as well, I suppose.'

'You have a problem with that?'

'Fuck, no,' replied Gregson. 'I have a rule. Never do a deal unless the other guy is making more money from it than you are. Chances are he's still ripping you off, but at least there's a possibility you might come out ahead.' He leant forward, resting his forearms on his knees and looking intently at Harry. 'Tell me the story,' he said.

Harry edged forward in his seat, meeting Gregson's cool, level gaze with an expression of placid determination. 'We talked about Cable Media the other day,' he started. 'My theory is that company just can't afford to pay for this satellite system it's building. The money isn't there.'

Gregson crushed the empty Coke tin in his right hand and lobbed it perfectly into the bin on the far side of the room; a broad grin creased up his face as he watched the trajectory of the missile towards its target. 'That's quite a theory,' he said.

'It is also potentially quite a market. Cable Media has a lot of debt outstanding. Debt which, if my numbers are right, it won't be able to pay back. Essentially the company is about to become a distressed debt play.'

The look on Gregson's face changed slowly; the boyish enthusiasm was replaced by something more grown-up, more serious, and Harry felt for a moment he had struck home. 'Well,' Gregson said slowly. 'Distressed debt is what we deal in.'

'And now you can start making a market in Cable Media debt, which should be worth billions.'

'What's the catch?'

'No catch, just a deal,' replied Harry firmly. 'I supply the research. Your salesmen start using it to trade the debt. And I collect a percentage of the commissions generated on the deals. The rest goes to your firm.'

Gregson stood up, walked towards the window and looked down at the trading floor below. 'It's a big company, with lots of the right connections,' he said, his eyes moving away from Harry. 'When we start trading the debt, the shit is going to hit the fan in cartloads. The position you are taking is potentially dynamite.'

'It is also a mysterious enterprise,' answered Harry. 'There are loose ends all over the place.'

Gregson walked back across the floor, standing next to Harry. 'Just how loose?' he asked.

Harry hesitated before replying, unsure of what he should say next. 'Take the death of the last chairman, Sir Ian Strang,' he said eventually, drawing out the words. 'I don't think it was ever satisfactorily explained. And it certainly placed a lot of power in the hands of Samuel Haverstone.'

'And power corrupts, right?' Gregson's expression hardened as he spoke. 'That's what you're saying.'

Harry shrugged. 'Along those lines. There's definitely something strange happening within that organisation. Something which we could turn to profitable advantage.'

Gregson laughed, his ribs shaking as he did so, and Harry could feel a large palm crashing down on his back. 'I like your guts, Mr Lamb. You're a loose cannon all right, but I'd rather have you on my deck than the other guy's.'

The gambit seemed to be working, Harry reflected; and the prize was certainly rich enough for him to feel a sudden rush of blood surging through his veins. 'So we have a deal,' he said.

'One condition,' answered Gregson, standing up again and walking away from Harry. 'If we're going to cut a deal, I want to be sure that not a word about this goes outside this firm. The knowledge has to stay with us. Nobody else gets a sniff.'

'You have my word on that.' Harry stood up, shaking Gregson warmly by the hand; he was an animal, of course, and probably a dangerous one, but there was an energy and enthusiasm to the man that was infectious. 'I'll get the research ready.'

'One word of advice, my man,' said Gregson, opening the door and letting in a blast of frenzied, anxious noise from the trading floor. 'There's an old saying on the Mississippi river. "Never sleep with someone with more problems than you. And never play poker with a man called Doc."'

'Meaning what, exactly?' asked Harry, allowing a quizzical look to drift across his face.

'Meaning I have a doctorate in mathematics,' replied Gregson, wagging a finger. 'And I'm probably a lot smarter than you.'

Julia's day had begun promisingly. In the morning, confirmation had come through of the bid for Staunton Tobacco; that had proved the insider dealing ring was still active and she figured that Croxley, Palmer were working with them. Then, just after she returned from a quick salad lunch at the café across the road, came a fresh bulletin from the Stock Exchange. Earlier that day the offshore companies had dumped their entire holding in Staunton. That, Julia reckoned, revealed two things. One was that the market chatter had read the situation wrongly; there was not going to be a higher bid for Staunton, her quarry knew that and they had decided to lock up their profits now. The other thing it told her was even more simple: they had bigger fish to fry.

Sure enough, less than an hour later another e-mail came through from the surveillance department at the Stock Exchange. The offshore companies had started moving into the market again. This time the buy orders were being placed in Riola, the French insurance company. As the numbers scrolled up on to her screen, Julia blew a low, sharp whistle; over the course of the morning the more than three dozen offshore companies she was tracking had, by working together, snapped up shares worth eight hundred million. And they were still buying.

Sitting alone in her office, Julia punched out seven digits on her phone.

'Trimble here,' said a voice on the other end of the line.

'It's me, Samantha,' said Julia.

There was a pause. 'Okay, what's up?' The splintered tone of his voice suggested he was not pleased to hear from her.

'I'd like to sell the position in Staunton. Immediately,' said Julia. 'And I'd like to reinvest the proceeds in Riola.'

'A big chance you're taking, there,' said Trimble.

'I'm feeling lucky.'

'It's your money. There seems to be a fair bit of trading in Riola today. What's your upper limit?'

'Anything up to forty-four francs a share,' said Julia. 'I'm not too worried about a couple of centimes. Just make sure the order is placed before the Paris market shuts.'

'Consider it done.'

The phone had gone dead, the conversation terminated as swiftly and curtly as it had begun. For a large customer, Julia had reflected, she was not exactly getting the red-carpet treatment; she could not be sure, of course, and it hardly amounted to hard evidence, but she suspected Croxley, Palmer had better things to do than serve Lexington Investments.

She had related the events of the day to Mitchell at just after five; the SFO, to Julia's surprise, tended to keep civil service hours and by the time she arrived at its Elm Street headquarters most of the people there seemed to be heading out of the doors. He had listened impassively while she ran through the details of the trades and Trimble's reaction to her orders. It was only when she had asked whether he had made any progress on getting copies of the autopsy report that his expression had changed.

Harry had made the request two days ago, at the same

time that he had asked her if she would like to have dinner. It had puzzled her for most of the evening after he had called; she was intrigued because she wanted to know if he was interested in her, or just in using her for some information he needed. He was an attractive man, there was no doubt, and when she put down the phone she was flattered for a moment that he had called; a sensation she recognised as a sign of potential romance. Yet he was older than she was; six years, which made a difference. And he had a child. Julia had experience of men with children and had learnt not to trust them; the children, she knew, always came first. Her last serious relationship had been with a divorced partner back at the consultancy and though she had been sure he loved her, when the hammer fell, she had been on the losing side of the auction. She had not had the emotional resources, she now realised, to outbid the child; the price was too high. Though it was more than a year now since the affair had ended the bruises remained.

Still, she reflected, a promise was a promise. After all, she owed him a favour.

The frown on Mitchell's face deepened and a cloud of suspicion started to mask his expression. 'I made some inquiries, yes,' he replied at length.

'And did you find anything?' asked Julia.

'Co-operation between the British and the Irish police is quite close, mainly because of terrorism,' said Mitchell. 'Such a request from the SFO for information from Ireland is unusual, and it would raise eyebrows over in the Republic if I were to ask for the report, so I went through a colleague in the National Criminal Intelligence Service. They got hold of a copy for me.'

Julia looked at him closely; there was, she suspected, something he was holding back; his eyes were moving through her, across to the other side of the room. 'May I see it?' she asked.

'You say you need this for a contact?' said Mitchell.

Julia nodded. 'A former broker at Croxley, Palmer. So far he has proved invaluable in assisting me with the case. I think he could be more helpful still. But he's doing his own research into this company. I feel if I can give him something, I might be able to get more information.'

Mitchell sighed. From his desk, he pulled out a small sheaf of papers, glancing at them briefly before putting them down. 'You're very new to detective work.' His voice was grave. 'I hope you're not being naïve.'

'I think I should follow my instincts,' she said. 'The point of my being here is to take a different approach.'

'And you feel you can trust him?'

The question took Julia sideways; she had not thought yet about whether she trusted Harry and, for an instant, she was not sure. 'I think so,' she replied, realising it was too late to back down now.

Mitchell picked up the sheaf of papers and handed them across the desk. 'Just be careful. I don't want you taking any risks you're not equipped to deal with.'

Sergei Lykanov had arrived in England after a complex journey lasting more than a week. Following his meeting with Chung, he had returned to his base; there were moments when he was assailed by doubts, yet they were passing and gradually disappeared as the days dragged by. In his bones he felt this was the right thing to do; not for his country or his profession, perhaps, but for himself. Within days, a message had arrived, telling him to find a plausible excuse for travelling towards Vladivostock; something that would not arouse any suspicions. That had been simple enough; there was another, smaller satellite base nearby and an inspection would not prompt any questions. On his first night there he was met by a contact in a bar, another Korean as far as Lykanov could tell, who supplied him with a complete set of false papers and a ticket for a haulage ship travelling down to South Korea. The journey took four days and on disembarking he was met again, this time with a fresh set of papers and a ticket for Tokyo. From there, after a stay of two nights in a hotel near the airport, he took a flight to London; the papers this time described him as a Polish businessman and the ticket was a return, the first half of which had already been used; as far as the British immigration officials would be aware, he was just a commercial traveller coming back after a five-day trip to Japan, with a stopover for the night in London before heading back to Warsaw. His passport was given no more than a cursory glance; it was a very professional way of bringing someone into the country, Lykanov had decided, as he set foot on English soil for the first time in his fifty years. Someone bearing his name would depart for Poland tomorrow and, so far as the British authorities were concerned, he would not be in the country.

He was met at Heathrow by Chung. The Korean greeted him warmly, welcoming him to Britain. His driver escorted them through the parking lot, towards a waiting Daimler, and drove them to central London. Together they stopped briefly in Bayswater, where Chung took him to a second-floor two-bedroom flat in a modern block; a modest apartment, decorated with formal, expensive, yet cold furniture. To Lykanov it looked luxurious. It was far superior to any of the state housing he had been familiar with back in Russia. These would be his living quarters for the next year, Chung explained; a maid would come by every day to clean, cook and stock the larder with food. A driver would collect him every morning and take him home in the evenings. There would not be any need for him to go out by himself, Chung had continued, and moving around the city without an escort was not permitted. Anyway, he would probably be too busy with his work.

Lykanov deposited his bag, a simple leather holdall he had owned for years, containing a few items of clothing and some photographs: one of his wife and one of his daughter, taken outside the academy in Moscow where she was studying. That done, he followed Chung back down to the waiting car, ready to be introduced to his new place of work. Arrangements had been made, he was reassured, to bring them out of the country should his sudden disappearance place them in any danger.

The office was in another part of the city and though Lykanov had scanned London many times via satellite, he was not familiar enough with its geography to recognise where he was being taken. They approached the building from the back, pulling up in a side-street and slipping through a back door. Chung nodded to a security guard, swiped a plastic card through the gate and led Lykanov inside. They made their way down a steel staircase into the foundations of the building; Lykanov was still too jet-lagged to keep an accurate count, but he estimated they were at least three floors below ground. Chung swiped the card again, opening a pair of steel doors. Together they walked towards them. 'This will be your headquarters for the next year,' said Chung calmly.

Lykanov looked cautiously into the gleaming room. Standing still in the doorway, his eyes flickered slightly as he started to register the equipment displayed before him. Towards the front there was a large Sony monitor, twelve feet by ten, of a type he recognised as having been designed for creating film special effects; it was capable of magnifying any image a hundredfold, then manipulating it in any of a thousand ways. Beneath were a series of standard monitors, each displaying the progress of a satellite around the globe, giving a moving fix on its precise position and indicating the range of territory it was able to survey; there were eighteen monitors in total in the display bank, though only four of them appeared to be currently operational. Below, there were a series of desks each with two display terminals and a keyboard, linked directly to the main monitor. It was a small room, no more than twenty-five feet across and with no natural light, but just from a casual glance Lykanov could guess that the equipment it contained had cost several millions.

He remained silent, making a tour of the room and its equipment. Though he had never seen any of it close up before, a lot of it he recognised; a mixture of American, Japanese and German technology, much of which he and his colleagues had studied back in Russia. Most of it was commercially available, sold to the companies operating broadcasting and telecoms satellites throughout the West.

'You should be able to oversee everything from here,' said Chung, standing close by him and resting his hand on Lykanov's shoulder. 'The satellites are of course controlled from a ground station, but there is a dedicated line connection between this room and the station. Their positions can be altered at your command. The feeds all come through to this control station and you should have all the computing power you need to get the analysis software up and running. If there is anything else you need just let me know. Money is no object.'

Lykanov nodded; it was, he decided, an impressive installation and the technical challenge of getting it working to full capacity would certainly be exciting. Only one thing puzzled him: the series of voice analysis monitors in one corner of the room. 'You have telecoms observation technology here as well?' he asked.

'That also will form part of your duties,' replied Chung. 'London, as you probably know, handles more voice traffic than any other city in the world. We have the capacity to monitor our targets via telecoms surveillance, as well as physical surveillance through the satellites. We would like you to build the software to integrate the two systems. When we select a target, we would like to be able to create as full a picture as possible of his or her movements. Ideally, there should be nothing we don't know.'

Lykanov took a deep breath. Integrating telecoms and satellite surveillance was certainly technically possible. It was just that it had never been done before. At least, not outside a government agency. And though he did not like to ask who his new employers were, he suspected he was not working for a government. They had their own experts, as good as any in the world, and they would not need him. 'What are we looking for?' he asked.

Chung shrugged, turning away from the scientist and starting to walk him back towards the door. 'For now, we just want you to build the system. As we start selecting targets you will be informed,' he replied crisply.

Cassandra was sitting cross-legged on the floor watching a *Muppets* video when Julia came into the room. She looked up briefly, said hello in a low, bashful voice and turned back towards the television. Julia leant down and kissed her on the forehead. 'Hello, Cassie,' she said softly. Cassie turned away. Tricky customers, children, thought Julia to herself.

Harry took her on a tour of the house; they wandered from the hallway into the sitting-room then back towards the large wood-panelled kitchen, which looked out on to about ten feet of garden; a swing and a trike were visible from the window. It was a standard Fulham family home; Julia had seen plenty of them since she moved up to London and had learnt all the correct appreciative noises to make. But there was also a strangely disconnected feel to it, as though all the pieces were there, but they had not quite been made to fit together. A family home without a proper family in it, she reflected.

Already she was wondering about the little girl, the house and where her own place might be. Why, she asked herself, am I unable to go on a date without worrying about the long-term relationship? Perhaps I should just enjoy myself more. Relax. Go with the flow.

Dinner at home had been her idea. Harry had suggested a restaurant, Kartouche in the Fulham Road, but Julia had protested; she did not want him to go to the trouble of getting the nanny to stay overnight and she would be happy to cook something for both of them. No, Harry had protested, he would make something. When she had mentioned it to one of her girl-friends yesterday, she had pointed out that she obviously just wanted to check out his house. Part of the inevitable vetting process. True, Julia conceded. The motive was obvious and, her girl-friend warned her, unlikely to be lost on Harry. 'Of course,' she had added, 'you can never tell with boys. They don't pick up on very much.'

A bottle of red Chilean wine was sitting on the table top. Harry poured her a glass and started stirring the pasta sauce that was already bubbling on the stove; it was the one dish he knew how to make from scratch and deciding what to cook had taken all of thirty seconds. Julia stood next to him, taking a careful, delicate sip of her wine and parrying some light-hearted banter about different types of pasta sauces. She found she was enjoying the attention he was lavishing on her; Harry gave the impression he had unlimited time. As perhaps he did. After all, right now he did not appear to have a job and, apart from his daughter, there were not many people in his life.

Julia volunteered to chop the tomatoes and wash the lettuce for the salad, while Harry put Cassandra to bed. He brought her into the kitchen briefly and she flashed a winning smile before he took her upstairs. 'I'll be five minutes,' he said warmly. 'That's all it usually takes to read one of Spot the Dog's adventures.'

It seemed like longer to Julia. She filled in the time checking the contents of his fridge-freezer, one of the largest collections of ready-prepared M&S meals she had ever seen, plus several tubs of Haagen-Dazs and a variety of different beers. One of her girl-friends had a theory that you could tell almost everything you needed to know about a man from his kitchen, but Julia was not sure she could tell very much, except that he lived alone and liked M&S food. Who doesn't? she asked herself.

Harry returned, took a gulp of his wine and started boiling the water for the pasta. He apologised for taking so long; Cassie had insisted he read the book twice, before she would turn out the light.

'You care about her very much, don't you,' said Julia.

'Of course. She's all I have.'

They talked about nothing serious during the meal; movies, plays, books they had read, places they had been. Julia told him about how she had grown up in Somerset, the daughter of a small market-town solicitor, read Economics at Cambridge, moved to the consultancy in London, and done her MBA. She had always rebelled at rural life, she explained; her sights were set on the glamour and wealth of the capital and she enjoyed London more than any other place she had ever lived. No, she could not imagine living anywhere else, although she had been offered a posting to either New York or Hong Kong last year. They were not for her. 'London is sometimes enough of a challenge for me.'

She learnt something, as well, about his life. He told her how he had been brought up in Kent, the son of a stockbroker, and had spent his life in conventional stockbroker-belt territory. After reading PPE at Oxford, he had never really had any doubts about moving into the City; it was what his family did and anyway, he pointed out, in the early eighties it was the place to make the most money. The pay was so high, you needed pretty good reasons not to work in the City and he had not been able to think of one. His eyes flickered away when he spoke about Amelia, as though it was something he did not really want to discuss; they had married when he was twenty-eight and she twenty-six. She was working in publishing, but really just wanted to get married and have children, and so did he. It was a pretty conventional and unremarkable middle-class English life, he noted. Until recently, at least.

It was not until Harry had started clearing the plates into the dishwasher that she mentioned the autopsy report. Julia took the sheaf of papers from her bag and handed them to him, putting them down on the wooden dining-table. She had already looked through the document and had no wish to read it again. She offered to make coffee while he read it, but Harry was already so engrossed he hardly noticed.

The report was written on Garda notepaper. It began by detailing the location of the cottage, its age, structure and ownership. Sir Ian Strang had booked it only a few days before, it noted, and had done so under an assumed name; the deposit was wired through to the owner's bank. His stay was indefinite; the first month was already paid for and an option taken on another month, at a cost of a further eight hundred pounds. The fire brigade had been alerted to the fire by a local farmer, but by the time they arrived it had almost burnt itself out. The cottage was entirely destroyed and the firemen had had to extinguish only the embers. It was not until they began sorting through the wreckage that they realised there had been anyone inside.

The remnants of two bodies had been found, but they were burnt beyond recognition; it was only through their dental records that they had been identified. Close to the fire, there was the body of a woman. A few feet away, a man's. Both were lying on the ground. Their flesh was too badly burnt for the pathologist to say much about the cause of death; they could have been killed by the flames, or they could have been dead before the fire started. It was impossible to say. The fire appeared to have been caused by a spark from the hearth catching the wooden floors, and the timber from which the cottage was built was so dry it would have burnt instantly. Once the flames encountered the high winds blowing that night it was not surprising the building was destroyed so quickly. It was plausible, the report concluded, that the fumes had suffocated the couple, rendering them unconscious, which would explain why they were lying on the floor and had not attempted to escape the inferno. But, the pathologist noted, deaths in house fires were more common when the victims were asleep; that way the fumes suffocated them before they had time to react. They might, of course, have been sleeping on the floor, but it seemed unlikely. The evidence was inconclusive, the report went on. If there were other suspicious circumstances surrounding the death the case would merit further investigation. If not, it would have to be put down in the files as unresolved.

Harry looked up from the report to find that Julia had put a cup of coffee in front of him. He smiled at her across the table, already feeling guilty for the minutes he had spent ignoring her, and was flattered by the warmth of the smile he received in return. 'Why would he book into the cottage under an assumed name?'

103

Julia shrugged. 'He was not with his wife,' she replied.

'She was not a hidden mistress,' he said, shaking his head. 'The old man had been divorced for years. No. There must have been another reason.'

'That he was running from something?'

'Exactly,' said Harry firmly. 'I can't think of any other plausible explanation, and I can't see why the police wouldn't pick up on that. Surely it's suspicious enough to justify further investigation, not the bland statement they made to the papers? It doesn't make any sense.'

There was a silence lasting several seconds. Julia looked across at Harry. There was a burning curiosity in his eyes, a look she had not seen before, and she realised he was briefly lost to her, his mind whistling through the possibilities, trying to find the connections. 'What's the deal with Cable Media?' she asked softly.

Harry took a sip of his coffee. 'The deal?'

'Why are you so interested in the company?' Julia continued firmly. 'Why does it matter to you?'

He looked at her closely, wondering how much to say. 'I think they had me sacked,' he answered calmly, realising it was the first time he had addressed the suspicion so directly, even to himself. 'I think they didn't like the position I was taking on their shares. In particular, I don't think they liked the research I was doing on the financing of their satellite system. I was becoming a problem. So they leant on Croxley, Palmer to have me dismissed.

Julia bent forward across the table, inching her palms across its surface. 'So move on,' she said. 'You've already had other job offers. Screw them. What does it matter?'

Harry leant back in his chair, and for a moment Julia wondered if he was drawing away from her; perhaps she had said the wrong thing. 'I suppose you're right. I should let it ride.' He moved forward in his chair again, resting his elbows on the table, and Julia noticed the tensing of his muscles as he did so. 'But I've never been very good at that. I guess they have just pissed me off. Part of me doesn't like the way big companies think they can just swat people aside, as if they didn't matter. It would be nice to think that just once they had messed with the wrong guy.'

The words were delivered calmly, but his eyes revealed a sense of purpose that Julia found instinctively appealing; in that instant, she wanted both to protect and to help him. 'So what do you want?' she asked.

'Revenge,' said Harry with an air of sombre finality. A silence hung in the air, before a broad grin started creasing up his face. 'Maybe. I have a few months off during which I can't work for anyone else. I might as well amuse myself with something other than watching videos with Cassie. If I have to see that damned *Muppets* vid again, I think I'll scream.'

Julia laughed, glancing down at her watch. It was almost twelve, time to go. She thanked Harry for a lovely meal and a delightful evening. Together they walked through the hallway, both of them aware that issues were being left unresolved, words unsaid. Julia leant by the doorway for a moment, feeling the cool night breeze against her skin, and looked into his strong blue eyes. 'We should do this again some time,' she said finally.

'Certainly,' Harry agreed. 'Soon.'

She leant across, kissing him on the cheek, allowing her lips to linger a fraction longer than was really necessary. His hand moved down to touch hers and she took hold of his fingers. By moving his face less than an inch, his lips met hers, resting there for a moment. 'Good-night,' she whispered.

8

Samuel Haverstone strode purposefully towards the podium. Dressed in a neatly tailored Prince-of-Wales check suit, with a pale-blue shirt and an Armani tie, his appearance was restrained and expensive. Above him a strip of thin neon tubing illuminated the stand, casting a pale light that ruffled through his carefully sculptured hair; greying fast, but still thick, it was slicked back, with a single lock falling over his forehead. Behind him, on a dark-blue screen, slanted lettering described him as the chairman and chief executive of Cable Media and he hesitated for a moment, allowing his audience to appreciate his presence, before beginning his speech.

The hundred or so people gathered for the Multi-media Strategies conference fell silent on his arrival, some of them leaning forward slightly to make sure they had a proper view of the speaker. Understandable, reflected Harry from his seat near the back of the conference room. Haverstone was certainly the man of the moment.

That month, Haverstone had made the *Vanity Fair* list of the hundred most important business people in the world; his début was at number eight, an impressive position, nestling between the guys from Intel and the team from Dreamworks. The company's PR machine had switched into hype mode, a state of mind they knew well, ensuring his inclusion had received plenty of coverage; there were several flattering profiles in the British broadsheets and both the *Wall Street Journal* and the *Washington Post* had run pieces. 'With the bold merger of his fast-growing European telecoms outfit with a staid but powerful British media company, Haverstone at a stroke transformed himself into one of the leading players in the information economy,' ran the breathless *Vanity Fair* description. 'His compelling vision of a convergence of telecoms and media markets has electrified the industry, and his new European satellite system promises to make his company the one outfit everyone has to do business with.'

'This has been a turbulent year for our industry,' began Haverstone, peering down at his audience with mock solemnity. 'Technology is changing, markets are changing and companies are changing at a pace that would have seemed terrifying just five years ago. There are winds of change blowing that have become a hurricane, sweeping aside established structures and flattening landscapes that were once marked by sharp natural divisions. Once there were telecoms companies that ran the phone system. There were film companies that ran the studios and the movie theatres. There were publishing companies that printed books and newspapers. And there were computing companies that made machines and designed software. We all thought we were in different industries and indeed, we have been in different industries. Then, we suddenly woke up one morning to find we were all in the same business. Communications.' He paused for a moment, allowing the word to rest pompously in the air. 'Of course, some of us woke up a little earlier that morning than others,' Haverstone added, hesitating, allowing a thin ripple of laughter to run through his audience before smiling benevolently himself. 'By creating the world's first integrated telecoms and entertainments company, I believe Cable Media has staked out a position as the most powerful player on the new landscape. Only our company has the ability both to create programming and to distribute it to the market. We are, or will become, the equivalent to the information economy of what the great oil companies were to the old industrial economy; the supplier of the essential lubricant that fuels the system.'

Harry sat back impassively, both soaking up the words and observing the man. He was the star speaker at the conference, the one person, himself included, they had all come to hear; the ticket had been booked when he was still at Croxley, Palmer and Harry had seen no reason to cancel it. Haverstone's delivery was impressive. The man had a command of his audience that came from deep within. It was not just his certain knowledge they were hanging on his every word that put him in control. He had a kind of serenity and a way of talking to the room as if he were just chatting to each person individually. It was a powerful performance.

On the screen behind the podium an image of a satellite flashed up; a spherical cylinder, with two massive silver panels stretching from both sides, capturing the sun's power to drive the electronics inside the machine. Along its side, in red luminous lettering, were the words Cable Media and, beneath those, Argus. Haverstone turned for a moment to admire the image, before looking back towards his audience. 'The Argus project is the boldest step forward yet taken by any company to supply the information economy,' he said. 'With this one system, Cable Media will be able to supply digital telephony, Internet and broadcasting capacity to every home in Europe. It will be the cheapest way by far of delivering information and will therefore, I believe, become the essential conduit for its distribution. This system will be the gateway through which information flows around the continent, and Cable Media will be the gatekeeper. The revenues it generates will be enormous. So will be the power that it confers on the company that controls it.'

There was an edge to the last sentence that made Harry sit up; Haverstone's lips curled slightly when he used the word power and his eyes, until then fixed placidly on the centre of the room, suddenly darted from right to left. It was as if he were scanning the room, hunting for any dissenting voices or expressions of scepticism. Finding none, his eyes rested again on the teleprompter as he began to contemplate the next sentence.

'Power is a useful commodity and often a valuable one,' he continued. 'But it has to be handled carefully. Power over our competitors is a natural and desirable thing. As a private company, we wish to defeat our rivals, just as they are free to defeat us. That is the free market. But control of information also puts this company in a uniquely powerful position within society. It is our responsibility to use that power for the general good and to contribute towards strengthening the societies that are also our markets. I would argue that Cable Media has already proved itself a reliable corporate citizen and that talk of restricting the reach of Argus, or our other distribution systems, is beside the point. This company can be trusted to act with restraint and dignity.' Haverstone looked around his audience once more, while tidying up the sheaf of papers on the podium, again rooting for any signs of disagreement or dissent. 'Thank you for your time this morning.'

A ripple of appreciative applause ran through the audience, though Harry felt no urge to participate.

Haverstone strode across the platform, a smile playing across his lips, and waited behind the desk for the first question from the audience. A fund manager asked whether the company was planning to extend the Argus system into America and Asia. Haverstone replied smugly that it would do so once it proved successful. Another analyst wanted to know whether Cable Media might move into providing Internet services directly and Haverstone said that it might do if and when a suitable acquisition became available.

Harry bided his time, waiting for the chairman to catch his half-raised arm. 'Could you explain exactly how the company plans to finance the investment in Argus?' he asked eventually. The question was delivered in a tone that was downbeat yet insistent.

Haverstone's eyes narrowed, as he stared directly at Harry. 'The details have all been set out in earlier documents,' he stated calmly.

'Not clearly,' replied Harry. 'Building the satellite system will cost far more than the company can support in debt.'

Haverstone ran a hand through his thick hair and a look of irritation passed across his face. 'I can assure you the declining cost of satellite technology combined with the steadily rising revenues from our existing operations will make the project self-financing very rapidly.'

Harry was about to press harder. 'Next question, please,' interrupted the conference chairman, looking for another raised hand. Haverstone leant across and whispered in his ear, 'Find out who that man is.'

It would have been useful to have some assistants, Lykanov reflected, as he unpacked the boxes and looked down at the array of computer equipment spread out on the floor. But assistance, he knew, would have been dangerous. Whoever it was he was working for, he could see they wanted to keep this project as secret as possible. And Lykanov had worked long enough for the military to know the first rule of secrecy: don't let anybody into the loop.

In the days since he had taken up residence in the underground bunker, the identity of his employers had puzzled him. Money did not appear to be an object. Wherever it was possible his instructions were to use materials that were commercially available. That was not so much of a problem as an amateur might suppose. In the last twenty years, much of the technology developed for military observation had found its way into a variety of computing and photographic applications. The difference between the military product and the commercial equivalent was often minimal; by buying the commercial version, Lykanov knew he could relatively simply engineer it back to its original use. But the preference for commercial equipment suggested his employers had no links with any government; if they had, they could simply have bought the military version.

Then there was the choice of targets. Satellites back in Russia, he knew, had been used for internal as well as external surveillance. But it was usually only for very broad tasks, keeping track of large groups of people. Individual surveillance was not usually considered worth the trouble. If the government wanted to monitor one of its own citizens within its own borders, there were usually simpler ways than using a satellite; a man on the ground could do the job more efficiently for several billion dollars less. A satellite would only be used for tracking an individual in territories to which agents had no access.

So why the girl? Lykanov pondered to himself.

Chung had issued the order earlier that day. It had been on his morning visit to the bunker, an arrival that now appeared to be established as part of the daily routine. The Korean appeared unannounced through the sliding steel door, pausing to inspect the premises before looking down at Lykanov. He placed the name of the woman, typed neatly on a single sheet of paper, on the desk in front of him.

Lykanov did not recognise the words. They meant nothing to him.

'I would like to locate the mobile phone number for this woman,' said Chung quietly.

'Any leads?'

'We know where she works, and the land line for her office and home,' replied Chung. 'It's just the mobile we need.'

'It should not be a problem,' said Lykanov, nodding as he spoke. 'We have access to the phone system from here. I can get back to you in a couple of hours.'

'Fine,' replied Chung. 'How is our project progressing?'

'Most of the equipment I asked for has arrived. It has not been installed yet, but that should not take very long.'

'Let me know if you need anything,' said Chung. 'The system must be perfect within the next few days.'

Locating the number had been easy. A separate bank of computers in the bunker had access to the phone company mainframes. How or why, Lykanov had no idea, but he knew it was not his place to ask questions. With access established, he merely had to instruct the computer to search its records for the mobile connection. It took time, but it was not a formidable task.

He went back to unpacking the boxes. The extra computers were needed to complete the building of the system, but more important was the software he had asked to be pre-loaded on to the machines; some of the most sophisticated voice and feature recognition technology available anywhere in the world, it was manufactured by Harlison, a small American company, who sold it to private security firms. Their best customers, he had learnt, were the big Las Vegas casinos, which used it to detect professional gamblers on their gaming floors. With only minimal modification, it would suit his purposes perfectly.

Julie could hear the slow insistent beeping, but for the moment she could not recall where she had left her mobile.

It was after eight and she had just returned home to her flat off Fulham Broadway. She had bought the place a little more than a year ago, and it was still unfinished; the carpet needed to be changed, and when she had the time and the money became available, she would have a new bathroom fitted. Perhaps a new kitchen as well. The bright, white surfaces she had inherited did nothing for her and she hankered after something more rustic; wood panelling and terracotta tiles would look a lot better, she had decided some months ago. She just needed to get the mortgage under control first.

The phone stopped after the fifth ring. Julia had still not found the mobile. Never mind, she told herself, they'll ring back, or leave a message.

She had been unable to decide what to wear that morning and the bedroom looked like a bombsite; there were clothes everywhere and the duvet had been left half spread across the floor. Tidying up, she found the mobile and put the machine into its charger. After sipping half a cup of coffee she unpacked her few items of shopping and switched on the TV; she liked the low noise in the background, even if she was not planning to watch anything.

In the kitchen, she began chopping up some tomatoes and lettuce, and opened a can of tuna; a salad was all she felt like this evening – or, at least, the most she felt her

113

last trip to the scales in the gym could justify. The flat had an empty, almost desolate feel to it tonight and Julia was still unsure if she enjoyed living alone; she had shared with a girl-friend before buying this place and it was the first time she had lived by herself. The privacy appealed to her; space and freedom were commodities she valued. But there were times when she missed the companionship of her girl-friends.

The mobile rang again, its tone interrupting her thoughts. Julia put down the food and walked briskly through to the sitting-room. She didn't want to miss the call again.

'Samantha Draper?' said a voice on the line.

Julia hesitated. She recognised the name, of course, but not the speaker; it was not Trimble, that much was certain. This voice was not English; American perhaps, or Pacific, it was impossible to tell. 'Yes,' she replied cautiously. How anyone would get this number and how they would connect it to the work she had been doing at the SFO she could not imagine. And yet, having set up the role, she felt she had little choice but to keep playing it. It was too late to back down now.

'You have made some very successful investments recently,' said the man.

'May I ask who this is, please?'

There was a chuckle on the line. 'That is of no immediate concern to you now,' he replied. 'You may hear from me again, you may not. You may meet me one day, you may not. It all depends.'

'Depends on what?' asked Julia.

'On what you do next.'

'I don't understand.'

'Then let me explain,' said the man. The tone this time was different, less amused and with an edge of cruelty to it. 'Your trading strategies at Lexington Investments appear to be very successful. As successful

114

as the trades made by some friends of mine. You appear to have been copying their tactics, and they would like you to stop. Rest assured, so long as you do as you are told, you need not hear any more about this.'

'I have no idea who you are, or what you are talking about,' said Julia.

'I believe you do.' The man's voice deepened to a low growl; the tone was relentless monotone, edged with menace. 'And let me assure you, you do not ever want to have to meet me. The consequences would be most unpleasant. You have been warned.'

Julia was about to speak; the threat angered her and she could feel her temper rising. Her hand, she noticed, was trembling slightly. She was about to ask again who he was and what right he had to make threatening phone calls. But the line had already gone dead.

The two blonde women had walked off together in the direction of the Ladies, sliding away from the table in their short skirts and high heels. Harry could not help admiring their legs as they disappeared from view; both had immaculate figures and their walk might have been purposefully calculated to pump up his testosterone. Indeed, it probably was; they had a swagger that suggested they knew exactly the effect they would have on any male audience.

Gregson took another slug of the double bourbon sitting on the table. 'Don't you just love those English Sloanes,' he said. 'Best whores in the world.'

Harry had not realised the women were paid for, but it came as no great surprise. Gregson was not the sort of man who would have time for friends or relationships; he would probably have trouble understanding any communication that did not involve money.

The invitation to dinner, when it was made the previous afternoon, had the feel of a command. Gregson had called, insisting it was time they got to know each other better and telling Harry firmly he would meet him at the Fifth Floor restaurant at Harvey Nichols the following night at eight. Although Harry had heard of the Fifth Floor, he had not been there before. The sight of the bar had confirmed his suspicions: a place for Eurotrash, ladies who lunch, girls who might want to be models some day and rich men in expensive designer suits who wanted to meet those sort of women.

Harry was expecting a business meeting to discuss the terms of their deal and the sight of the women took him by surprise. They introduced themselves as Rachel and Kirstin. Both wore obviously expensive clothes, bright red lipstick and chattered happily about books and films. Harry enjoyed their company; Julia aside, he realised he had spent too little time with women recently and from the way she melted at his every word he suspected Kirstin might have taken a shine to him.

'Kirstin is yours if you want her,' said Gregson. 'Or you can fuck Rachel if you prefer. They're both pretty good pieces of ass.'

'Are they literally hookers?' asked Harry.

'Now that's a very precise question for this time of night,' replied Gregson. 'Back where I come from, we always drew a fine line between hookers and whores. Hookers were hard-working girls who turned tricks at ten bucks a time. Whores are ladies with expensive tastes who don't want to get up in the morning and go to the office. They like fine jewellery and good coke, get off on presents, preferably cash, and they don't mind lying on their backs. That makes these girls whores.'

'We'll see how things go,' said Harry cautiously.

'You a married man?' asked Gregson.

'Not any more,' replied Harry. 'My wife died a little while ago.'

'Too bad,' said Gregson, his tone void of any

116

sympathy. 'Still, it saves you the cost of a divorce lawyer. I hate those guys. I was married myself once, but I'm not going down that road again. No sir. Not unless she's a lot richer than me and I can take her to the cleaners. And there aren't many good-looking ladies with more money than me.'

Harry sipped his champagne; it was the third bottle Gregson had ordered that evening, most of it drunk by the two women. 'Are we ready to move with our deal?' he asked.

Gregson looked at him closely. 'Are you just into this for the money, Harry?' he inquired. 'Or is it something personal?'

Harry shrugged. 'Just for the money,' he replied. 'Sure, I never had great relations with Cable Media when I was working as an analyst and covering the stock. But this is just business. We've seen an opportunity, so we should take it.'

Harry was conscious, as the words fell from his lips, that they were mostly untrue and he looked for any signs that Gregson might have picked up on the subterfuge. This was not about the money. It was about discovering more about Cable Media and about why he had lost his job. But Gregson was not a man he felt any compunction about lying to. He probably expected it.

'Have you ever met Haverstone?'

'Not face to face,' replied Harry. 'Just at company meetings.'

'I hear he's a mean guy,' said Gregson, pronouncing the word mean with heavy emphasis. 'I hear he doesn't like guys crapping in his garden.'

'That doesn't bother me,' said Harry.

'Fine. There's just one thing I want you to do for me. I need a guarantee that all your work, everything you've done so far, will be held in my office. This research is dynamite and I have to be sure the firm keeps control.'

117

Harry nodded. 'I have no problem with that. When can we start?'

'Monday morning,' said Gregson, clenching his fist as he spoke. 'No time to waste. I have a feeling Cable Media is going to start blowing up quite soon, and we need to be ready for it.'

'It's a deal.' Harry stood to let the two women, their make-up freshly primed, back to the table. Kirstin allowed her hand briefly to brush his back as she walked past, but he ignored the touch. She was attractive, and in another place and another mood he might have wanted her. But not now and not like this. He would take Gregson's money and he would use his firm as a vehicle, but he did not feel like taking his women as well; there was only so much whoring a man could do in one week.

Glancing at his watch, Harry started to explain that it was time for him to leave; the nanny would be waiting for him, he said. Both women looked surprised to see him go, but not disappointed, Harry noted; they were presumably getting paid anyway, he decided, and the less work they had to do the better. 'You must be a very attentive father,' said Kirstin softly. 'I admire that in a man.'

Harry let the remark pass; he had no great desire to prolong the conversation. Gregson followed him through the bar, now brimming with well-cut suits and low-cut dresses, and stood next to him waiting for the lift back down to the street. 'You have a lot of self-control,' he said. 'Not many men would have passed up the chance to screw those girls.'

Harry laughed. 'Perhaps I'm just shy.'

'I don't think so. Discipline. It's a rare thing in the world these days. And dangerous in an opponent.'

Gregson paused, a look of concentration passing across his face, before slapping Harry heartily on the back. 'How much do you know, exactly, Mr Lamb?'

'Enough,' replied Harry crisply. 'Quite enough to make this deal work.'

'But not too much,' said Gregson.

'Too much for what?' asked Harry.

Gregson hesitated, rubbing his chin with his hand, before looking back up, his eyes burning with concentration. 'Too much for your own good, I suppose,' he replied.

9

The man from the computing and telecoms division of Scotland Yard had a slow, ponderous expression; he was dressed in a light-brown suit, with a pink shirt and a striped tie, and an unkempt moustache draped uneasily across his upper lip. Julia did not much like the look of him; his eyes shifted nervously in their sockets and his habit of rubbing his palms constantly across his wide stomach had started to irritate her. Still, he was the expert, and potentially her best hope of cracking this case.

Mitchell had called Alan Weatherspoon to the SFO for an early-morning meeting. The previous evening Julia had written a memo to her superior and sent it through to his office by fax. It had explained that, in her opinion, their best chance of cracking the insider dealing ring was to track the money to its source. They had already established a British link; the connection with Croxley, Palmer had proved that much. It seemed obvious the money was being accumulated by a person or group of people with connections, or a base, in the UK. And, if that was the case, it seemed likely, too, that the fortune reaped from the conspiracy was also finding its way back to Britain. Otherwise, what would be the point?

The problem was to find some way of tracing the money. They knew the group of companies being used as fronts for the ring, but the banks in the Cayman Islands and other offshore centres would never reveal who the true owners were; and, indeed, the probability was that there was a whole layer of front companies masking where control of the funds really lay. There was, however, one other possibility. If the money was being routed back to Britain, it would probably be via an electronic funds transfer from one bank to another. If it were possible to eavesdrop on the electronic transfer, it might tell them where the money was going. That, in turn, might tell them who was operating the insider dealing ring. If the technology existed to plant an electronic eavesdrop on the line, it was worth a shot.

Mitchell turned to Weatherspoon, scrutinising the man closely. He knew the resources devoted to tracking electronic crime had grown dramatically in the last three or four years; it was, after all, one of the great growth industries of the nineties and every effort was being made to keep up to speed with the cyber-criminals. A whole unit over at Scotland Yard was now dedicated to tracking computer fraud. Weatherspoon, according to his contacts over there, was the best man they had. If he couldn't find a way to plant a bug the chances were it could not be done. 'Well,' Mitchell asked carefully. 'Is it possible?'

Weatherspoon was still holding Julia's memo in his lap, his eyes scanning the words and the fingers of his right hand softly stroking his stomach. 'It is certainly an ingenious idea,' he replied.

Julia smiled to herself. 'It would crack the case right open,' she said enthusiastically.

'Technically, it's not absolutely impossible, just very difficult.' Weatherspoon said slowly. 'An electronic funds transfer is really just a message between two computers, an instruction to exchange money from one account to another. It travels down a modem, much like any other communication between computers. And, like any piece of telecoms traffic, it can be intercepted.' He paused, switching his eyes from Julia to Mitchell and back again, as if he was unsure which of them to address directly. 'The eavesdrop is really just a matter of filing a request with the telecoms company, so that the call gets re-routed via our office before reaching its final destination. The problem is not so much placing the tap, but finding the information. Something in excess of twenty million calls a day come into London from overseas and there's no way we can search through that lot. Now, we can narrow that to calls coming from the Cayman Islands, assuming we just try to track one of these companies. From Cayman, the calls will be a lot fewer. Perhaps no more than a few thousand a day, if we're lucky. Also, we are only interested in calls between computers, so we can weed out any human communication. That cuts the numbers further. But then it could be weeks before our target makes a call, so that puts the number up again.'

'But we can access the call so long as we can find it?' asked Julia.

Weatherspoon nodded. 'Sure, so long as it's not coded. A funds transfer usually contains a description of the account being drawn on, the account where the funds are being deposited and of course the amount. Since we have the names of the companies we are tracing, it should be quite easy. Company X sends so much to Company Y. We can just read it and tell you who is collecting the money. Our best bet would be to route every call from the Cayman Islands via a computer in our office over a period of about a week. We log everything on to our computer, then tell it to discard all the voice traffic. Then we do a search, until we find the

122

name of the company we are looking for. It will require a bit of time to set up and a lot of computing power. But that aside, I think it's feasible. Hard work, but feasible. So long as we can get permission.'

'Permission?' asked Julia.

Mitchell turned to face her. 'The police, and the SFO as well, are allowed to tap phones,' he explained. 'But all wiretaps need to be authorised by the Home Office before they can be started. And to get permission we need to establish a clear case for thinking a crime has been committed within British jurisdiction. We might have enough here, but I'm not sure. We might need more evidence.'

Julia shook her head. 'We don't need permission,' she stated firmly.

Both Mitchell and Weatherspoon looked at her closely, their faces betraying surprise at her forceful interruption. 'I don't think we're tapping any phones exactly,' she continued. 'The way I see it we don't want to know what these people are saying to each other, not at this stage, anyway. We just want to know who they're calling. That doesn't count as a tap. Once we've found out who they're talking to, we take it from there.

Mitchell smiled, turning towards Weatherspoon. 'What do you think?' he asked.

Weatherspoon hesitated before replying. 'She could be right. Within the technical definition of the law this isn't really a tap. Just a look at who's calling whom from a particular destination.'

'Fine,' said Mitchell. 'We'll go ahead, then. What do you need?'

Weatherspoon shrugged. 'Just your authorisation to contact the telecoms company to get permission to divert incoming calls from the Cayman Islands via our system.'

'I'll get in touch with the relevant people at British Telecom,' said Mitchell.

Weatherspoon shook his head. 'As I recall, the lines into and out of the Cayman Islands are handled by one of the other international operators now. I think that traffic is handled by Cable Media. You'll need to get in touch with them.'

The hand leant heavily on Lykanov's shoulder, a thick, cold touch, which communicated neither pleasure or warmth. 'Good work,' said Chung.

'The number was easy to find,' said Lykanov with a shrug. 'It was no problem.'

The Korean had emerged from the dim light at the back of the long thin room. It was late morning, though nothing except the digital clock on the wall gave any sense of time; daylight never penetrated the basement. The place was sealed and sanitised; perfect, he had already decided, for work that was likely to become very messy.

'Are all the computers installed?'

'In place? Yes,' replied Lykanov. 'But there is more to this task than buying the equipment. The thing is to make it work.'

'That's why you are here,' said Chung. 'How long do you need?'

'A few days at least,' answered Lykanov.

'And then we can have perfect visibility?'

'Nothing is perfect, my friend,' said Lykanov, looking down at his screen. 'You should know that by now.'

Chung rested his elbows on the desktop, peering into the Russian's eyes. 'But as close as humanly possible, that can be achieved.'

'It is true, yes,' agreed Lykanov. 'We can have good, if not perfect, visibility over London and over the rest of Europe.'

'Before the end of the week.'

'I will do my best.'

Chung nodded, sliding his fingers over the blank and empty screen. 'Remember,' he whispered softly, 'we need to be able to see and hear everything.'

'Like gods,' said Lykanov.

Chung smiled, his lips creasing and his eyes narrowing as he did so. It was meant as a joke, but the man had failed to capture it; a difference of culture, Lykanov supposed; or perhaps just one of outlook.

'I would not have put it like that,' Chung said. 'But if you insist, I suppose I can accept the comparison.'

It was a smell Harry had read about, but never experienced before; an acrid stench, mixing sweat, insecurity and greed in equal measure. The smell of fear.

His desk was towards the back of Gregson's trading floor. A sheer black metal surface, with a Reuters terminal and his own workstation, a picture of Cassie in the right-hand corner. The essential ornaments he liked to have around him while he worked. Not that he planned to be here long. Just a few months, according to the agreement he had drawn up with the firm. And then only part-time, enough to get the show on the road, but not the regular seven-to-seven hours that were worked in the City. He could do without that, no matter how much was at stake.

Part of him, he confessed, felt good about being back in an office. It was a month since he had left Croxley, Palmer and there was only so much time, he realised, a man could spend at home. It might have been different if Amelia had still been alive; they could have done things together with Cassie, as a family. But he found that after dropping her off at playgroup, time hung heavily on his hands. He needed to be involved in something and for the next couple of months this would fit the bill perfectly. He could make some money; more than enough, if everything worked out well, to pay for Cassie's education. And he could teach whoever at Cable Media had insisted on his dismissal a lesson: that this time they had messed with the wrong man. Yes, thought Harry. It's good to be back. For now.

For the two days he had been in the office he had been preparing the firm to start trading in Cable Media debt. He had turned his old research into a pair of well-written briefing notes for the sales force. One stated cogently all the reasons why Cable Media was about to disappear down a financial plughole. It argued that the Argus project was unfeasible, the company was spending too much money building the satellites and its revenues forecasts were way too optimistic. It would face a crunch, and soon. When it did so, any banker left holding its debt could start thinking about early retirement. The salesman would use those arguments, and anything else that sprang to mind, to start shaking loose some of the holders of the debt. Anyone turning nervous after they saw the research could unload their debt now; they would not get all their money back, but they would get a lot more than they were likely to, once the receivers moved in.

The other paper took a very different line. It argued that Cable Media debt was a sound and solid investment, with excellent prospects of both the capital and interest being repaid, although perhaps not precisely on schedule; the satellites would produce fantastic revenues once the system was working at full capacity, and the rest of the company's media and telecoms holdings would keep generating cash at a furious rate. There was nothing for investors to worry about. And at the discounted rates it was now trading at, the debt should produce a capital gain.

Harry had felt less comfortable writing the second note for the salesmen; the arguments all rang false even

126

as he was tapping them into his screen. But he understood the rules of the game. If the firm was to make a market, there had to be buyers as well as sellers. It was useless buying in millions of pounds of Cable Media debt, just to sit on it. Particularly if you felt the company might go bust at any moment. The second note would be needed when they started selling the debt they had bought, hopefully at a higher price than they had paid for it.

'How we doing?' boomed Gregson, standing close to Harry's desk. 'Are we porking anybody yet?'

The man had sidled up behind him without Harry hearing so much as a footstep; a remarkable feat, given that he was more than six foot tall and carried a growing roll of middle-aged weight around his stomach. Harry swivelled his eyes upwards. 'We're just softening them up so far,' he replied. 'I don't think anyone has actually bitten yet.'

Gregson leant closely over the back of Harry's chair. 'Stroke them,' he said. 'Bankers and women. No difference. Feed them a line, caress them, make them wet. Pretty soon they'll be begging you to stuff them.'

'The salesmen are doing just that,' said Harry. 'But it takes time. Cable Media is blue-chip. They haven't borrowed money from just anyone. These are nice, respectable institutions. They aren't about to lie back at the click of our fingers.'

'How long?'

Harry shrugged. 'Hard to read, right now. I reckon a few days. Perhaps a week. Then we'll start seeing some sellers.'

Gregson stood back, his hands clasped together. 'Sooner than that, I think,' he said softly. 'This story could be about to break.'

10

The memory was warm in his hands. He could still feel her lips on his, and the soft touch of her finger-tips on the back of his neck. There was, he sensed, a trace of her perfume lingering in the hallway, left over from when they had said good-night.

Harry had woken early; it was just after six thirty, and he was already grinding some coffee beans in the kitchen and wondering how soon he should wake Cassie. He had been out with Julia the previous evening, to the theatre and dinner, the latest he had stayed out since Amelia had died; and the most fun he had had as well. It had been a reasonably good play and Harry had probably drunk more than he should have over dinner. He had wanted the evening to last and ordering more drinks was a way of postponing their departure.

Harry poured the ground coffee into the cafetiere, filling it with water. They had ridden home together in a taxi and Julia had come inside briefly for another drink; Harry was already feeling guilty about how late he had kept Lucy up and was slightly embarrassed to be arriving home with another woman. Lucy had scanned her slightly suspiciously before saying good-night and he wondered briefly if she was jealous. Probably not, he decided; she was more likely to see Julia as a threat to her job. The drink had been no more than a formality; neither of them seemed interested in the bottle of white wine Harry had pulled from the fridge. He had held her body tightly to his and kissed her on the lips and Julia had responded by holding him close to her, resting her face on his chest. They had stayed on the sofa for half an hour or so, talking and kissing. Harry had felt strangely juvenile; this was hardly the way a man in his mid-thirties with a daughter to look after was supposed to behave.

He took a sip of strong black coffee. It had been such a long time that he was unsure of the ground rules. Perhaps that was what getting older did to you. A decade ago, he would have been desperate for her to stay the night and would have moved her swiftly towards the bedroom; he would have summoned up whatever words were necessary to sweep away her doubts. Yet last night when she had mentioned that it was time to go, he had merely made some feeble remark about how she could stay if she wanted to. 'Not tonight, but soon,' she had replied softly, kissing him gently on the lips. He had not asked again, happy enough with the promise and content to let the relationship simmer slowly. Maturity, perhaps, or nervousness. It was hard to tell. He just hoped she didn't mistake his reserve for indifference. It was only when he had woken up that he'd realised how much he would have liked to have taken her to bed.

Taking another slug of coffee, Harry wandered upstairs to wake Cassie. Lucy had the morning off, so he would have to get her to the playgroup today. She was still asleep when he stepped into her bedroom; her eyes were closed and her arms were wrapped tightly around her teddy. Harry kissed her gently on the cheek before shaking her shoulders. 'Time to get up, princess,' he said.

Cassie awoke with a start, as if she had been interrupted in her dream; a trait she inherited from her mother, Harry reflected. She rubbed her eyes and sat up, still holding the bear in her hands. 'Good morning, Daddy,' she said. 'Good morning, Teddy.'

'Time for breakfast, princess,' said Harry.

Cassie scampered off in the direction of the bathroom, while Harry went back to the kitchen and started making some toast. He picked up the newspapers on his way down, flinging them to one side while he poured another cup of coffee and retrieved some orange juice from the fridge for Cassie. It was only while he was pouring the juice that he noticed the headline in the *FT*. 'DEBT CRISIS TALKS AT CABLE MEDIA', it read. It extended across the top of section two of the paper and Harry grabbed it anxiously. I was right, he thought to himself.

Cable Media, the entertainment and telecoms conglomerate, is holding debt rescheduling talks with its bankers, it emerged last night. The company is understood to be having problems with the financing of its Argus project to build a system of broadcasting and telecoms satellites across Europe.

The company has borrowed £5 billion from a group of around seventy European, American and Japanese banks to finance the project. It is believed to need to borrow substantially more money in order to complete the system. Already it appears to be having problems meeting the interest payment schedules on the debt.

From the corner of the kitchen, Harry could smell the toast burning. Bugger, he muttered to himself. He jumped up, retrieving the bread from the toaster and flinging another couple of slices into the machine before returning to the paper.

> Sources close to the lead banks said last night that interest payment schedules were not currently being met and that a group of the major banks were seeking urgent talks with the company. 'Nobody seems to have much idea what is happening over there, or what exactly the problems are,' said one senior banker. 'Right now, we just want to clarify the situation.'

Fools, muttered Harry under his breath. He retrieved the toast and took some Marmite from the cupboard. He could hear Cassie running down the stairs. 'Can Teddy have some breakfast as well?' she asked, dragging the bear behind her as she came into the room.

'Only if he's very hungry,' answered Harry, ruffling her hair.

'Don't know if he's hungry,' said Cassie.

Harry decided he couldn't see the point in debating the issue and put some more toast into the machine. He glanced back towards the paper.

> A spokesman for Cable Media said the company was aware its bankers had asked for meetings and that these would be scheduled shortly. 'It is no more than a temporary problem,' he said. 'A matter of re-negotiating some of the terms of the debts.' However, other sources indicated that problems within some of the other divisions, particularly within its film business, might be causing cashflow problems at the company. Analysts point out that Cable Media is very highly geared and that the company was relying on buoyant revenues from its entertainment businesses to fund the debt on the new satellite system.

Cassie tugged on his sleeve. 'How can we tell if Teddy is hungry?' she asked.

'I don't know,' replied Harry, trying to hide the irritation in his voice. 'Try asking him.'

Cassie looked disappointed. 'He doesn't like to say,' she said sullenly. 'I think he's shy.'

Harry rolled his eyes; just at the moment he wasn't that bothered by whether the bear was hungry or not. 'Just give him some toast, princess,' he said. 'It's almost time for your playgroup and we need to get you dressed.'

'Is Daddy coming to school?' asked Cassie.

Harry picked her up, gave her a hug and sat her down on the table next to the paper. His eyes glanced at the rest of the story, but the reporter seemed to have run out of fresh material; it was a recap from the cuts. 'Daddy can't go to school, because he has to go to work,' he said.

'And Daddy already knows everything,' said Cassie.

Well, Harry thought to himself, not quite everything. He hadn't known anything like this was going to appear in the papers, although he suspected that Gregson might have done. And he had not suspected Cable Media was so close to the crunch that it would already have to start talks with its bankers. There was more to this story than he yet realised. 'Daddy certainly knows that you need to hurry up,' he said. He glanced at his watch. It was already past eight. And this, he decided, was likely to be a busy day.

Julia was finding it hard to concentrate that morning; her mind kept fluttering back to the previous evening. She was wondering if she had done and said the right things. Perhaps she should have stayed the night. There were moments when she had wanted to and he'd been certain he wanted her too as well. And yet they were swiftly followed by moments when she was not so sure; when she wondered if she had not been pushing things too far, too fast. Harry was a nice guy, good-looking, in

132

a rugged, very masculine way, polite and attentive, funny. She felt sure her girl-friends would be telling her to snap him up before some other woman got her hands on him; indeed, she would be telling them the same thing if the roles were reversed.

Still, she was uncertain. It was partly Cassie. She seemed like a nice enough little girl and Harry was devoted to her; he was obviously a good father and that was part of his appeal. But she could not be sure how she felt about intruding on another family. Nor could she ever be positive about how Harry felt about his former wife; she might always feel she was a replacement, not the woman he really loved. A stepmother, she thought to herself with a shudder. It was not a role she had ever imagined for herself, nor one she could even begin to feel comfortable with. Better get myself a broomstick, she decided with a smile. And start growing my finger-nails.

A small kitchenette, decorated with the most hideous lino she had ever seen, occupied a corner of her isolated office. It was little more than the size of a cupboard. Julia slipped inside, flicking on the kettle and making herself a cup of peppermint tea, her second of the morning. Being by herself all day made her drink more, she realised; it was the one way to take a break from her screen. Never try this again, she told herself. Isolation is no fun at all.

An e-mail was waiting for her, its icon flashing in a corner of her screen. She clicked on the mouse and the message scrolled down. 'I think we have a trace,' it read. At last, thought Julia. A breakthrough. She picked up the phone and punched in Weatherspoon's number. 'Are you sure?' she asked crisply, without even introducing herself.

'I think so,' Weatherspoon replied.

'Tell me about it,' said Julia. She could sense that her

133

breathing was quickening slightly as she spoke.

'We have been monitoring the electronic traffic coming in from the Cayman Islands over the last few days,' said Weatherspoon slowly. 'The computers here have been logging all the calls and searching them for an identification.'

In her mind, Julia could picture him rubbing a hand across his stomach and, silently, she was urging him to hurry up. 'And you found something?' she asked.

There was a pause. 'Yesterday, a transfer of one hundred million sterling to an account in London from one of the offshore companies you are monitoring.'

Her fingers gripped the receiver tightly. 'Who is it?' she asked.

'A company called Turevul Trading, based here in London,' answered Weatherspoon. 'The money was lodged yesterday.'

'Keep looking,' said Julia. 'We need to find out if anything is coming from any of the other companies.'

She hung up and logged on to a fresh page on her screen. Flicking on the modem, she dialled into Companies House, tapping in the name of the company at the prompt. The words disappeared down the line and Julia sat back while the timer on the screen counted down the seconds until it could make a delivery.

First things first, she told herself. I need to find out more about this company.

It took almost three minutes for the computer to find the accounts for Turevul Trading. The minute they became available she flashed them up on to her screen.

Turevul Trading:
Founded 2.10.1997
Issued share capital: £100
Registered address: 121 Bishopsgate, London EC1
Directors: Kenneth Jacobs, David Sharp

Purposes: General commodity trading
No accounts have yet been filed for this company

Julia sat back and stared at the screen. Turevul had been formed at roughly the same time as the insider dealing ring had started its operations. Now it appeared that at least some of the profits were being run into a trading company in London. But why? If they just wanted to make some illicit money in the markets, why bring the money back to Britain? Why not just leave it in a series of secret offshore accounts, ready to be enjoyed once they decided they had made enough? Why take the extra risks?

Richard Gregson leant back against his desk, a can of diet Coke in one hand, a rumpled newspaper in the other. A smile was playing on his lips and his eyes were alight, illuminated by a mixture of amusement and desire. 'I guess you play soccer,' he said.

Harry just nodded.

'Then you might know what I mean by the phrase "kick 'em when they're down",' he continued.

'I think I get the general drift,' replied Harry.

Gregson shook his head. 'In college football round-abouts where I grew up, the man goes down on the turf and that is when you have him where you want him. Nobody scores a touchdown when they're lying on the grass. Get them down and keep them down.'

Harry glanced across at his Reuters screen; the Cable Media share price was already down by thirty pence in morning trading and still seemed to be slipping. He watched the red pixels glowing on the display with a sense of growing satisfaction. His old colleagues at Croxley, Palmer would know now that he had been right all along: the company was overstretched and sooner or later that was going to be reflected in its share

135

price. He might even give Trimble a call later on. There was nothing wrong with a little gloating. 'It certainly looks as if our friends at Cable Media are down this morning,' he said.

'The point is to keep them down,' said Gregson. 'No getting up off the grass. And no last-minute touchdowns.'

The office had been humming by the time Harry arrived at work. It was later than he would have liked, but Cassie had to be dropped off at the playgroup and they did not open their doors until eight thirty. By the time he arrived at his desk at nine the phones were already busy; London's bankers were usually at their desks by eight and they would have digested the morning's papers by now. Plenty of them had already been told by the salesmen the firm was in the market for Cable Media debt. A few were by now getting cold feet and were looking to sell.

'We have shaken quite a few loose this morning,' said Harry. 'Not in volumes yet, but the drift is starting. I reckon we took about twenty million in debt on to our books so far, but there should be more to come. It's just a matter of time.'

'What kind of prices are we getting?' asked Gregson.

'At the moment we're quoting eighty pence in the pound,' replied Harry. 'That's kind of low, I suspect. We might need to edge it up a little if we're going to get any serious selling.'

Gregson shook his head firmly. 'I reckon we come down. Start quoting seventy pence in the pound and keep edging it down.'

Harry looked up at the man; there was a swagger in his voice and in his manner which suggested total confidence, but he himself was unsure if that was the right move. They needed to offer a reasonable price if they were to attract sellers. 'It might be too low to get any volumes going,' he said.

Gregson bent forward, his face leaning across the desk. 'Create the impression of chaos,' he said, raising a single finger. 'First law of the debt markets. The further the price sinks, the more nervous the market gets. They think we might know something they don't. The less we offer them, the more they want to give us.'

It's a warped psychology, Harry decided, but there was a chance Gregson might be right; the market was a strange mistress and its logic rarely moved in straight lines. 'Okay,' he said with a smile. 'We'll take it down to seventy and keep pushing until we find the bottom.'

'That's the spirit,' said Gregson, slapping Harry loudly on the back. 'Remember what the gold prospectors used to say. "The big deposits are always way down low. Just stray nuggets on the surface." So we get down lower.'

John Mitchell was talking on the phone when Julia walked into his office; the receiver was clasped tightly to his chin, his brow was furrowed and he appeared to be whispering. He waved a hand in her direction, motioning her to sit down. Talking to his wife, perhaps, thought Julia. Or a girl-friend.

She stood in the far corner of the room, ignoring his invitation; she was too hyped up by the events of the morning to relax. She glanced around the office. It still appeared to her to be dreary and drab, bereft of any ornamentation, or much sign of life; a joyless tone pervaded the place, which she supposed suited its prosecutorial role. It was not meant to be a place that promoted anything other than grey, and sometimes vengeful, authority.

'What's up?' asked Mitchell, replacing the phone and turning to her.

He had agreed to see her instantly after she had put a

call through to his secretary and the cab ride across from her dummy office had taken little more than twenty minutes. All through the journey she had been thinking about what to say. 'We made a breakthrough,' replied Julia, her voice touched with pride.

His eyebrows arched slightly. He leant forward on his desk, an expression of concern playing on his face. His hands were clasped. 'Tell me about it,' he said.

'The company. We've tracked the organisation in London the insider dealing ring is feeding money to. It's called Turevul Trading.'

'How much?' asked Mitchell.

'A hundred million,' replied Julia. 'But of course there could be much more. This is just one transfer. I've looked up its accounts and that has given me the name of the directors, but apart from that it doesn't say very much. The company has been running for less than a year.'

'When did you find this out?'

'Just this morning.'

He pursed his lips and looked towards his window. 'So we know they are using the money in Britain,' he said at length.

Julia walked over to the desk, sitting on its edge. 'But what for? That's what I cannot understand. There could be hundreds of millions transferred to this trading company. It must be for something.'

'True,' mused Mitchell. 'I suspect, however, that we're getting closer. The question is where do we go next?'

'Investigate the company,' stated Julia. 'We know they're involved and that at least some people at Croxley, Palmer are too. If we find out more about them, it should provide us with the connections we need.'

'Start with the directors,' said Mitchell. 'Find out

everything you can about them, but preferably without arousing their suspicion.'

'Myself?' asked Julia. She was unsure if this was a task she was qualified for, and indeed whether it was the kind of skill she wanted to acquire.

'You've been running the case pretty well so far,' replied Mitchell. 'If you feel you're getting out of your depth, I'll assign someone else to help you. But for now I'd like you to keep running with the ball.'

Julia nodded. 'I've already been warned.'

Mitchell stood up. His expression was concerned, surprised and, Julia suspected, a little annoyed. 'A few days ago,' she continued. 'I got a call on my mobile asking for Samantha Draper. I don't know who it was. A man's voice. He told me not to carry on making investments in the way that I, she rather, was. I didn't think too much about it at the time. But it worried me.'

'Bugger it,' said Mitchell. 'How would they get your mobile number?'

Julia shrugged. The question had been bothering her as well. 'I don't know.'

'Whoever it is we're dealing with,' said Mitchell, 'they certainly appear to have a lot of information at their disposal.'

'Information is what they deal in,' said Julia.

'Be careful and let me know the moment you get any more calls. You should have told me sooner.' Mitchell looked at her carefully and she was unable to tell whether his expression was one of annoyance or concern. 'Information can be dangerous material.'

11

Lykanov looked at the photograph closely, searching for any distinguishing features. The jowls were saggy and grey, the balding patch on the top of the head slightly uneven, the shoulders slumped and a thin roll of excess fat could be detected between the collar and chin. He could be one of many thousand middle-aged men in London. There was little to set him apart. Never mind, he thought to himself. The computer would take care of that.

The picture had been scanned into a PC using a simple, off-the-shelf photo-processing programme, a type used by thousands of magazines. It had been converted into digital form and analysed. Lykanov now had a perfect take on the man; a description, in precise mathematical code, of every inflection of his skull, the dimensions of each feature on his face and a measurement of every mole on his skin.

Leaning back in his chair, he lit up a Marlboro; he had given up smoking Russian cigarettes almost a decade earlier, but the prospect of unlimited quantities of Western brands had been too much for him to resist. He was back up to sixty a day within a week of taking his first drag. What the hell, he had told himself. It's time to start enjoying myself.

Turning to his screen, he looked down at the display. He could see the figure of the man at the door quite clearly: the same grey hair, the slumped shoulders, the balding patch. It certainly looked like his target — hundreds of observations and thousands of pictures had been fed down from the satellites to track him from his office to this location. But the computers would provide the evidence. Keying a series of commands into his keyboard, Lykanov instructed the machine to run a match on the man in the photograph against the one on the display screen. While the microprocessors ran through a million calculations, he lit up another cigarette, enjoying the taste of the nicotine on the back of his throat. An early payment on the good life, he told himself.

'Match confirmed,' read the line of text displayed on the screen in front of him. 'Identification of target.'

'Probability of error?' keyed Lykanov into the machine.

Up on to the screen flashed: '0.02%.'

Lykanov noted the figure mentally. It looked good and he was sure it was accurate. Getting the recognition software into place had been a huge task and had occupied his time solidly for most of the past three days. He had known what needed to be done. The technology of tracking individuals from space was well known to surveillance specialists on both sides of the Cold War for many years; in his old job the KGB had taken a special interest in the ability of satellites to monitor anyone they might want to keep an eye on and the budgets for that part of the operation had always been generous. Even so, he had never installed a system single-handedly before and he could not help feeling a touch of professional pride at the results of his work.

'It's him, then,' said a voice from behind his back.

A thin, acrid trail of cigar smoke had already alerted Lykanov to Chung's presence in the room; as usual, the

Korean had walked in unannounced and without any of the formalities of greeting.

'It's definitely him,' answered Lykanov. 'No question. There could be two or three men in London with a similar profile, but it is not possible that they would have travelled to this place from the same office. Not unless he works with his twin brother. It's him.'

'And the woman?' Chung pointed down at the doorway displayed on the screen, where a lady could be seen opening the door. Even with the poor definition it was possible to detect a welcoming smile on her face.

Lykanov shrugged. 'It is impossible to say who she is, with this information only,' he replied. 'An identification would take a lot more work.'

'But it is not his wife?' said Chung.

'We have seen that his wife is a brunette,' answered Lykanov. 'This lady is a blonde. So I would say that is not his wife.'

Chung nodded. 'Can we print out that picture?' he asked. 'And see if we can locate a phone or fax number for that address.'

Lykanov pressed a command on the computer and signalled Chung towards the printer where a clear, sharp colour image of the man being greeted at the door would be available within moments. He turned back towards the keyboard and started tapping in a series of commands; he had already programmed the software to locate the phone numbers of any of his targets and he knew the computer would complete the search within minutes.

There was an eerie stillness inside the office. As Harry stepped through the door, the controlled fury of the trading floor was still ringing in his ears, it's noise inhabiting his mind, closing down any other thoughts. But when he shut the door behind him it died quickly and suddenly, as though it had been strangled, and a fierce calm descended upon him. He could see the noise, and perhaps even feel it, but it could no longer be heard.

Gregson was leaning back in his chair; so far he was virtually horizontal, with his feet slung up on the desk and his eyes fixed firmly on the ceiling above him. 'How are we scoring?' he asked lazily.

'Not bad,' answered Harry. 'Dribs and drabs are starting to come our way, and we've pushed the price down to about sixty-five pence in the pound. I reckon we took about fifteen million today. The bankers are rattled, but they aren't quite ready to bail out yet.'

'Lemmings,' said Gregson. 'Know what they are?'

Harry smiled; he figured he could already guess where this was leading, but decided to play along with the game. 'Small, fluffy creatures. They like to jump off cliffs.'

Gregson swung his feet on to the floor, swivelling round in his chair and sitting up suddenly. He looked directly in front of him. 'Nope, they're small fluffy creatures in pin-striped double-breasted suits and they like to work in banks,' he said. 'Or any other big financial institution. They sit around all day on their arses, ogling the secretaries, but too frightened to fuck them. They look at millions and millions, but they get too scared to take any of it for themselves. Basically they are very frustrated men. So then one day they see this great big cliff, with all those rocks, and waves crashing at the bottom and so on. And they walk up to the edge, start peering over, look down at those mean and deadly rocks and start thinking to themselves, what the fuck. Who gives a shit. Let's jump.' Gregson lifted his feet back up on the desk and stared at the ceiling. 'Point is, people get lemmings wrong,' he continued. 'Folks think they're jumping because all the other guys are going over. It isn't quite like that. They jump because they're all frightened. Each guy thinks he's making an individual choice. Just turns out they're all the same, so they all reach the same conclusion at the same time.'

'I think they're just peering over the edge at the moment,' said Harry. 'Only a very few are jumping. I guess they aren't quite frightened enough yet.'

'True,' said Gregson. 'You have to be plenty scared to jump. Scared out of your wits.'

Harry walked towards the bar, choosing a diet Coke for Gregson and placing it on his desk, and picked up a can of Perrier for himself. He took a long swig of water before saying, 'Then we have to make them more scared.'

'Absolutely,' agreed Gregson, pulling the tab on his can. 'Like something out of *Friday the Thirteenth*. Get them sweating for their fucking lives. What have you got?'

'We could feed some of our research to the press,' replied Harry. 'Get some sympathetic articles about the squeeze on Cable Media's cashflow. That should rattle their cages.'

Gregson nodded thoughtfully and started sipping his drink. 'Not bad, not too bad,' he said slowly. 'But it's only a spine-tingler. Not out-of-your-wits fucking terrifying.'

'What have you got?' asked Harry.

'You,' answered Gregson.

Harry smiled. 'Thanks for the compliment. But I don't think I'm that frightening.'

'Too right, you are,' barked Gregson. He swung his legs back down to the floor, standing up, this time, and walking across to the window, his eyes gazing down on the trading floor. 'To a banker you are. Didn't you say you reckoned you'd been sacked by those lily-livered brokers for doing critical research on Cable Media?

144

Research that turned out to be pretty much on the button, but which those guys didn't want to see delivered to the market?' He turned to face Harry directly. 'I reckon we feed that story to the press,' he said. 'It makes it seem like Cable Media has a lot to hide about its debt position. Like they were desperate to stop any serious analysis getting to the market. That makes them look bad. Very bad. It reeks of a cover-up. Release that line and those bankers are going to start getting very twitchy. The whole gig is going to start looking very ugly, like something they don't want to be involved with, no sir, not at all. Quite a few are even going to feel like jumping.'

Harry nodded. Gregson's logic had a twisted, perverse credibility to it, which, though disturbing, he could appreciate. But he was not sure he wanted to be involved; it was too personal. 'I have another idea,' he said.

'Shoot,' said Gregson, looking back down towards the trading floor.

'We leek the details of the autopsy report on Sir Ian Strang.'

Gregson remained silent and motionless, his eyes tracking the movement of the traders down below. 'What autopsy report?' he asked.

'There was a report soon after his death, which made the circumstances sound very strange,' said Harry.

'I don't see what that has to do with anything.'

Harry stood, walked towards the window and glanced down briefly at the trading floor. He could see some of the salesmen he had been dealing with, the phones clasped tightly to their chins, their mouths working overtime, their fingers jabbing the air as they spoke. 'It doesn't directly have any connection, at least not that we know about,' he said. 'But it's all part of creating the right atmosphere. Of spooking the opposition. Don't

145

you get it? A debt crisis. A chairman who might have been murdered. It all looks pretty frightening.'

Gregson turned to Harry and smiled. 'I like the way your mind works,' he said.

'Then we should arrange to feed the information to the market?'

'Don't even fucking dream about it.'

'Why not?' asked Harry.

'Too dangerous.'

'Dangerous?' repeated Harry. 'Why?'

'Don't you ever get frightened, Mr Lamb?'

Harry shook his head. 'Not often,' he replied. 'Should I?'

'With a mind like yours and the amount you appear to know, most certainly, sir, most certainly.'

Julia tapped her notes feverishly into the machine; she had come into the office early, keen to carry on with her work. The place was absolutely empty at this time of the morning; the few companies that shared her building were mostly sales organisations, with staff rarely at their desks, or fronts for trading organisations that she suspected barely existed. There was a sense of impermanence to the place, as if everyone there were just passing through, killing time until the next opportunity came their way. Much like myself, she decided.

The memo was being written to herself, although Mitchell had impressed upon her the importance of keeping detailed notes at every stage of the investigation. Put down everything that happens, no matter how trivial, he had told her; it might turn out to be important later on. So far she had set out everything they had discovered about the details of the insider dealing operation. At the bottom, largely for her own illumination, she tapped a single word into the machine: *why?*

She took a sip on the peppermint tea she had just made herself; she had been worrying over the past few days that she was drinking too much coffee and was determined to cut down. Various conjectures and suppositions were running through her mind, and to clarify her thoughts Julia began tapping them into the machine: a series of half-illuminated facts with, she realised, no sign of a thread connecting one to the other. This is not good, she told herself. I need more information.

She put a call through to a contact Mitchell had given her at the Home Office: a man within the records department, he assured her, who could find everything it was possible to know about any individual. 'Can you run a check on Kenneth Jacobs and David Sharp?' she asked, before giving him the dates of birth she had retrieved from the Companies House files for extra identification.

'How soon?' he asked.

'As soon as possible,' Julia replied, aware that all the requests going into that library were for immediate delivery.

He assured her that he would do his best and Julia put down the phone. I will just have to wait, she decided. Investigative work, she was starting to realise, entailed a lot of waiting – and a lot of dead-ends.

The fax machine clicked into action. Softly, although no one could hear it under the sound of the Rachmaninov piano concerto playing in the background, its chips started decoding the lines of digital code feeding down the phone line. Gradually a picture started to emerge from the top of the machine, sliding out millimetre by millimetre as the image began to reassemble itself.

It had been lying there, silent and inert, for several minutes before Sir Daniel Soames disentangled himself from the skilful embrace of the blonde lady and walked across the room to the machine. He was puzzled when he saw the covering letter marking it for his attention; no one would have known that he could be contacted at this address. As he flipped down to the image underneath, his breath quickened and he could feel a slight trembling in his fingers. This was his worst nightmare come to life, converted into twelve inches of shiny fax paper.

The picture, though imperfectly transmitted, was quite clear. It showed himself, visibly recognisable, being greeted at the door by Sonya. It was clearly taken from high above, perhaps from one of the tall buildings on the other side of the road, but the touch of his lips on hers was visible, as was the hand she slipped round his waist.

He walked across to the window, edging aside the curtain, scanning the tops of the buildings opposite to see if he could spot the location from which the photograph might have been taken. But he could see nothing.

At his side, he could hear the phone ringing. Sonya picked it up, holding it to her ear for a brief moment, before passing it across to Sir Daniel. 'It's for you,' she said.

'Caught in the act, Sir Daniel,' a voice said slowly.

For a moment he was silent, too stunned to speak. His eyes flashed across to Sonya and she could detect a seam of anger; whether it was directed at her or the man on the phone she could not yet tell. 'Who is this?' he asked eventually.

'An observer,' replied the man. 'I might say a dis-interested observer, but that would not be strictly accurate.'

Sir Daniel looked again at the woman. Beautiful though she was, he could not at this moment say she was worth it. A terrible mistake. 'How did you get the picture?' he asked, straining to conceal the tone of mounting despair in his voice.

148

'Never mind. The question we need to ask is how much you would like to keep the photograph strictly between ourselves.'

A deal, thought Sir Daniel. At least the man wants to trade; it might be possible to reason with him. 'I think I would prefer its circulation to be as limited as possible,' he said stiffly.

The man allowed a silence to hang over the line for several seconds before responding. 'I can see that. For the Director of Public Prosecutions to be found visiting the home of a high-class whore would really be quite embarrassing. She has other visitors, you know. Gentlemen friends, not all of whom are as distinguished and legitimate as yourself. Our surveillance equipment is quite good, as I am sure you can imagine, and there are plenty of other photographs we could fax through.'

'That won't be necessary,' said Sir Daniel. He was already starting to dislike Sonya.

'Some of the papers would be most interested,' the man continued. 'For once I would imagine they would have a genuine public-interest defence for publishing this kind of sleaze. They wouldn't even run the risk of breaching their code of conduct. And then there is your wife. I imagine she would be very disappointed to learn what you have been doing. Not to mention your colleagues in the government.'

Sir Daniel's heart sank; the man was obviously a professional blackmailer of some kind and skilled at his unpleasant trade. He was calculating how much he would be prepared to spend to pay him off. A lot, certainly, that he already sensed, but not everything; no man's reputation was worth everything. Not any more. 'What do you want?' he asked.

'Now that is a better class of question,' said the man. 'It shows a man who is willing to negotiate. And I also am a reasonable man. I have no desire to cause you any

149

embarrassment. I merely wish to encourage you to make sure your work is being done professionally. And to urge you to control some of your more enthusiastic subordinates more effectively.'

He doesn't want money, thought Sir Daniel with relief; that at least was something to be grateful for. 'Go on. I am always ready to take advice.'

'The Serious Fraud Office is currently investigating what they believe to be a large insider dealing ring operating out of the City of London,' said the man softly. 'I advise you that their inquiries are unjustified. Quite possibly a waste of public money. It would be better for all of us if the case were quietly dropped.'

Sir Daniel hesitated for a moment. Interference with an ongoing case was dishonourable, no question about that. But then, the SFO was dropping cases all the time; sometimes they seemed to be going down like flies. One more could hardly make much difference. 'Who's in charge?' he asked.

'A man named John Mitchell. I trust this can be arranged immediately. If so, we shall have no need to trouble you again.'

It could, Sir Daniel reasoned to himself, be done discreetly; as part of some overall review of ongoing cases at the SFO, perhaps. Presented, possibly, as part of a redirection of resources. There need be nothing sinister about that. 'I think that can be arranged,' he stated firmly. 'Is that all?'

'Absolutely,' answered the man, the pleasure evident in his tone. 'I am sorry to have troubled you. And do enjoy the rest of your evening.'

Chung clicked the off button on his mobile and slipped the receiver inside his jacket pocket. Leaning over the desk, he tapped a centi-metre of cigar ash into the ashtray that now appeared to be stationed permanently on the side of Lykanov's desk. 'Good work,' he said, patting the Russian on the shoulder. 'Everything seems to be going satisfactorily.'

Lykanov glanced down at the display on his screen; it still showed the doorway and the scene of the man going inside from an hour earlier, frozen in time and space. To use several billion pounds' worth of the best surveillance equipment in the world just to catch a man on a visit to his mistress suddenly struck him as a spiteful waste of technology; there must, surely, be something better you could do with so much money and engineering talent. The poor bastard, Lykanov thought to himself; a man should be safe somewhere.

12

The trade was the largest Julia had yet seen; mind-numbing amounts of money were passing across her computer screen, enough to suggest that her targets were becoming both restless and reckless. Enough, also, to suggest they were tiring of the shadows. They wanted to start playing in the open. How can they possibly believe they can get away with this? she wondered to herself.

Details had just come through from the surveillance department at the Stock Exchange; each of the forty offshore companies she was tracking had been active in the market that week. And they had all been pursuing the same stock: Stansky, an industrial conglomerate that manufactured everything from heating equipment to handguns. So far, the main companies on her list had purchased about a billion of stock between them, enough in itself to start causing ripples in the market and driving the price up; the normal daily turnover in the stock was about two hundred and fifty million and that had now jumped by fifty per cent. They were obviously confident something was about to happen to turn a huge profit on their investment. Something big. And very soon.

She had already put a call through to Trimble. It had

been earlier in the morning and she was not quite sure why she had done it; she was feeling jumpy, she supposed, frustrated at the slow pace of the investigation. She had wanted to move things along.

The broker had not sounded pleased when she introduced herself as Samantha Draper. 'Haven't heard from you for some time,' he had said sullenly. 'Thought you had taken a holiday or something.'

Julia ignored the remark. You haven't heard from me since the threatening phone call, she thought to herself, a call you probably organised and which you hoped would be enough to frighten me off the case. 'I've been sitting on my profits,' she said casually. 'Trying not to be greedy. But I'm interested in this Stansky situation. The price seems to be moving up sharply. For no apparent reason.'

There had been a silence on the other end of the line. 'What's your theory?' he asked.

'Heavy buying, perhaps ahead of a bid,' replied Julia. 'Any murmurs like that in the market?'

'Not that we have heard. Thinking of buying?'

Not yet, Julia had told him. She was, she explained, just monitoring the situation and she promised to keep in touch. Trimble hung up without saying goodbye and she had switched off the tape, making a record of the conversation in her notes. He was clearly still hiding something; many of the orders for the stock had been placed through Croxley, Palmer and Trimble would know who the buyers were. He would also be aware that she was still on the trail, and that she had not been intimidated by the phone call.

The fact that they had her mobile number still worried her; it meant, presumably, that they knew who she was and why she was after them. She shuddered slightly at the thought, wondering how far she should take this thing.

A message from the librarian she had contacted at the Home Office came through on her e-mail. He had completed the search on the two directors of Turevul Trading and the results were mysterious. As far as their records were concerned, neither man existed. They had been conjured out of thin air. Julia read the message a couple of times before putting it to one side. How was that possible? she asked herself. Could a company be formed with directors who had false names?

A quick check with an official at Companies House revealed it could be done. When a company was formed, it was usually just necessary to give names of directors and list the other companies they were involved with. There was no need to provide rigorous proof of identity. Random checks were carried out, but unquestionably some false identities slipped through the system. It was certainly no harder than getting a false passport, probably a lot easier. Even so, setting up a company with directors who did not exist was clearly a criminal offence. If it was found that the company had been formed with false information it could be shut down and its assets frozen, while an investigation was started.

Julia tapped her notes into her computer. She took a swig of the cup of coffee at her side; the peppermint tea had been disposed of for today. Getting closer, she thought to herself. If the assets within Turevul Trading could be frozen they could start opening up the company. If they could find out who was controlling it they would be close to cracking open the insider dealing ring. She was, she realised, starting to feel encouraged. There was light at the end of the tunnel, and she might soon bring the case to a conclusion.

She punched through a call to Mitchell on her phone. 'I need a meeting,' she told his secretary.

He was busy for the morning, the secretary told her.

But they could meet later this afternoon. They would talk then. Mr Mitchell, she added, had already asked to see Julia urgently.

Harry caught sight of Gregson on the far side of the trading floor. He was talking to some of the other salesmen; his face was animated and he appeared to be laughing as he swapped stories with the dealers. He was enjoying himself. The trades were going well, perhaps, reasoned Harry. Or perhaps he was just smirking over the piece that had appeared in the paper that morning.

Time to wipe the smile off his face, thought Harry. He strode across the trading floor, walking purposefully, standing just behind Gregson. A story was being finished: something about a couple of girls he had met the other night, a few lines of coke and a pair of aggrieved boy-friends. The traders were smirking, lapping up the description of the night and waiting for the punchline. 'We need to talk,' demanded Harry.

Gregson turned, looking down imperiously and slipping an arm round Harry's shoulder. 'In a moment, Mr Lamb,' he said. He turned back towards his audience. 'Now, seems this lady couldn't handle the coke as well as she thought,' he continued.

'Right now,' said Harry.

Gregson shrugged and smiled at the traders. 'In my office, okay,' he said to Harry.

Together, they walked silently across the floor and up to the glass-encased office. Gregson shut the door silently behind him, fixing Harry with a cold stare. 'What seems to be the problem, Mr Lamb?' he asked.

The story had appeared in the diary section of the *Daily Telegraph's* City pages; a discreet location, but one where it could be guaranteed most people in the City would read it. It made mention of the rumours of a debt crisis at Cable Media, and described how Harry had left

Croxley, Palmer some weeks earlier in mysterious circumstances. The word, according to the paper, was that he had been about to publish some critical research on the company, concentrating on its ability to finance the cost of the Argus system; the same system now plunging the company into a crisis. 'We make no comment on whether these events are related,' it concluded archly. 'But it certainly seems the research would have been timely and clients may regret not having had the chance to read it. Criticising Cable Media, however, can damage a man's career.'

Harry stood with his back to the trading floor. 'I thought I said I didn't want to have my name used,' he said angrily. 'My departure from Croxley has nothing to do with what I'm doing here. At least, not for public consumption.'

'Hey, buddy,' snapped Gregson. 'Don't start coming across like some two-bit débutante. I have no time for cockteasers in this organisation. You start dating with this firm, you better be prepared to go down and get dirty.' He jabbed a finger in the air, pointing it towards Harry. 'There's a job to be done here and a lot of money at stake. You play with me, you play by my rules.'

'Then you should have asked me first,' countered Harry, his face reddening with anger.

Gregson moved closer to him, slipping an arm round his shoulder, an expression of closeness Harry found distasteful. 'Perhaps, Mr Lamb,' he said. 'But, heck, I'd have done it anyway, so it wouldn't have made much difference. Information is there to be used. The thing is, if you don't use it your advantage, somebody else will, so it might as well be done right.' He took his arm from Harry's shoulder and waved out across the trading floor. 'Think of the orders we are going to start taking,' he continued. 'The bankers will be real frightened now. As scared as small children at Hallowe'en. They think that anyone who messes with Cable Media might lose their job. First thing they want to do is wash their hands of the whole thing. Get that debt off their books, fast as they can. And, right now, we are the only buyers. We're going to make a fortune and you have a healthy percentage. So tell me. Would you rather be right or rich?'

Right, thought Harry to himself, but he was not about to admit that now. 'And we don't use the information about Strang?'

Gregson's eyes narrowed. 'I thought I told you,' he replied. 'That stays under wraps.'

'Unless we need to blow the story right open.'

'We already have blown the story open,' said Gregson. He stood closer to Harry, looking down at him. 'Heck, I'm sorry if I pissed you off. But listen. If you want to play softball, then go to the park. If you stay here, you're playing hardball. And we play to win.'

The crisp sheets of paper slipped silently through the laser printer and landed without a sound on the tray. Chung picked them up, holding them neatly in his left hand, his brow furrowing as he read through the words. The girl clearly knew too much, he decided.

He looked across the room at the Russian, noting with distaste the curls of cigarette smoke wafting around his head. Cigars he enjoyed, but heavy nicotine he had always abhorred, yet the man had simply paid no attention to his orders not to smoke. Still, what is there to be done? For the moment, he was useful and could hardly be dismissed for smoking on the premises. At least he was inhaling Western brand and not some vile Russian tobacco. 'What time were these calls made?' he asked.

'This morning,' replied Lykanov wearily.

'And we are sure these are all of them?'

'Quite certain,' Lykanov answered. 'The tap on her

phone is perfect. Any phone traffic via that building, whatever phone she might use, is diverted via this system before reaching its destination. The computer picks up her voice. We have everything.'

Chung nodded gravely. It was clear from the transcripts that her investigation was proceeding and she had not yet been told to drop the matter. It was also clear that his earlier warning had made no impact on her. She was brave, but also careless. The worst sort of fool, Chung decided. He would have to make sure she was stopped, and quickly.

Mitchell looked nervous when Julia stepped into his office. She sat down on the chair opposite his desk, acutely aware of the silence hanging between them. 'They are getting bolder,' she said.

Mitchell raised his eyes, peering at her through his glasses, but said nothing.

'There was another trade this week,' she continued. 'A big one. I mentioned it to the guy at Croxley, Palmer, but he acted as if nothing were happening. It seems to me they are getting greedy, and sloppy as well. They must, I think, suspect we are on to them, but they are acting as if they don't care. It can't be long before they make a stupid mistake.'

The words seemed to move right past him; Mitchell heard, but he was not listening and Julia could see from his expression she was making no impact. He leant forward on the desk, taking off his glasses and spreading his palms out in front of him. 'It's over,' he said quietly.

Julia hesitated. Over, she thought to herself. What exactly could be over?

'I'm afraid the case is closed,' he continued.

Momentarily, she was too surprised to react; the words themselves were comprehensible, but they made no sense. It was hard to believe she had heard correctly.

'What do you mean?' she asked.

Mitchell turned on his swivel chair, looking out of the office window; it was as if he wanted to speak, but found it too difficult to do so while looking at her directly. 'An order,' he replied slowly. 'From the office of the Director of Public Prosecutions. They told me that this case was no longer a priority and they wanted us to stop working on it immediately.'

'Did they give any reason?' asked Julia. The shock was slow to sink in and it was taking her time to formulate a meaningful response.

Mitchell sighed, emphasising his empathy with her question, but kept his eyes fixed firmly on the window. 'Officially, there has been a review of the cases the SFO is currently working on,' he said. 'That happens all the time. The Director of Public Prosecutions' office goes through our files, indicating which cases they want followed up with maximum vigour, those they want pushed to the back of the queue and those they want dropped completely. This one fell into the category of cases to be dropped.'

'It doesn't make any sense,' protested Julia, wishing he would look at her directly. 'I thought insider dealing was a priority for this office. And this is the biggest case yet uncovered. If we aren't going to go after these guys, then who are we going after?' Julia noticed she was using the word 'we' as if she had worked here all her life. Starting to identify with the organisation, forgetting that I'm just here on a temporary secondment. But she was irritated to have had the work of the last month swept away by a bureaucratic whim that made no sense. It was insulting to the effort they had put in. It was also wrong.

'The line from the DPP's office is that we've spent too much time chasing insider dealing cases without producing any results,' continued Mitchell. 'They think we should be spending more time on corporate fraud.

159

Things that impact on the ordinary consumer. Sorry, correct that. The ordinary voter.'

'But this case could have made all the difference,' said Julia. 'It isn't just a big case, it's also one we have a realistic chance of cracking. It could change everything if we landed some big prosecutions.'

Mitchell turned away from the window, looking at her directly; he could detect the anger in her voice and he sympathised with it; but he could also detect the determination in her eyes and found it disturbing. 'Public service can be a frustrating calling,' he said. 'I agree with you, as it happens. This is a stupid decision. It's dumb and it's wrong. But we have to live with it. I have already fought the battle and lost. Let it rest.'

Julia sat back in her chair. 'So what do I do now?' she asked. Her tone, she was aware, bordered on the petulant, but there was nothing she could do about that. Nor was there much she cared to do about it. Right now, she did not feel like doing very much at all. At least, not for this organisation.

'I'll find you something else to work on,' said Mitchell. 'Something which has more chance of working out. If I may say so, I have been hugely impressed by your skill and dedication. This isn't your fault. It's just one of those things.'

Julia leant forward on the desk, a conspiratorial look clouding her face. 'We have a lead,' she said.

Mitchell raised his hands, as if he did not want to hear about it; this case had already gone far enough, he had decided, and he did not want it to go any further.

'The directors of Turevul Trading filed false names,' she added. 'If we can find out more about who filed the papers we could have the real breakthrough. The one that could lead us to the culprits. As you said, we already have the evidence, so once we have the culprits on the case we go to court. We might be just days away.'

Mitchell stretched out his hands across the desk, touching her wrists. 'Don't even think about it.'

'Why not?' asked Julia. 'If we had the right sort of evidence they would have to proceed with the case. They couldn't ignore it.'

'Because that is not how the real world works,' said Mitchell sternly. 'When a case is dropped, it's dead. End of story.'

'I suppose so,' Julia spoke sullenly. 'I was just thinking . . .'

'Don't think,' said Mitchell. 'Not about this. Not any more. Trust me. There's something odd going on and I don't think you should be involved with it any more.'

'A few more days,' said Julia. 'That's all it would take.'

Mitchell gazed into her eyes; he could tell how resourceful and tough she was, and he admired that. It had been for those very qualities he had insisted on hiring her; she had been perfect for the role he had in mind and she had played her part better than he would have expected. But it was time to stop. 'There are things you don't know about this case,' he said slowly. 'Take a couple of days off, and forget it.'

13

The voice on the line sounded sullen and uninterested. Harry cupped the phone to his ear, listening to the low, futile whinging of the banker he was speaking to. The man was trying to wriggle, he decided. He thought perhaps he should sell. Then again, he thought perhaps he should hold on. He was in the grip of a funk of indecision. And it is my job to make him come off the fence, decided Harry. 'What do I have to say to get an answer here?' he asked.

It was starting to become possible to adopt a more aggressive tone in the market. Ever since the statement the company had made through the Stock Exchange early yesterday morning, the firm had found it a lot easier to shake loose holders of Cable Media debt; the problem had been keeping them off the line. The announcement had stated the company was in talks with its bankers about rescheduling its debts. The formal reason was some unexpected cost overruns in building the Argus satellite system; the exact problem Harry had noted some weeks ago.

The statement went on to stress that the company was not in any long-term financial difficulties, but talks about changing the terms of its debts would start immediately. The reaction in the market, as anyone could have predicted, had been swift, savage and brutal. Its share price had dropped from the sky, reminding Harry of why he had been advising clients at Croxley, Palmer to steer clear of the stock. Holders of Cable Media debt had begun bailing out. Nobody knew yet what the outcome of the debt restructuring was likely to be. But they could tell that holding any form of Cable Media was going to be a lot less profitable than they had imagined, and plenty of them wanted out.

'We are still not convinced this is the time to sell,' said the banker. 'I think we would prefer to wait and see what happens in the talks between the company and its creditors.'

'The former chairman was waiting to see what happened,' said Harry. 'It didn't do him much good.'

'What do you mean by that?'

Harry wasn't sure what he meant; the words jumped from his lips instinctively, with no thought or planning. 'He died. Of course, you already know that. It's why Samuel Haverstone has unrestricted power at that company. Kind of convenient for him, although it might also help explain why the business has got into this sort of mess.'

'I don't see your point,' said the banker obtusely.

'You haven't heard the rumours then, I guess,' answered Harry.

'What rumours?'

'That Sir Ian Strang didn't die from natural causes,' replied Harry, spelling out the words slowly. 'It's nothing but a rumour, of course, but it's gaining currency on the trading floors. All I'm saying is that if you think the price of Cable Media paper is going up again any time soon, then think again. Ours might be the best price you see for a long time. Possibly ever.'

The banker hesitated and, though he was miles away,

Harry was sure he could read his expression: dumb fear. 'I'll think about our position, Mr Lamb,' he said. 'And we'll get back to you.'

'You do that,' said Harry, putting down the receiver. Caught him, he thought to himself. The banker would come back, he decided. Soon. And when he did, he would sell.

A row of lights flashing on his phone indicated more calls were waiting, but for the moment Harry did not feel like playing the salesman. He stretched his arms, yawning with exhaustion, and glanced around the rest of the trading floor. It was already late in the afternoon. For the past thirty-six hours the floor had been humming, speaking to bankers around the world who were looking to unload Cable Media debt. A few of the salesmen had been here all night, taking calls from the Far East where, Harry calculated, the company had about a billion in debts outstanding; the Japanese were always quick sellers when any sort of problems emerged. Several of his team were pushing endurance beyond its natural limits and, judging by some of the furtive conversations in the Gents, some were snorting a few lines of coke to keep themselves going. But this was an opportunity to clock up some serious bonuses and none of them wanted to blow it.

Extra salesmen had been drafted in from around the firm to work on Cable Media and Harry had already briefed them early that morning, pumping them with the lines to use and instructing them on what buttons to press; all of them were quick learners and although they did not have much idea of the detail of what they were talking about, they delivered their lines with passion and commitment. Each time he glanced across the floor from his own phone, he could see the clenching of fists and slapping of desktops that told him another sale had been made. A rough and ready calculation indicated about a billion and a half in sterling of Cable Media debt had been turned over in the last thirty-six hours, even though the prices quoted were still dropping. Most of it had been taken on to Gregson's books. And more was coming.

It was a great deal, reflected Harry. And one that should make him a tidy sum. Only one thought troubled him. It was all very well taking these mountains of Cable Media debt on to the firm's books. But what were they going to do with it all? So far, they had found plenty of sellers. But they weren't finding any buyers. Nor did they appear to be trying.

I'm glad it isn't my money we're playing with here, he decided. After all, if the company's paper was as useless as the salesmen kept telling the bankers there was a limit to how much you wanted to hold of it.

Up above, on the podium, he could see Gregson surveying the scene. His eyes robotically scanned the traders, locking on to them one by one, following their lips as they punched home their lines. Gregson caught his eye and beckoned him, his long arm outstretched. The lights on his phone were still flashing and Harry briefly wondered if he should take a couple of calls before responding; an act of calculated defiance, he suspected, but also a way of reminding the man he was freelance. Not one of the minions, constantly at the beck and call of the boss.

'I thought I told you not to talk about Strang,' said Gregson. He was standing in the doorway of his office, towering a full half foot above Harry. Anger was vividly written in the square features of his heavy face, in the tone of his voice and the creases across his brow. But there was something else as well, something Harry could not quite place. Suspicion, perhaps. An expression, anyway, which suggested he was looking at Harry in a different light.

Gregson turned, walking into his office, leaving Harry with little choice but to follow. He stepped into the cubicle, leaving the door open, but Gregson swept passed him, closing it firmly, shutting out the noise of the trading floor. He looked down at Harry, his eyes alive, darting over him, peering into him. 'I'm told you've been spreading rumours in the market about the death of the Cable Media chairman,' he declared. 'What the fuck do you have to say for yourself?'

Harry shrugged. He had not thought about mentioning Strang and had certainly not prepared himself for this confrontation. He was not so sure it had been a good idea; not then and certainly not now. Still, there was no backing down. He was damned if he was going to admit it had just been a spur-of-the-moment thing. That would be weakness. 'Put it this way,' he replied. 'My role here is to create a market in Cable Media debt and I'm working for myself, not for you. I was going to use the Strang thing anyway, so it doesn't make much difference whether I asked you or not.' He looked up at Gregson, wondering if he was aware his own words were being quoted back at him; from the look on his face he judged he did, but it had done nothing to soften his anger. A thin smile crossed Gregson's lips. 'You really are a loose cannon, Mr Lamb,' he said.

Harry attempted a grin. 'As you said, if you want to play softball, go to the park.'

Gregson turned, standing close to the fishtank running down the side of the office. 'I meant it,' he agreed. 'But I don't think I intended for you to play hardball with me.'

'Playing hardball with the market, nothing more,' said Harry stonily. 'Just loosening a few reluctant sellers. No harm done. At least not as far as I can see. It's just a rumour.'

'Well, you sure are playing hardball now, Mr Lamb, and I hope you know how to hit a home run.'

Julia looked down at the files on her desk, but for now they held no interest. She had already leafed through the reams of neatly calculated pages, with their rows of tables, graphs and statistics. But she found it impossible to get her mind to connect with the information. It was elsewhere, exploring different avenues and pondering other premises.

Mitchell had, as promised, put her on to a fresh case that morning, but she had not yet been allocated a new desk at the headquarters of the Serious Fraud Office. The rent on the dummy office was paid until the end of the month and she supposed she was entitled to use it still; it was somewhere to work, she decided, until they found her some space in Elm Street. They had not spoken of the insider dealing ring again. His manner with her had been more formal, as though he were embarrassed about what happened; it had certainly diminished his authority, proving that he was really little more than a functionary, a cog in the machine, and she guessed he was uncomfortable with that role.

Her new case concerned a suspected instance of false accounting at an industrial and building conglomerate. It was thought the directors had been fiddling the books to support their share price; a fraud, definitely, and a crime punishable by a prison sentence if they were unlucky. But not something Julia found she could get terribly excited about. Surely it happened all the time, she told herself. These guys just became too enthusiastic and that seemed to her a mistake rather than a crime.

For the first time in weeks she found herself wondering what she was doing in this place. During the pursuit, she had paid little attention to her surroundings, immersing herself in the immediacy of the chase. It was an adrenalin rush, a thrill. She had little time or interest in getting to know her colleagues, or exploring the hierarchy and culture of the organisation. Everything had been poured into the investigation. And now it was gone.

Idly, she began to leaf through the files once more, trying to concentrate on the numbers. She knew that if she started analysing the audit records, checking the official numbers against the internal figures revealed during the investigation, she would have the beginnings of a case. Turning on the computer, she called up a spreadsheet programme and started creating a new set of files. The work needed to be done, she decided, and she might as well get on with it.

She reached for the phone, tapping out the number of the man she had spoken to yesterday at Companies House. She got through instantly, but hesitated when she heard his voice on the line. Why am I doing this? she asked herself. The case is closed. 'I was wondering if you had made any progress with Turevul Trading?' she inquired.

'Some,' replied the official. 'It was definitely created using false names for the directors. You were right about that.'

'And is there any way of discovering who really established the company?' asked Julia.

'One lead,' came the reply. Julia cupped the phone a little closer to her ear, glancing round the room; it was a reflex action, since the office was, as always, empty and there was no one who could possibly overhear her. 'We have the name of the accountants who filed the forms to create the company. An outfit called Davidson & Slode, on the fringes of the City. They would, of course, know who they were working for.'

'Thanks,' said Julia, jotting down the name on a pad on her desk.

'Should we freeze this company?' asked the official.

'We have enough evidence that an offence has been committed.'

Julia sighed. 'Not just yet,' she replied. 'At least not without checking with your superiors. The case appears to have been closed.' She thanked the official for his work and put down the phone.

Turning back to her computer, she started peering into the spreadsheet, crunching in some of the numbers from the files on her desk. As she did so, her eyes glanced at the name jotted down on her notebook. They had a lead, she reflected to herself. A good lead. Through that accounting firm they should be able to find out who had created Turevul Trading. And if they could do that, they would discover who was behind the insider dealing ring. They were no more than inches away from cracking the case wide open. To abandon it now made no sense, she decided. No sense at all. Tapping out three numbers, she was put through to directory enquiries, asked for the number of Davidson & Slode and scribbled down the seven digits. There they were on the notepad, staring up at her, tempting her to call, to start making inquiries.

Get a grip, Julia reflected, and don't become emotionally involved. After all, it makes no difference to you in the long run whether the case is cracked or not. It doesn't really matter; not enough, anyway, to disobey a direct order. There were other things she wanted to do with her life. Like getting back to her career. Like making some money. Like finding a proper relationship.

At her side, she could hear the mobile in her bag ringing. She fished it out, wondering if it might be Harry confirming the arrangements for dinner this evening.

'Miss Draper,' said the voice on the line.

Julia hesitated, unsure if she should respond.

'Or perhaps I should call you Miss Porter,' he continued.

Julia glanced out of the window, but could see

nothing apart from the grey clouds streaking the sky and the muffled snarl of traffic on the streets below.

'You travel under a number of different guises, it appears,' said the man, his tone low and hushed, but cloaked in an unmistakable air of menace. 'And I don't think I like any of them.'

'Who is this?' asked Julia

'You don't know by now?'

'No,' said Julia.

'Which, if I may say so, demonstrates how little progress you have made with your case.'

'Which case?'

The voice on the line chuckled; his laugh was mirthless and dry, communicating threats rather than humour. 'The case which has been dropped,' he continued, 'but which you appear to be minded to pursue.'

'The case has been dropped,' said Julia.

'Indeed, officially dropped,' the man concurred. 'But you do not seem to be following orders. Let me advise you one last time. It would be in your best interest not to take this any further. You have been given your instructions. Now follow them.'

'I'll make my own decision, thanks.' Julia's voice seethed with sarcasm. The tone was wrong, perhaps, she reflected. But she had had enough of being pushed around today. Quite enough.

'The warning is clear enough,' said the man. 'You make your own choices.'

'I'll do just that,' Julia countered angrily. 'And you go fuck yourself.'

She snapped the mobile shut, killing the line and flinging the phone across the desk. It lay amid her half-open and abandoned files. Inwardly, she was seething, an anger that seemed to start somewhere around her gut and filtered up through the rest of her body. Her fingers, she could feel, were trembling. Her mind was rattled and, for the moment, her thoughts were confused; a swirling mass of disconnected instincts and emotions. Who was this man? she wondered. How could he have access to her phone system? How could he know so much? And how seriously should she take his threats? If there was one thing she could not stand, it was being given orders; instructions delivered by a threatening, anonymous voice on a phone line. It offended every sense inside her, prickling her nerves and loosening her reason. It was, she realised, a kind of violation; an invasion of her privacy and independence. She had been right, she decided, to tell him to go fuck himself.

Ten miles away, in a different part of the City, Chung hesitated for a moment, looking at the disconnected receiver, before putting down the phone. It was a while, he reflected, since a woman had told him to go fuck himself and it was not an experience he enjoyed. The warnings were not working, he decided. She would have to be dealt with another way.

Alone in her empty office, Julia reached out for her mobile, stowing it away in her bag. Her eyes fell on the number of the accounting firm, scribbled on her notepad. She ripped out the sheet of paper, tucking it into her filofax and sliding that too into her bag. We'll see, she thought to herself. Collecting her coat and the rest of her belongings, she swung her bag over her shoulder and walked through the office towards the door. She had seen and heard enough for today.

The kiss was long and slow and lingering. Harry held her in his arms, embracing her, and as he did so he could feel every muscle in her body tense, a response that indicated the depths of her desire. His lips moved gradually from her mouth to her neck, puckering at her skin, and his fingers drew smoothly up her back, feeling the soft flesh beneath her dress.

Julia held his in her arms, enjoying every second of the moment and surrendering herself to his touch; it had been a trying, nervous day, and she was overwhelmed by the need to release some of the anger and energy building within her. His embrace seemed the most natural release available and she pressed her body closer to his.

Harry disengaged himself from her arms, kissing her eyes gently. 'Cassie is waiting in the car,' he said softly. 'You should get your things.'

Dating a man with a child was a lot of trouble, Julia reflected, but she supposed it was something she was going to have to get used to; few men, she had learnt over the years, were perfect. 'Give me one moment,' she replied. 'Bring her in for a glass of juice or something.'

They had arranged to go out to dinner together and Harry had said he would drop Cassie off at Lucy's house, where she could stay over until morning; neither of them had said anything about it, but it seemed to Julia the perfect opportunity for them to spend the night together without having to worry about any interruptions from the toddler. About time too, she decided, as she collected a few essential items of make-up and slipped a toothbrush into her bag. Given that this was their fourth date, the moment had come to get beyond heavy petting. At this rate of progress she was starting to feel like a teenager again.

By the time she came back downstairs, Harry was in the kitchen pouring a glass of juice for Cassie. 'Hello, Cassie,' said Julia brightly.

Cassie smiled up at her, but held on tight to the seam of the brown cords Harry was wearing.

'Hello,' she said. 'Are you going somewhere?'

'Just to dinner with your daddy,' replied Julia.

Cassie nodded. 'Fish fingers,' she said. 'I often have fish fingers when I have supper with Daddy.'

Julia smiled. 'Well, perhaps I will have that then,' she replied.

From the corner, Harry observed cautiously how Cassie and Julia communicated. She was often distant with strangers, observing them warily and sometimes disappearing to her room without saying a word. Sometimes he would find her there later, sobbing on her bed, clutching her teddy close to her chest. It was in moments such as those Harry missed Amelia most terribly; the sight of Cassie doing without her reawakened all the old agonies in his heart most painfully. But with Julia she seemed to be gradually relaxing, building up a rapport that was rare and valuable. I suppose I'll have to get used to Cassie vetting my girlfriends, he decided. Let's hope she has reasonable taste.

'Hop back into the car, princess,' said Harry. 'Daddy will be with you in one moment.'

Cassie puckered her lips and shook her head, as if she were about to refuse, but when she caught the stern look in Harry's eye she changed her mind and started walking towards the door. 'One minute,' whispered Harry, patting her head.

'She's a very sweet little girl,' said Julia.

'And you're a very sweet big girl,' said Harry, taking Julia in his arms.

Her lips moved up towards his. Harry could feel her arms sliding round his back, moving along his spine, and the nerves tingled beneath her fingers. He pressed his mouth into her neck, running his tongue up towards her ear.

'I hope there's room for more than one girl in your life,' said Julia.

'Sure,' whispered Harry. 'One big and one small.'

She smiled, pressing her mouth against his. 'Okay,' she said, when the kiss was finished.

The sound of the explosion ripped through the

hallway with a shattering thud; it was a noise so terrifyingly loud and sudden that for a moment Harry just froze. He could feel Julia in his arms, yet he was disconnected from time and reality, as though, for a few seconds, all the wires had been pulled. Time stopped, and when it resumed its progress it seemed to move in slow motion, stretching seconds into minutes. Strange sound, he thought, in a way that was almost abstract. Very loud and very close. A plane overhead, perhaps. No, it was too loud. A car backfiring. No, too loud for that as well. Could it be a building being demolished nearby? No, it was too late for that. Those thoughts meandered through his head for what seemed like minutes, but was, in reality, only a fraction of a second. Then it struck him. An explosion. Outside.

He dropped his arms from Julia, flinging himself through the front door and tumbling out into the street. As he saw the debris all around him, his knees started to buckle beneath him and his hands rose to his face. No sound escaped his lips, but inwardly he was screaming; a shout of horror that seemed to travel from his throat down into his gut.

Not much was left of his car. He could, he supposed, just make out the chassis, but it was engulfed in flames; bright, amber lashes of fire, whipping upwards, driven higher by the wind. In front of him, just a couple of feet from his face, he could smell the burning leather of what could be a seat. It was impossible to tell. The searing heat scorched his face and the acrid, rotten smell of combusted petroleum flooded his nostrils, bringing vomit to Harry's throat. He coughed violently, his guts wrenching inside. Swirls of heavy black smoke obscured his vision and stung his eyes.

Moving forward, he plunged desperately into the smoke, ignoring the hot, burning rubbish all around him. 'My God, where is she?' he said aloud. He heard the words and for a moment found himself wondering who was speaking. He could feel Julia behind him, but ignored her, his mind capable of focusing on just one thing. Part of him had already given up hope, was trying to cope with the unimaginable horror of finding her broken body, of having to watch her charred flesh slowly disintegrate. He knew it was more than he could bear.

Harry went closer to the remains of the car, his eyes moving feverishly through the wreckage. He raised his hands, shielding his face from the heat, but keeping his eyes open, scanning the kerbside, desperate for some sight of her.

Her body was lying some ten feet away, crashed up against the kerb. 'Cassie,' Harry screamed, his voice roaring the words. He flung himself in her direction, a flame lashing against his jacket as he did so. There was no sign of movement; Cassandra lay perfectly still against the roadside, frozen and motionless, with a thin trickle of blood seeping from her forehead. Her dress was scrunched up around her waist, its fabric blackened. To her side, a large black metal object was still burning, its flames illuminating her face.

Harry kicked the burning lump of metal to one side, ignoring the pain that shot through his foot as he did so. He knelt down next to her body. 'Stay with me, my darling,' he said. The smoke hit the back of his throat as he opened his mouth and he started coughing violently again. Cassie seemed so peaceful lying at the roadside, almost eerily at rest, that for a strange, still moment Harry was almost reluctant to disturb her. He bent down carefully and cradled her in his arms. He held her close to his chest, starting to stand up, anxious to get her away from the fumes. Instinctively, he put his hand to her wrist, searching for a pulse.

14

Samuel Haverstone trod carefully down the steep metal steps, the steel heel caps of his suede half-brogue shoes clacking against the iron staircase. The noise echoed around the slim concrete chamber, reverberating downwards into the hidden depths of the building. His ears caught the sound of his feet and he smiled to himself; an expression of indulgent self-congratulation that was purely for his own consumption. The sweet sound of my own arrival, he thought to himself, wondering if some of the floors in the chief executive's suite should be resurfaced; stainless steel tiles, perhaps, or aluminium. Zinc even. Something that would make a crisp noise every time he approached, that would let people know he had arrived.

He had not ventured down into this part of the building before. The plans, of course, he had seen many times. It had been part of the architecture of the new headquarters, a priority when he had chosen this as the base of Cable Media soon after the merger. A deep underground lair had been part of the stipulation, something below car-park level, tucked away. A place which, if necessary, could be kept hidden from the world.

That some of the great multinationals headquartered

in London would have built underground nuclear shelters, back in the days of high paranoia during the Cold War, was not something he would have imagined. It seemed senseless now, but he supposed it had a certain logic back then; after all, some of the company's operations might be left standing after a nuclear blast and though capital might be destroyed, its controllers would want to carry on. When he stumbled across this building, vacated by a giant chemicals company, he realised at once that it was perfect. Not only was the building above the ground suitably grand, imperial even, to represent the communications giant he was creating, but the shelter for the directors would provide perfect cover. Hardly anyone even knew of its existence, and those who did could easily be taken care of.

Up to now, he had deliberately kept away from his creation. Fingerprints, he knew, were dangerous and though he had been careful to dust over his own tracks, he was aware that everything had to be done at as much distance as possible; should questions ever be asked, it would help to give his denials maximum plausibility. Yet this evening was different. He was tempted to see his work close up and to take the full measure of what he had designed. And he was curious to see how the night had gone.

He was, Haverstone reflected, so close now to everything he had desired. Caution be damned!

The door ahead looked innocuous enough: a single sheet of steel, with a fire hazard warning above it and a numerical keypad on the right-hand side for security. A notice above the door warned visitors that admission was strictly prohibited, and the voltage sign indicated that behind it lay nothing more sinister than an emergency power generator. Haverstone knew differently, but few people would spot anything unusual; the power generated within this part of the building was a sort few people could imagine. A power, Haverstone decided, that only the truly inspired could comprehend, which in its majesty and reach nobody beyond himself could truly appreciate.

He punched five digits into the keypad and waited while the computer checked the code. A green light on the keypad indicated the numbers had been verified and, inside the door, Haverstone could hear the locks sliding away. He turned the handle and pushed the heavy door open, his eyes swerving furtively through the room inside.

The pale light surprised him. For himself, he preferred stronger strips of neon; he liked the glaze and glimmer of bright illumination and always tried to insist that every corner of his office was fiercely lit. Still, he supposed they had their reasons. He stepped carefully inside, enjoying the acrid smell of the cigar and cigarette smoke that hung heavily throughout the room. Haverstone did not smoke, apart from a very occasional cigar at formal dinners, but often hired smokers; indeed, for certain situations, he practically insisted on it. He did not care for men who were too concerned about their health; it was impossible to tell whether they were cowards or not. After all, if they were not prepared to hazard a cigarette, what risks would they take?

The Russian and the Korean were hunched over a computer screen, peering intently into their equipment. Haverstone walked across the room, his eyes scanning the fabulous array of machinery stacked against the walls, and stood next to the two men. 'Good evening,' he said curtly.

Chung turned to face him; his expression was deferential and polite, but maintained its own impassive dignity. 'Good evening, sir,' he replied. 'I don't believe you have met Sergei Lykanov.'

The Russian took a drag on his Marlboro, looking up

behind him. With a flick of his wrist, Chung indicated he should stand and Lykanov rose heavily to his feet, extending a hand.

Haverstone took it with both of his. 'I have heard so much about you,' he said warmly. 'You are among the best in the world in your field, or so I am told. That is as it should be. We hire nothing but the best here.'

Lykanov eyed the man standing before him. So this is the person I am working for. He cut a modest, unprepossessing figure, somehow different from what Lykanov had imagined; he had pictured someone rougher than this neatly manicured specimen. Haverstone stood no more than five foot six inches, was wearing a perfectly tailored Prince-of-Wales check suit, with a blue-striped shirt. His grey hair was neatly combed and his double-breasted jacket buttoned up. One hand was in his pocket and his handshake was soft, verging on the limp; the Russian suspected he did not enjoy touching other men.

'I have heard little about you,' said Lykanov. 'But I am glad to meet you at last.'

Haverstone nodded, his green eyes scanning Lykanov intently. He was much as he would have imagined; a large bear of a man, with shoulders disappearing into the rolls of excess flesh around his torso. His appearance was scruffy and dishevelled, and his eyes were bloodshot: a combination of alcohol, nicotine and hard work. An engineer, Haverstone decided. They were much the same breed of men the world over. 'I hope you have everything you need,' he said.

'Almost everything,' answered Lykanov. 'Certainly much more than was available to us in Russia.'

'That is good,' said Haverstone. 'If there's anything else, don't hesitate to ask.' He turned towards Chung. 'How has the work of the evening progressed? Do we have any information yet?'

179

Chung pointed down to the screen. 'The bomb has been detonated, as requested, sir,' he replied.

On the monitor Haverstone could see the display. He peered forward, resting his elbows on the work surface next to the overflowing ashtray. He loved satellite images; the intimacy and privacy of them fascinated him. They had done for years. Ever since he first started working in the communications industry he had been captivated by the capabilities of the orbiting hunks of steel and silicon, entranced by their power and subtlety. They were, for him, the most perfect machines of the twentieth century. And now they were his.

The image, captured from thousands of feet above, yet clear and crisp as if they had been watching from across the road, showed the fired, burning hulk of a car. Haverstone could see the lie of the street, the neat, suburban west London house and the debris scattered across the road. He saw the damage, but, though he was scanning every detail of the image, he could not yet see its consequences. 'Did you get them?' he said, looking at Chung as he spoke.

'It is impossible to say as yet, sir,' he replied. 'Lykanov had a camera timed to take a picture at the moment the car was primed to explode. As you can see, we have captured the detonation. From this angle we are not able to see what victims might have been claimed. The next set of pictures should reveal that. But I am sure nobody would have survived an explosion of that force.'

'How soon can we have the evidence?' asked Haverstone. He was looking directly at Lykanov, his expression petulant and demanding, his eyes boring through the other man, as though he were not used to waiting for an answer.

Meet the new boss, same as the old boss, thought the Russian, remembering some lines from a song of his youth. 'We need to wait for the satellite to be in precise position over this exact location,' he replied with a shrug. 'No more than a few minutes now, according to my calculations. Then we shall have our answer.'

'I'll wait,' said Haverstone, his tone rich and smug. 'Those two people have proved very annoying. I would like to see them dead.'

Harry cradled Cassandra in his arms, holding on desperately to her tiny, limp body. Water filled his eyes, but whether it was the stinging of the smoke or the emotion of the moment it was impossible for him to say. He held on tightly to her wrist, hugging the faint pulse he could feel there, and wrapped his torn sleeve around her head, hoping to staunch the bleeding. 'Get an ambulance,' he said to Julia, the words choking in his throat. 'Get an ambulance as quickly as possible. Please.'

He looked down again at his daughter, listening gratefully to every tired breath that escaped her lips. Hang in there, darling, he muttered, not sure if he were talking aloud or just to himself. Hang in hard and tough.

How long he had to wait for the ambulance he would be unable, later, to recollect. It seemed like a lifetime; a lifetime during which a mass of memories crowded and cluttered his mind: of her birth, of her first few months, of her mother's death, of the many moments of happiness and grief they had shared; memories which might have given them both strength to pull through, but which, just now, seemed to sap his spirit. To lose her now, he realised, would be more than he could live with. He would be utterly broken.

Julia was already at his side by the time the spinning, screeching sirens of the ambulance broke his thoughts. Two men climbed out, carrying a stretcher between them, and started to take Cassie away from him. Briefly, without thinking about it, Harry resisted, his mind unable to focus on who they were and what they were doing. Then, grateful yet also strangely reluctant to release her, he handed her into their outstretched arms. Standing up behind them, with Julia close at his side, he started to climb in, but the men prevented him. 'In the police car behind,' they said, pointing past their own vehicle. The police would escort them to the emergency unit at the Chelsea and Westminster Hospital. There was no time to lose.

Harry looked around him and started to comprehend the unfolding scene. Ahead he could see the burning wreck of his car, already surrounded by a couple of policemen, scrutinising the damage. He could see a fire engine pull up to the kerb, the men starting to clamber out of the machine; the fire seemed close to burning itself out, but they would still want to extinguish the remaining flames. Little was left of the motor, and the roadside where it had stood was blackened and charred. He could see the ambulance pull away, but for the moment he felt too bewildered to do anything other than watch it disappear down the road. A seam of loss opened up in his chest; they are taking her away from me, he thought.

Above, he saw a policeman leaning forward, a trace of sweat visible on his brow. 'Was that your car, sir?' he asked.

Harry just nodded, wiping the sweat away from his face as he did so.

'And your little girl, sir?' he continued.

'Cassandra,' answered Harry. 'Is she all right?'

'She's alive, sir,' the policeman replied, the words ground out in a flat monotone. 'She has been taken to the hospital.'

'I must be with her,' said Harry.

'We can take you there,' said the policeman. 'But we will have to ask you a few questions along the way.'

182

Harry nodded again, rising unsteadily to his feet; the policeman took his shoulder, helping him to stand. He could see that his leg was shaking, but he felt strangely disconnected from the moment, as if he were watching himself from a distance. He could tell Julia was at his side, standing close by, and he turned to look at her, catching her eye; he could read the sympathy there and he was grateful for it. But he also saw bemusement and bafflement written across her face.

The policeman held the car door open and Harry climbed into the back seat, Julia sitting next to him. Questions, he thought. Of course, they will want to ask questions. But he was damned if he could think of the answers. He had no idea what had just happened. None at all.

He turned to look at Julia, noticing for the first time how drawn and worried she appeared. 'Are you okay?' He felt bad for having taken so long to ask.

She leant across and gripped his hand, squeezing it tight in her own. 'Of course,' she replied. 'Are you all right?'

Harry wiped his brow once more. 'Of course,' he answered. 'I'm okay. It's Cassie I'm worried about.'

Lykanov looked back down at the screen. Tapping a series of commands into his keyboard, he pulled up a tracking ,a piece of sophisticated positioning software that gave him a constant reading on the location of the satellites under his control and the ground they were covering. It told him it would be possible to capture another image of the site within the next seventeen seconds. The computer already had the co-ordinates of the street they wanted to observe and a simple instruction commanded the machine to feed through a photograph of the site as soon as it could be made available.

Haverstone leant over his shoulder, the gold of his

signet ring tapping against the metal frame of the machinery. 'How good is the system?' he asked.

'Pretty good,' answered Lykanov. 'Not up to the CIA systems, but as good as anything we have in Russia, for sure. Probably much better than anything operated by any other intelligence agency outside of America. Much better than any in private hands anywhere in the world, that much is definite. Assuming this is in private hands.'

'Has he been told much of who he is working for?' asked Haverstone.

Chung shook his head. 'He has been told no more than necessary,' he said. 'As you instructed.'

A hand descended upon Lykanov's shoulder; the touch was light and delicate, the Russian noted. Effeminate almost, as if he were unwilling to communicate anything but the most distant regard. 'At some stage we must become better acquainted,' said Haverstone. 'But for now I can say you are working for one of the most successful private corporations in the world. And one of the most powerful.'

There was a solemnity to the way the words were delivered that struck Lykanov as disturbing; as though the man were making a formal speech to a large auditorium, not speaking to two other men in a darkened room hidden deep underground. He turned to face his employer. 'As long as my wages are paid I don't mind too much who I work for,' he replied. 'That is something you learn under communism.'

Haverstone looked disappointed with the answer and appeared to be pondering a reply; he had already withdrawn his hand from Lykanov's shoulder. But his attention was distracted by an icon displayed on the screen in front of them. It flashed, blinking on and off every second, and showed an envelope superimposed upon a small satellite. The photo they were waiting for was ready.

184

Lykanov keyed the image up on to the monitor and could feel Chung's hot breath on the back of his neck as he peered down to take a close look.

The burning hulk of the car could still be discerned, but it had been joined now by three police cars, an ambulance and a fire engine. In the corner Lykanov could see a man sitting on the kerb, a woman close by him, whom he judged to be their prey. And he could see what appeared to be a stretcher being carried towards the ambulance.

'Zoom in closer,' said Chung, his voice cool yet hurried.

Lykanov enlarged the image, focusing on the man sitting on the kerb. Harry and Julia could be seen clearly now, their faces dirty and downcast.

'Fuck it,' muttered Chung quietly, the words compressed between his tight lips.

'They are alive,' said Haverstone slowly.

Chung composed himself instantly, standing upright and turning to face Haverstone directly. 'It appears they have survived, sir,' he said.

'I can see that,' said Haverstone.

Lykanov shifted the angle of the image slightly, focusing on the stretcher. He could make out the shape of a small body, crumpled on the makeshift resting place, and with blood clearly visible around her head and eyes. Two men were carrying the stretcher and though the child was obviously injured, he could see that her face was not covered. 'The child is alive as well,' he said flatly. 'If she were dead, they would have covered her.'

'A failure,' muttered Haverstone. He shook his head as he spoke. 'I am not pleased when an operation does not go according to plan.'

'The outcome is always uncertain, sir,' said Chung quietly. 'We agreed on a car explosion, you'll recall, because we did not want a lengthy police investigation at this delicate time. Unfortunately the target was not in the vehicle at the time the device detonated.'

'Bloody unfortunately,' said Haverstone.

'But I think we can be assured those two people will have been effectively warned by now,' Chung went on. 'They should not be foolish enough to continue with their games.'

'And if they are?' asked Haverstone.

'Then we can always deal with them another way.'

Harry paced nervously round the waiting room of the casualty department, his limbs aching from the tension of the past few hours and his head racked with anger, denial and doubt. His back felt sore and his breath came in short, nervous bursts, leaving him unable to focus or concentrate.

The night had already drawn in around him and, inside the hospital, the detritus of the city had arrived. The same tramp had asked him three times if he had a cigarette and by the third time Harry had lost his patience, telling the man to piss off. He had been angered by a brutish young thug who swung through the heavy doors, a cigarette dangling in his mouth, despite the no smoking sign, and with blood still spattered across his tight white T-shirt. Elsewhere, the waiting room was filled with sad and sorry-looking specimens, their eyes growing more vacant and empty as the hours ticked by. The unruly ghastliness of the place ground on Harry's nerves, making him more and more irritable.

He glanced up at the clock on the wall. It was just after ten. The doctors had said they would have to treat Cassie for severe concussion and possible burns. That had been two hours ago and although he had since asked one of the nurses how it was going, she had replied that nothing could be said until the doctor emerged from the operating theatre. She was sorry, she said sympathetically, but there was nothing that could be done. He paced the dismal waiting room, walking until his legs ached, in the vain hope it might ease his tension and clear his mind.

The interview with the police officer had filled the first half-hour or so of the wait. The man had introduced himself as Inspector Williams; he explained it was unnecessary to go back to the station in the circumstances, and sat next to him in the casualty department. 'Tell me what happened,' he said sympathetically.

Harry ran through the sequence of events. He explained how Cassie had gone out to the car ahead of him, and that the next thing he heard had been an explosion, the sound of his car blowing apart.

'Had it been left unattended during the day?' asked Williams.

Harry nodded. 'I don't drive to work,' he replied.

The policeman looked at him directly. 'I have to ask blunt questions sometimes,' he said. 'Do you think someone is trying to kill you?'

Harry was shaken at first. He supposed, in retrospect, the thought had already crossed his mind, drifting, perhaps, through his subconscious, but it had not yet surfaced. At least not openly. 'I can't imagine it,' he replied. 'It seems impossible.'

Inspector Williams asked him some more questions, getting a detailed description of his work, his family, his life. He could find little there to arouse his suspicions, however, and Harry could soon tell he was starting to lose interest. 'What do you think happened?' he asked.

The Inspector hesitated before replying. 'It could be something quite simple, sir,' he replied. 'For a car to explode is unusual, but not absolutely impossible. It happens from time to time. A fuel leak can flood petrol into the engine and if one of the spark plugs accidentally ignites an explosion can be the result. Then again, a very tiny explosive device near the fuel tank would produce the same thing.'

'It could have been a bomb?' asked Harry. The surprise was evident in his voice.

'Only could have been, sir,' Inspector Williams replied. 'We will have to examine what is left of your car. There may be too much damage to the fuel tank to tell if there was a leak, but if there was an explosive device we may well be able to trace it. I shouldn't think so, though, sir. In my experience people don't often try to blow up stockbrokers.'

The conversation had been rattling through Harry's mind for the hour or so since the Inspector had left. He had taken Harry's address and promised to be in touch tomorrow, and wished Cassie all the best. At the time, Harry was glad to see him go. Just then, he wanted to be alone. He needed to know how his daughter was and anything else was just a distraction.

Julia was at his side when the doctor emerged from the operating room. She had stayed with him throughout the ordeal and he was grateful for her presence, even though there was little he could think of to say to her. Sometimes he just held her hand. Sometimes, he just sat, his head slumped on his fists, peering down at the floor.

The casualty unit brought dark and unhappy images flooding back into his mind. It had been somewhere much like this a little over a year ago that he had waited for news of Amelia after the accident. The same late-night vigil, the same tired nurses, the same ugly patients littered around the room. The same sense of terror and uncertainty. And the same sense of helplessness. Utter and total helplessness.

It was, he reflected, the sense of your destiny being wrenched from your own control that he hated the most. First her and now me, he wondered to himself. Was that possible?

The doctor approached them carefully, sitting down on the chair next to Harry. She looked young to him; late twenties perhaps, possibly touching thirty. Her expression was serious, yet reserved. Harry could read nothing on her face. 'How is she?' he asked.

The doctor seemed to wait before replying, as if pondering the answer; a moment which, for Harry, appeared to stretch into an eternity. 'She's alive,' she said.

Harry could hear himself exhaling a sigh of relief, but at the same time felt a pang in his chest; the word 'alive' seemed the best that could be said about Cassie. 'Will she be all right?'

'She lost a lot of blood,' said the doctor carefully. 'It was lucky she arrived here so soon because she would not have lived much longer. We have bandaged up the cuts and those shouldn't cause any permanent damage. But the blood loss has sent her into a temporary coma and it's still too early for us to say whether she will pull through. She seems like a strong little girl, but we'll have to wait a few days. We have her in intensive care.'

Harry nodded, trying to digest the words as they were spoken. Part of him was relieved she had lived through the explosion; that it had not captured her immediately. He knew he should be grateful; it could have been much worse. Yet part of him was still terrified; he could feel the fear, circulating through his veins and shivering through his spine. He had never felt so frightened and was unsure how he could cope with the agony of waiting. 'Can I see her?' he asked.

The doctor stood and led him through the doors, along a thin, gloomy corridor to the intensive care unit. Cassie was in a room by herself and Harry could feel his heart jump as he saw her stretched out in the cot, her arm attached to a strip of plastic tubing, an electronic display at her side giving a constant reading of her heartbeat. Harry found himself glancing immediately across at the machine, his eyes fixed on the monitor, checking that she had survived another few seconds. He knelt down on the floor beside the cot, his hand reaching out, stroking her softly across her bandaged brow. 'Princess,' he said. 'Pull through.'

Her expression remained unchanged while he spoke. Her eyes were closed and he could hear her soft breath, and see her chest rising and falling. She seemed lost and distant; it was a deeper and more peaceful sleep than he was familiar with.

He could feel Julia's palms softly kneading the back of his neck and her touch was comforting. She, too, was peering into the cot, looking into the small bed, searching for signs of recovery. The doctor stood at their side and for a few minutes Harry was happy just to kneel there, gazing into the closed eyes of his only child.

When eventually he stood up, it was hard to wrench his eyes away from her. The doctor was clearly becoming impatient and Harry knew there was nothing he could do. Julia took his arm and led him towards the door, but he paused, desperate to take one last look at her before he departed. As he glanced back at Cassie a horrible thought pulsated through his mind, a thought he could neither deny nor control. This might be the last time I see her alive.

15

The limousine fought its way slowly through the early morning traffic clogging up the Embankment. Across the Thames a trace of mist was still hanging in the air, obscuring the view from the shaded window. Richard Gregson glanced out through the mist across the river. It was still and peaceful at this time of the morning, with hardly a ripple disturbing its surface. He looked at his watch, noting that it was still not seven thirty, and he could not recall if he had seen it this early before. He doubted it. He was not by nature an early riser, preferring to slumber away the effects of a hangover until eight or nine. And he doubted if he would see the river this early again soon. It was not, he reflected, his time of day.

If there was one thing he disliked in particular about Samuel Haverstone it was his mania for calling breakfast meetings. Normally, he would have refused. Indeed, he had done his best to arrange another time when the call came through late last night. Lunch, Sam, he had protested. Or dinner, he had added. Even better. Hook up with a couple of starlets from one of his television stations and make a night of it. Have some fun.

But no. There had been a petulant tone in

Haverstone's voice as he reeled through a list of important engagements he already had lined up for the next day. It was a voice Gregson had come to recognise over the last few months; whining and self-important, it was at once pleading and insistent, leaving little room for disagreement.

The car pulled up outside the back entrance of the company's West End headquarters. Gregson thanked the driver, told him to wait around the corner and stepped inside. The security guard checked his appointment and waved him towards the lift. Gregson always used the back door on his rare visits to this building; to be seen coming through the grandiose lobby would be to invite suspicion, the last thing they needed at this stage in their plans.

Haverstone was sitting alone in his office, looking as though he might have already been there for several hours. Rebuilt since Cable Media had taken possession of the building, the office measured forty feet by twenty and had been furnished in a style that seemed more appropriate for minor royalty than the chairman of a public company. The carpet lay thick under one's feet and the walls were painted a pale yellow; portraits were strung across them at regular intervals. At the back of the office sat an imposing antique desk. To one side were a set of deep, tanned leather sofas and armchairs, at the other a bank of display screens, an incongruously modern touch in an otherwise strictly nineteenth-century room. Thirty screens made up the display, each broadcasting a different Cable Media product, all with the sound turned down. They were mostly breakfast shows at this time of the day and Gregson had seldom seen so many pastel studios gathered together, or so many air-brushed blondes mouthing silent platitudes at the same time. Garbage, he thought to himself. But useful garbage. And profitable as well.

Haverstone had a spread of newspapers across his desk and was flicking through their pages; all Cable Media titles, Gregson noted. His eyes darted from story to story, seldom lingering for more than a second, and a smile of satisfaction was playing upon his face.

Gregson stood close to the desk, peering down at the man in front of him. 'So what was so god-damn important that we couldn't talk about it on the phone?' he asked. The voice was croaky and rough; it always took Gregson a couple of hours in the morning to get his vocal chords working smoothly.

Haverstone glanced up at his guest, his expression playful and amused. 'You better than anyone should understand why I don't trust the phone,' he replied.

'True,' answered Gregson, helping himself to a cup of coffee from the counter and sitting down on one of the leather sofas opposite the desk. 'Fucking freaky, if you ask me,' he continued. 'The thought of your spooks listening in on anything a man does.'

'Freaky, yes,' answered Haverstone thoughtfully. 'But intriguing also, don't you think?'

Gregson shrugged. 'Just hope the creeps aren't watching my ass all day.' He paused, smiling and chuckling to himself. 'Mind you, the blonde I took home last night. If the spooks have found a way of capturing that, I'd sure appreciate a copy.'

Haverstone nodded. 'I don't think the technology is that sophisticated yet,' he answered.

'Yeah, well, be sure to let me know,' said Gregson. 'So what's up? Why the party? You know I hate being dragged away from a lady in the morning. I've told you that.'

'They lived.' Haverstone spoke in a precise, clipped tone, delivering the words with cold accuracy. His features were calm and composed, betraying no emotions.

'Who?'

'Mr Lamb and Miss Porter,' said Haverstone, with a small flick of his wrist.

Gregson put his coffee down on the table, staring upwards at the man behind the desk. 'I thought it was a car bomb,' he said. 'Nobody survives them.'

'They do if they are inside the house when it goes off,' said Haverstone.

'Then your Korean friend will just have to keep trying,' said Gregson.

'Of course,' replied Haverstone. 'It is being taken care of. I felt you should know in case Mr Lamb shows up at your office this morning.'

'Very considerate,' said Gregson sourly. 'How much more time do we need?'

'Depends,' replied Haverstone. 'How much of the debt does your firm now control?'

'Last night it was twenty-eight per cent,' answered Gregson.

Haverstone nodded, a thoughtful expression creasing up his brow. 'Good, but not quite good enough,' he said. 'I suspect we need to accelerate the process a little.'

'By starting the talks?' said Gregson.

Haverstone nodded again. 'I think it is time,' he replied, looking across directly at Gregson and leaving the words hanging in the air.

Gregson chuckled, taking a long swig of his coffee. 'I love it when the game gets serious,' he said.

The night had taken a heavy toll. Harry took two aspirin, washing them down with a large mug of black coffee. His head was still aching and he had been unable to sleep; the tiredness was clouding his mind, his thoughts painfully slow and sluggish. His nerves, he sensed, were shot through, severed from any rational way of working, and he knew he needed to rest. But rest was impossible. Not until he had found out what had happened. A call to the hospital had told him that there was no change in Cassie's condition. They would contact him immediately if she woke.

Julia looked almost as badly beaten as he did. Her face was drawn, the lipstick long since gone, and faint lines were visible beneath her eyes now the mascara had faded. 'Not much of a way to spend our first night together,' he said, attempting a smile. 'I'm sorry.'

She reached out and touched his hand across the table, grateful for the humour, but too exhausted to laugh. 'It's okay.' She smiled. 'It isn't your fault.'

He scanned her face, hoping briefly to find some explanation there, but realising as he did so that she knew no more than he did. 'Whose fault is it?' he asked. 'What do you think happened?'

Julia shrugged. 'You mean was it an accident or deliberate?'

Harry nodded. 'We have to know.'

Julia sighed, stood up and poured herself another cup of coffee. This was no time to cut back on her caffeine intake, she realised. 'I think I should tell you something,' she said.

Harry looked across at her, his interest suddenly engaged. 'What?' he asked.

'I've been receiving threats,' Julia replied, sitting down again. The information had been weighing on her mind for the past few hours. She was aware, almost as soon as it happened, that the phone calls might in some way be related to the explosion, but she had not wanted to speak about it. It seemed too much of an admission that she might, even remotely, be responsible for what had happened to Cassandra, and she was not sure if she could bear that. It was a form of denial, she supposed, but not something she could continue for much longer. He had a right to know.

She started to explain how the investigation had been stopped suddenly by Mitchell, without any warning and with no clear explanation of why the decision had been made; as if he could neither understand nor explain it himself. 'There were phone calls,' she said slowly, catching her breath as she spoke. 'Warning me not to continue and saying I did so at my own risk.'

'Who from?' asked Harry, looking up.

'A man,' Julia replied. 'He didn't give his name. The strange thing was he called me on my mobile and he seemed to have a very good idea what I was up to. And he said that if I didn't stop the investigation, something nasty would happen. This might be it.' She leant across the table and slipped her fingers over Harry's hand. 'If so, I want you to know how sorry I am. If I had thought it was serious I would never have let either you or Cassie come anywhere near me.'

Harry took her hand and held it in his for a moment; he examined the lines on her opened palm and wondered briefly why she had not mentioned the threats. A casual disregard for danger, perhaps, as though nothing and nobody could really touch her. A misplaced sense of machismo; a common enough feature among women who worked in a very masculine world; they often appeared to believe they had to take enormous risks just to prove they had bigger balls than the men. Or just an innocent inability to believe that anyone could really be threatening her life. If so, that was dumb; when you were investigating a criminal racket potentially worth billions you had to figure you were up against some pretty heavy characters.

The possibilities flickered through his mind and, as he weighed the different options, he realised how little he knew her. 'I, too, have a confession to make,' he said heavily.

196

Julia looked up, her eyes suddenly alive with curiosity. 'Yes?' she inquired softly.

'Gregson was very angry with me when I used the information about Sir Ian Strang to start shaking loose some nervous sellers of Cable Media debt.'

'What did he say?' asked Julia. 'Did he threaten you?'

'Not in so many words,' answered Harry. 'But he was angry. It was definitely something he didn't want used again. It struck me that there was something odd about his attitude. Strang was probably murdered, at least if the initial police report from Ireland is to be believed. Whoever was responsible for that, well, they are murderers. If they got the impression I knew something about the case and if they thought I was spreading rumours about it, who knows what they might do.'

'Try to murder you as well,' Julia suggested softly.

Harry shrugged, his hand still holding on to hers. 'Let's face it,' he said. 'It has to be a possibility.'

Julia leant back in her chair. Her eyes, Harry noticed, betrayed a flash of vulnerability, but her mouth and her brow indicated defiance. She did not have the look of someone who was about to surrender and Harry was grateful for that as well; the more he thought about what had just happened to Cassie, the more he was minded to fight back.

'It seems as if there might be someone who is trying to kill you,' she said firmly. 'And also me.'

'The question is which.' Harry attempted a smile.

'We need to find out,' said Julia, 'or they will succeed.'

Gregson was standing in the centre of the trading floor, leaning over one of the junior traders, a pale-faced boy Harry was not sure he recognised. His arms were raised high above his head, as if he were about to strike his helpless victim, but the scene was being played out in silence; Harry knew he would not be able to hear what

197

was being said across the roar of the trading floor.

He sat down at his desk and started scrolling through some of the files on his screen. He was not sure if it had been the right idea to come to work today. It would take his mind off Cassie for a while; he felt so hopeless just sitting around waiting for the phone to ring. And as Julia pointed out, they both needed to go in to the office, if only to see how much they could discover about what was happening to them.

'The boss is in a foul mood today,' remarked one of his colleagues from a nearby desk.

'What's up?' asked Harry, loading the question with a nonchalant indifference.

'Fuck knows,' came the reply. 'Bad line of coke last night, perhaps. He's taking it out on everyone. Charlie has already been canned, and he's giving Bazza all kinds of shit. We're keeping our heads down until lunchtime.'

Harry nodded and returned to his screen. He checked his Reuters panel, noticing immediately that Cable Media was down already by 80p and a red asterix was flashing next to its stock quote. He clicked on the market, pulling up the stories to read. Four had already been filed by the Reuters financial correspondents. 'CABLE MEDIA ANNOUNCES TALKS WITH BANKS OVER DEBT RESTRUCTURING'; 'CABLE MEDIA STOCK SLIDES AS DEBT TALKS REVEALED'; 'BANKS REASSURE MARKET CABLE EXPOSURE LIMITED'; and 'MARKET SPECULATES CABLE MEDIA DEBT CRISIS COULD TAKE WEEKS TO RESOLVE'. He pulled up the final story, knowing that would be the most up to date, his eyes flicking through the words as they scrolled on to his screen. With Cassie in hospital, the deals suddenly seemed trivial and pointless.

London: 8.58. The giant media conglomerate Cable

Media today announced it had started formal talks with its bankers about rescheduling several billion pounds of debts. The market reacted badly to the news, taking 80p off the price of Cable Media shares in early trading. A statement from the company before the market opened said it had asked the consortium of bankers to start immediate talks about rescheduling its debts. It said delays in completing its ambitious Argus telecoms and broadcasting system had meant the prospect of immediate revenues from that investment had now been postponed, and disappointing cashflows in its film division and rising newsprint costs in its print media subsidiaries had reduced revenues from other operations.

In the market this morning there was speculation that Cable Media would be seeking either a temporary standstill on its debts, which some analysts believe could last for up to a year, or a debt to equity swap. 'The problems obviously go a lot deeper than anyone imagined,' said one. 'This mess will take a long time to sort out.'

Harry glanced anxiously around the room. The traders were buried in their phones, keeping their heads down; partly, he suspected, to avoid the attentions of Gregson, who appeared to have moved on to another trader, and partly to deal with the volume of calls coming in. It would, of course, be a terrific morning to be trading Cable Media debt. A shame, he reflected briefly, that I'm unlikely to be around to enjoy it.

'How's the market looking?' he asked the first trader to come off the phone.

'Hot,' came the immediate reply. 'The people we have been trying to shake loose for weeks are now begging us to take this rubbish off their hands. We are just about the only show in town right now.'

'What kind of prices are we offering?' asked Harry.

'About sixty pence on the pound right now,' the trader responded. 'But it could go lower. Anywhere down to fifty pence. What do you reckon?'

Harry shrugged. He should be in the thick of things, marshalling the troops and directing the game, he realised. This was, after all, the moment he had come here for and he should be in his element. But just now he had too many other things on his mind. Far too many other things. He no longer cared.

'You're looking like some vomit on the side of the street,' boomed a voice loudly from behind his back. 'Load yourself up with some caffeine and come and talk to me.'

Harry turned round, realising as he did so that he hardly needed to; he would by now have recognised Gregson's voice anywhere. By the time he had turned, the man had his back to him and was striding up the stairs towards his office.

Caffeine was good advice. He filled up a cup from the machine, stirring in a sachet of sugar; he had not slept since the night before and he needed something, anything, to pull him through the next few hours.

When he walked into the office, Gregson was already seated behind his desk, his hand squeezing a can of Coke. 'So what happened?' he demanded. 'Too busy balling some slut to come in to work? You look like shit.'

'Actually,' Harry replied softly, 'someone tried to kill me.' Understatement, he realised, was probably lost on this man, but for the moment he found he didn't mind. He would say whatever he felt like saying.

Gregson smiled. 'I've taken some pretty extreme measures against jerks who show up late in the morning. But usually I just can them. What happened?'

Harry hardly felt like divulging the details; he had said what he intended to say and for now he just wanted to see the man's reaction. He explained about the explosion of the car, telling him of the injuries to his daughter, all the time keeping his voice as level as he could manage. He had no wish to display any emotion to Gregson. 'I was exaggerating when I said someone was trying to kill me,' he finished. 'It might have been an accident. But I have no way of knowing, so I have to be on my guard.'

'Who would want to kill you, Mr Lamb?' replied Gregson. 'Been porking any gangsters' wives?' The man's voice was steady but his eyes were piercing and cold.

'I thought I'd listen to your theories.'

'My theories?' said Gregson, his eyebrows lifting. 'What would I know?'

Harry shrugged. 'You're a smart guy. Any ideas?'

Gregson laughed, shaking his head. 'Only guy ever wanted to kill me was some black dude after I mistook his wife for a whore in a Vegas casino. Happens all the time. Lot of those black chicks dress like hookers.'

'What about the people who killed Sir Ian Strang?' Harry allowed the sentence to hang in the air, scrutinising Gregson's reaction to the words. He wished he had a camera; a snapshot of the moment would have been useful to study later, since the fleeting glance of anxiety was so brief he could not be sure he had witnessed it. Perhaps, perhaps not. After half a second it was impossible to tell, the look having long been replaced by one of calm serenity.

'What are you talking about?' asked Gregson.

'Somebody killed him,' said Harry. 'They might also have tried to kill me. Alternatively, somebody connected with Cable Media. Anything is possible.'

Gregson stood up and walked towards Harry, slipping an arm round his shoulder. Momentarily, Harry found himself recoiling from the man's heavy touch, but he allowed his arm to remain there, unsure how to react.

'Take some time off, my boy,' Gregson said. 'You're under a lot of pressure. Go see how the kid is doing, and clear this shit out of your mind. I can understand how you feel, but it's all nonsense. If anybody was pissed about what is going on in this firm, anyone at Cable Media that is, then it's me they would be trying to kill. And my car is right over there in the parking lot, safe and sound. So quit worrying and come back when this is all over.'

Harry frowned, pulling away from underneath Gregson's outstretched arm and standing two feet away from him. 'This is a crucial time for the operation,' he said.

Gregson slapped his hands together in annoyance. 'Listen up,' he said. 'Things can run okay without you. You've done some great work in setting this thing up, but it can run smoothly enough now. Everything is under control.'

'How much do we have?' asked Harry. 'Of their debts. On the books right now.'

Gregson shrugged. 'Getting up close to thirty per cent,' he replied. 'Something around that level. Coming in all the time since the story broke this morning.'

'And when do we start selling?'

'Selling?' asked Gregson. 'What do you mean?'

'Selling the debt,' insisted Harry. 'I thought we were here to make a market, not just to buy everything in sight while the price keeps dropping.'

Gregson walked back to his desk, taking a swig from his Coke can and pressing the thin metal between his palms. 'Whenever,' he said casually. 'As soon as we think the price is right. You get some rest, recover from this accident and we'll worry about that later.'

The wait outside Mitchell's office seemed to take for ever and as the minutes ticked by Julia found that her anxiety levels were rising. She was no longer sure this was the right thing to be doing; perhaps she should have listened to Harry and taken the rest of the day to see how the situation unfolded. For all she knew there might be another attempt on her life at any moment. Perhaps right now, here in this building.

She had checked in at her old desk briefly, exchanging just a few words with her colleagues. A couple remarked on how tired she was looking, asking her if everything was okay and she reassured them curtly that she was just having trouble sleeping. Mitchell's secretary said he was busy for most of the morning, but Julia insisted it was extremely urgent; she would come up straight away, she said, and hang around the office until he had time to see her.

From her desk she collected the files she had already printed and downloaded the rest from her computer on to a floppy; she was not sure when she might need them, nor when she might be back. The more she thought about it, the less she felt like hanging about a place where she could be easily located.

Mitchell seemed surprised when she walked into his office. Concerned even. His eyes narrowed and he focused intently upon her. 'Are you all right?' he asked, his voice gentle and, Julia suspected, worried.

She sat down opposite his desk and tried to compose herself, before explaining the events of the past twenty-four hours. She finished by stating that she could not be sure whether the explosion had been an accident or not. 'But I'm nervous. You can understand that.'

'You're right to be worried,' said Mitchell flatly.

'Do you know anything?' Even as she uttered it, the question struck Julia as too direct, but she could think of no other way of phrasing it.

'Only that you're right to be careful,' he replied. 'Tell me about the man you were with.'

Julia noticed he seemed faintly embarrassed, as if he were inquiring into her personal life, which in a way he was; yet she and Harry had not had much time to establish a private life. 'He's involved in the City.'

'Are you sure you can trust him?'

It had not occurred to Julia that Harry was someone she should be suspicious of and the question took her sideways, leaving her momentarily struggling for an articulate response. Her eyes were cast down and she could sense she was blushing. 'Yes,' she replied.

'Yet you know he was involved with the brokerage that we have established has connections with the insider dealing ring.'

Julia nodded, unsure what he was driving at. She chose her words carefully. 'It's possible an attack was directed at him,' she said. 'But he couldn't be involved. After all, it was his daughter who was injured.'

Mitchell pondered the words. 'You're probably right,' he said. 'But in these situations you have to be alert to every possibility. No matter how fantastic it might appear. If Mr Lamb is involved, he's got a lot at stake.'

'I've remained alert so far. What do you think I should do next?'

Mitchell looked out of the window behind him. 'First we need to establish from the police whether it was a bomb, or just an accidental explosion,' he replied.

'In the meantime we can reopen the investigation into the insider dealing ring?'

Mitchell shook his head. 'On no account do that, Julia,' he said firmly. 'That would be the worst thing to do. We have strict orders.'

'But it's obviously much more serious now,' Julia protested. 'These people are no longer just fraudsters. They might be murderers as well.'

Mitchell laid his palms on the desk and the look in his

eyes was hard and unyielding. 'Don't even think about it, Julia,' he said. 'You're in enough trouble already.'

Julia surveyed the man momentarily, noting the tension in his voice. 'What do you know about this case that you aren't telling me?' she asked.

'I can't tell you,' Mitchell replied stonily. 'It's too sensitive.'

'I have a right to know,' demanded Julia angrily. 'My life might be at stake.'

Mitchell turned away, looking towards the window. 'Believe me, it's better for you not to know.'

16

The neon light filtered down on to the bank of monitors, spreading a pale artificial light across the room. Years living within an underground base had accustomed Lykanov to working in near darkness and, by now, he believed his eyes were better adjusted to the pixelated glow of the cathode-ray tube than to any form of natural light; he understood its fractions and colours, and he could read its messages, sometimes instinctively, without even thinking.

Working the system into manageable shape had been a mammoth task, consuming up to twenty hours a day during the last couple of weeks, but he figured he was starting to get the kind of information flows his employers had demanded. It was still some way below its optimum capabilities, but he believed the machines were starting to perform.

All the satellites were now fixed in a stable orbit, covering the whole of the European continent, and each was sending down a constant flow of hundreds of images a minute, filed away in the massive hard disks installed on the mainframes in another part of the building. Each satellite was equipped with ten high-density cameras, powered by the solar panels spreading from the wings of the machines; the cameras had been manufactured by a small engineering company based in the Slovak Republic, which had once supplied parts for the Soviet spy systems; it was familiar with the technology needed and, for a generous price, would build it discreetly. They had been fitted secretly to the communications satellites before they were launched and were unlikely to be observed amid the mass of data-retrieval and transmission devices fitted to a broadcasting and telecoms machine. Not that anyone was going to spot them, Lykanov reflected; orbit was one of the few places these days where you were safe from prying electronic eyes.

The software for rudimentary analysis had been installed. Each image downloaded from the satellite would be converted into digital form and stored in long lines of binary code. The computers had been programmed to recognise human forms and could do so with a success rate of ninety-eight per cent. For each person whose image was captured, another file was created and the details stored in a separate set of code. At the same time, pictures of several hundred people his employers wanted tracked had been fed into the computer and their images, too, had been converted into digital format, providing an effective fingerprint for every one. Performing millions of calculations every second, the computer checked the code for each of its targets, comparing it with the thousands of images it was downloading every day. From its calculations, it could produce a report at any time, tracking the movement of all the individuals it had been assigned to follow. Their fingerprints were everywhere and the computers, working alongside the satellites, could follow them wherever they went. There was no hiding place.

New targets could be slotted into the system at any time; several dozen bankers, politicians and industrialists had been added in the last few weeks alone. Because every image downloaded from the satellite was stored in the mainframes in digital code a new target could be selected and, once an image had been fed into the system, an analysis of his or her movements over the past few weeks could be generated within hours. Lykanov had already completed a number of trial runs, keying in random people whose pictures he had torn from newspapers and magazines, and found the system was working well. It was not always perfect and there were always glitches. But it would do for now. And within a few months, with some tweaking and some careful work, he felt confident it would be perfect. The Argus would see, store and remember everything that had happened within Europe.

The work, he decided, torching up another Marlboro, was going well.

Integrating the telecoms network into the system had not been quite so easy. It was not a technology he was intimately familiar with; phones had been routinely bugged by his old Soviet paymasters, but that had not been something he had ever been required to work on. Still, some of his colleagues had, and he reckoned he had learnt enough from decades working on remote electronic surveillance to make the system work.

The basic technique for phone tracking, Lykanov was aware, was based on voice recognition. Each individual voice has a distinctive quality which, when analysed on a computer, can be translated into a series of waves; the technique had first been developed by criminologists, for use as evidence in courts when taped telephone conversations formed part of the evidence. Once the wave had been mapped it could be stored in the computer and the pattern of each person's voice was as distinctive as his or her fingerprint. Meanwhile, all the millions of phone calls processed every day to which his employers seemed to have access could be simultaneously analysed to identify the voice patterns of the people speaking. Again, just as was the case with the visual surveillance, a bank of voice patterns for the target list could be stored by the mainframes. Crunching millions of numbers a second, the computer could keep track of it, comparing it constantly with the flow of telecoms traffic moving through the system. Within seconds, as soon as one of the target list came on the line, the computers would log into the conversation, capture it, store it and produce a printout for later reference. The system automatically located the call and recorded every word, each time a target picked up the phone.

Of course, it still was not perfect. Even when reduced to digital code, voice recognition was fuzzy and any interference on the line pushed the system towards breaking point. Of the target calls the computers were retrieving, Lykanov reckoned there was about a ten per cent error rate; acceptable but far from perfect. The rogue calls, calls made by people who sounded very like those on the target list, and when interference on the line disrupted the pattern, could usually be easily identified and cast aside. How many calls by targets were getting through without being picked up by the computers. Lykanov could not be quite sure. He reckoned it was probably less than one in fifty.

And with patience, the system could be tweaked and smoothed until it was perfect. Then they would capture everything.

From the dim recesses of the bunker Lykanov could catch a faint scent of expensive cologne puncturing the acrid smell of cigarette smoke that now permeated the small, enclosed space; it was a smell he had learnt to recognise as the announcement of Samuel Haverstone's arrival. From the English papers and the television that he had started glancing at most mornings, he recognised him as the chief executive of Cable Media, although he had not been introduced with that title. From that information he had started to figure out where the basic satellite platforms were coming from; the machines flung into the sky, to broadcast television and carry telecoms traffic, were clearly rigged to act as spy satellites as well. It was a technological trick which, once he thought about it, would pose no great engineering challenges; a hunk of metal floating above the earth could be put to many purposes and collecting surveillance data was just one of them. There was no reason why any particular satellite could not be configured to perform several tasks simultaneously. It was just a matter of putting the right equipment on board.

Neither Haverstone nor the Korean had troubled himself to inform Lykanov of the purpose of his mission; an omission that rankled with him increasingly as the weeks dragged by. Even back in Russia, his masters had spun some fabricated lines about the advancement of world socialism in the old days, or, more recently, the protection of the motherland. Most of it had been lies, of course. He recognised that and had done so for years. But at least they had tried to give his work some purpose. These men just treated him as a hired hand; a technician who could supply the information they needed.

He was well paid, he knew, and he was starting to appreciate the subtle pleasure of watching money pile up in an offshore bank account; his few hours each day away from the control centre were often spent pondering his investments and thinking about what he would do with the money when he was free of this place. He knew the first half-million dollars had already been lodged in an account created for him in the Cayman Islands, a place where it would be safe from any subsequent investigations, and he had been assured that the next half-million would arrive there shortly. He pondered ways of discreetly moving it in chunks to other destinations, perhaps in Switzerland and Luxembourg, and placing some of it in his wife's and daughter's names. He did not feel comfortable with having all his money in one place, and he did not necessarily want his employers to know where their money had gone.

Lykanov glanced at his watch; it was just after nine and he would soon be finishing for the day. Most of the system was in place now and he saw no need to work through the night this evening. He needed some rest.

'How is the target identification progressing?' asked Haverstone.

'Not bad,' replied Lykanov. He started to explain how the computers had now taken over most of the routine surveillance, keeping a constant track on the targets he had selected.

'The two young people we saw last night, do we know what they have been doing?' asked Haverstone.

Lykanov tapped a series of numbers into a keyboard, the code for the two targets identified, the details of which had already been fed into the computer. He sat back and lit another cigarette, while the computer started crunching the analysis, enjoying the hit of nicotine on the back of his throat. Right now, he could have used a drink, preferably vodka. But he was not sure if he was allowed to drink on the premises and he did not yet feel comfortable enough to ask.

Both Haverstone and Chung leant forward as a series of images scrolled upwards on to Lykanov's monitor. The display clearly showed a picture of Harry, first entering the office of Gregson & Heath, then leaving, then outside the hospital, then departing again. Another set of pictures displayed Julia, entering the headquarters of the Serious Fraud Office, then leaving. Another picture showed her going into her house; there were

211

none of her exiting, suggesting she was still inside. To the side of the pictures there was a brief text of a telephone conversation, captured by the analysis of the telecoms traffic moving through the system. Harry had called Julia early in the afternoon to suggest that he would visit her after he left the hospital; he explained that he had no news of Cassie, but he would see what the doctors had to say later. He would, he promised, see her that night at her home. She replied that she would stay in and wait for him, and said goodbye.

A thin smile spread across Haverstone's lips as his eyes digested the words and pictures on the screen. It had been a lot of money, a fabulous amount, he reflected, but now that he could see the results he knew it was worth it. Every penny. The range of knowledge it put at his disposal was staggering. And knowledge, as he constantly reminded himself, converted effortlessly into power: the hardest and most valuable of the world's currencies. 'Information,' he said softly, to nobody in particular. 'Raw and complete. The most perfect thing in the world.' He patted Lykanov on the shoulder. 'This is tremendous work. Really tremendous.'

'If they are both going to be in the same house later on,' said Chung, his voice cold and level, 'this might be a good opportunity to finish the job.'

Haverstone sighed. 'I suppose so,' he said. His eyes looked down again at the screen, briefly lost in childish wonder. He took the mouse and started scrolling up and down, moving the images into and out of view, occasionally clicking on a picture to enlarge it, his eyes widening as he did so. 'Perfection,' he muttered under his breath. 'Sheer perfection.'

Harry sat inert by the hospital bed, his body barely moving, his breath subdued and slow, his mind emptied, momentarily, of any thoughts. Before him,

212

Cassie lay perfectly still, her back arching slightly with each weakening breath, but her face remaining placid and expressionless, her eyes closed and her hands still. He reached down to clasp her, holding her tiny palm in his. Her skin felt warm. He could detect life there and feel her pulse moving; but there was no reaction when he touched her. It was like holding on to something lifeless.

He rubbed his hand across her brow and wondered briefly if he should pray. He was not a religious man and never had been; he and Amelia had not even had Cassie christened, an omission he now regretted. But then, who could have foreseen that things would ever come to this? He sighed deeply, taking hold of her hand again. I could never have known, he told himself again. It was unimaginable.

At his side a nurse appeared and had begun readjusting the tube of fluid that ran into a vein in Cassie's left arm. Harry looked up at the woman: early thirties, dark hair, large but not yet fat. She seemed aware that Harry wanted silence and, though she nodded in his direction, she did not say anything.

'Any progress?' asked Harry.

The nurse looked at Cassie, an expression of genuine sympathy illuminating her eyes. 'She's still with us,' she replied. 'The doctors are doing everything they can.'

Harry looked down at the floor, unwilling for now to contemplate the implications of what she was saying. 'You've seen worse?' he inquired eventually, his voice touched with hope.

'I have, and I've seen them get up and start smiling and running around again,' the nurse answered. 'And it's a joyous thing to behold, that it is.' She walked round the bed and touched Harry briefly on the shoulder. 'You should be going. Visiting hours are almost over and there is a gentleman waiting to see you.'

213

Harry nodded, looking down at Cassie once again and, although knowing she was unable to respond was painful, it was impossible to take his eyes away. 'I'll see you soon,' he said to the nurse.

He walked along the corridor of the intensive care ward, his shoulders hunched and his mind heavy. Most of the people along this ward seemed to be very old, or at least middle-aged; there was some sort of sense to their being here. But not Cassie. She was too young, and this was no place for her.

The policeman was waiting at the end of the corridor. Inspector Williams had the look of a man who was used to hanging around hospitals; he had an expression of easy familiarity that only comes from a close knowledge of your surroundings and his face betrayed little sign of interest in the task before him. 'Mr Lamb,' he said, extending a hand. 'How is the little girl?'

'Still in pretty bad shape, I'm afraid,' answered Harry. 'The doctors have no real idea yet whether she will recover or not. They think they might have to operate.'

The Inspector motioned Harry towards a seat in the lobby, sitting down next to him. 'The laboratory has completed its investigation,' he said. 'So I thought I should see you in person.'

His interest suddenly captured, Harry looked up, scanning the policeman's face for a sign of what he might be about to hear. But there was nothing there he could read; just a neutral look of practised sympathy. Something they learn at police school, Harry supposed. 'Was it an accident?' he asked.

'The laboratory results confirm that interpretation,' Inspector William replied carefully. 'They found no evidence to suggest the car had been tampered with deliberately.'

'What caused the explosion?' asked Harry. 'Could they tell?'

'The most obvious explanation is a leak from the fuel pipe into the spark plugs. That floods the area with petrol, an ignition plug misfires producing a spark and suddenly the whole thing goes up,' said the Inspector. 'It's rare, but it does happen from time to time. All cases of this sort are notified to the manufacturer to see if there's anything they can do about safety.'

'Bloody German cars,' muttered Harry. 'I thought they were supposed to be reliable.'

The policeman smiled. 'No car is ever a hundred per cent safe. Anyway, I wanted to let you know, to put your mind at rest.'

Harry stood up and shook the Inspector's hand. 'Thanks,' he said.

'I hope the little girl makes a full recovery. She looks like a fighter.'

Harry nodded his agreement, and said good-night, watching as the policeman turned and left. He sat down, observing as a man on a trolley was wheeled towards the operating theatre, and thinking about whether he could stand it if Cassie had to make the same journey. A sense of helplessness overwhelmed him and he wondered momentarily what he would do if she died. Could he carry on? For now, it was impossible to say.

At least no one is trying to kill either me or Julia, he decided. It was an accident; the first piece of good news he had had in what seemed like a lifetime. Now I can just focus on looking after Cassie, doing everything I can for her and putting our lives back together. I must tell Julia, he realised. She would be worried sick, and she had a right to know.

The chief executive of Harrington's Bank stepped carefully into the offices of Cable Media. Malcolm Fielding had not been here before, even though the company was one of his bank's largest debtors.

215

Harrington's was by now a massive financial conglomerate which, as well as branches on every high
street, owned the stockbrokers Croxley, Palmer, a fund
management firm, an investment bank and a building
society. Even when a company had borrowed more than
a billion, the account did not usually merit the personal
attention of the chief executive. He left that to his
subordinates.

He had met Haverstone two or three times on social
occasions, but never one to one, and he had to confess
he was intrigued when he received the invitation for an
early-evening drink. The man had a reputation, and
reputations were always interesting to encounter. He
was a larger-than-life figure, and those were rare among
the ranks of grey men who controlled the world's
industrial and financial powers.

Thirty-five years ago, he reflected as he walked
through the glitzy marbled lobby towards the steel-and-
glass lifts, banking had been the centre of the commercial
universe. When he had joined Harrington's as a young
graduate he had imagined he would be working for an
institution that dealt in as much power as any government ministry, certainly more than any of its industrial
rivals. Even a decade ago he reckoned that would still
have held true. But now the scales had slipped. These
days, it was the information barons who appeared to hold
sway. Judging by the long and respectful magazine profiles, it was men such as Haverstone, with their iron grip
on the flow of knowledge, who were lauded as the most
powerful in the world. And perhaps, he reflected, it was
even true. Perhaps it really was information rather than
money that now kept the world spinning.

A secretary met him by the door and led him through
the chairman's suite. Haverstone certainly lived well,
Fielding decided. Bankers were not known for their
modest surroundings, but he would have hesitated

before decorating his office like a small palace. The chairman appeared to have a whole floor to himself, complete with several offices and, as far as he could judge, a lavish apartment as an annexe. And he didn't even live here; the apartment, Fielding supposed, was just there should he decide to work overnight in the office, or should he feel like a rest in the afternoon. If they spent money so freely, perhaps it was not that surprising Cable Media had run into financial difficulties.

The handshake was warm, yet uncompromising. Fielding was surprised at how slight a man Haverstone appeared to be; just a little over five and a half foot, slimly built, with a long neck and an almost feminine awareness of his appearance. 'So good of you to drop by, Malcolm,' he said with a thin smile.

'No trouble, Samuel,' Fielding replied, noticing they were on first-name terms already. Owing someone the best part of a billion pounds does make you pretty close, he decided.

Haverstone poured two glasses of whisky from a decanter, mixing his own with ice and soda; Fielding took his neat. The bank of monitors along the wall cast an eerie light over the room, but the sound was turned down and the backdrop was no more than a minor distraction. Haverstone, Fielding noted, seemed strangely calm and relaxed – at least for a man who could be about to see his empire unravel.

'You appear to have hit a rough patch,' said Fielding.

Haverstone looked at him closely, taking a delicate sip of his drink. His green eyes scanned the man, as though he were trying to read him, but his face concealed any conclusions he might have drawn from his examination. 'I am sure between us we can resolve this,' he replied stiffly.

'Just how bad is it?' asked Fielding. 'Between ourselves.'

'Not as bad as it looks,' answered Haverstone.

Fielding nodded; he was sure he had heard that line before and he doubted its truth.

'Of course, the costs of the Argus project have come in higher than we originally forecast,' Haverstone continued, sitting down on one of the black sofas next to his desk and motioning Fielding to do the same. 'That often happens with an ambitious piece of technology, as I am sure you are aware. The hardware always takes longer to get into the sky than you hoped and the market takes longer to develop. Then there are unforeseen circumstances to cope with. As you probably know, we had been planning to fund the new satellite system partly through bank borrowings and partly through cashflow from our existing businesses. Now there has been a slight downturn in the rest of the company; a couple of movies that didn't achieve the take we hoped for at the box-office, a few pop groups who haven't delivered their new albums on time, a rise in the cost of newsprint and so on. A matter of tens of millions here and there, but it all adds up.'

'With the result that you are in serious difficulties,' interjected Fielding.

'It depends how you define serious,' responded Haverstone. 'Think of it as a wound. There is serious as in needing surgery and a period of recuperation. And there is serious as in fatal. Our blood has been drawn, that much I will admit, but that is all. Surgery and recuperation is all that is needed. Afterwards the company will recover and be stronger than ever.'

'What kind of surgery do you have in mind?' asked Fielding. 'An amputation, by any chance?'

Haverstone smiled, but Fielding could detect the man recoiling from the sound of the words. 'We could consider raising immediate cash by selling some of our subsidiaries. Getting rid of one or two divisions would

218

no doubt raise enough money to complete the satellite system, but it would be wrong. The beauty of this corporation is its ability to control all the means for creating, processing and distributing the information globally. That is our strength. To sacrifice that because of a few short-term cashflow difficulties would be a terrible mistake. We must preserve the integrity of the company, or we have nothing.'

Fielding had seen enough examples of short-term cashflow difficulties to become immediately suspicious; somehow the short-term seemed to last an eternity. But for now he was not ready to make any decisions. He would listen to the man and see what he had to say. 'What other alternatives are there?' he asked.

Haverstone paused before replying; his right hand was playing with the corner of the cuff on his double-breasted suit and his eyes had moved up to the bank of monitors, where he was scanning the display of channels. 'Two possibilities,' he answered eventually. 'One is that we could come to some arrangement with the consortium of bankers to postpone interest on the debt until the Argus project is finished. The other is that we arrange for the debt to be converted into equity.'

'I am speaking in a purely personal capacity and I have no idea what the other bankers will say,' said Fielding gradually. 'But I think it unlikely that we will agree to postponing the interest. Not when the cash could relatively easily be raised by selling some of the subsidiaries.'

Haverstone nodded; he knew Fielding was speaking only for himself, but since, in his experience, all bankers tended to think in the same way, he was sure he could take this man as a proxy for the rest. 'And a debt for equity conversion?'

'That would make the debt holders major share-holders in Cable Media.'

'True,' said Haverstone, his eyes narrowing and focusing directly on the banker opposite.

'I am not sure many of the banks involved would want to become shareholders in the company,' said Fielding. 'We are, after all, financiers, not media people. It is not an industry we are likely to understand.'

'But it is the industry of the future,' said Haverstone. 'The one that really counts, the essential raw material of the twenty-first century.'

'If the numbers add up, we shall certainly think about it,' said Fielding slowly. 'But I suspect we might prefer some disposals.'

Haverstone finished the remains of his drink and stood up. 'Don't worry,' he said. 'The numbers will add up.'

He showed Fielding to the door, leaving the banker to ponder the implications of the conversation as he rode down in the lift towards his waiting Jaguar. It was a strange meeting, he reflected. Odd that Haverstone had wanted to display so much of his hand so early; companies usually waited until the last possible minute before coming up with any serious proposals. And curious that he seemed so keen to convert the debt into equity; it was usually an option that was only explored when all the other possibilities had been rejected.

Alone once again, Haverstone stood briefly before the bank of monitors, gazing up at the display; he loved to watch with the sound down, marvelling at the flow of images from around the world, each of them under his personal control. Briefly he wondered if he should slip downstairs to talk to the Russian. It might be interesting to turn the satellites on to that Fielding man; it could be useful to discover how he spent his free time and it might even be possible to teach him, in precise and embarrassing detail, exactly why information was more powerful even than money. Yes, he decided, that could well be amusing.

Taking a mobile phone, he punched up a number for Gregson. The man sounded distracted when he answered the call; probably fooling around with one of those cheap call girls he liked to spend his time with, reflected Haverstone. It was a weakness in him, he had decided long ago, but when you were playing for stakes such as these you could not spend too much time worrying about some of the company you had to keep. 'I think he'll go for it, Richard,' he said into the phone.

'A done deal, or just fishing?' asked Gregson.

'Just fishing at the moment,' replied Haverstone. 'But he will be on board before too long. The seed is planted.'

As the taxi pulled up along the pavement Harry could still see the marks of the explosion on the edge of the road; the kerb was blackened and the residents' parking lines had been demolished for several feet. If I still had a car, at least I could park, thought Harry. A miracle in itself around this part of town.

It seemed strange to be back at the scene of the event. The last twenty-four hours were, by now, a jagged heap of fragmented memories and it was only as the evening drew in that he began to realise he had hardly slept; adrenalin had kept him going, yet now the chemical rush was fading and he could feel his eyelids start to sag, and his muscles to ache. Perhaps tonight he could relax, he thought to himself. Have a drink or two and something to eat. And finally get some sleep.

Julia met him at the door, asking immediately how Cassie was getting along. Her face fell when he told her the doctors thought they might have to operate and he could see the sympathy was genuine. She ran her fingers through his hair and told him to try not to worry; her touch was the first sign of reassurance Harry had felt all day. 'I'm sure she'll be all right,' she said softly.

221

'I hope so.'

He lay in her arms for a moment, allowing her to cradle him, relaxing under the soothing touch of her finger-tips upon his brow. His mind wandered, drifting back to the memory of Cassie alone in her bed, with nothing apart from the inanimate pulse monitor alongside her. An accident, he told himself again. There was nothing you could have done.

He looked up, marvelling at the deep-brown clarity of Julia's eyes, and his lips moved towards her. They kissed chastely, tasting each other, but without the desire, for now, to explore any further. 'I spoke to the police this evening,' he said as their lips parted.

'And?'

'They said the lab had concluded it was just an accident. A freak. Something that could have happened to anyone.' He could tell she was relieved. '

At least no one's trying to kill us,' said Julia softly.

Lykanov could hear the phone ringing at his side, but he took a couple of drags on his Marlboro before replying. He was not sure this was a call he wanted to take.

The image on the screen before him was crystal clear; or at least as clear as he could hope for in the circumstances. There was heavy cloud cover over the part of west London he had been instructed to monitor that evening, but he knew his machine could look through clouds like sheets of thin ice. The satellites had been equipped with microwave sensing devices, allowing them to peer through the clouds and reconstruct an image of what lay below; the satellite beamed down a microwave radio signal across its target area, then collected the signals bouncing back from the earth, in much the same way radar did with sound-waves. The data collected allowed the machine to calculate a digital impression of what lay below. The images were not as good as the information captured using a direct photograph: they were much fuzzier and the reconstruction meant the margin for error was wider. The clouds, which amateurs sometimes supposed might protect them from the remote sensors in the sky, were really no cover at all. His satellites could see straight through them.

'Have you located the target?' asked Chung.

Lykanov had answered the phone on the fourth ring. 'Target identified,' he said warily.

'Where is he?' demanded Chung.

'He entered the house we have been monitoring about ten minutes ago.'

'You are sure it's him?'

Lykanov glanced at the screen; the picture, through the cloud, was too fuzzy to be recognised by a human eye, but a digital analysis of the figure matched perfectly with the digital description of the target he had fed into the computer some days earlier. 'It's him,' he replied.

Chung replaced the mobile phone in its slot next to the gearbox of his silver-grey Lexus. He glanced at his watch; it was just after nine. In fifteen minutes, maximum, he would reach his destination. That was fine, he decided. They would still be there. There was no need to hurry. He patted the inside pocket of his black overcoat and felt the solid steel of the Walter & Koch pistol. This time there would be no mistakes.

The red wine tasted good against the back of Julia's throat and she allowed herself another sip before taking the call. She had just opened the bottle, and poured a glass for both Harry and herself; she wanted, she realised, something to calm her mind and quieten the anxieties that had been tormenting her for the last twenty-four hours. The thought that she might have been responsible, even indirectly, for Cassie's injuries

223

was more than she could bear. And the suspicion that she might herself be the target of an attack was more than she imagined she could handle; the phone threats she had been able, slightly to her own surprise, to shrug off casually, but the reality of danger scared her witless. It was time to relax and start putting all that behind her.

'Julia,' said the man on the line when she finally picked up the phone.

She recognised Mitchell's voice and the urgency in his tone. 'Yes.'

'Bad news, I'm afraid.'

Julia could feel her pulse quicken and she placed the glass of wine nervously on the desk next to the phone. 'What?'

'I managed to get a copy of the lab reports,' said Mitchell. 'That explosion. It was not an accident. The car had been primed.'

There was a pause, left hanging on the air. For a moment Julia could think of nothing to say; her senses had deserted her, abandoning the scene, panicked into flight. Her mind had emptied and she had been left literally speechless. Her mouth opened and the muscles in her throat started to flex, but the words would not come.

'I think you're in danger,' said Mitchell eventually.

Harry had already stood up; he had seen the fear descend upon Julia's face and was starting to wonder what was happening. He was already edgy, alert to danger everywhere, and he was not about to take anything for granted.

'But the police told Harry it was an accident,' she said eventually, the words slipping reluctantly from her lips. 'Just now. This evening. There must be some mistake.'

This time it was Mitchell's turn to pause; he had not expected this and was unsure how to react; the danger he had placed her in was worse than he had imagined.

'They must be lying,' he said at length. 'I saw the report from the lab. A small explosive device was placed next to the fuel tank, with a timer to make it go off at the right time. The lab found traces on the fuel tank, and that explanation squared precisely with the size and force of the explosion. There can be no doubt.'

'Why would they lie?' asked Julia, desperation starting to creep into her voice. 'Why would they say it was an accident?'

'You don't want to know, Julia,' said Mitchell carefully. 'You're up against something much bigger than I think you can even begin to realise. Something much more than just an insider dealing ring. I don't think it's safe for us to talk on the phone.'

'What shall I do?' inquired Julia.

Harry was standing closer to her now and she looked into his eyes. 'Tell me what to do,' she repeated into the phone.

'Come in,' said Mitchell. 'I think we should take you into some sort of protective custody while we get this sorted out. I'll start arranging it now. But you must come in. This is too dangerous for you and Lamb to handle on your own.'

Julia leant into the phone. 'I need to think,' she whispered. 'I'll call you back.'

'Don't think, Julia,' said Mitchell. 'It's too dangerous.'

Julia put down the phone, taking a deep breath before looking back up at Harry. 'Mitchell says he has seen the lab report on the car,' she said. 'It wasn't an accident.'

'Is he certain?'

Julia nodded. 'He seemed sure.'

He took her in his arms and held her tight, aware that panic was starting to show in her eyes.

'What will we do?' she asked.

'Get your coat,' said Harry firmly. 'We're getting out of here right now.'

225

17

The window frame felt loose beneath Harry's fingers and as he edged it up the first few millimetres he was surprised at how easy it was to shift so far. After a quick inspection of the building, he had found all the doors were bolted. He sensed there might be no way in; they were not burglars and Harry could not imagine how to break in. The window was their one hope. The muscles in his forearms strained against the wood, tensing as he tried to break it free. The window, he guessed, had not been opened for years and the paint had congealed around its edges. He drew a deep breath, heaved against it once more and could feel the frame vibrate as it started to slide upwards.

As he peered into the darkness behind, Harry realised he had lost track of what was driving him; forces he had not known he possessed, that much was clear. Normally, an act such as this would have been beyond his comprehension. But in the last couple of hours he had been running on pure adrenalin, and it was taking him in new and unexpected directions.

Julia had tagged along in his wake, reluctant to follow, but also reluctant to leave him. There was an anger within him that she could understand, yet which was also frightening. It was a side of his character she had not seen before. We need time, she kept saying to herself. Time to compose ourselves, and to decide what to do next.

Harry yanked the window open far enough to slip inside, extending a hand as he stood on the floor, pulling Julia along behind him. The office was dark and only the pale light of the street lamps outside cast a few dim shadows into the room. She stood next to him, casting her eyes over the small office, adjusting to the pale light. What the hell is he doing? she thought to herself.

The last hour had passed in a fit of anxiety. When Harry had told her to grab her coat she had not disagreed. He was right, she reflected. It was clear someone was trying to kill them and, also, that the police were not planning to do anything about it. The attempt had failed, that much they knew. But there was no reason to suppose the same people would not try again. Indeed, the only safe assumption was that another attempt would be made, and next time they might not be so lucky.

Harry had seemed agitated. 'What leads do we have?' he had asked her, as they climbed into her Golf. She mentioned the accounting firm, the one solid piece of information she had collected from her investigations within the Serious Fraud Office; the firm from which the insider dealing ring had been controlled and the one place she could think of that might tell them who or what was controlling it.

'Let's go,' Harry had insisted. 'Right now.'

At first Julia had been unsure. 'You don't think we should back off?' she'd asked, after Harry had started driving in the direction of the City. 'Aren't we in too deep already?'

'Exactly,' replied Harry, a look of grim determination on his face. 'They're already trying to kill us. Nothing we do now will make any difference. This can't make the situation any worse.'

Involuntarily, she admired his ability to keep his wits about him. It was one of the many things that made him attractive and for that alone she was prepared to go along on the trip. He was right. Nothing could get any worse now.

Unless, of course, they were caught.

The thought struck her as they stood in the gloomy room, wondering where to begin. There appeared to be no one around and if there were alarms they did not seem to have triggered them yet. As far as she could tell there were no cameras on the walls, but perhaps they had just escaped her eye.

Harry seemed dangerously oblivious to the risks they were running. While Julia could feel herself trembling, he was rock steady, his eyes darting feverishly round the room. There was a hardness about him as he moved through the empty desks, she noticed, an aura of sense and purpose, combined with an almost abnormal intensity.

He flicked the power switch on one of the desktop computers, his fingers playing on the keyboard as he scrolled through the files. He took a floppy from a pile, slotting it into a hard drive. 'Download everything you can,' he said sharply, looking across at Julia. 'Save anything that looks useful.'

Julia took a floppy from the pile and followed his instructions. On the screen was displayed a long list of files; she couldn't be bothered to calculate how many, but it looked like several hundred. Some, just from the file names, seemed to relate to offshore accounts and others appeared to contain details of share trades. If there was anything here it would most probably be within those files. She started downloading them on to the floppy, not troubling herself to look at any of the information as it was transferred. There would be time to look through it all later, she decided. She glanced across at Harry, busy with his own terminal. 'How much do you think we need?' Julia asked.

Harry shrugged. 'I don't know. Let's give it ten minutes or so. Then we should get out of here.'

Kim Chung pulled up at the far end of the modest terraced street. He left the Lexus on a double-yellow line; a parking ticket was the least of his worries. Just so long as the car was still there when he returned, he decided. He would need it.

He pulled the collar of his overcoat up around his neck and walked slowly down the street. There was nobody out, but he kept his eyes doggedly to the ground; should someone pass he knew from long experience it was impossible for anyone to identify you later if they had not seen your face, nor peered into your eyes. A light drizzle was falling as he walked and, inwardly, he composed himself, preparing his mind for the intense concentration that would be needed in the next few minutes. No matter how many people you had killed, he reflected, everyone was different, and it was always crucial to close down every target with the same thoroughness and professionalism. This was not a game for amateurs.

He stood five yards from the house, observing it from a distance. As far as he could tell, there were no lights on, but that meant nothing. They might well be in bed. Indeed, for all he knew, they could be making love. The thought amused Chung and he allowed a thin smile to spread across his lips. He had never assassinated anyone while they were making love, but he had heard a bullet to the head during the act produced the most sensational orgasm. He shrugged to himself. One would never know, he decided, and one would never care to find out.

He walked slowly to the front door and rang the bell. A couple of minutes passed without any sign of anyone appearing before he pressed it again. He waited two more minutes before pulling the gun from his pocket and checking that the silencer was still attached. He pressed the pistol to the lock, spreading his overcoat to hide it from view and to muffle the tiny thud that would escape from the silencer. He squeezed the trigger, standing back slightly to examine the damage. The lock was blown away and carefully he pushed the door open.

No lights were on. Chung stepped inside, adjusting his eyes to the darkness. He walked through the hall, keeping his ears alert, waiting for some sign of habitation. There was nothing he could detect. He checked the kitchen first, then the sitting-room. Both were empty. He walked upstairs, taking less care to remain silent now; he already suspected that there was no one in. He checked the first bedroom, then the bathroom. Nothing. He lingered for a few minutes, riffling through some clothes and papers lying open in the bedroom. None of it was of any interest. He walked back downstairs, through the hallway and out into the street, closing the door carefully behind him.

Back in the car he put through a call to Lykanov on his mobile. 'Gone,' he said quietly to the Russian. 'I need to know where.'

'What happened?' asked Lykanov.

'Never mind,' replied Chung. 'I have to find them. Now.'

Lykanov turned to his monitor and called up the image. It took several minutes for the information to be downloaded from the satellites and analysed by the computer system, but the movements were already clear. 'We have a trace,' he said into the open mobile line. 'They have headed east. I will have the direction and the address of their destination shortly.'

Chung pulled the car away from the kerb, turning in the direction of the City. Once he had the location, he knew there would be no time to lose.

Harry looked up from the computer screen and glanced around the darkened room. He could feel his pulse throbbing and for the first time since they had entered this office the dangers suddenly became apparent to him; he listened to the eerie silence, anxious to know whether they were about to be discovered. 'I think we should go,' he said. 'We probably have enough.'

Julia nodded, relieved the ordeal was about to end. She waited for the file she was downloading to transfer itself to the floppy, flipped the disk out of its socket and slipped it into her pocket. Harry did the same, taking her by the arm and leading her to the window. He checked the street, making sure no one could see them leave, before helping her through. He followed, standing next to her on the empty dark street. 'Walk casually away,' he whispered. 'We should act as if nothing is happening.'

They turned out of the side-street and into the main road. Some traffic was moving and the lamps were brighter, but the street was still empty; there were few residents here among the offices on the fringes of the City. Harry slipped his arm round Julia and they started walking. So far, he had no idea where they were going, nor what they were trying to achieve. That would come, he figured. Once they had had time to think.

The Lexus pulled up a few yards ahead of them, although Harry barely noticed it at the time – big Japanese cars were not a rare sight in this part of town. A man in a trench coat climbed out, while Harry and Julia sauntered in his direction. Harry paid him little attention as they passed, but as they went further down the street, he was aware that the man was now walking steadily behind them, always ten yards behind, never varying his pace, keeping a steady distance. He glanced round and noticed the other averting his eyes. Harry gripped Julia a little more tightly to his side and quickened his pace.

Behind him, Chung did the same, walking faster, maintaining the ten yards between them; this was a relatively empty part of town, he reasoned, and it would not be long before he found a moment to strike.

There was no time to get back to her car, Harry decided. They would have to think of something else. Up ahead, he spotted the reassuring orange light of a black cab coming from a side-street and his hand reached out into the air, waving it down. It pulled up to the kerb and Harry opened the door for Julia, bundling her inside, saying nothing to the driver; he did not want to delay a moment more than was necessary. Looking through the back window, he could see the tall man briefly staring up at him, before turning on his heel and walking back down the street.

Chung strolled in the direction of his parked Lexus. There would be little point in following them now, he realised; the taxi would be long gone by the time he retrieved his own vehicle. It did not matter much, he told himself as he walked the last few yards. There was nowhere they could hide and nowhere they could run to. The satellites would find them, and sooner or later they would be his.

18

As Harry gazed out on the rising sun, watching the dawn seep slowly over the river, his senses briefly calmed; a new day, he told himself. From the gentle breathing he could hear behind him, he could tell Julia was still asleep. He would not wake her, he decided, taking a sip of the Coke he had opened from the mini-bar. A few minutes of peace and solitude and reflection were needed; there were so many threads running through his mind, he could only start to untangle them by himself.

The view from the hotel window was quiet and calm. From the ninth floor room he could see out over a small estate of newly finished houses, eerily deserted since none of them had yet been sold, to a wharf that had been converted into an office and retail unit and on to the river beyond. Harry had rarely ventured into the docklands before and for a few moments he allowed himself just to unwind and take in the scenery. He had slept only fitfully and his mind was still crowded with uncounted fears. He was unable to last more than a minute without wondering about Cassie.

After climbing into the taxi the night before, Harry had had little idea where he wanted to go; escape was the one word looping endlessly in his mind. His nerves were edgy and his energy sapped, yet he'd still had enough strength to realise the man he had seen was most likely a dangerous opponent and there was no way he wanted to encounter him on the street. It was possible, of course, that he was just a solitary individual out for an evening stroll. But Harry doubted it. The last couple of days had taught him to trust nobody.

At first, he'd just told the taxi driver to head east, checking constantly to see if the man was following; he had already resolved that should he see anyone on their tail he would go straight to Scotland Yard and insist on being taken into custody. There was no sign of the car, however. Harry figured the man realised his prey had escaped him for the evening and a pursuit, for now, was useless. No doubt he believed he would get another chance. He asked the driver if he knew of any hotels in the area which might have a room for the night. The driver cast them a nudge-nudge look as he turned to face them; probably assumes I'm a married guy taking his secretary for a quickie before going home to the wife, Harry decided, conscious he was looking slightly embarrassed. The driver suggested the Travelodge in Rotherhithe, just past Wapping. 'Fine,' Harry had said. It sounded a suitably obscure spot. 'Take us there as quickly as possible.'

He was relieved when they had a room and even more pleased to discover that for another twenty pounds they could have one with a computer; he was anxious to discover what was on the disks they had captured, but hardly felt like heading home to use his own PC. He handed over his credit card, feeling slightly sheepish when the receptionist asked if they had any bags. Harry just shook his head and decided to ignore the prim expression on the face of the brunette completing the booking.

The room was plain and functional, with a double

bed, a TV and a desk with a computer. Julia ordered a couple of sandwiches from room service and disappeared into the shower, returning fifteen minutes later, her hair washed, wrapped in a large white dressing-gown the hotel provided. Harry moved across the room, giving her a hug before taking a shower himself; he realised as he did so it was the first time he had seen her even partially naked, and her body felt warm and tender beneath his embrace. The contact was comforting rather than sexually charged; he had been through too much in the last couple of days to contemplate making a move on her, although the thought did cross his mind as he was showering. Life goes on, he reflected.

They ate the sandwiches practically in silence; Harry was hardly hungry, but realised he had to force some food down his throat before he collapsed. His taste-buds seemed to have abandoned him; the stuff he was chewing was neither good nor bad, just calories, energy to keep him ticking forward. 'How do you feel?' he asked Julia.

'Terrible,' she replied with an attempt at a smile. 'Nervous, afraid and exhausted. I think I need some sleep.'

They had drifted lazily towards the bed and lay there, wrapped in each other's arms. He ran his fingers through her hair and caressed the back of her neck.

'That feels nice,' she'd whispered, practically under her breath.

Before he could reply, he had drifted off to sleep and within less than a minute she too was slumbering peacefully in his arms.

Harry recollected the moment tenderly as he gazed out into the dawn. It drifted through his mind, clashing with memories of the other evenings they had spent together, and with snatches of time spent with Amelia.

He thought about Cassie, a knot tightening in his stomach as he did so. Please God, let her be okay.

The light was brighter now. It was just after six thirty and the sun was rising steadily over the City, glistening off the murky brown water of the Thames. How could the pieces of this jigsaw be put together? he wondered. Where could he find the key that might unlock the riddle? So far, he realised, they had just been confronted with an increasingly bizarre and seemingly unconnected series of events. Somewhere there had to be a thread linking everything.

Every problem is solvable, Harry told himself, with thought and dedication. Right now, he could not figure what the thread might be. Yet, now that he had some sense of the danger they had stumbled into he felt sure the answer must be there somewhere. It was just a matter of rooting through everything that had happened to them during the past few weeks. Within seemingly ordinary events he might find the answer.

Harry put a call through to room service, ordering two continental breakfasts. Sitting on the bed next to Julia, he began rubbing the back of her neck until gradually she awoke.

She looked up at him, her eyes sad, yet also tempting. She smiled and kissed him on the lips.

'Good morning,' he said softly.

Julia hugged him, resting her head against his chest. 'How're we doing?' she asked.

Harry smiled. 'Probably better than could be expected.'

The coffee tasted good and Harry could feel the caffeine kicking some energy back into his veins. He chewed his way through a croissant, spreading it thickly with butter and jam, and the sugar helped to revive him. By the time they had finished breakfast, he was feeling almost human again.

'We could go to the police,' said Julia.

Harry nodded, looking directly at her across the small table. 'We could,' he answered carefully. 'And if you think that's the best thing I'll go with you.'

'But you don't want to?'

'If the police were on our side, they would have given us the accurate lab report on the explosion. It's a horrible thought, but I don't believe we can trust them. Right now, I'm not sure we can trust anyone.'

'Then we run,' said Julia. There was a distant look in her eyes, reflective and remorseful, and it was clear she could hardly contemplate the prospect. 'And keep running until this is all over. Whenever that might be.'

Harry shook his head. 'We don't run,' he replied. 'Two reasons. We don't know how. We wouldn't be any good at it. And we haven't done anything. So why should we run away? It isn't fair. And anyway, I couldn't leave Cassie behind.'

'What else can we do?'

'We fight back.'

'Meaning?'

Harry leant across the table, grabbing her out-stretched palm. 'We discover who is trying to kill us. We discover why. And we discover a way of defeating them.'

'You make it sound so easy.' There was a breath-lessness in her voice that indicated she was nervous and exhilarated at the same time.

'I don't imagine for a moment it will be easy,' he said. 'It will be difficult. And I imagine it will be dangerous as well. But right now it's the only thing I think we can do.' He edged forward in his seat, gripping her palm tighter between his hands. 'But I don't think you should be with me. I don't necessarily rate the chances that high. Fifty – fifty perhaps, but I'm an incurable optimist. You should probably get down to the City airport and get on the first flight to anywhere, somewhere far away from

237

here, and stay away until this is over. I'll find a way of contacting you when it ends. If you don't hear from me you'll know I haven't succeeded and you'll have made the right decision. I don't think you need to be involved any further. It isn't safe.'

Her eyes flashed up to meet his. The anger was unexpected, a reminder, he noted, of how little he knew her. 'I'm not going anywhere,' Julia said firmly. 'I am staying right here with you. We started out on this thing together, and we'll finish it together.'

The conference chamber just down the corridor from the chief executive's office was known as the crisis room. Malcolm Fielding had forgotten why, exactly. He seemed to recollect it had acquired the nickname some time during the late eighties, a time when Harrington's Bank appeared constantly to be trying to bail out some crashed conglomerate. Long, tense financial negotiations, often conducted through the night, had always been held there.

Fielding had been fully briefed by his staff before convening the meeting. The position of Cable Media did indeed look dire. The company had overspent wildly, according to the calculations made by the bank's analysts. Money had been poured into its media divisions, extending its product range with little thought for the returns it might earn. The telecoms division was making good money, but competition was increasing and the company would obviously come under pressure to cut its charges. It was hard to see how that operation could carry the rest of the business indefinitely. But the real black hole was the satellite system. It appeared to have cost far more than the company forecast; indeed, it was hard for the number crunchers to figure out how so much had been spent, although it had to be admitted that new technology often came in a lot more pricey than anyone imagined. Its prospects were hard to evaluate. It was leading-edge equipment, no question. And if it worked as planned it would put the company in a dominant position in both the broadcasting and telecoms industries throughout Europe, both East and West. But there was no clear indication of when it could be expected to start earning money, and, for the bankers, it was impossible to justify supporting it for ever.

Two proposals were up for discussion. Either the bankers could put their own men into the company, evict the present management and start selling off some of the juicier media assets to dig it out of a financial pit. Or it could convert the debt into equity and hope that eventually the business would be making enough profits to justify holding the shares. Neither struck Fielding as particularly attractive, but that, he reflected, was the nature of banking. You rarely got to play the nice guy.

Fielding eyed Richard Gregson suspiciously as he walked into the crisis room. He had only once met the man, but had formed a distaste for him that was both professional and personal. At first Gregson had just been treated as an interloper by the City establishment, one of the many mavericks who washed up in the square mile and usually vanished as quickly as they came, often amid some horrific scandal that damaged everyone's reputation. But Gregson's success in the market and his seemingly endless supply of money had made him a force. Fielding found him brash and vulgar, a man who was either ignorant of the codes that governed City life or chose deliberately to break them. He would have preferred him not to be present at the meeting this morning. Yet his firm now held so much of Cable Media's debt that it was impossible to ignore him.

That was another lesson he had learnt about banking over the years. You were seldom allowed the luxury of choosing your enemies. They chose you.

At least Gregson was wearing a suit, Fielding noted as he shook his hand: some flash Italian creation, however, with a very loud tie and tasselled loafers, which only compounded his distaste for the man.

'I guess I'm more important on this ball game than you are Malcolm,' said Gregson with a broad grin. 'Can't help saying I get a kick out of that.'

Fielding frowned. 'I would have thought we were all here to discover what is best for the company, the shareholders and the debtors,' he replied stiffly.

'Might be,' said Gregson with a laugh. 'Personally I'm just here to discover what kind of balls British bankers have. Leave them at home with their wives, that's what I hear.'

Fielding took his chair at the head of the long, wooden table. There were twenty people around the room, all men, dressed in dark suits and black shoes. All the major British banks were represented; so too were the big German, French and Japanese banks. Cable Media's advisers were present, and the Bank of England, too, had sent along an observer; the potential bankruptcy of a major British company was always a matter of concern to them.

The introductions made, Fielding opened with a brief preamble. The bankers would have studied the available documents and would know that their decision would eventually come down to a straight choice: send in their own men or accept the debt-for-equity conversion the company was pushing. He suspected most of the bankers would prefer the first route; they hated to back high-risk projects and disliked holding vast quantities of shares in a single company.

Gregson was the wild card in an otherwise predictable pack. He had seldom been involved in this kind of negotiation before and he was a trader, not a banker. It was impossible to tell which way he would jump.

After making his opening statement, Fielding asked for observations. He went carefully around the table, looking to each man for his thoughts. As the numbers started tallying up, he sensed his first guess had been right. Most of the bankers seemed to prefer an immediate solution. They expressed their views cautiously, but they did not want to back this company much longer. They would prefer their own people to begin selling the assets for whatever they were worth. 'And your view, Mr Gregson,' said Fielding.

'I reckon you guys need to start going to the gym more often,' he kicked off, his eyes darting around the table. 'You're all soft and flabby, and you don't like taking risks. The raw truth is you're putty. Cable Media, I reckon, is a great business and Haverstone has been doing a great job. Sure he needs some backing and the short-term cashflows aren't what they might be. Who gives a fuck. Take the conversion and you end up with a pile of cheap shares in the most powerful company in the world's most powerful industry. Looks like a good deal to me.'

'Your views will be noted, Richard,' said Fielding.

'My views will be more than noted,' interrupted Gregson. 'I reckon my firm now speaks for more than forty per cent of the debt. That makes me the most important voice here, and I'm still buying. Pretty soon I may well own more than fifty per cent. Then I'll be in a position to call the shots.'

'Until then, this committee will decide what happens,' said Fielding severely.

Gregson shrugged. 'Looks like I'm the only person around here who didn't leave his balls at home.'

Fielding took a moment to gather his thoughts. It was clear that Gregson was going to be a tougher customer than he had imagined; his worst nightmare made flesh. Either he didn't know the rules, or he was deliberately ignoring them. Committees of bankers worked by consensus, not confrontation. After all, they always knew they would be meeting again soon and any enemies you made now would not have to wait long before they could take their revenge. Gregson did not seem concerned by any of that. He wanted this conversion to go ahead, no matter what the cost to the other holders of the debt. 'I think we should study this matter for at least another week,' Fielding said. 'In the meantime I suggest we hold talks with the directors of Cable Media to establish a clearer idea of their position.'

'A week is too long,' interrupted Gregson. 'I suggest we get this cleared soon. By Friday lunch-time at the latest.'

'That is just four days away,' said Fielding. It struck him as an impossibly short deadline and he could see little sense in hurrying.

'Four days is long enough,' snapped Gregson. 'I don't see how the company can be expected to survive while nobody knows what's going to happen. This is typical of the way bankers operate. Let the thing bleed until it dies. I say we resolve the situation now.'

The expressions around the table worried Fielding. Some were intimidated, some worried, others embarrassed. None of them was sure how to handle the situation. It was up to him, as chairman of the committee, to find a solution. He went round the table canvassing opinions. There seemed to be a majority in favour of delay, but not strongly enough to defeat Gregson. He was the largest holder of the debt and his views counted.

'We should convene again at midday on Friday,' said Fielding eventually. 'By then I think we can have a concrete proposal for a conversion of equity into debt before us. We can take a vote then.' He looked across at

Gregson, noting with distaste the idle smirk playing on his face. 'That will be the time for the final decision.'

'That's okay by me,' said Gregson. 'I'm looking forward to finding myself and the people I represent as the biggest shareholders in Cable Media.'

'There are still four days to go,' said Fielding. 'A lot can happen.'

Gregson walked across the room, standing close to Fielding, looking down at the man. 'A lot has already happened,' he said.

Between them Harry and Julia had collected twelve floppies; six each, all they had been able to manage in the time available, but also the bulk of the records that appeared to refer to offshore companies. Slotting the first one in to the hotel computer, Harry started scrolling through the list of files. At an initial glance he reckoned there must be at least a couple of thousand pages of information. Most of it he knew would be useless, of no relevance to anyone except the tax dodgers and money launderers who probably made up the bulk of the accounting firm's clients. But somewhere within the files there had to be some clues. Perhaps even an answer. 'What exactly do you think we should be looking for?' he asked Julia.

From her work at the Serious Fraud Office Julia knew the accounting firm's records should hold the key. Turevul Trading, the company that operated the insider dealing ring, had been established through this firm. That was enough to make it clear the company was in some way involved with the ring. Somewhere within these files they might find out who had asked for Turevul to be created, perhaps even who controlled the profits. 'Any mention of Turevul Trading,' she answered. 'We need to find out who controls it. That was always the missing link in the investigation.'

Harry nodded. 'It was just after you located the name of this firm that they tried to blow us up,' he said. 'My bet is you were on the right tracks and getting a little too close for their comfort.'

'We should find out.' Julia rested her hand on Harry's shoulder.

For the next hour he punched up files, scrolling through them, checking the financial records and the names of the companies mentioned. It was boring work. The firm seemed to have a lot of clients with offshore dealings and subsidiaries; mostly general trading companies, import and export outfits, and a few small financial firms operating on the wilder fringes of the London markets. There were plenty of those around, Harry knew from experience, and almost none of them were legitimate.

It was a tiring, mind-numbing task, heavy on their eyes and wearing on their nerves. The print was small, the numbers dense and Harry could feel his mind starting to ache from the amount of information he was trying to process. At times he could see the symbols on the screen blurring up before him and had to wrench himself back. Concentrate, he told himself. Everything may depend upon it.

The clock on the wall was ticking close to midday before he spotted anything that might be relevant to their investigation. It was somewhere between the first and second hundred files they had scanned through that the words Turevul leapt out, catching Harry's eye first. He flicked the mouse next to the name and flashed up instantly on to the screen the details of the firm's dealings with that company.

Harry could feel his pulse quickening as he started scrolling through the information. It appeared the company had been set up late last year at the instigation of two men identified only by their initials: RG and SH.

In retrospect it would strike Harry as incredible that it took him a couple of minutes to realise who they were. 'Richard Gregson and Samuel Haverstone,' he said quietly, wondering, even as he spoke, whether he should believe it.

Julia peered forward into the screen; she wanted to check for herself there had been no mistake, that the initials Harry had just read out and the connection he had just made were accurate. 'How could they be involved in this thing?' she said, the tone of her voice betraying both puzzlement and surprise. 'It doesn't make any sense.'

'It makes plenty of sense. Think about it. If they are the two men controlling the insider dealing ring it explains why they wanted both of us dead. You because you were becoming too persistent in your investigation and were perhaps getting too close to the answer. Me because of my involvement with both Gregson and Haverstone. There must be something I've said or done which has offended them enough for them to want me out of the picture. The car bomb falls into place, now. The explosion would be a perfect way of eliminating both of us at the same time.' He paused, aware that the words had been tumbling out of his mind without editing; that his thoughts were running away with themselves, veering into unexpected directions. 'It makes a lot of sense,' he repeated. 'More than I would have imagined.'

'But why you?' asked Julia. 'You were working for Gregson. Why on earth would he get you on the payroll and then try to eliminate you?'

Harry could feel his heat thumping. He had never liked Gregson; inwardly, he cursed himself for having ignored his first gut reaction. The thought that he might, however inadvertently, have helped a man who was now ultimately responsible for the injuries to his daughter, who had tried to kill both himself and Julia, sickened him; his stomach was churning and he could feel his fists clenching as he glared into the silent, neutral computer screen. 'I can't be sure,' he said. 'But my guess is it might be because I showed too much interest in the death of Sir Ian Strang. Also in why exactly Gregson was piling up such a huge position in the debts of Haverstone's company. My bet is that I started out by being a useful idiot, someone who could be manipulated, but ended up looking like a dangerous character. Potentially even an opponent.'

Julia leant back in her chair, removing her palm from Harry's shoulder and wiping a trace of moisture from her forehead. She turned to look at him directly. 'And are you a dangerous character?' she asked. It was a serious question; at this moment she was not quite sure she knew what drove him and she felt she needed to get closer. If she were to spend the next few days at his side, perhaps even entrust her life to him, she had to know.

'I think those two men are about to discover just how dangerous I can be,' Harry replied firmly.

Lykanov had rarely seen such a collection of faceless-looking men. The dozen photographs spread out before him were all of males in their forties, with neatly cut and parted hair, regulation black or grey suits. There was, to the naked eye, little to tell one from another. No matter, he reflected. The naked eye would not be required to detect them. The computer, he felt sure, would find enough distinguishing features to produce a digital map. And that would be enough for the satellites to keep a silent, distant watch on their movements.

With only cursory interest he checked the phone records. Tapes of each man at the banking committee meeting earlier that day had already been fed into the computer and an accurate digital map of their speech patterns had been generated for all of them. He had run a couple of tests feeding tape loops into the phone system and the computers had done their job well; the calls had first been detected, then logged. A printout of their conversation anywhere around Europe could be conjured up at the touch of a button. 'Everything is working,' he told Chung.

The Korean was sitting in the far corner of the room, a trail of cigar smoke curling around his face. He seemed in a dark and distant mood today, Lykanov noted. His manner, always cold, had acquired a frozen edge; his brooding added to the dark gloom of the room to create an atmosphere of ugly tension.

Chung walked closer to the control desk. He glanced down at the screen, punching up at random the list of phone calls logged on the display. Several showed calls from the bankers back to their head offices, describing details of the discussion and requesting guidance for what positions they should take before a final decision had to be made on Friday. Most seemed to be against the debt-to-equity conversion, but it was still early days. They would need a full printout of those conversations. Haverstone would expect to see it on his desk before the day was finished.

'The man and the woman,' asked Chung. 'Any trace?'

Lykanov could hardly resist a smile. Many years working in the Soviet Union had taught him never to laugh openly at his paymasters, but he knew how to smile to himself and the expression remained firmly buried beneath his impassive lips. He had thought the previous evening that he had seen the last of that particular couple; the Korean had left with a grim expression, and even though they had fled the house by the time he arrived, Chung had been given precise co-ordinates of their destination. When he had arrived earlier today requesting that the satellites resume their search for the pair, he had known at once they had survived. He was not quite sure why it pleased him so much. Perhaps it was because he always rooted for the underdog, whether in sport, politics or love. Or possibly it was because he enjoyed a chase and this was turning into an exciting contest. It might even be because he harboured few sympathies for the men he was now working for; they seemed cruel and unyielding, with little thought for anything nobler than their own immediate gain. 'Nothing yet,' he replied flatly. 'The satellites are still searching.'

The trail had been lost after Harry and Julia had climbed into the taxi last night. Lykanov had told Chung that had he been given some details of the car, even a registration number, he could have tracked it to its destination. Without that it was impossible. At first he had seemed annoyed, as much with himself as the Russian, but he relaxed once he was told a fix on their location could still be made. The satellites were trained on every square inch of the city and it had their details. As soon as they showed themselves in the open they would be spotted and the system was rigged to alert him the moment the target was found.

'Keep watching,' said Chung. 'I need to know immediately we have a trace. At any time of the day or night. Is that understood?'

Lykanov nodded, lighting up another Marlboro. He remained silent, watching carefully, while Chung turned and left the room. He was, he reflected, not sorry to see him go.

The journey from the bunker to the chief executive's suite took several minutes. There were still plenty of people around the building at this time of day, but Chung paid no attention to them, nor they to him. They were ordinary people, going about their ordinary jobs, and they were of no concern to him.

Chung was surprised to find Gregson with Haverstone, yet he masked his expression behind an inscrutable glare. He had met the American several times before and he knew of his role in the events that were to unfold in the next few days. But he did not work for him directly and felt he had no control over him. No leverage. Chung was uncomfortable with people over whom he held no sway. As a rule he avoided the company of those who were not in some way indebted to him.

'Those two pranksters are still at large, I hear,' said Gregson, looking directly across the room at him.

Chung nodded stiffly. 'That is so,' he said softly.

'Disappointing news.' Gregson's tone dripped sarcasm.

'It is being dealt with.'

'I hope so,' said Haverstone. 'We have four more days. I don't care too much what happens after that, but this week there must be no distractions. That would be intolerable. Everything has to run like clockwork.'

'It has been taken care of,' said Chung. 'A trace will be discovered soon then our two young friends will be disposed of. And anyway, it is impossible for them to go anywhere, or to contact anyone, without being discovered. So even if they do survive it will only be by doing nothing, in which case they pose no threat.' He walked closer to the two men, laying a printout of phone records on the desk. 'I have just checked with the Russian,' he continued. 'The phone calls of all the bankers on the committee are being monitored and logged. The system appears to be working well. From these records you will know every move your opponents are making.'

Haverstone collected the sheaf of papers from the desk, his eyes falling upon them with unconcealed glee; his pupils widened slightly as he drew the information from the paper, passing each sheet across to Gregson when he had finished with it. 'They are crumbling,' he said, a lighter tone entering his voice.

'Like cookies,' said Gregson. 'Like we always said they would. I could see it at the meeting this morning. Men with no stomach for a fight. No stomach at all.'

Haverstone walked across the room to the window. He gazed down at the glimmering lights below, then looked across at the bank of television screens. 'Soon all of this will be mine,' he said softly, looking at no one and speaking to himself as much as his audience.

'Ours,' corrected Gregson.

Haverstone turned, a waspish smile playing on his lips. 'Forgive the slip, Richard,' he said. 'Ours. Soon all this will be ours. The greatest accumulation of data amassed in the twentieth century. A resource such as no one has ever created before. Absolute control of all the information flowing through the continent. All of it ours, not just to manage, but to control, in perpetuity.' He looked towards the two men, his eyes gleaming with desire. 'And there are just four more days to wait.'

19

Watching, looking down from above, Harry decided, was better than doing nothing. His fingers held on to her hand, clasping it tight, keeping track of her pulse. Senseless, of course, he reflected; it was unlikely she would start disappearing before his very eyes and, even if she did, there would be nothing he could do. Yet it made him feel better; there was a sense that he was doing something, playing some part in her recovery.

The doctor at his side was busy checking the readings on the pulse monitor. Harry scanned her face, looking for some sign of the prognosis, and from the frown playing on her forehead he could tell she was concerned. 'She's not doing as well as we would hope, Mr Lamb,' she said. 'Surgery may still be our best option.'

Harry could hear the breath escaping from his lips; he had prepared himself for this moment but nevertheless the words rattled in his ears. If it had to be, he decided, better it should be done quickly; he was not sure how much longer he could endure the agony of waiting. 'What are the chances?' he asked, raising his eyes to look at the doctor directly. There was, he knew, a look of boyish pleading in them. He was slightly embarrassed by it; part of him felt he should be more manly, that he should be able to roll with this punch. Yet he couldn't help himself; he was desperate for Cassie to survive and it was impossible to disguise his longing.

'Good,' the doctor replied. 'Probably about seventy-thirty. In your favour. Normally it would be pretty straightforward, but because of her age and weakened condition we can't be certain.'

Harry looked down again at Cassie's unmoving form. Seeing her lying so still was strange. She was normally such a restless child, wriggling even as she slept and constantly in motion when she was awake. Now she just lay there, perfectly still, almost as if she were already dead. He leant forward, lifting her from the bed and holding her tight to his chest. 'Be strong, my darling,' he whispered.

'We'll monitor the situation for a few more days. But if there isn't an improvement, we'll have to operate.'

Harry nodded. 'I'll be here every day.'

'Parents are allowed to be present during operations. Sometimes it seems to help, although others find it too traumatic. You might want to think about that.'

'I'll be there,' said Harry firmly. 'I wouldn't leave her for anything.'

He walked out of the swing doors that led away from the intensive care ward and along a narrow corridor towards the elevator. His feet were heavy and it took almost all his will-power to keep moving. Too much was happening, he decided, and too quickly. He could not be certain if he was doing the right thing, nor whether his reactions were leading him in the right direction. He was, he guessed, running on instinct. He needed to find some time to reflect. He felt sure he now knew who was responsible for Cassie's injuries and might still be responsible for her death. But he could not yet know why. Nor how he would take his revenge.

He stood outside, enjoying the sunshine for a brief

moment, watching the traffic flowing down the Fulham Road. Ordinary life, he reflected to himself. It seemed so distant.

Later, he could not quite recall how long he had been standing there; no more than a minute or two he was certain, before his thoughts were interrupted by an announcement from inside the building. 'Is there a Mr Lamb here?' The voice echoed round the lobby of the hospital. At first, Harry could not tell where it was coming from and he looked around the desolate group of sickly patients and uninterested visitors, scanning the faces, trying to decide who had spoken. 'That's me,' he said eventually to the man at the desk.

'Urgent call for you,' said the porter, holding out a phone.

Harry tried to conceal the look of surprise on his face. Only Julia would know he was here and surely wouldn't call unless something terrible had happened. His pulse quickened slightly as he took the receiver, waiting to hear the worst; I've already had enough bad news today, he thought, pressing the phone to his ear.

'Mr Lamb?'

Harry couldn't recognise the voice. 'Yes,' he replied sharply.

'We have not spoken before.' The tone was cold and distant. 'But I believe we are aware of each other. You have my apologies for what happened to your little girl. Trust me, that was not intended. It was you and your lady friend I meant to destroy.'

'Who is this?' demanded Harry angrily. The question was futile. He already knew who it was; there was no face or name he could put to it, but he was aware what the voice represented.

The chuckle on the other end of the line was slow and mirthless, as if deliberately calculated to provoke and annoy. 'You don't want to know who I am. Knowledge is dangerous and you have already stumbled across too much of it. You should have realised that by now.'

Harry was holding the phone tight to his ear, his fist trembling with anger.

'I called to say two things,' the voice continued, grinding out the words in a relentlessly grey monotone. 'Keep yourself out of other people's affairs, and remember, we can find you anywhere. We know everything.'

Three miles away, deep underground, beneath a thin strip of neon, Chung replaced the phone with a soft click. He turned towards Lykanov and smiled. 'Good work,' he said softly. 'Now keep an eye on where he goes next. And keep looking for the girl.'

John Mitchell was already half-way through his cappuccino when Julia entered the room. The Dome café behind the Opera House had been the only place she could think of to meet; not too close to their office and busy enough with tourists for them to be relatively inconspicuous. She was not sure if they were being tracked, indeed, she still found the idea difficult to contemplate seriously, but Harry had warned her to be careful and she was sure he was right. They could leave nothing to chance.

His eyes were cold and distant as he greeted her, running the length of her face and body; Julia felt as though she might be a piece of rare porcelain, being examined for cracks or fragments. On the surface she looked fine, she supposed; just another working girl taking a break from the office. It was what was happening inside that worried her. 'Is everything okay?' he asked.

'Not really,' she replied. She started to explain. Earlier that day she and Harry checked out of the hotel, taking their disks and the information they had discovered with them. Harry had insisted on going to the

254

hospital to check on Cassie's progress, while she arranged a meeting with Mitchell. They needed to discover where he stood; there had to be someone in a position of power they could trust and, for the moment, he was the only person she could think of.

After ordering a large cappuccino from the waiter, she ran briefly through the events of the past twenty-four hours. She told him about how Harry had been informed by the police that the explosion was an accident and how, on hearing his view that it had been deliberate, they had decided they had no choice but to flee. 'Are you sure it was some kind of bomb?' she asked

Mitchell nodded. 'No question. I got a copy of the lab report.'

'Then there's only one conclusion to be drawn,' said Julia. 'Whoever we are dealing with also has some kind of leverage over the police. Why else would they lie to us, other than to cover up for their friends and to lull us into a false sense of security?'

Mitchell's head was resting in his hands, his coffee ignored, as he listened to the story. 'You may be right,' he replied. 'I managed to get a raw copy of the lab report. But it would appear the police dealing with the case decided to ignore it.'

'And lie to us,' added Julia.

'It fits together,' said Mitchell slowly, 'and becomes a kind of pattern. First the insider dealing case was dropped, for no apparent reason and just when we were starting to make good progress. I'm sure the order came from very high up, perhaps even someone in the government. Next, the police lie to you over the explosion. It would seem that whoever we are dealing with has some very influential friends. Or some kind of leverage that can make the authorities bend to their will.'

'Last night you told me to come in,' said Julia, 'to return to the office, and to turn everything over to the

SFO and the police. Do you still think that?'

Mitchell thought for a moment, taking another sip of his coffee. 'Yes,' he replied, his voice heavy as he spoke. 'You're not equipped to fight this thing by yourself. Come back with me to the office, bring Lamb in, and we'll do everything we can to protect you.'

'You can guarantee our safety?' asked Julia.

Mitchell shook his head and Julia knew her decision was being made for her. 'Nobody can do that now,' he answered. 'But it's your best chance.'

'I don't think Harry would stand for it.'

'Then you come in,' said Mitchell.

Julia looked down, stirring her coffee with her spoon. 'I don't think I can leave him now. He needs me.'

Mitchell's look darkened as he digested the words. 'A man you've just met, Julia,' he said sternly. 'You should put your own safety first.'

'I know it sounds crazy, but I don't think I have any other choice.'

'It's your funeral.' Mitchell shrugged, the line delivered without a hint of humour.

Julia peered up into his eyes. 'You said some days ago there where things you couldn't tell me. I don't think you've been completely honest with me, right from the start, from the time you chose me for this assignment.' She hesitated, listening to the words as they tumbled from her lips, unsure how to continue. 'If we're to survive, I think it's time you told me everything you know.'

Mitchell glanced down at her; she was pulling strings, he could tell, playing the vulnerable female. It was an old and artful trick, yet an effective one. And she had a point, he decided; she was entitled to the truth. It was too late to play games now. 'You should never have carried on with the investigation after I told you to stop,' he said sternly.

Julia looked away. 'I know. That's history now. I don't think I had any idea what was involved – mainly because you didn't tell me.'

Mitchell sighed, taking another long gulp of coffee. 'Okay,' he said at length. 'It's like this. The insider ring has been known about for some time, both within the surveillance department of the Stock Exchange and the SFO. A crime of that size doesn't go unnoticed for long. The trouble was we could never get any authorisation to crack it. The people running it have influence. Powerful influence. Deploying a completely unknown investigator, such as yourself, was the only way forward I could think of.'

'Who are these people?' asked Julia.

Mitchell looked away. 'We don't know precisely.'

'The truth,' said Julia, levelling her stare directly into his eyes. 'You owe me that.'

'It's true that we don't know exactly who they are,' Mitchell replied. 'But I know two things. One is that they have powerful access to information systems. That's how they're running the insider dealing ring; the raw data for their trades has to be coming from somewhere. The other thing we know is that they have friends within the security services. That's why earlier attempts at an investigation have been stopped. My guess all along has been that they have some kind of surveillance system under their control and are sharing it with the security services in return for protection from investigation.'

'Is that possible?' asked Julia. 'Why would the security services want to do a deal with anyone? Particularly criminals.'

Mitchell nodded. 'British surveillance has always been heavily dependent on the Americans. More so than anyone could imagine. They have almost no independent capability, mainly because they don't have the money and no one will give it to them. But they would like their own surveillance. My guess is that if some kind of private capacity were being built in this country the security services might well protect it in return for access to the data. That's quite possible. It's also wrong. I and some of the other senior people at the SFO have known this for some time and have felt it should be stopped. I'm afraid you've become involved in our attempt. More than you should ever have been allowed to.'

Julia remained silent for a moment, allowing information to filter through her mind. She felt as if a veil had been lifted from her face and she could see clearly for the first time; it was frightening, but also a relief. At least she had some idea of what was happening to her and why. For the first time she felt she was starting to make some sense of everything that had happened in the past few weeks. 'We already know who it is.' The statement was delivered point-blank, but with a just a hint of a feminine smile. Julia could not help but feel pleased by the look of astonishment and curiosity that flashed across Mitchell's face. She realised now that she was ahead of him, not just tagging along behind.

'Who?' he asked.

Julia hesitated. She could not be sure whether she should tell him; she had not discussed it with Harry and to reveal too much without checking first with him struck her as a betrayal of their relationship. 'I don't think I should say just yet,' she replied. 'Anyone who knows is likely to be a target.'

'But you're certain you know?'

'Sure,' replied Julia. 'Not in terms of proof. But the evidence fits together well enough. It's compelling. So, yes, enough to be sure.'

Mitchell looked at her closely; he already had a high opinion of her logic and tenacity, but now he admired her guts as well. 'Then you must find the evidence,' he said. 'That's the way out. It will be dangerous and difficult, but it's the best way.'

'And when we find it?' asked Julia. 'What then? That's what makes me so angry. If what you're saying is true, how can we know anyone will act upon it?'

'If it's compelling enough, it will do. If the case is strong enough, there's always a way.'

'And will you help?'

'I can't if I don't know the names.'

'Don't play games,' cautioned Julia. 'I can't say who it is, not without talking to Harry first. But if we need help later on, can I rely on you?'

'Certainly.' The answer was delivered stiffly, with a flicker of hesitation, and Julia was no longer sure he was telling the truth. He reached inside his jacket pocket and fished out a pen and a slip of paper, writing down a pair of numbers. 'It might be safer to contact me at home, away from the office. And if you feel that's too dangerous, leave a message with my sister and tell me where to contact you. I'll do so immediately, I promise.'

Julia drained her coffee, collecting the remnants of the sugary foam with her spoon; the sweetness momentarily soothed her and set her mind at rest. She thanked him and stood up to leave.

'A few words of advice,' said Mitchell. 'The chances are you can't outgun your opponents. Nor can you evade them for ever. But you might be able to outsmart them. Just remember. You must think of everything, every possible vulnerability, and try to shut it down.'

'It frightens me.'

'That's good. It should. It's the people who aren't scared who make the worst mistakes.'

At her side, Julia was aware of a waitress leaning over the table. 'Are you Miss Porter?' she asked.

Julia nodded.

'There's a phone call for you,' the waitress continued.

'For me?' questioned Julia. She stood up and walked towards the phone on the counter. Surely nobody could know she was here. Not even Harry. It was impossible. Absolutely impossible.

'You have been taking too many risks,' said the voice on the line as she cupped the receiver to her ear.

Julia recognised the tone instantly; the same distant and cold voice that had delivered the threats days ago. 'Who are you?' she demanded.

'A variety of different people,' the man replied. 'All of them willing to do whatever is necessary to prevent you getting any further.'

'You won't succeed,' said Julia angrily.

'I think I probably already have. Just remember we can see everything.'

Chung replaced the receiver, and looked across at the Russian. 'How long has she been there?' he asked.

Lykanov shrugged wearily. 'Ten or fifteen minutes,' he replied.

'Is she with anyone?'

'There is no way of knowing,' Lykanov replied. 'She went in alone. How am I to know who else might be inside the café?'

'Keep watching.'

Lykanov turned to look up at the Korean, torching another cigarette as he did so. 'Why play games?' he asked. 'If you want to finish with them, just do it. We know where they are. I don't see any point in toying with them first.'

Chung's eyes narrowed and he chuckled to himself. 'This is London, not Moscow,' he said softly. 'You can't gun down people in broad daylight. Just keep tracking them until you find them in a quiet enough spot. Then I shall finish the game.'

'Who is this Lamb character, exactly?' asked Fielding.

The question was pitched at two of his advisers; bright young men fresh from business school who worked in the chief executive's office. Since the meeting of the banking committee yesterday, both of them had been researching Cable Media and this was just one of the angles they had uncovered. Even so, it looked a trifle embarrassing for the bank, that had to be admitted. Fielding was already in a foul mood and this could not be counted on to lighten the atmosphere.

'He worked down at Croxley, Palmer as a media analyst,' replied Simon Killick, the more senior of the two and the one who earned his colleague's gratitude by regularly volunteering to broach delicate subjects. 'He was quite good, apparently, at least according to the Extel rankings. He did some research a couple of months ago, which appeared to demonstrate Cable Media was getting in way over its head with the satellite project.'

'Perhaps we should get him up here,' remarked Fielding caustically. 'He might be a useful man to talk to.'

'Not sure that will be possible sir,' responded Killick, shifting from one foot to the other. 'It seems he was fired just over a month ago.'

Fielding had often wondered why his predecessor had been so keen to acquire a stockbroking firm and generally avoided looking at its figures; they were just too depressing. He found the miserable returns and the lavish bonuses paid to all the staff an affront, and tried to keep Croxley, Palmer as far from the front of his mind as possible. Now he could recollect why. It appeared to have an uncanny ability to irritate him. 'Why exactly was he fired?'

'It was a request from the company.'

Fielding looked up sharply, unsure if he should be believing what he was hearing. 'Explain,' he requested harshly, in a tone that invited no argument.

'It seems some of the analysis he had prepared and some of the stuff he was saying to clients was rather offensive to Samuel Haverstone,' answered Killick. 'His line was that the Argus system was far too expensive and would never make a decent return, at least not in the short term. Haverstone got in touch with Arnold Webber over at Croxley, Palmer and said he wanted the guy out on his ear. Said he was making rather too many waves. Anyhow, as we understand it, Haverstone also pointed out how much money Cable Media had borrowed from Harrington's, how they could take their business elsewhere if they wanted to, plenty of people queuing up to lend them money and so on.'

'Not any more, they aren't,' interjected Fielding.

Killick shook his head. 'No, probably not, sir. Webber maintains he protested a bit, but when Haverstone pointed out that Croxley could easily be cut out of any deals involving Cable Media he didn't have much choice but to buckle. The firm can't afford to annoy a company of that size, particularly when it is so active in the market. And anyway, Lamb wasn't anyone special. He was just an analyst. They are expendable.'

Though he was reluctant to say so, Fielding had to admit the story rang true. Analysts were always disposable and they could also be very annoying; he could recall being furious when one of the Croxley financial team had put out a note criticising the performance of Harrington's. Even so, it was embarrassing to have sacked a man just for being right. 'How good was the analysis?' he asked.

'Spot on,' replied Killick cheerfully. 'It predicted the cashflow crisis and even hinted it might be imminent. Lamb was well ahead of the pack. The Cable Media share price was still rising sharply at the time.'

'And where is he now?'

Killick shrugged, turning to his colleague, who merely looked away. 'I don't think anybody quite knows,' he replied. 'He was told to clear his desk immediately. That is standard practice down at Croxley, I believe. Nobody hangs around.'

Fielding looked up. 'Then find him,' he commanded. 'I think I would like to speak to Mr Lamb. It would be interesting to talk to somebody who actually understands that company.'

'Find him?' asked Killick. 'You don't think we should check first whether we might be leaving ourselves open to some kind of wrongful dismissal charge? Perhaps we should run it past the legal department first.'

Fielding shook his head. 'I don't think we should check anything,' he replied firmly. 'I have three days to sort out this mess. I think you should find him immediately.'

Harry glanced at his watch nervously. She was only five minutes late, but he had already been sitting there for almost half an hour and his patience was starting to fray. He had drunk one cup of coffee and was ordering his second. She should be along some time soon, he tried to reassure himself. Be patient.

Glancing around the café, located on the strip of smart shops and bars opposite Harrods, Harry found it hard to concentrate. The events of the last couple of hours had shaken his nerves and the words he could recollect from the phone conversation were still ringing in his ears. He was sure they'd been followed last night and now this. Whoever it was they were up against, they seemed to have almost perfect knowledge of their movements, as if they could see everything. For now, he appeared safe, but he wasn't at all confident that would last. The man had found him before and no doubt would locate him again soon.

We know everything – the phrase still reverberated around Harry's mind. How was it possible to be located with such ease? Nobody, Julia aside, would have known he was heading for either place. For a brief, terrifying moment he considered whether he should be suspicious of her, but quickly dismissed the thought. There was no way she could have contacted the man, even if she had wanted to, and that was in any case incomprehensible. No, he decided, that was not the answer. It had to be something else. The soft touch of her finger against his shoulder broke his thoughts. Harry was surprised he had not seen her come in and cursed himself inwardly; he had been too busy mulling over different possibilities to keep a check on his surroundings. A mistake. He glanced up into her eyes and, though she smiled down at him, he could tell she was worried; there was a look of nervousness, a heightened sense of anxiety, which her smile could not mask. He waved at the waitress, indicating he wanted another cappuccino. 'What's up?' he asked.

'I was seen,' Julia replied. 'The same man who made the threatening call before. He contacted me again while I was having coffee with Mitchell.' She glanced over her shoulder, scanning the collection of jewelled women thronging around the café, as if she expected him to walk through the doors at any moment.

'Where was this?' asked Harry. 'And when?'

'About twenty minutes ago,' replied Julia. 'In Covent Garden.'

'I heard from him as well,' said Harry.

Julia looked startled; her eyes darted up from the coffee that had just been put down in front of her and her hand reached out across the table to hold his. 'Where?' she asked.

'It was when I was coming out of the hospital,' he said. 'About an hour ago. A phone call to the lobby just after I left.'

Julia took a quick sip of her cappuccino; she was definitely drinking too much caffeine, she reflected briefly, but she would worry about that another time. 'He seems to be everywhere.'

'Or at least anywhere we go,' said Harry. 'It's frightening how easily he seems to locate us.'

'Mitchell might have told him,' pondered Julia. 'I thought I could trust him and he promised to help, but I can't be sure.'

Harry shook his head. 'Possible but unlikely,' he said. 'It would explain how he knew where you were. But it doesn't explain how he knew I was at the hospital. Neither Mitchell nor anyone else would have known that. It was a reasonable guess, I suppose, that I would go there some time and he might just have been staking out the place. But then, how would he know you were in Covent Garden?'

Julia looked lost; in her eyes Harry could detect a sense of helplessness, as though the mystery were about to overwhelm her and as if she were close to admitting defeat.

She started to explain everything Mitchell had told her, the words tumbling from her mouth in a garbled rush, making little sense as she spoke the sentences.

Harry looked at her intently, soaking up every word, his mind racing forward, calculating the possibilities. 'Then there is only one option,' he said when she had finished.

'Which is?'

'We keep moving.' He put a five-pound note down on the table and stood up, collecting her hand as he did so. He brushed past the other customers, walking purposefully towards the door, his eyes darting along the street as he stepped into the sunshine. He half expected to see some strange and malevolent figure waiting for them and his muscles were tensed, preparing for the confrontation.

265

'Where shall we go?' asked Julia.

Harry gripped her tighter by the hand, drawing reassurance from the feel of her next to him. 'I don't know yet,' he answered. 'Somewhere. Anywhere. Where we can't be seen, and where we can figure out what's happening to us.' He looked nervously about him as he stepped out into the busy street. The sun was shining, and the shoppers and tourists stepped past them, their feet ambling down the crowded pavement, paying little attention to their surroundings. To everyone else it was just another normal weekday afternoon. Harry held Julia close, steering her towards the road. He looked around him once more, his sense of paranoia increasing. Suddenly, the most trivial sights had become threatening; streets that had once seemed so safe and secure were now heavy with menace. He shivered slightly, looking up at the bright sky and wondering how his opponent could know so much. 'Here,' he said, guiding her into an electronics shop.

Julia followed him without a word, remaining silent as he stood in front of the counter, looking down at a row of laptop computers.

'What do you have in stock?' Harry asked the first salesman who came into view.

'There's quite a range, depending on what . . .'

'The most powerful,' he interrupted.

'That would be the Hitachi,' said the salesman. 'It has . . .'

'I'll take it,' Harry snapped, fishing out his wallet and putting down a gold credit card on the counter. He hesitated slightly at the thought of his card being traced, but he needed the laptop.

The salesman fingered the biro sticking up from the breast pocket of his short-sleeved shirt. He seemed surprised; few sales were as easy as that, particularly the expensive ones, and he was already calculating the commission. He took the card and started processing the transaction. At his side, a colleague asked if there was a Mr Lamb in the shop. The salesman glanced down at the card: that was the name he saw there. He looked up at Harry, his voice betraying his surprise. 'There seems to be a phone call for you,' he said.

Harry took the receiver warily. 'Stop running, Mr Lamb,' said Chung. 'Surely you realise by now that you will have to give yourself up soon.'

'It's him,' said Harry, looking across at Julia.

'Let's get out of here,' she said.

'Fuck off,' he muttered into the phone, replacing the receiver. He looked up at the salesman. 'Are we ready yet?'

The salesman nodded, handing over the computer. 'Would you like a box?'

Harry shook his head. 'No time,' he snapped. He took Julia by the arm and stepped out again into the street. 'Do you see anyone?' he asked.

Her eyes were already scanning the pavements, searching for anyone who might be monitoring their movements. 'Nothing,' she replied. 'But they must be watching us.'

He grabbed her by the hand. 'Keep moving,' he said breathlessly.

Julia stopped, looked up at him, wondering for a moment whether she could still recognise him. 'I think it's time we went to the police. Mitchell said he could protect us. We can't do this any more. We should trust him.'

Harry was already starting to walk away. 'I don't trust anyone,' he said sharply.

20

Lykanov took the flask from his coat pocket and poured a measured shot of vodka into the glass resting next to the computer screen. With a swift movement of his left hand he tipped the clear liquid into the back of his throat, swilling it around his tonsils before allowing it to sink towards his stomach. It was good liquor; better than the rough moonshine he had grown used to drinking during his many years on Russian military bases, and he took a moment to enjoy its hard, intemperate flavour.

It had been a long night. Judging by his watch, it was now morning and he had spent most of the last twenty-four hours here. He didn't mind that so much. The flat he had been provided with was cold and soulless. It was not and never would be a home. When this job was over, when his money was safely stored away and he could start living his new life, it would be a joy to leave.

Already the first two hundred thousand of the money deposited for him in the Cayman Islands had been transferred to an account he had opened for himself in Switzerland. It would be safe there and the rest, when he judged the moment was right, would be switched to other accounts located in different financial centres around the world. This, Lykanov knew, was his one shot at serious wealth and he was not going to let it slip through his fingers now.

For the moment, an end to this vigil did not appear to be in sight. He had been instructed by Chung to keep a precise eye on his equipment, checking for any sighting of the two people he had been monitoring for the last couple of days. The instructions had been fed into the satellites and he did not expect the task to be very difficult; after all, it had located one of them at the hospital and the other in the Covent Garden area without any difficulty. At the sound of footsteps descending the stairs, Lykanov put away the vodka; he did not want to be caught with the stuff on the premises.

'Any progress?' snapped Chung from across the room. 'I was expecting we might have something by now.'

Lykanov turned, glancing back at the man; he appeared rested and clean-shaven, as though he were completely relaxed about his work. 'Nothing,' he replied. 'Not a single sighting.'

Chung walked across the room, drawing closer, leaning over Lykanov's shoulder to peer down at the screen himself. 'I thought this equipment could detect them anywhere in Europe,' he said. 'I thought that was the entire point.'

'Sure it can detect them,' said Lykanov. 'Anywhere they show themselves outside, or even if they are exposed to a window at the right angle. You know the capabilities of the system and you saw how well it worked yesterday.'

'True, true,' muttered Chung. 'I saw it work well enough. So why is it not effective now? I need to know where they are.'

Lykanov shrugged, throwing his hands a few inches up in the air. 'It just hasn't found them,' he answered. 'The only information we have is some calls coming into the man's house.'

'Calls?' questioned Chung. 'Who from?'

Lykanov punched a button on his keyboard, bringing a display up on to his screen; he had already programmed the computers monitoring telecoms traffic to keep tabs on all the incoming and outgoing calls of his targets and to trace the source of the calls. You never could tell when you might want to know who was trying to contact your prey. 'A few from these residential numbers, a few from the hospital,' he said, pointing to the display. 'And a couple from the head office of Harrington's Bank.'

'What did the messages say?'

Lykanov punched another couple of keys, bringing a fresh display up on the screen. 'Message recorded: Tuesday, 16.42: This is Simon Killick calling for Harry Lamb from the chief executive's office at Harrington's. He would very much like to meet with you urgently. Could you call me back to fix an appointment? Thanks,' it read. The next display detailed a message delivered earlier that morning. 'Message recorded: Wednesday, 8.37. This is Simon Killick calling again. I really would be grateful if you could get back to me. We know you may be angry about what happened at Croxley, Palmer, but the chief executive thinks it could all have been a terrible mistake. Please call back as soon as possible. The chief executive is very keen to discuss your views on Cable Media.'

'Get me a printout of that,' snapped Chung. He started walking towards the printer to collect the document. He would have to show this to Haverstone. There was not much question about that. If Fielding wanted to talk to Lamb, that was suspicious. And he would have to make sure the conversation never took place.

Harry glanced down at the newspaper headline and for

a moment could scarcely believe his eyes. He double-checked, anxious to make sure it was true, then started running through the prominent *FT* story. How could I have been so stupid? he asked himself. Suddenly everything made sense.

CABLE MEDIA PLANS EQUITY SWAP
Cable Media, the telecoms and media giant, is proposing a massive debt for equity swap that would convert most of its outstanding debts into shares in the company. The company has put a detailed set of proposals to its bankers and a decision is due to be made at a special meeting of the banking committee on Friday. If the proposals are accepted, it would give the current debtors slightly more than fifty per cent of the equity in the company.

Harry stretched his muscles and tried to clear his head. It had been a long and difficult night, and yet, he supposed, he had slept okay; as well as could be expected, given the circumstances. He had never tried living rough before. Nor had he ever contemplated the prospect. It was not much of a life, he reflected. Not something he imagined he could handle for more than a few days. For now, it would have to do. As far as he could see it was their only option.

The memory of the day before was still burning in his mind. She had been reluctant at first. But faced with the choice of staying at his side, or turning herself over to the police, Julia had stayed with him. What other choice does either of us have? he reflected. For better or worse, fate has thrown us into this together and we have no one else to turn to.

'Where exactly are we going?' she had asked, as he moved down the street.

Harry had shaken his head; he wished he could tell

her, but he had yet to formulate a plan. 'We're just moving,' he'd replied. 'And we keep moving until we reach a conclusion.'

That had been late yesterday afternoon; about sixteen hours ago, he now realised from glancing down at his watch. At first they had hopped on the Piccadilly Line, riding up to King's Cross, travelling most of the distance in silence, both of them too preoccupied with their own thoughts to say very much. At the station, Harry suggested switching on to the Circle Line. 'At least there we can just sit for a while and not have to keep changing trains,' he'd remarked.

They had ridden the train for several hours, talking, mulling over their options. Harry spoke most of the time, reeling through the possibilities, weighing different alternatives, evaluating every angle. None of them made much sense. Every avenue seemed closed and, if he were being honest, he could not see much chance of escape. Nothing he could think of looked as if it would work.

'We can't ride the tube for ever,' Julia had said eventually. 'Apart from anything else, it closes down at night.'

It was true, Harry knew, but for the moment he was out of ideas. 'I don't know where we can go,' he'd replied. 'Home is out. We could go to a hotel, but frankly I don't trust it. They can trace our credit cards, I'm sure. All through today they seemed to know wherever we were. If I'm right, as soon as we get out of here, they'll spot us. Once we're in a quite secluded space, I don't think they'll just call. They'll try to kill us.'

Julia nodded. 'Okay, so we stay underground.'

'As you said, it shuts down.'

'Perhaps,' said Julia. 'But the tunnels go on for ever and some of them must be practically empty. Particularly the part they're still building.'

The idea had struck Harry as slightly crazy, but no worse than some of the ones he had proposed to her over the past couple of days, and in the absence of anything else, he felt he should play along. The extension of the Jubilee Line from central London down into Docklands was still being built and for all they knew it might be virtually empty. At least at night. It was certainly unlikely to be guarded; after all, who would want to break into an empty tube tunnel? There was nothing there.

At Embankment station, on the Circle Line, they stepped out on to the platform. The extension was meant to start close to here, according to the maps, and there must be an entrance somewhere. Harry walked in the direction of the building site, with Julia following along behind. A barricade boarded off the area under construction, but there was a door in the flimsy plywood contraption. It was not locked. Harry opened it and went through; before him lay a long corridor, stretching for fifty yards or so and dimly lit by a row of lamps spaced at ten-yard intervals. When finished, Harry guessed it would lead down to the Jubilee Line platform.

They started walking down, turning at the bottom of the corner, and climbed down a motionless escalator. A platform stretched out before them, empty and bleak. It looked much like any other tube station, except it was strangely clean. None of the fixtures was yet fitted along the walls, nor were there any posters or litter along the tracks. There was a smell of disinfectant, of freshly unwrapped plastic and newly laid cement, adding to the pristine atmosphere. The light was murky and dim, beamed down from a row of makeshift lamps; the headlamps to illuminate the platform had not yet been fitted and half-shadows played ominously along the walls.

Harry led the way, walking the length of the platform.

It turned towards the end and a doorway beckoned. He stepped inside. It led to a small room, about eight feet by ten, with a series of panels and displays still encased in their plastic wrappings. Some kind of station room, Harry figured, for security, or for controlling the line. 'We could always stay here for the night,' he said, looking at Julia. From the expression on her face he could tell she did not relish the prospect; a slight wrinkling of her nose indicated she had seen better and, in truth, so had he. But for now it would have to do.

It had been reasonably warm. Spring was already on its way and the insulation down here was good, though an empty breeze whistled constantly through the tunnel. In the distance, the rolling of the trains could still be heard, rattling along their tracks. Harry took some of the cardboard boxes and flattened them out on the floor, covering them with plastic sheeting. He slipped, as quietly as possible, back the way they came and collected some Cokes, some crisps and some chocolate bars from the kiosk back at the main station. They had eaten the small meal practically in silence, both of them too exhausted to say very much. Together they lay down on the cardboard, holding on to each other for additional warmth, and slowly drifted into a restless sleep. 'Don't worry, everything will be all right eventually,' Harry had whispered.

'I hope so,' Julia had replied, her voice drowsy.

Harry had woken up first, He had rubbed his eyes and could feel already the tension and pain in his muscles; that's what you got, he supposed, from sleeping rough. There was no form of natural light down here and no way of telling the time apart from looking at his watch. It was just after seven. Trying not to disturb Julia, he crept back towards the station, keeping a close eye out for guards. There appeared to be no one around; work here was just about complete, he figured, and there might well not be anyone about until it was almost time for the new line to open. He collected some more supplies and a newspaper from the kiosk, and put a call through to the hospital. When, after twenty or so rings, no one had answered he hung up. He didn't want to leave Julia for too long. She already looked worried enough.

The taste of the Coke in his mouth felt strange; it was too sweet, too fizzy and too cold for first thing in the morning, yet it was the only form of caffeine he could find. There were several cafés close to the station where he could have collected coffee, but he still did not feel safe stepping outside. They had lucked into this hiding place and he felt relatively certain they could stay here for at least a couple of days without being discovered. He did not want to do anything that might blow their cover; even if they survived, there was not much chance of them finding anywhere so secure.

It was then, while Julia disappeared to find somewhere to wash, that he started reading the *FT* story, and one part of the mystery began to unlock itself; for a brief, elated moment Harry could feel the pieces of the jigsaw coming together.

Perhaps there was something she could detect in his manner when Julia returned to the small station room; a lightening of his mood, or the trace of a smile around his lips. 'What is it?' she asked.

He handed her the newspaper. 'What do you make of that?'

She started reading and Harry could tell she too was intrigued. 'What do you think it means?'

Harry took a sip of his Coke. 'This is just a theory, but let me try it out on you,' he began. 'We discovered yesterday that both Gregson and Haverstone are involved in the insider dealing ring. Indeed, they might well be the men controlling it. That would make sense.

Neither of them, from what I know about them, is the kind of man who would want to play second fiddle to anyone. Okay, that's progress. But it raises as many questions as it answers. Such as how would they control the ring? And what might its purpose be?'

'And you think this might have something to do with it?'

'It's like pieces of a jigsaw,' replied Harry. 'That's one part of the picture and this is another, a different corner.'

'And your theory?'

'Gregson's firm, with my help I have to admit, has been buying up vast quantities of the debt in Cable Media,' said Harry, his brow tightening and his fist kneading one another. 'At first I thought it was just making a market in the debt, but after a while I wasn't so sure. The firm kept buying the debt whenever we could shake loose some sellers. We never seemed to sell any on. Indeed, there was no interest in selling. The position just kept getting bigger and bigger. Dangerously so, even for a firm as wild as Gregson & Heath.'

'And now it appears that debt is going to be converted into equity,' interrupted Julia. She was starting to catch the flow of his thought.

'Exactly,' said Harry. 'So the holders of the debt will, by Friday afternoon, become big shareholders in Cable Media. But what if that was the plan all along? It seems crazy, I know, perhaps too crazy to be true. But what if the plan was to drive Cable Media to the edge of bankruptcy, buy up the debt, then convert it into equity? And what if you were pouring the profits from an insider dealing operation into that scheme? Then you would end up as the owner of the company and at a bargain basement price. It would be one of the great financial coups of all time.'

Julia hesitated. 'Is that plausible?' she asked.

'Don't you remember what Sherlock Holmes used to say? When you've eliminated the possible, it's time to start considering the impossible. It explains why Gregson and Haverstone would be co-operating. They'd need each other to make a plan like that work. Gregson to buy the debt and Haverstone to make the conversion. The end result is that the two of them finish up controlling the most powerful communications empire in the world. That, I suspect, for both of them would be a game worth playing.'

'It adds up,' said Julia. 'But it's just a theory. Theories are no good without proof.'

Harry turned, drawing her close to his side. 'Then we prove it. The whole thing. That's the only way we'll ever get out of this.'

She looked into his eyes and could see the intensity behind the words. Then her eyes wandered over the small dingy room, a place that was partly a haven, but which also looked strangely like a place of incarceration. Right, she thought to herself. Prove it. From a tiny empty underground room in a deserted part of the tube. It was going to be a lot harder than Harry suggested.

Richard Gregson was not sure why they always met in Haverstone's office. Indeed, he was having trouble remembering when he had ever seen the man outside this building. Sure, he was known to show up occasionally at industry conferences. He would sometimes jump on a plane someplace to sign a deal, and there were occasions when he would pose artfully for one of the many magazine articles, where he would drool on about the importance of the digital age. But most of the time he was right here, locked up on the eleventh floor, pacing his Olympian office, playing with his toys. Outside this place the man did not appear to have any kind of life. This was his existence.

Haverstone should get out more, he decided. Mix a little. Perhaps even meet some women. So far as he knew, the guy was not even married. Never seemed to have any kind of relationship, not even fooling around with any of the hundreds of young media wannabes crowding his empire. Nothing seemed to turn him on. At least nothing that wasn't spinning at a few thousand miles an hour one hundred miles above the surface of the earth. There were times, and this was one of them, when Gregson suspected the man was not just in it for the money. That, he figured, was a mistake. It could even turn out to be dangerous.

The elevator moved swiftly up to the top of the building, not stopping on the way. Haverstone had explained once how a special device had been fitted that meant, when the security guard touched the right button, the lift would make the journey undisturbed; requests from more junior staff for it to stop would be ignored. What kind of weirdo does that? Gregson wondered. Somebody who was very particular about the kind of people he met in the lift, somebody who didn't like to mix with his fellow men.

He stepped out and glanced down the corridor. As for me, he reflected, this is just another scam. A way of making a pile of money and one of the best I've ever encountered. A way of earning a living and a good one, too. Nothing else. It's strictly business.

Haverstone was sitting behind his desk when Gregson found him. As so often, it was littered with newspapers and magazines, some of which the company owned, others trophies he would no doubt like to buy. Haverstone had been just a telecoms guy, a business-man, when they had first met. He had a fascination with media, but that was understandable; it was one of the fastest growing industries in the world and one of the most profitable. Although Gregson did not buy into all the digital revolution bullshit, he could see the point of convergence and regarded Haverstone's interest as legitimate. It was a way of making money and that, in his book, was always okay. Yet now the man seemed different. By degrees, he had become a fanatic, and Gregson could not be sure what he was dealing with any more.

'A bulletin from the front line?' asked Haverstone. He had looked up from his desk, a sly grin playing upon his lips.

'Everything is falling into place,' replied Gregson. 'We have enough of the debt in our pockets already to make this swing and some of the bankers are still falling our way. My boys are shaking them loose one by one.'

'Good, good,' said Haverstone, standing up from behind his desk and walking across the room to shake Gregson warmly by the hand. 'I think one or two of the other bankers, even those who don't sell, will come down on our side. Our team have been monitoring them closely and have discovered some interesting facts. Enough to make sure they know what is in their and our best interests.'

'That's quite a system we have downstairs,' said Gregson with a shake of his head. He had yet to witness the satellite tracking system in person, but he was well acquainted with its capabilities. Indeed, ever since the plan had first been discussed between them it had been central to all their objectives. The possibilities of a perfect observation station had appealed to Gregson instinctively; after all, what more could any trader ask for than a machine that updated him constantly on what all his rivals were doing? Markets, he had learnt through many years of experience, were little more than rivers of information and whoever controlled it could also control the flow. Or, at least, that was the theory. So far it seemed to be working out pretty well.

'It is more than a system,' said Haverstone. 'It is a cornerstone.'

'Of what, exactly?'

Haverstone turned away, looking up at the bank of television screens running along the side of the office, his attention briefly distracted by the series of flickering images. 'An empire, of course,' he replied.

'It's silicon and steel,' said Gregson. 'Nothing else. Don't romanticise. It's risky.'

Haverstone shook his head. 'It is more than that,' he said slowly. 'All empires have a technological foundation. The Mongols with the stirrup, the English with the longbow. A single, crucial technology can create an empire. Of course, those were different times. People thought of empire in terms of land and people and gold. We know differently.'

'Sure,' said Gregson caustically. 'We know it's just about the money. That's the only kind of empire that anyone gives a damn for any more.'

'Not quite,' said Haverstone. 'An empire of the mind, that is what we are creating. One where we control every point of contact between the individual and the outside world. Through their newspapers and magazines, through films and television and radio, through their telephones and computers. The information and the knowledge, all of it will be filtered through this company. Everything they know and can imagine, all of it will come from here. Now, that is an empire, and one that is fitting for the third millennium.'

'To you, perhaps, but I'm just in it for the money.'

Haverstone turned slightly, walking closer to Gregson and slipping a hand on to his shoulder. 'Your trouble, Richard,' he said, 'is that you have no imagination.'

'And your trouble is that you have too much.'

Haverstone walked back to his desk, sitting down,

and continued flicking through the magazines. 'You can never have too much imagination,' he said sourly. 'It is what makes us human.'

21

Harry looked first left, then right, before slipping through the slender wooden door. Watching, he realised, was starting to become an instinct. Looking over his shoulder, checking his back, keeping an eye on his shadow, all of them had been unnatural to him. Now he imagined that the dangers might lurk around every corner, and, with that knowledge, his carefree, easy manner had abandoned him. He had become nervous and fidgety, anxious about what might be going to happen next. It disturbed him. This was not the sort of person he admired, nor the kind he wanted to become. For now, however, this was the type of man he would have to be.

A bank of pay phones lay immediately to his right, stretching along the edge of the station. He walked casually towards them, noting that a couple were free. After putting the money into the slot he dialled his own number, keying in four digits to the touch-tone phone that would enable him to check his messages. There were three or four from friends wondering where he was, two from Cassie's nanny, with the same request, two from the hospital and three from Malcolm Fielding's office, each more urgent than the last.

It was the message from Fielding that hooked his

attention. Why would the head of Harrington's want to talk to him? he wondered. Now, of all times. He had never wanted to talk to him while he was working there. What, he asked himself, was the connection?

Harry glanced around the station forecourt, wondering about his next move. He needed to call the hospital and would like to ring Fielding. He could turn out to be a useful ally during the next couple of days and there was plenty they had learnt that might well place him on their side. But he was unsure if it was safe. So far, the ability of their enemies to track them seemed uncanny. Very little appeared to escape their scrutiny. And he knew enough about Cable Media's involvement in the telecoms business to be certain it was not safe to make the phone call. That was not a risk he was prepared to take. At least, not without finding some way of protecting himself.

For a brief moment he could feel his heart sinking. Despair started to overwhelm him. I can't move around, he realised, nor can I even make a phone call without being detected. Anything I do will lead to my discovery. The situation looked completely hopeless. He was trapped, incarcerated, safe only so long as he remained hidden underground.

Taking a deep breath, Harry walked across to one of three men selling copies of the homeless magazine *Big Issue* near the entrance to the station. 'Fancy earning a tenner, mate?' he started.

The man was dressed in faded denims and a rough-looking overcoat, had long, greying hair and a straggly beard. The stale scent of cheap, strong lager hung over him. 'Don't mind,' he answered in the slurred Scottish accent that had always struck Harry as compulsory among London's beggars. 'What do you want?'

'Make a couple of phone calls, that's all,' replied Harry.

The man nodded his assent and followed Harry back towards the pay phones. Harry dialled the number and handed the receiver over to the beggar.

'Simon Killick here,' said the voice on the line.

'Tell him it's Harry Lamb calling,' whispered Harry. The beggar repeated the words into the phone.

In his office at Harrington headquarters Killick sat up sharply; he had been wondering all day where Lamb might have got to and had already been pondering how to break it delicately to the chief executive that the man seemed to have vanished from the face of the earth. 'Thank God you got the message,' he exclaimed. 'We've been looking for you everywhere.'

Harry could hear the words and whispered a reply into the ear of the beggar. 'Do you still want to meet?'

'I'll check the diary and fix you a time right away.'

'No,' said the beggar, after listening to Harry's instructions. 'I can't come to the office. It isn't safe. If Fielding wants a meeting it has to be at a place of my choosing and on my terms.'

There was something about Lamb's voice that Killick found disconcerting; he knew that stockbrokers hired some barrow boys, but he would have expected an analyst to sound more middle-class. And Lamb was hardly a Scottish name, so why the accent? It puzzled him, yet the chief executive had been very insistent about the meeting and he saw little choice but to play along. 'Okay,' he answered. 'Where and when?'

Harry glanced up at the tube map before replying. 'There's a long walkway connecting Bank and Monument stations in the City,' said the beggar carefully. 'Meet me there at seven thirty tonight. Tell Fielding not to worry about recognising me. I'll spot him and make the approach when I judge it's safe.'

Killick was momentarily lost for words. This was, without question, turning into the most bizarre conversation he had ever had. 'I'm not sure all this cloak-and-dagger stuff is really necessary,' he started. He was starting to get an inkling of why Croxley, Palmer might have wanted this Mr Lamb out of their organisation.

'That just shows how little you know about the situation,' said the beggar, after taking instructions from Harry.

'I suppose I can pass the message through to the chief executive, but I can't . . .'

'Just tell him I'll be there,' interrupted the beggar, before listening to what Harry wanted him to say next. 'If he wants to find out what's really happening to his money he should be there as well.' Harry reached across the beggar to click the switch, shutting off the line.

The beggar replaced the handset, looking across at Harry. 'You're fucking mad, you are, man,' he said.

'I suppose I might be,' he replied with a smile. He dialled the number for the hospital, got the beggar to announce himself as Harry Lamb again and heard the nurse on duty state that Cassie's condition had not altered. His heart sank and he was overcome with an immense urge to see her. He took a tenner from his pocket and handed it to the beggar. 'Thanks for your help.' Turning, he scanned the station, satisfying himself that no one was watching. Sauntering casually towards the plywood he slipped through the door, drawing as little attention towards himself as possible, and began walking quickly through the long empty tunnel.

Julia had been busy while he was away. The same dim light was shining down on the small room and it took Harry a moment to adjust his eyes to the gloom and isolation of the surroundings after the bright bustle of the main station. Fortunately, there was a power point within the room, hidden inside one of the panelled

285

cabinets, and she had managed to connect the computer. She had also found a phone socket and had hooked that to the machine's internal modem. 'At least we have some electronics at our disposal,' she said as Harry entered the room.

He nodded, recognising that in many ways she was more able than him, and he admired both her tenacity and her courage. Many men would have buckled under the kind of pressure they had been subjected to, yet she had shown no signs of surrendering. Of pressure, yes. Her face looked tired and there were strain lines around her mouth. But of surrender, no. He found her strength reassuring. I must not let her down by weakening myself, he told himself. That would be a betrayal. And there had been enough of those already. 'Fielding contacted me, via my home number,' he said. 'I arranged to meet him later tonight, further down the tube.'

Julia looked both surprised and intrigued. 'The gameplan?' she asked, glancing up briefly.

Harry smiled, an expression that was both forced and natural at the same time. 'I don't know for certain,' he replied. 'We've been relying on instinct up until now. But he's a powerful man and my suspicion is he's being taken for a ride by Haverstone. I think he might be an ally.'

She stood up and walked the few yards that separated them. 'I think we have to decide what we're going to do,' she said.

'You mean talk about our relationship?' asked Harry with a smile.

'Not yet, stupid,' she answered lightly. 'Although I might raise that later, particularly if you expect me to spend the night here again. I am a girl after all.'

Harry knew well enough what Julia wanted to talk about and was aware she was right. If they were to survive, and if he was to see Cassie again, they had to plan as carefully as possible. Any mistakes and they would most probably be finished. 'Review what we know,' he said. 'We know Gregson and Haverstone are working together on the insider dealing ring. We believe they are also working together on buying up Cable Media's debt and converting it into equity. My guess is that has been the plan all along. The insider dealing ring was established to raise the money and the finances of Cable Media were deliberately destroyed to make the conversion possible. Basically, it's a plot to get control, personal control, of the company as cheaply as possible. It's quite a scheme. In a way you have to admire them.'

'It's a fine theory, but that's all it is,' said Julia. 'There are two things we still need to figure out. One is how to prove it. The other is how we use the information.' She bit her thumb-nail, her face serious.

'Take things in sequence,' replied Harry. 'We know they've tried to kill us. That suggests to me we already have enough information to make us potentially fatal to their plan.'

'But what is it we know?'

Harry stood up and started pacing round the room. He stretched his muscles as he walked, hoping to flex his mind at the same time; his limbs were still aching from the previous night and he realised it would be several days at least before he found himself in a comfortable bed again. If ever. 'Two possibilities,' he said. 'One is that we've discovered that Gregson and Haverstone are the men behind Turevul Trading and hence the people who control the insider dealing ring. The other is that we know Sir Ian Strang was murdered.'

Julia paused before replying. 'But we've only just found out about Turevul. Surely the key question is what did we know when the car exploded. That alone was dangerous enough for them to attempt to assassinate us.'

'Okay,' said Harry. 'One possibility was that you were pursuing the case even after it had been dropped and you had the name of the accounting firm. That was a breakthrough and could have been sufficient cause. The other was Strang. We already had that dossier from the Irish police and we knew he was attempting to organise a shareholder revolt to get rid of Haverstone before he died. I only thought it was a vague possibility he had been murdered. It seemed too unlikely, not the sort of thing that happens in real life. But now we know they're capable of killing people it doesn't seem so unlikely any more. Indeed, I would say it was practically definite. They had to get Strang out of the way for the scheme to work. My bet is that his death was at about the same time as the insider dealing ring started its operations.'

'Did you mention to anyone how much you knew about Strang?' asked Julia.

Harry snapped his fists together. It was an expression of annoyance with himself; he had just realised how wilfully he had blundered into this situation and how carelessly he had placed himself, Cassie and Julia in such extreme danger. 'Fuck it,' he muttered, almost under his breath. 'I spoke to Gregson about it just a few days ago. Of course, I didn't have any idea then that he was involved. Christ, what a stupid thing to do.'

Julia frowned. 'You weren't to know,' she said shortly. 'If only we could find a way of cracking that mystery,' she continued, her voice hardening as she pronounced the words. 'That might unlock the door.'

Harry looked up at her, his eyes widening. 'He might have left a message,' he said.

'What d'you mean?' she demanded impatiently.

'I told you he made some phone calls to fund managers the night he died,' replied Harry quickly. 'Apparently he also said something about a website. If we can find that, it might provide some of the answers.'

Malcolm Fielding looked up at his subordinate with a weary expression. It had been a long day and he was tired. Keeping track of all the bank's activities was enough of a job in itself – ever since that Leeson guy had single-handedly brought down Barings he had redoubled his efforts to keep track of every aspect of its operations with a zeal that bordered on paranoia. A crisis on top of the normal workload only heightened his anxiety. Particularly one as intractable as this. Perhaps I am devoting too much attention to this issue, he pondered. After all, there was no reason why he should not let the conversion go ahead. The bank would end up with a pile of Cable Media stock and though he had a feeling it would turn out to be a very bad deal, it would hardly threaten the whole bank. Perhaps he should just let it ride.

No, he decided. Gregson was taking the banks for fools, of that he was certain, and something about the man's behaviour seemed very suspicious. He wanted to find out more about what was happening. 'He wants to meet where?' he asked.

'In the tunnel connecting Bank and Monument tube stations,' replied Killick cautiously. 'It is a very long tunnel, sir,' he added. He was not sure if Fielding had ever been on the tube, although he supposed he must have been, at least when he was younger.

'Did he say why?'

Killick shook his head. 'No, sir,' he replied. 'He just said that if you wanted to know what was really happening at Cable Media you should meet him there at seven thirty this evening. I told him we would rather arrange a meeting in your office, but he insisted it was there or nowhere. He hung up after that.'

Fielding thought for a moment before replying. It sounded ridiculous; meeting a man at the tube station, as though they were hiding from someone. But if he was taking the need for secrecy this serious, perhaps he really did have something extraordinary to say. 'Tell him we'll be there,' he said eventually.

'He didn't leave a number,' commented Killick. 'He just said to be there. That's all.'

'Then tell my driver to be ready at seven,' Fielding muttered irritably.

The next two hours were consumed with internal meetings and by the time Fielding stepped into the gleaming blue Jaguar at seven his mood had lightened a little. Banking could be a dull business sometimes, he reflected, as the car drew away from the kerb and headed into the early-evening City traffic. From time to time you needed a crisis to keep your interest going.

He had reviewed the notes Lamb had published during his time with the bank. He seemed a sensible analyst and though he could understand the reasons why he had been sacked, it was a matter of regret. His work was lucid and intelligent, and he was clearly a capable man. The least he could do, Fielding decided, was to listen to him; he had, after all, suggested the meeting himself.

Killick provided the right change for the ticket machine. It was a long time since he had been on the tube; he had not set foot underground since he had first joined the board of the bank a decade ago and had been given a chauffeur, and he was out of the habit of carrying small change.

They had entered at Bank station and Killick pointed the way down from the Central Line to the Circle Line platform at Monument. After riding down the escalator, they followed the corridor round and started to walk through the long stretch of tunnel that connected the two stations. It was busy with City workers making their way home for the evening and as Fielding strolled through the tunnel he could see no sign of the man he was looking for.

'Good evening, Mr Fielding,' said Harry.

The man standing to his right was just over six foot, dressed in a dark-grey suit, but had a remarkably dishevelled appearance, Fielding noted. He did not appear to have shaved for a couple of days, and his hair could use a wash and comb. His clothes were badly creased and the collar on his shirt looked decidedly grubby. His face was drawn and there were lines under his eyes, as though he had not been sleeping well. He definitely looked as if he were going rapidly to seed. Not a good sign, Fielding decided. 'Mr Lamb?' he inquired.

'Pleased to meet you, sir,' said Harry, extending a hand. 'Thanks for coming.'

The handshake was firm, and Fielding was immediately aware of the difference between the way he looked and the way he sounded. His appearance had the air of a man who was flipping out, losing all touch with reality, but his voice was hard and decisive, everything he would expect from a serious young City executive. *I wonder what has happened to him in the few weeks since he left Croxley, Palmer?* 'My car is waiting upstairs,' he said. 'We could go somewhere and get a drink if you like.'

Harry shook his head. 'I don't think you want to be seen with me,' he replied. 'It might not be safe.'

Fielding had a healthy respect for paranoia; it was often a useful attribute for survival in the markets, but he was starting to suspect this character might be taking it too far. 'Just as you say,' he said carefully. 'We can talk here if you prefer.'

He followed Harry down towards the platform, motioning to Killick to wait behind; this would be a conversation better held in private, he decided, and no matter how crazy Lamb might turn out to be, in such a public place he would be quite safe. Harry chose a couple of bright-green plastic platform seats and

291

suggested to Fielding that they talk there. The banker nodded. 'I am sorry about what happened at Croxley, Palmer,' he said. 'I have investigated and it appears you were sacked after they came under pressure over some of the notes you had written and some of the things you were saying to the market. It is ironic, I know, because as it happens you were quite right. You have my apologies, for what that is worth. If there is anything I can do to help you find a different job, or if you want to come back to the bank, just let me know.'

Harry turned to look at him and smiled. 'I suspected all along that bastard Haverstone had me sacked. Of course, that wasn't what they told me at the time. They said something about being a loose cannon.'

'That might be true.'

'Yes,' Harry agreed, with a sharp nod of his head. 'Plenty loose just now, that much is certain.'

'As you are probably aware, the bank is involved in negotiations with Cable Media,' said Fielding. 'You know more about the company than anyone. I wanted to hear your insights.'

Harry looked up directly, trying to gauge the depth of the man; he had been aware of Fielding as a very distant figure when he worked for Croxley, Palmer, but he had never met him before. He had a reputation as a consensual, mild-mannered leader, good on the detail and the paperwork, weak on vision. He was not known as a risk-taker and what he was about to propose involved taking a big chance. 'How far do you want to take this thing?' he asked.

'How far does it go?'

'A long way.'

'Tell me about it.'

It was a risk, Harry was well aware. But, the way he saw it, he had little choice. He could not fight this thing on his own. And Fielding was the only person he could imagine who might have an interest in helping him. 'Okay,' he said.

He started by explaining about his own investigation into Cable Media after he was sacked from Croxley, Palmer. He mentioned how he met Julia and that she was investigating an insider dealing ring. He told Fielding about the explosion and the events of the following twenty-four hours. Then he started drawing out the conclusions; that Gregson and Haverstone had established the insider dealing ring; that some of the senior staff at Croxley, Palmer appeared to be helping them; that they were taking a huge position in Cable Media debt and were planning to take personal control of the company at the meeting on Friday.

'So the way I see it, you're the ones who are losing out,' said Harry, looking directly at Fielding. He was trying to judge the man's reaction, yet found he was being met only by an empty indifference, an expression he suspected the banker had learnt over many years of listening to fantastic stories, mainly from people trying to borrow money. 'Haverstone wanted the company to fail to meet its interest payments, that was part of the plan. He did it deliberately, because he knew he could force you to convert the debts into equity. I just happen to be in the way, so he's having me rubbed out. He has already injured my daughter, and he'll take me and Julia just as soon as he gets the chance. I have to stop him and I want you to help me.'

Fielding listened, transfixed. The story was different from what he had expected: a saga from some strange, parallel universe, where none of the normal rules seemed to apply. He was not sure he could believe it; indeed, for now, he was not even sure he could comprehend it. 'This all sounds quite fantastic,' he said slowly. 'Do you have any evidence?'

Harry hesitated. 'Evidence,' he replied. 'What kind of evidence would convince you?'

'Direct connections,' said Fielding. 'If it could be demonstrated that Gregson and Haverstone were running an insider dealing ring and if it could be proved that they were using that money to buy up the debt in Cable Media, it would seem to me proof that a major fraud was being perpetrated. Then I might be convinced.'

Harry nodded. 'And what do I get?' he asked. 'I deliver the proof, okay, but then what do you do?'

'Harrington's is a very large bank,' said Fielding. 'It is not without influence. As you said, it is as much in our interests as yours to stop these men. Deliver the proof and I will make sure they are dealt with. You have my word on that.'

'Your word is your bond, I suppose.' Harry didn't bother to stifle the sarcasm in his voice.

'For men of my generation that is sometimes still true,' said Fielding stiffly. 'I suspect you are just going to have to trust me.'

'How long do I have?' asked Harry. He had started to realise he had misjudged Fielding's reaction. This was, perhaps, a man who could be trusted.

'The creditors meeting is at midday on Friday,' said Fielding. 'Nothing need happen until then. If you can deliver the proof in time, we can take them down. If not, I fear it will be too late.'

Harry drew a deep breath. 'I'll make it,' he said. 'And if I don't, I'll have bust my guts trying.'

Fielding drew a card from his wallet and handed it to Harry. 'My direct line, and a home number and a mobile number are on this card. When you find anything, let me know. I'll be waiting to hear from you.'

A train pulled up at the platform, the third since they had started talking. Harry stood up, shook Fielding by the hand and walked towards the open doors. 'Until Friday.'

22

The air had turned hot and acrid and sticky. Perhaps it was the ventilation? wondered Lykanov. Oxygen, he well knew, once piped through several hundred feet of steel tubing was never perfect; it lost its freshness and its energy. Or perhaps it was the fact that neither he nor the Korean had moved from this spot for the best part of the last forty-eight hours. Whatever. It was now becoming suffocating.

Over the last few hours the search had turned cold, darkening the atmosphere still further. The instructions had been clear and explicit. to find the man and woman, and to keep them under close surveillance until they delivered themselves into a situation where they could be dealt with. Lykanov had no doubt the intention was to kill them. It was cruel, he decided, and probably not even necessary. But for the moment, that was no concern of his. For now, he was just following orders.

The failure of his systems to locate the prey was starting to trouble him. He knew from long experience that any kind of intelligence operation was far from perfect; there were always ways for targets to evade detection, so long as they were patient and cunning and experienced. It was a game of cat and mouse. Yet these two, so far as he knew, had no experience. They were rank amateurs.

It was impossible to imagine they could have any idea of the technology pursuing them; its power and reach were beyond the comprehension of the layman. Normally, a prey could only perfect an escape if he knew exactly what he was evading; only then could he take the kind of actions necessary to keep out of sight. But these amateurs knew very little about the true nature of the hunt. That thought comforted Lykanov; pretty soon they would make a mistake. They would reveal themselves.

'Has the search progressed?'

The voice was low and insistent. Lykanov recognised it at once, although he had only heard it a couple of times before; it had the kind of bullying, relentless persistence that was familiar among the political officers back at his old underground base. It's a type, Lykanov decided, one that you probably find in every country and often in positions of power; demanding and unreasonable, it was a voice that belongs to men who were used to getting their own way and interpreted any kind of denial as a personal challenge. It was not a type he liked, even if he had been forced to grow used to it over the years.

Haverstone was standing close to him now, peering down at the screens; it was clear from his expression that he did not understand the technology, yet would petulantly attempt to push it as far as possible.

'We are receiving very little fresh information, sir,' replied Lykanov.

'The monitoring of the other targets is progressing very well,' interrupted Chung.

Haverstone nodded. 'What have we found?' he asked.

'Enough on most of the bankers to keep them in line at the meeting tomorrow morning,' answered Chung.

'Some of them are squeaky clean, of course, that is to be expected. But a few have secrets to hide that are now in our possession. Enough to be embarrassing and to ensure that we should not have too much trouble securing their support.'

'But no sign of Mr Lamb and Miss Porter?'

Chung shook his head and Lykanov could tell from his expression that he was not a man who enjoyed admitting to any kind of failure. 'Not yet,' he answered. 'So far, they appear to have evaded our systems.'

'How is that possible? I thought we could see everything.'

Lykanov noted Haverstone was looking directly at him now and it was he who was expected to answer. 'We can see almost everything. So long as it is in the open air we should be able to detect it.'

'What about a disguise? asked Haverstone. 'If they disguised themselves, could we still see them?'

'I have thought of that and it is possible,' answered Lykanov. 'But I think it is unlikely they could escape detection for long. I have also instructed the computer to search for body types. Particularly skulls. Those are fairly distinctive and we have a good map of both of theirs. Just dyeing their hair or growing a beard or whatever would not do them any good. The system should still be able to detect them. If it sees them, that is.'

'So why hasn't it found them?'

'They haven't shown themselves, I imagine. They must be hiding. The system cannot see inside buildings.'

'And nothing on the phone records?'

Lykanov shook his head. 'It's impossible to disguise your voice. At least not so that it will not be detected by a voice scanner. As far as we can tell they have not made a single phone call.'

'Are you sure?'

Lykanov was pretty sure; the voice scanner was sophisticated and could pick out patterns of speech no matter how much the speaker tried to disguise him or herself. Even trained actors had not been able to defeat the system and he was confident a couple of amateurs would not have the wits to evade it. 'They have not made any phone calls,' he replied firmly.

'I don't like it,' said Haverstone. 'It is almost as if they are deliberately trying to evade detection.'

Chung paused for a moment; that possibility had occurred to him as well and the thought made him nervous. 'That is unlikely,' he said carefully.

'But not impossible.'

'Not impossible, no, sir.'

'Then they must be stopped.' Haverstone's voice started to tremble with barely concealed rage. 'Nothing must be allowed to stop me owning this company. Is that understood?'

'Nothing will stop us,' Chung assured him. 'Two amateurs on the run don't have a chance against a system of this complexity.'

'Just make sure that is true,' said Haverstone angrily. 'Use any means necessary. But make certain they are stopped. They are the only thing that can stand in my way now.'

Age, perhaps, reflected Harry. The aching in his limbs was worse now, more acute than it had been the night before and there was a numbing pain in his spine. Living rough was not an option for a man of thirty-five. Maybe when he was in his teens or early twenties he could have hacked it; he could remember sleeping on plenty of floors after late-night parties many years ago. But he no longer had the strength for it. Those days were behind him and he was not sure he could bear this much longer.

Sooner or later they would have to break cover. Of

that he had little doubt. They could only stand this subterranean existence for another day, perhaps. One more night at most. That, he sensed, would be about all he could take. Beyond that, he didn't believe he could survive being parted from Cassie any more.

He glanced down at his watch; it was just after eight in the morning. He held Julia closer to him, anxious to feel her warmth and taking a momentary pleasure in her presence beside him. Her hair was starting to lose its gloss, and her clothes were crumpled and stained. I don't suppose I look much better myself, he thought. He could already feel the stubble on his chin turning into a beard, and the grease around his hair was thick and uncomfortable. Not good circumstances in which to get to know a woman, he mused.

Sleep was necessary. Another aspect of getting older perhaps; there was a time when he would have happily stayed up all night, but no longer. He needed to rest and his head, he knew, would have to be clear if he were to have any chance of solving the problems that lay ahead. Yet rest was difficult, without anything resembling a bed to lie down on or even any food to eat. He had snatched a few hours of fitful sleep, amid the tossing and turning, but it was not enough; his head was spinning and his vision blurred. He could use some coffee, but knew he would have to settle for one of the cans of warm Coke he had collected the previous night.

Harry stepped out on to the platform and took a quick piss against the wall in one of the small, darkened connecting tunnels; he had been using the same spot for the last twenty-four hours and it was starting to acquire a stale, acrid smell. His head was beginning to lighten and it was with something approaching a sense of anticipation that he returned to the small lair he and Julia had made for themselves.

After his meeting with Fielding they had talked briefly

of what needed to be done. As long as they could prove the conspiracy Gregson and Haverstone had concocted, Harry felt certain Fielding would stand by his word.

'We could just be delivering ourselves straight into the enemy camp,' Julia argued, her voice touched with nervousness.

'I know,' Harry had replied. 'I just don't see any other options. Neither of us can run for ever and I don't think we can stay down here much longer. This is our one chance. We either take it or we don't. It's as simple as that.'

Julia shook her head slowly and Harry could detect the look of mystified sadness in her eyes; he had felt the same sense of mounting desperation himself, but knew it might be fatal to admit any weaknesses and preferred to keep his terrors safely wrapped up within him. 'How did we ever get into this situation?' she had asked.

Harry had just shrugged; he knew there was no answer to that question and that any attempt to find one would only increase their anxiety. There was no time for introspection.

Disturbed by his absence, Julia was slowly waking by the time Harry returned to the room. She yawned and stretched, and he offered her a Coke. 'Good morning,' he said softly.

She sat up and kissed him on the cheek. 'Domestic bliss.' She smiled. 'Just what I always dreamed of. My own underground hovel and a man who hasn't shaved for three days.'

Harry laughed, grateful for her humour. But there was work to be done and not much time left. They had today and if they could not collect enough evidence to prove their case within the next twenty-four hours they were probably finished.

By tomorrow, they had to compile evidence that Gregson was buying up Cable Media debt; they needed proof that it was being funded by the insider dealing ring controlled by the two men; they had to find out exactly what had happened to Sir Ian Strang; and to find a way of getting to the meeting at noon tomorrow safely and intact. It was a big task, yet Harry sensed that at least some of it might be possible. And if some of it could be achieved, there was no reason why all of it should not be managed. With luck and persistence.

While Harry had been meeting Fielding, Julia had been studying the disks they had stolen from the accounting firm. The computer had been set up in a corner of the small room and was running on maximum power. The information had been downloaded and she had spent several hours on its analysis. Her ability to diagnose forensically a set of complex accounts was one asset out of many qualities that Harry was beginning to admire in Julia.

The important nuggets of information were in the details of the records. The accounts for Turevul Trading showed a steady influx of cash into the company, amounting to hundreds of millions over a period of a year or so. By matching it against the record of profits she could recall from studying the insider dealing ring, Julia had produced a set of records that left little doubt where the money from the ring was going; the match between the profits on those illegal trades and the inflow of funds into Turevul was perfect.

On the debit side, the records merely showed a variety of investments in different financial instruments; normal enough for an offshore trading company. Harry was convinced the money was being used to buy up the debts of Cable Media. There was nothing here to suggest that, yet he felt it to be true. A feeling was not good enough, however. They had to prove it.

'Can you get inside the system of Gregson's firm?' asked Julia. 'If you could, we might be able to find some evidence of who is the ultimate owner of the debts.'

'True,' answered Harry slowly. He had not thought of that possibility, but she was probably right. The ownership of the debts had to be logged somewhere within the system and there was no reason why he should not be able to find it. The computer was already set up and the modem was connected to a phone socket. He sat down at the machine and dialled into the company, tapped in his password and found himself within the system. One advantage of Gregson's firm was that because the man worked on the hoof so much a lot of the administration was in permanent chaos; it did not surprise Harry very much that no one had bothered to cancel his password.

Each trader was required to log every trade into a terminal on his or her desk; every time they bought a chunk of debt from one of the banks it would be recorded in the computer, which would then organise the necessary transfer of papers. From the displays he could drag up on screen, Harry could see that the trading had been fierce in the few days since he had last been in the office; the firm currently controlled more than forty per cent of Cable Media's debts.

That told him nothing about who now owned it. As far as he could tell from the trading records, there was no sign that the firm had been selling Cable Media debt; it was being bought but not sold. At a rough calculation it meant that more than a billion of the debt had been taken on to its books; Gregson, he knew, did not have that kind of money so the ownership had to be passed on somewhere. His guess was that Turevul Trading was taking on the liabilities. The proof had to be somewhere in the system. 'I'll just have to go deeper into the records,' he said to Julia. 'It must be in here somewhere.'

'Keep searching,' she encouraged. 'You'll find it eventually.'

He started tracking through the back office records, sorting his way through layers of client accounts, error accounts, trading accounts and ledger reconciliations. So far as he could tell, the ownership of Cable Media debt was invariably transferred to a nominee account, identified just by a number: 0024810. A couple of initial attempts to penetrate the security wall failed; each time he requested details of ownership of the account, a message flashed up on the screen: 'Access denied. Please refer to system supervisor.' Harry thought for a moment. There had to be a way through. A hacker would have no trouble he decided. But he was no expert; computers had never interested him very much.

Keep it simple, he told himself. Computers are dumb creatures.

He logged off from the system, closing down the connection. Rebooting the machine, he logged in again, this time keying in Gregson's name; he must have access to the ownership file, he figured. 'Password', flashed up a message on the screen. His mind was a blank; there was, he realised, almost no way of knowing what Gregson's password might be.

'Go back,' said Julia, leaning over his shoulder.

He turned to face her. 'You know something about hacking?'

Julia shrugged. 'A couple of classes at the consultancy,' she replied. 'Not much, but this is a simple trick that might just work.' Her fingers started running across the keyboard. 'If you come out of Windows and back into the DOS system you can search the words most commonly used,' she continued. 'Discard the obvious words and the password is usually in the top ten.' She waited while the commands she had fed into the machine were processed. On the modem, Harry could see a series of small red lights flashing, as the information was relayed down the line and the answers

303

came back through the system. A list of words started to scroll up on the screen: 'And, if, but, is, no, because, debt, this, trade, yes, bonus, equity, you, will, my, never, can, casino, their, before . . .'

'Which do you think?' asked Julia.

'No question,' answered Harry. 'Casino. The guy loves gambling.' He turned to the screen, switched back into Windows and went into Gregson's system. When the password request flashed up, he tapped 'casino' into the modem and pressed execute. It took only moments for the machine to digest the data, but to Harry the time stretched into hours; if this did not work he had no idea what would. When he saw Gregson's system start to open, he slapped his hand against the machine in relief. 'I think I'm through,' he said, his voice touched with excitement.

Julia stood by his shoulder, peering down at the small laptop, while Harry scrolled through the pages displayed on the screen. He clicked forward, working his way towards the nominee account that was holding the debt in Cable Media. 'Detail transactions,' he commanded. A series of numbers flashed up on to the screen. Both Harry and Julia leant forward, their eyes squinting at the pixels before them.

'Gotcha,' whispered Harry under his breath.

The page they had discovered listed the holdings of the debt. Hundreds of transactions were recorded, one for each significant trade. The first column of each display showed the amount of debt that was bought, and against each one was a record of a debit drawn on one of several offshore bank accounts. In the third column of the display the ultimate owner of the debt was recorded; in each case it stated simply Turevul Trading. There was no question the company had, over the course of the past few weeks, acquired several billion pounds' worth of debt in Cable Media. 'I knew it,' said

Harry. 'That's the proof. They're trying to take control of the company.'

'But why?' asked Julia.

'Same old story,' said Harry with a shrug. 'Money and power. Mostly power, I suppose. After all, both of them already have plenty of money.

Richard Gregson was getting nervous. The traders spread out across the dealing floor could tell from the mistimed swagger in his step that something was up; his shoulders were hunched and the usual menacing smile that lit up his thickset features had been replaced by a ferocious grimace. A couple of them commented on it as he walked by. There was no particular reason for his mood to have swung: no disasters on the trading floor, no bad trades crashing through the system. Everything seemed to be going fine. Their positions were squared. No one was losing any money, and the trade in Cable Media was still a roaring success.

'Where the fuck is Lamb?' asked Gregson when he arrived at the centre of the room.

'Nobody has seen him for a couple of days,' answered Terry Semple, one of the older traders on the floor and one of the few who felt confident enough about his prospects elsewhere to treat Gregson's wayward moods with something approaching the contempt his colleagues felt they deserved. 'Not since the beginning of the week.'

'Then who the fuck has been examining the records of our trades in Cable Media?' demanded Gregson.

A nervous silence slithered through the room; dealers glanced down at their phones, but for the moment thought better of answering them. A few looked anxiously at their screens. They all knew they were meant to record every trade on the computer, a duty they took seriously, but they also knew they were not supposed to examine any of the records. The instructions were quite clear. Only senior executives had access to those. Any attempt to peer into the entrails of the system would be met with instant dismissal. Plenty of misdemeanours were tolerated within the company, but snooping was not among them. 'Nobody would do that, boss,' replied Semple. 'You know that.'

'If I find a single person here guilty of a breach of trust I will do three things,' Gregson snarled. 'One, I will sack you. Two, I will make sure you never work in the markets again. Three, I will fuck your wives, girl-friends, or daughters and possibly all three, maybe at the same time. Now get the fuck back to work.'

He turned and strode back across the floor, leaving a huddle of terrorised staff in his wake. Angrily he climbed the stairs to his office, slamming the door behind him. He grabbed the phone from his desk and put through a call to Haverstone. This intrusion had made him nervous. Having Lamb on the outside made him nervous. And having a deadline less than twenty-four hours away made him nervous. The deal was drawing to a close and it was time to finish it off. Any loose ends were bad for his blood pressure and needed to be shut down. Immediately. 'Someone's been looking at our records,' he barked into the phone as soon as he heard Haverstone's voice on the line.

There was a pause, slow and calculating, during which Gregson could feel the tension rising. 'Who?' asked Haverstone.

'How the fuck should I know?' asked Gregson. 'My guess is Lamb. That boy is trouble. I don't think we should ever have involved him in our plans.'

'He was too perfect to miss,' said Haverstone. 'After all, once he started writing critical research on the company, drafting him into the debt dealing operation was too good an opportunity to pass up. This thing

306

would never have gone so smoothly without his help. He has, however, outlived his usefulness.'

'More like a crab than a pawn,' snapped Gregson. 'He bites back.'

Haverstone laughed softly. 'Whatever,' he said. 'He is still a very small creature in a wide and dangerous sea. Don't worry. He is being dealt with. I don't think he will be around to trouble us much longer.'

'Just make sure he isn't. And remember, if anything goes wrong with this gig, both us are going down together. Big time.'

Haverstone replaced the receiver and glanced up briefly at the bank of television screens; he found the soft lights of the cathode-ray tubes strangely reassuring and sometimes switched off all the others so he could rest in their warm, comforting glow. If Lamb had been studying the records of the holdings of Cable Media debt that indeed could be worrying. But, he felt sure, there was nothing he need fear; the boy might collect some damaging information, but there would be no way he could ever use it. Chung would see to that.

He put through a call to the Korean, still hunkered down in the bunker, studying the satellite images and wondering why his prey had eluded him. 'It seems Lamb has been trying to access the records over at Gregson's firm,' he said softly. 'He needs to be stopped.'

Chung nodded into the receiver. 'We might be able to trace the call,' he suggested.

'Then do it.'

To Harry it seemed he had been surfing for hours now, and his eyes were starting to feel the strain. The Netscape display had been held on to his screen continuously and the effort of waiting for the machine to crunch through the endless commands he was feeding it was getting on his nerves. Be patient, he told himself. The answer must be in there somewhere. But where? By comparison, a needle in a haystack would have been easier to find.

On reflection, he could not quite understand how it had taken him so long to make his move. That morning he had slipped outside to the stations forecourt, still watching nervously for anyone who might be following him. He approached the same man he had spoken to yesterday and this time offered him twenty quid.

The call took Alan Broat by surprise. The tramp explained, in his slurred speech, that he was calling on behalf of Harry Lamb and that he needed more information on the last call Sir Ian Strang had made. Desperately. Was the call made to the office? he asked.

Broat had replied that it was; he often worked late and that evening had been no different. So might the call be taped? the beggar had asked, after taking instructions from Harry. Probably, Broat had replied. All the calls into the office were. It was standard practice in the City now to tape all the phone traffic. Whether the tapes would still be in the system he really had no idea.

Harry whispered a short sentence into the tramp's ear. 'Lamb needs to listen to the tape and he is ready to trade some valuable information,' the man hissed into the phone.

At his side, Harry waited impatiently for the answer; fund managers were suckers for inside information and he was betting Broat would tumble for the trick. Okay, came the reply. Broat said he would see if the tape could be retrieved and suggested they call back one of the technicians in the compliance department in half an hour. 'Make sure Lamb remembers the tip,' he added.

Getting the tramp to the phone again cost another tenner, but Harry knew it was well worth it. The

308

technician said they had located the tape and could play it back to him. Harry had taken the receiver and cupped it close to his ear. He could hear Sir Ian explain to Broat that he felt Haverstone was getting out of control at Cable Media and that he was looking for support among the shareholders to restructure the board. They had discussed the situation for a few minutes and Broat had said he would be happy to listen to a full explanation next week. It was the last sentence that captured Harry's attention. 'If anything happens to me, I suggest you look up a website I have recorded,' Sir Ian explained. 'But of course, you'd have to be up on your mythology to find it. Still, I'll see you next week.'

The more Harry thought about it, the more it made sense. If you want to record a message somewhere, to put it in a place where it could be found and yet remain secret, and where it would be virtually impossible to destroy, what better solution than to create a website? No one would find it unless they were looking for it and had been told where it could be found. And unless they located the server on which it was stored there was no way of wiping it. It was a perfect hiding place.

All he had to do now was find it.

'He definitely said you had to know your Greek mythology to find it,' said Harry, the words muttered almost under his breath, as if he were not expecting a reply.

'Zeus, Hercules,' said Julia. 'Have you tried those?'

'Endless websites with those words in them, but none of them is relevant,' replied Harry.

'Then think more rationally. Haverstone, Strang, Cable Media, are there any mythological connections there?'

Harry paused briefly. 'Argus,' he replied. 'Could that be it?'

'I thought it was a local newspaper title,' said Julia. 'The *Shropshire Argus* and so on.'

Harry shook his head. 'I wish I'd paid more attention during my Greek classes at school. I think it might be some sort of mythological creature. We need a dictionary.'

Both of them glanced around the dim, cold room, before Julia pointed back at the computer. 'You'll find one on the web.'

Of course, thought Harry. He turned back to the screen, calling up a search engine, instructing it to look for sites on mythology. Within minutes he had found a dictionary. 'Argus', he tapped into the machine, pressing the mouse on the word as soon as a list of hyperlinks downloaded onto his machine. He began reading the words from the screen. 'A creature from Greek mythology with a thousand eyes.'

'There are a lot of eyes following us,' said Julia with a shrug.

It was past lunch-time and both of them were feeling hungry; the chocolate bars they had been living on had already made Harry feel nauseous. Julia volunteered to collect some sandwiches from one of the shops outside the station. 'We need to eat,' she told Harry. 'We can't go on like this without some proper nourishment. I'm sure I can make it a dozen yards to a café without anyone seeing me.'

Harry was reluctantly forced to concede the point. They desperately needed the food; it was a day and a half since he had eaten anything more substantial than a chocolate bar and the thought of another made him feel sick inside. 'Be careful,' he warned her. 'Try not to look at anyone.'

He returned to the screen, trying to clear his mind and concentrate on the immediate problem. Okay, he told himself, the Argus was a mythical creature, so that must have been what Strang was talking about. Know your mythology, he had said. He turned back to the dictionary, looking for more details. A hyperlink took him to another page. Argus, it transpired, was a giant with a thousand eyes. Zeus had turned his beloved Io into a heifer to protect her from the goddess Hera and it was Argus's task to defend her. Hermes, the god of riches and trade, killed Argus, rescued Io and returned her to Zeus. Hermes, thought Harry to himself, the slayer of Argus.

He tried www.hermes.com but only found the home page of the scarf manufacturer. Something else, he told himself. He tried www.hermestrang.com. This time, after a search lasting more than a minute, a single home page listing appeared on the screen. He clicked on the link and waited for the connection to be made.

'Welcome to the Home Page of Sir Ian Strang,' flashed up a message on the screen. 'If you wish to continue, please press enter.'

Harry moved the mouse downwards, clicking on the flashing sign. He could hear the hard drive crunching through the connections as he did so and it seemed to take an age for the page to be downloaded, although in reality it was just a couple of minutes. A Netscape icon flashed up, asking if the system had the capacity to accept real-time video. A video? thought Harry to himself. He had not expected that. Yes, he told the machine, hoping the capacity on his laptop was large enough to deal with the footage. He waited nervously while the clip downloaded itself, his pulse quickening as he did so.

Within seconds, the screen flashed on to a pale background and a fresh image appeared. Harry leant back, listening in amazement as the message reeled forward. For a moment, he sat transfixed, rooted to the spot, amazed and horrified by what the dead man had to say. As the lecture rolled forward, he could feel a sense of terror rising through his chest while the revelations poured forth. Suddenly, everything clicked into place. 'Oh, my God,' he muttered under his breath. His first thought was for Julia and for her safety. It was madness, he now realised, for her to go outside at all. Even for a few yards. They could see everything.

The computer still switched on, the screen glowing in the dim light, he fled from the room. Running along the platform, he could feel his legs beginning to shake beneath him. One thought pounded through his head, relentless and incessant: if they were not safe here, where would they be safe?

Harry could see her in the distance, two bags tucked beneath her elbows. He rushed towards her, taking her in his arms; he could not imagine what he might be protecting her from, nor what use he might be, but the urge to cradle her was overwhelming. 'Thank God you're all right,' he said, trying to catch his breath as the words tumbled from his mouth.

'Don't worry,' she said, her tone betraying her surprise at how agitated he was. 'Nobody saw me. We're quite safe.'

Harry shook his head furiously. 'Nothing is safe,' he said hurriedly.

23

The icon flashed up brightly on the screen, flickering in the dim lights but remaining silent and inert; it had nothing to announce itself but a small grey box of pixels, surrounded by a black border. 'Target identified,' it read.

Lykanov did not notice it at first. He had wandered off to the Gents, stopping on the way back for a quiet smoke in the far corner of the room. The constant glow of the monitors had given him a headache more than a day ago, but after thirty-six hours of trying to locate his prey the tension had eased; he had no idea where they might be and no particular expectation of finding them any time soon. 'Shit,' he muttered under his breath, as the icon on the screen captured his attention. He was already wondering how long it had been there and how much time might have been lost by his failure to catch the message immediately.

He punched a series of commands into the computer, instructing it to bring up its latest set of images, at the same time putting a call through to Chung. By the time the pictures appeared, the Korean was already at his side, peering hungrily into the screen. 'They are starting to make mistakes,' Chung whispered softly.

The image was not well defined. To the naked eye, Lykanov realised, it would look like little more than the usual crowd of stressed office workers walking through a busy street. It would be hard even for someone in the thick of the crowd to identify the person they were looking for. For someone thousands of feet above the scene, it would be impossible. That was the beauty of mechanised surveillance. It could locate targets that would always evade human observation.

Amid the sea of figures, he thought he could recognise a head of long brown hair, but it could belong to countless thousands of women in London. The computer, Lykanov knew, was way ahead of him. He instructed the machine to scan and zoom, and sat back in his leather chair while the image started to enlarge itself before his eyes. Slowly, through the crowd, she began to emerge on the terminal. Within less than two minutes, the face of a woman was clearly visible on the screen.

'That's her,' said Chung, his tone rising and a note of triumph entering his voice. 'Where is this and how long ago?'

Lykanov started tapping commands into his keyboard. A panel in the corner of the screen drew a map of London, a flashing red circle identifying the target's location as the small pedestrian street running up from Embankment tube station to Charing Cross. In a corner of the panel the time read 14:22, about half an hour ago.

'Can we get any more pictures?' asked Chung.

Lykanov shook his head. 'It takes the satellite three minutes to do a scan of the inner London area, so it would only pick her up if she were still on the street three minutes later. Obviously she had gone by then. From the direction she is facing, I would say she is heading into the subway. That would explain why we are not picking up any more images. If they are 'underground we would not be able to detect them.'

'Underground, yes,' repeated Chung. 'That would explain it. How much progress are we making on tracing that phone call?'

Lykanov walked across to a second computer and checked a display on the monitor. He had been informed earlier that day that his employers wanted to locate the source of a single call into a firm in London made earlier that day. It was a difficult task, but, he suspected, not impossible. All electronic exchanges keep sophisticated records of calls made, mainly for providing itemised bills for customers, a relatively recent innovation in telecoms technology which had made the work of electronic snoopers a lot easier. Tracing a call backwards depended on whether the correct codes had been captured; if they had, it was simply a matter of the computer performing a few hundred million searches to find the location. 'We have a trace,' he announced, after looking at the display.

On the screen, eleven digits were displayed. 'Where is that?' asked Chung, looking down at the screen.

A series of commands tapped into the keyboard would yield the answer within seconds; finding a location for a number was a simple matter of checking through the main telecoms computers. An address flashed up on the screen. 'Customer: London Transport. Location: Jubilee Line extension, Embankment station, traffic control room.'

Chung turned round from the screen, pacing away from Lykanov. 'They are hiding underground,' he muttered. 'Quite smart.'

'It is almost as if they knew we were tracking them from the sky,' said Lykanov.

'Perhaps, perhaps not,' answered Chung. 'I suspect not. If they knew that the woman would not have stepped outside. No, I think it was a lucky choice on their part. And their luck has just started to run out.' He paced back towards the Russian, resting an arm on his shoulder. 'Keep the satellites trained on the central London area and see if you can find a way of making sure it checks every entrance to a tube station,' he said. He touched the revolver in his breast pocket, feeling reassured by the presence of eight ounces of cold, hard steel next to his chest. 'Make sure you contact me as soon as you get another trace.'

Lykanov lit another cigarette while he waited for the Korean to leave the room; he took long, slow drags, letting the nicotine do his thinking for him. In the distance, he could hear the steel door snap shut and the muffled tread of another man's shoe leather against metal steps. He turned back towards the screen. Underground, he thought to himself. They had obviously sensed they were being tracked and had taken the one escape route still open to them: getting clear out of sight of the sky. Clever, he decided. It was just a shame they had not realised the phone call they had made could be traced and that it was madness to step outside, even for a few brief seconds.

On his computer, he dialled into the Citibank account set up in his name in the Cayman Islands. He scrolled down to the balance statement. The account was empty. The money, as he had instructed, had now been spirited away; it was beyond the reach of his employers. It was his and his alone. I am a wealthy man, he reflected. Perhaps I can be choosier about whom I work for. Perhaps even start working for myself.

Lykanov looked back down at the screen. He could tell from the telecoms codes displayed on the computer that it had not located a voice call; it had been made by a computer to another computer, probably, he figured, via an Internet connection. He asked the computer to locate an e-mail address for the target and sat back, lighting another Marlboro while the machine searched for an answer. The cigarette was no more than half smoked by the time the e-mail address appeared on the screen.

Lykanov cast his eyes over the bunker, allowing his thoughts to drift. The power his employers were attempting to accumulate was worse than anything he had witnessed in his homeland, even during the darkest and most corrupt days of the old regime; an absolute and total contempt for privacy that even the KGB might have considered undignified. The world did not need any more of their sort and he, Lykanov decided, was tiring of spending his life in the service of petty tyrants. I am my own man, he thought to himself. With my own money in the bank. I may do as I please. Lighting yet another cigarette, he looked up again at the e-mail address and started running his fingers gently across the keyboard.

Harry took Julia roughly by the arm and started steering her back towards the tube station. He knew it had been a mistake to allow her to step outside for even a couple of minutes and yet, he reflected, neither of them could have been expected to know how much of a mistake. Until now, they could not have dreamt just how powerful were the forces they were trying to fight.

As they rode down the escalator, he explained what he had discovered. Julia soaked up the information impassively; she had heard so much bad news over the past few days that she was no longer sure anything could have much impact upon her. I don't think I can do this any more, she told herself, the phrase echoing around her mind, repeating itself, like a tape caught in a loop.

He could tell from the look in her eye she was badly shaken; there was a tremble in her lips and a distant, haunted expression on her face. She remained perfectly silent and, for the moment, Harry could think of nothing to say to her. No words of reassurance or comfort came easily to mind. It was, he realised, no use pretending. Their predicament was truly horrible.

Together they went in silence through the slim doorway and down into the empty tunnel. From the noise of the station, they moved swiftly into a place of eerie stillness; the quiet of the platform contrasted sharply with the world they had left behind. Harry could hear every step his feet made against the concrete, painfully aware how loudly he was advertising his approach to anyone who might be nearby.

The door to the small room on the unused platform was still slightly ajar, as Harry had left it. He approached it carefully, anxious to discover whether they had been found yet, but seeing nothing. Everything was as before. For a few minutes, at least, they were safe. 'Get everything together,' said Harry. 'I don't think we should hang around.'

Without a word, Julia started putting the disks into their carrier bag and was about to unplug the computer when she noticed the icon flashing on the screen. 'We have a message, Harry,' she whispered, her voice so low she could hardly hear it herself.

He looked across at her. 'A message,' he repeated.

Julia pointed down at the computer. The icon was unmistakable and so was the small text box in the right-hand corner of the screen. 'Message pending,' it read.

'So they've found us,' said Harry, looking around, his ears straining for the sound of feet moving along the platform.

'Read it,' said Julia.

Harry braced himself. Part of him wanted to discover what it said. Another part simply wanted to escape, to find some other place where they might be safe for a few hours. Somewhere where nobody was watching them, where, for a little while at least, they could take their lives back. Looking down at the inert screen, his curiosity took control. Almost involuntarily his hand moved down to the mouse, clicking on the icon that would bring the message up on to the screen.

The text box sprang into view, a narrow window, shaded by a pale-blue border. Julia leant forward, resting her arms on Harry's shoulders, to catch a glimpse of the words. 'If I am blind, I cannot see,' they read. 'If I am deaf, I cannot hear. Good luck. The engineer.'

'What d'you think it means?' asked Harry.

'I think it might mean we have a friend on the other side, or at least a well-wisher.'

'Do we reply?' asked Harry.

'I don't see why not,' she answered. 'We don't have anything going for us. Take a chance.'

She was right, Harry decided. You took your luck where you found it. Peering at the screen, he pulled down the reply box with the mouse and started tapping into the keyboard. 'How can you be blinded?' he wrote. 'And how can you be deafened?'

Three miles away, Lykanov glanced down at his screen, noting the message that was waiting for him. He was surprised the prey had responded so quickly. But then, he decided, there was a sort of community among people who, for one reason or another, found themselves forced to spend their lives underground.

How can I be blinded and how can I be deafened, he wondered? He lit another cigarette and thought for a few seconds. It was an interesting technical question. Of that there could be little doubt.

The few lights along the dark and empty platform were half illuminated and cast only a pale, sickly glow in the bare corridor. Chung trod cautiously along the concrete

319

stretching beneath him, conscious of the thin echo of his shuffling feet. If his prey were here he wanted to make sure they were not alerted to his presence. It was always better if an attack had the element of surprise. Particularly when you were going in for the kill.

His eyes rooted along the length of the platform, attempting to discover where his target might be located. Torchlight would have been useful, but risked revealing his approach. Instead, he scoured the corridor, trying to locate any possible hiding place. The phone trace had pin-pointed this part of the tube network, but it was impossible to find any kind of map that would tell him precisely where they might be. He would just have to hunt them out himself.

It was clear there was nowhere suitable on the platform and his pace quickened slightly. Perhaps among the corridors towards the back. On reaching the end, Chung turned into a small connecting corridor. To his right he could see a little glass-fronted room, shrouded in darkness. From his pocket he quietly withdrew a gun and held it lightly in his fist. He did not suspect they were armed, but Harry was a decent-sized man; he was not a trained fighter, but if his life depended upon it he would fight, and fight hard. Even amateurs, Chung knew from past experience, could find unexpected strength when it came to a decisive struggle.

He could hear no sounds inside and by the time he slid the door open he was already starting to doubt whether they were there. His eyes moved around the small, darkened room. On the floor he could see some Coke cans and some chocolate bar wrappers. To one corner were some flattened cardboard boxes, crushed, as though people had been sleeping on them. In the centre of the floor a rat nibbled on the remains of some food. He knelt on the cold concrete floor, noticing the rat scampering away as he did so. Chung pressed his hand against one of the cardboard boxes, feeling the traces of warmth left on its surface. There could be little doubt someone had been very recently here. He sniffed the air. If it had been a tramp, there would be the stale smell of alcohol, but he could detect nothing. It was them, he decided. It had to be.

He swept his torch around the tiny room, watching the pale shadows flicker across the walls. Quietly, his feet no more than shuffling, he stepped back out on to the platform, casting his light up and down the tunnel. To his right, towards the entrance, he could dimly hear the rattle of a train along the tracks. Not that way, he thought to himself. If you wanted to escape through the tunnels you would not walk towards the trains.

He drew a coin from his pocket, throwing it down on to the tracks. It fell on the metal rail and bounced harmlessly to the ground below. No sparks, noticed Chung. The track had been built, but it had not yet been electrified. For now, it would be safe to walk through the tunnel. He lowered himself from the platform. Holding his torch firmly in his left hand, leaving his right hand free to reach for his pistol, Chung started walking down the length of the track. He took short and careful steps, hoping to quieten the sound of his feet against the metal. Looking up ahead, he could see the tunnel stretching before him and, as he approached the darkness, he flicked off the torch, replacing it in his pocket. Better to approach my prey without light, he decided. There is no point in letting them know I am here.

Harry's eyes could not cope with the darkness. However hard he stretched and strained his pupils, it was impossible to see further than a couple of feet ahead and to tell where she might have gone. 'Julia,' he said, raising his voice above a whisper for the first time. 'Where are you?'

She had left no more than ten minutes earlier. Why she had chosen that moment to crack he couldn't say. He supposed he should have seen it coming. The nights spent down in the tunnel had started to tell upon her nerves and he had sensed all along she was struggling to control her fright. Struggling too much, he reflected. Sometimes you had to allow your emotions some space, let your fears speak, but Julia was not a woman who permitted herself that kind of freedom. She was too anxious to maintain the impression of having everything under control.

It was only when they had received the reply from the man who called himself the engineer that she had slipped. 'I have to get out of here,' she had snapped at him suddenly, her eyes alight with a mixture of anxiety and anger. 'I've seen enough.' His response, Harry realised now, was wrong, but he too was hanging on to an emotional cliff's edge, barely able to keep his own head together. When she had turned on her heels and started stalking out along the platform, then down on to the tracks, he had remained silent, just watching her as she left.

There was no reply to his question. He heard the words echoing through the tunnel, repeated five, six, then seven times, but though his ears were strained there was only an eerie silence. The darkness engulfed him and the chill of the whistling wind was beginning to tense his muscles. He was wondering whether to speak again, trying to form a sentence in his mind, when, in the distance, he heard a faint noise. It was a painful, unnatural sound; more of a choke than a sob, someone trying to hold back their tears. Harry began edging forward along the tracks, allowing his ears to guide him, not wanting to speak until he drew closer. Inwardly, he cursed the darkness; he was not used to guiding himself by sound alone and his progress was pitifully slow.

'Julia,' Harry said again, softening his voice to muffle the echo.

'Here,' he heard her say.

The voice was coming from a distance, how far he couldn't say. The tone was cracked and throaty, and although he could not see her he could sense the tears in her eyes. Slowly, he crept back along the track. He placed his hands against the wall, hoping that it would guide him closer to her, feeling its dampness against his palms. Beneath his feet, he could hear a tiny rustling movement. Mice or rats, he supposed.

The hand appeared to come from nowhere. Harry had been edging his way through the darkness, wondering if he had been distracted by an echo, when her fingers suddenly reached out in front of him. He recoiled, as if by instinct, slipping back. Then, realising it was Julia, he slipped his hand into hers, drawing her towards him, cradling her in his arms. Her face was damp, the tears still wet on her cheek, and he ran his fingers through her hair. 'Are you okay?' he asked.

Julia swallowed, as though trying to stifle her feelings. He could feel her head nodding in his arms. 'I just lost it, that's all,' she said slowly. 'I don't think I can take this much longer.'

Chung strained his ears, hoping to catch the sounds of voices carried by the wind blowing through the tunnel. At first it was no more than a few muffled noises of uncertain origin and direction. He paced forward and the noise became clearer. A man, that much he could tell. And, unless he was mistaken, one of the words he had caught was 'Julia'. It was them, he decided. There could be no doubt.

Inwardly Chung cursed himself for not having brought along some night vision goggles. Whispers of light fell through the tunnel, but it was impossible to discern anything more than the occasional shadow on the wall. Slowly, he crept forward, keeping close to the wall, feeling his way through the blackness. How far this strip lasted he could not be sure. Until the next station, he supposed. Half a mile, or a mile perhaps. It mattered little. He would find them.

'Ssh,' whispered Harry in Julia's ear. He kept his voice as low as possible, no more than breathing level. He could tell her face had frozen and from the tensing of her muscles that she was frightened. 'I think I heard something.'

Harry listened to the wind, unsure whether the noise he had detected was just the breeze, a group of rats, or the tread of a foot against the metal rails. Take no chances, he told himself. Assume it's them and plan accordingly.

He looked up ahead. There was no sign of a light at the end of the tunnel. How far it might be to the next station he had no way of knowing. A mile, perhaps. Even then, it might just be an empty shell. An abandoned, deserted place, from which the workmen had moved on. A perfect killing ground, he reflected grimly. 'I think we should go back,' he whispered to Julia. 'It's our best chance.'

Was that a voice? wondered Chung. Or just the whistling of the wind? It was impossible to tell. But if he were inclined to make a bet, he would wager it was the former. He edged forward, holding the torch in his hand. Get as close as possible, he decided, then switch the thing on and he would have them in his sights.

There was a chill in the air and he pulled the collar of his coat up around his neck. He could smell the mixture of concrete and machine oil filtering through the tunnel. The ground underneath felt hard and cold and, softly though he was walking, he was aware of the tread of his feet against the rails. His eyes scanned the wall, looking for any shadows, but he could see nothing. And his ears listened to the movement of the air, but he could hear nothing.

By counting his paces, Chung calculated he might have advanced half a kilometre down the tunnel, perhaps a third of the way towards the next station. He walked forward, measuring each pace as he did so. At five hundred metres, he decided, he would break cover and use the torch. After all, they could not escape from here and he might miss them in the darkness.

Harry felt his way along the wall, holding Julia's hand as he did so. It was damp and cold to the touch. His pulse began racing as he heard the regular tread of the feet along the rails draw closer. There could be no doubt now, he realised. It was a person, and whoever it was would be looking for them.

Harry fought to curb the overwhelming instinct to turn and run. His ears straining into the silence, he felt his way further along the wall. The alcove was no more than a dip. A space for electricity fittings, Harry supposed. Whatever. It would do for now. He slipped into it, pulling Julia up behind him, holding her tight to his chest. He put a hand over her mouth.

The darkness inside the alcove was complete; an enveloping, womb-like blackness from which there could be no escape. The sound of the breath escaping from his nostrils ricocheted around Harry's ears. He could feel Julia's heartbeat thudding throughout her entire body and closed his eyes in a silent prayer.

The steps in the tunnel grew louder. Harry stayed perfectly still, slowing his breathing and clutching Julia closer to his chest. They both were holding their breath, too afraid to move or even to exhale.

Harry's mind was racing. How many were there. Could he and Julia be spotted? The footsteps stopped. Whoever was out there could only be a few feet away on the other side of the tunnel. The silence stretched on and on, becoming suffocating in its intensity. Just when he was sure he could not bear the tension any longer, the footsteps continued, moving down the tunnel. Harry listened and counted. If each pace was a foot, then he should allow a couple of hundred of them before he started to make his way back to the station. It was a gamble they had no choice but to take. 'Come,' he whispered to Julia eventually. 'Let's go.'

Far enough, thought Chung to himself. There was too much risk of missing them in the dark. He moved to the middle of the tracks, and clicked the switch on his torch. The light beamed out, suddenly illuminating the surroundings. Chung glanced instantly around, scanning the walls as far as he could see. There was no sign of them. 'I know you are here,' he shouted, allowing the words to echo around him. Chung paused, listening to the same words five times as the sound bounced off the enclosed walls. 'Don't think you can escape,' he yelled.

He waited, listening to the echo, hoping to hear his prey. Perhaps they would make some sound that would betray their location. 'Come and confront me now, it is your best chance,' he went on. 'You might be able to save yourself, but you cannot save your daughter. I have her hospital staked out. We have to deal with each other sooner or later. It might as well be now.'

Somewhere behind him, Chung fancied he could hear the sound of thudding footsteps along the rails. They were running, he realised. How far away they were he could not tell. Two hundred yards perhaps. No more. Thrusting the torch ahead of him, he started to run back towards the station.

24

John Mitchell had been relieved to hear from his sister. She called through to his office at just after three thirty, saying she had received a message from a man telling him to call Julia at four and leaving a number. No, she said, he did not sound like a middle-class Londoner – he had a Scottish accent and sounded quite drunk.

It was a long time since he had heard from Julia and just to know that she was still alive was something; he had hardly slept the night before, knowing she was on the run. Of course, Julia had to take her own share of the blame; she was an intelligent woman and she could have been more careful. She should have stopped investigating the case when he told her to. Police work was like that sometimes. It was wise to take orders even when they did not make much sense. But Julia was not to know that. She was fresh and keen and inexperienced, and it was his fault for putting her on the case in the first place. She was his responsibility and he would do whatever he could to help, no matter what the cost.

He stepped out of the building at ten to four and walked down the street to a call box. Instinct told him this was not a call he should make from the office. He doubted that his telephone was being monitored, but experience had told him it was always best to take precautions. They were up against strange and powerful forces, that much was certain, and he did not want to take any chances.

The phone rang four times before it was answered. He recognised Julia's voice at once. 'Thank God you're safe,' he said. 'Is everything okay?'

'Could be better,' she said.

'Have you made any progress?' he asked.

'Some,' she replied. 'I think we know what's going on and how to stop it.'

'Tell me about it,' said Mitchell. He was curious, but at the same time impressed; for a young woman in a terrible situation the calm and composure in her voice indicated a resolution and determination he would not have thought possible. She was a class act, yet he suspected that there was an element of bravura in her performance; there were vulnerabilities there, he felt sure, that she did not feel confident enough to admit. It was as if she felt that at any sign of weakness she would crack completely. A real professional would not be so reserved about admitting her fears.

'I can't.' Her voice was flat. 'Not on the phone. It's too dangerous.'

'I'm in a call box,' said Mitchell. 'I can't be sure my phone isn't tapped, but this should be secure. Nobody can tap every phone in London.'

Julia hesitated before replying. 'Right now, I'm not confident any form of communication at all is safe,' she said. 'You said you would do what you could to help. Fine. If you want to live up to that promise you have to play it my way or not at all.'

'Okay,' said Mitchell. 'Just tell me what you want.'

'Not yet,' said Julia. 'Call this number at four thirty. A man will answer the phone. We'll be relying on you, so try to do everything we ask.'

The line was dead, but Mitchell could not help holding on to the receiver for a few more seconds after she cut him off. He would certainly follow whatever instructions he was given; he owed her that much. He glanced at his watch. It was now four fifteen. He wandered off in the direction of a coffee bar, preparing to sit out the few minutes until he could call her again. He was intrigued to discover what she wanted, but also anxious. Whatever it was, she appeared to be playing a game way above her head.

Julia turned towards Harry. 'Okay,' she said. 'The call is made. Where do we go now?'

Harry cast his eyes up and down the length of the platform, scanning the faces of the people waiting for the next train. They looked innocent enough. Commuters and tourists, most of them just impatient for their train to arrive. But it was impossible to say for sure. Any one of them could be watching. 'We move quickly to the next phone box,' he answered. 'It won't be too long before they trace that call.'

Since escaping from the tunnel, both he and Julia had a better idea of the risks they were running. Nothing, he realised now, could be left to chance. Nor could he assume any movement they made would not be detected.

As soon as he had heard the voice behind him in the tunnel and seen the flash of a torch around the curve, Harry had taken Julia by the arm and started running. They covered the distance back to the station in just over a minute, clambering desperately up on to the ledge, dashing along the platform, towards the trains. Harry had not wanted to waste time looking back, but he could hear the swift clattering of feet along the rails behind him.

Together, they had rushed down on to the Circle

Line platform. It was crowded and the indicator told them the train was approaching. Harry had scanned the entrance, but could see nothing suspicious. When the train came in, he chose the fullest carriage and stood by the door. As it started to pull away, Harry thought he could see an oriental man move swiftly down the stairs, his eyes darting along the platform. He was certain it was the man who had been chasing him; the first time he had laid eyes upon him, but not, he felt sure, the last.

They had ridden for a couple of stops, before switching lines, doubling back on their tracks and making their way to Leicester Square station, where Harry had suggested Julia should call Mitchell. It would be traced, for sure, but contact had to be established. It was the only way of making use of the information the engineer had provided them with.

Once the call was made, they moved straight back down to the platform. Keep moving, Harry told himself again and again. It was their only hope.

The phone rang twice on Malcolm Fielding's desk before he picked it up. A pair of senior executives from the bank's Hong Kong subsidiary were in his office, running through their plans for the Asia-Pacific region for the coming year. He had told his secretary he did not want to be disturbed for the next twenty minutes, but this call was coming through on his direct line, a number known only to a very few of the most senior people within the bank, all of whom had strict instructions only to use it in an emergency. He apologised for the interruption before taking the call.

'I'm calling for Harry Lamb,' said a voice on the line. 'He can't speak to you himself, so you'll have to listen to me.'

The man's voice sounded rough and unsteady, not the sort of person Fielding was used to dealing with.

'How do I know you are speaking for him?' he asked.

There was a pause, lasting half a minute or so, before the man returned with a precise description of their meeting the previous evening. Okay, thought Fielding. Just the two of us were there and no one else could have those details. 'Fine,' he answered. 'What does Mr Lamb want to tell me?'

'First a question,' said the voice. 'Is the creditors meeting still scheduled for noon tomorrow?'

'Yes,' replied Fielding. 'No change.'

'Then Mr Lamb would like to be there to make a presentation that will answer all your questions about the deal. Is that okay?'

'Can he tell me what he will say?'

There was a pause before the man replied. 'No, not now. He says it's too dangerous. Everything will be made clear tomorrow at noon.'

Fielding thought for a moment. He had a choice, he figured, and no more than a couple of seconds to make up his mind. 'Tell him he is welcome to come along and make his presentation,' he said. 'I will make arrangements with security for him to be admitted to the head office.'

'One more thing,' said the man.

'What?' asked Fielding nervously.

'Make sure you have your best security people close at hand.'

Fielding listened as the phone clicked dead and looked up anxiously at the two men waiting to continue their talk about the bank's loan book among the developing Pacific economies. Suddenly, Fielding found he had lost interest. His mind was still fuddled and his stomach churning. He took a sip of tea and tried to calm himself. It was one of those split-second judgements when you had to decide instantly what to do and could rely on little more than the instinct of the moment.

If he had said no, he would have had to go along with whatever Gregson and Haverstone were trying to pull. That would be safer, but it was also offensive; he did not trust either man and the thought of them stealing from his bank filled him with revulsion. Alternatively, he could play along with Lamb, let him into the meeting and face what potentially could be one of the most embarrassing gatherings of his life. If he levelled accusations against a man such as Haverstone that could not be proved it could be fatal for the reputation of both him and his bank. It would certainly cost him his job and possibly the bank untold billions in lost business.

He hoped he had done the right thing. He felt that he had, but could not be sure. It was a gamble and it would be eighteen hours before he knew whether it had come off. Eighteen hours in which to wonder what information it was, exactly, that Mr Lamb had. And whether it would prove decisive.

Mitchell checked his watch before making the call; he had chosen a different phone booth this time, just to err on the side of caution. He slipped the phone card into the slot and started tapping out the seven digits Julia had given him earlier.

The phone rang just once before someone picked it up. 'Yes,' said a man's voice.

Mitchell did not recognise the voice and could not place the accent exactly; it might be Scottish, or somewhere around the Borders, but it sounded rough and slurred, as though he had been drinking. 'I was asked to call this number to receive some instructions,' he said.

'Right,' replied the man. 'Two things. There will be a meeting of the creditors of Cable Media at noon tomorrow at the head office of Harrington's Bank in the City. She would like you to be there.'

'Okay,' he answered. That should be easy enough to arrange, thought Mitchell. The SFO had good links with all the major clearing banks and they should not have any objection to him sitting in on a meeting as an observer, so long as he signed the usual confidentiality papers. If there was any trouble, he could always find a way of leaning on them.

'And she wants you to find out how to turn off the electricity on central London for about half an hour or so.'

'What?' asked Mitchell, hardly able to stifle his surprise.

'I'm just relaying what I'm told, mate,' said the man. 'That is what the lady says she wants to know. She says they will probably need to find their way into the computer of the central electricity generating board and flick a few switches. Just find the way to do it and call her back with the information.'

Mitchell thought for a moment. 'Can I speak to her?' he asked.

There was a pause. 'No,' said the man. 'She says not. It's not safe. Either help her like you promised, or not. That's the deal.'

This was madness, Mitchell decided. Whether he could find that information in a short time he had no idea; he did not doubt it was theoretically possible to shut down the power supply, since there were all sorts of potential emergencies when it might be necessary. What he did doubt, however, was that it was a good idea. Whatever it was that Harry and Julia were about to try to pull off, it sounded far too dangerous. Complex plans, in his judgement, were always a mistake. If something could go wrong it would. You could rely on it. 'Tell her I'll try,' he said. 'How can I contact her?'

'Call this number at eight this evening,' replied the man, reeling off another list of seven digits.

'Okay,' said Mitchell. 'Can you tell her something for me? Say that I think this is madness. She should come in, along with Lamb, and leave this to the authorities. Make sure she understands that.'

The man grunted and hung up the receiver. He turned to Harry and Julia, who had been standing anxiously at his side during the conversation. 'He says you shouldn't try it. Says you should give yourselves up to the authorities and let them handle it.'

'No way,' replied Harry. He handed over a fresh ten-pound note to the man, who tucked it into the back of his faded and stained jeans, and collected his copies of the *Big Issue* from the floor of the call box.

'Thanks,' he said. 'And good luck. Whatever the fuck it is you might be doing, I hope you get away with it.'

'Cheers, mate,' said Harry breezily. 'We'll need all the luck we can get.' He pulled Julia to his side, casting anxious glances up and down the tube station, before leading her towards the platform. 'We'd better get out of here,' he said. 'It isn't safe to hang around.'

The phone rang only once before Mitchell heard the sound of the receiver being picked up. Another strange voice answered, and Mitchell told him he needed to speak to his friends. The voice told him he would be passing it over to someone else shortly. Mitchell should talk into the phone and give his instructions. Neither of his friends would speak. It was not safe. When he was finished, he should hang up.

Mitchell suspected the security precautions they were taking were excessive. This was, after all, a payphone speaking to another payphone. It should be impossible to trace the call. 'You can speak now,' said the voice on the line and Mitchell could hear the sound of the receiver being passed across. To whom he did not know.

Finding the information that was required of him had

not been easy. Mitchell had known it was theoretically possible to shut down the power system, but how it might be done he had no idea. Still, he figured one of his contacts within the police would know and he had plenty of old friends within the force. He pretended he was investigating a group of financial terrorists who were blackmailing some banks with threats to shut down their power and so destroy their dealing systems for hours. He needed to know if the threat was credible and whether the blackmailer knew the precise method of switching off the supply. The answer was that it was complex, but possible. Anyone who had access to the right computers and knew the right codes could certainly do it. What codes? Mitchell had asked. The man laughed down the phone and only when Mitchell had convinced him that it was no joke did he get the information he required. More than his fair share of favours had been called in this evening.

He repeated the instructions over the phone, spelling out the exact steps slowly and precisely, making sure the person on the other end of the line had plenty of time to write down the details they needed. Whether it would actually work, he had no idea.

The more he thought about it the more he was mystified by what they might be planning. And the less sure he became that he should be helping them. Still, he reflected, a promise was a promise. He would not forgive himself if he backed out now. 'Good luck,' he said when he had finished detailing the instructions. There was no reply, but he could hear the click as he was cut off. Too dangerous to utter even a single word, Mitchell decided. Well, he would see them soon enough. He might even find out what was going on.

The atmosphere within Haverstone's office was tense and cold. Chung had already read the transcripts

Lykanov had printed out of the system and he knew the implications were worrying. He handed them over to Haverstone with a shrug, as though they meant little, but he knew the man would not be pleased.

Haverstone took the five sheets of A4 paper and started scanning the contents. Over his shoulder, Gregson was reading at the same time, darting through the words. He was trying to imagine the circumstances in which the conversation took place, but was finding it hard to do so. The thought of an old stuffed shirt like Fielding mixing himself up in this kind of drama was incomprehensible. He was having trouble believing this was real. 'Are we sure this is Fielding talking?' asked Haverstone.

From the nervous twitch in his voice, Chung could tell he was simmering, but was trying to preserve his cool. Over several years of working together Chung had never seen the man lose his temper. His fury was just swallowed and internalised. He never relaxed enough to become angry. It was one of many characteristics that made him such edgy, dangerous company. 'Quite certain, sir,' Chung replied.

'But the other speaker? It is not Lamb.'

'No,' said Chung. 'The voice recognition system would have picked it up if it had been. We obtained this from a standard monitor we have been running on Fielding's phone. Otherwise we would have picked it up a lot earlier.'

'And do we know who this other man is?'

Chung shook his head. 'My guess is they are just using someone else to make their calls for them,' he said. 'There is no way the voice recognition system could pick up on that. In fact I am certain. We picked up a trace of the woman earlier today making a call from a phone box, but she told the person she was calling to ring another number later. That would have been when the real conversation took place.'

'Let me get this absolutely straight,' said Gregson, his eyes peering fiercely down at the sheets of paper. 'We spend millions on the best technology available, technology that's meant to enable us to track any phone call made anywhere, and they can just sidestep it by getting someone else to make their calls. Is that what you're telling me?'

Chung nodded softly; it was embarrassing, but there was no choice but to admit it. The system had been outwitted. 'I think that is the case, yes,' he answered.

'So we have no idea what calls Lamb might have been making?' asked Haverstone.

'No,' replied Chung. 'If he is using decoys then he could have been talking to various people and we would not know about it.'

'So this guy and his girl-friend are out on the loose somewhere, getting up to fuck knows what and there's not a single god-damn thing we can do about it?' asked Gregson.

'I don't think the situation is that extreme,' said Chung.

'Do we have any idea where they are?' Gregson wanted to know.

'Some,' answered Chung. 'We managed to trace the call into your computer system and it came from a part of the Underground system.'

'The Underground?' said Haverstone quizzically.

'It appears, sir, that for the last couple of days they have been hiding in one of the newer parts of the Underground. On the line that is currently being built.'

'Smart,' snorted Gregson. 'It should be pretty empty down there. And it's about the only place in London where there's not a single fucking chance in a million of being spotted by a satellite.'

'We had a trace earlier today,' said Chung. 'The

337

woman went out briefly and the satellites spotted her. I checked their location and found the place where I believe they have been hiding. Unfortunately, by the time I arrived they had already left.'

'Another fuck-up,' muttered Gregson.

'Not quite,' said Chung. 'At least we now know where they are hiding. Not the precise location, but the general vicinity. That is to our advantage.'

'How much do you think they know?' asked Gregson. The question was directed towards Haverstone.

'Plenty, judging by this evidence,' he replied. 'But perhaps not quite enough. If the woman showed herself then it would appear they do not know about the satellites, or at least not how powerful they are. And if they don't know about that they don't really know anything.'

'So what kind of stunt are they planning to pull at the meeting tomorrow?' asked Gregson. He was sitting on the edge of the desk now, grinding his fists together, and his eyes were moving feverishly around the room. A few beads of sweat had appeared on his brow.

'I don't know,' answered Haverstone. He looked across at Chung. 'What's your guess?'

'I don't think it matters, sir,' said Chung softly. 'They will never attend the meeting.'

'You are sure of that?' asked Haverstone.

'Quite certain, sir,' said Chung. 'One reason is that we can assume they are hiding somewhere on the tube system. There is no reason to change their location now. I will organise a reliable group of men to make a search tonight. We should find them. Even if we don't there is no way they can make it to Harrington's Bank without showing themselves. It is not accessible from underground. At some point they have to surface and the satellites will find them. Once located, I shall make sure they are taken out.'

Haverstone looked briefly reassured by the answer. 'The satellites can't fail?' he asked.

'It is unheard of,' answered Chung.

'I should hope so,' said Gregson. 'I don't like the idea of those two showing their faces tomorrow. It could be deadly.'

'Don't worry,' said Haverstone calmly. 'Just make sure you are there yourself. Everything will be taken care of. I think Chung is right. They have caused a certain amount of trouble. But it is impossible for them to succeed.'

'They seem to be doing okay so far,' snapped Gregson.

'But there is still one other crucial weapon we can deploy to our advantage,' said Chung slowly, looking across at the American. 'The little girl.'

25

Harry glanced down at the sheet of paper on which he had written the instructions. He turned to look at Julia, who had been standing at his side while he scribbled down the notes.

'I think it's possible,' she said.

'Can it be done via a computer?' he asked.

'According to these instructions, yes,' she replied. 'But we only get one shot at it. We set the clock ticking then make our run and hope it works.'

'I'm ready to take my chances,' said Harry grimly. 'If you are.'

The call from Mitchell had been received at a phone box inside South Kensington tube station, yet one more stop on what seemed to be a never-ending journey through the Underground. His limbs were weary and his eyes tired; his clothes, he was sure, stank of sweat and tension. Another fifteen hours or so, he told himself. Hold everything together. Just try to pull through.

The burden of the knowledge they possessed weighed heavily on him now. Harry knew they had the information they needed. If they could only make it to the meeting they could stop Haverstone dead in his tracks. Yet he also knew the knowledge was dangerous.

He realised now why they were so desperate that neither he nor Julia should survive the night. He was aware of precisely what was at stake and it did nothing to comfort him.

Thoughts of Cassie crowded his mind. They had been informed by the hospital that a decision to operate would be made in the next twelve hours or so. He wanted to go and see her, to hold her hand through the night, and desperately to be with her if the operation was necessary. He sensed that his mere presence by her side might help to give her the strength to pull through. But he knew at the same time it would be dangerous. To go anywhere near the hospital could be fatal. He would be located and that would risk everything, including Cassie herself.

The man in the tunnel had said something about the little girl. It's my weakness, he admitted to himself sadly. I will have to be there. And they will know that. There was no way he could evade confronting his enemies for ever.

Together, with Harry holding tightly on to Julia's hand, they descended the escalator and made their way back to the platform. It was a wearying and dismal sight; they had both seen enough tube trains in the past two days to last a lifetime, and the grimy netherworld they were inhabiting had grown dark and ugly. Neither of them had decided precisely where they were going any more. They knew only that they had to keep moving and find some safe place to spend the night. Somewhere where they could plug in their computer and make sure they could prepare everything for tomorrow. And where they could be sure they would not be discovered. Somewhere they could start bringing the journey to its close.

They knew it was impossible to expose themselves to daylight, to enter the outside world at all, even for a

341

moment. To do so was madness. It simply invited detection. 'Heathrow,' said Harry eventually.

'We can't leave now,' said Julia. Part of her wanted to get on a plane, to go somewhere far away, to leave all this behind them. That would, in a sense, be a blissful liberation; they would be together and safe. Yet, no matter how much she might wish it, she knew it was not possible. They could not abandon the fight now. Not when they were so close. And Harry could never leave Cassie behind. It was more than she could ever ask of him.

Harry shook his head. 'No point in getting on a plane,' he said flatly. 'We know far too much now. They would never leave us alone. And neither of us knows how to run.'

'Then why the airport?' asked Julia.

'Think about it,' said Harry. 'We can get there on the Underground. It's the only place in London where you can climb out of the tube into a shopping area even at night. We can get everything we need and make sure we never expose ourselves to the outside sky. It's perfect.'

Julia thought for a moment. 'We can even spend the night there without arousing any suspicion. Lots of people are hanging around waiting for their flights. Get something to eat.'

Harry nodded. 'We can pick up the Piccadilly Line here and be there just after eight. That should give us enough time.'

Lykanov peered down at the screen, checking every programme. His instructions were clear: find any trace of the prey and find it immediately. So far nothing had appeared. Neither the satellites nor the telecoms system could sniff out their target. That, he decided, was to be expected. A surveillance system was only effective so long as it was one step ahead of the person it was

342

tracking. That was the trouble with his current employers. They expected to be able to see everything. They did not understand the limitations of the system.

The suspects knew now what they were up against. To Lykanov, it seemed a matter of simple observation. The satellites were perfect ammunition against a target who did not suspect their existence. But, like any surveillance system, once you knew it was there, and were aware of its capabilities, it was possible to take evasive action, particularly in a big city. They knew and that would make their task easier.

'Any sight?' asked Chung.

The Korean was leaning over his shoulder and Lykanov could smell the alcohol on his breath. He could have done with a drink himself, but the bottle of vodka he had smuggled into the bunker had already been emptied and since he had not left the place for three days himself he had not been able to replenish his supplies. 'Nothing,' he replied. 'No trace anywhere. Not from the satellites or the phone system.'

'How is that possible?' The speaker this time was Haverstone, standing at the back of the room, his face obscured in the pale half-light.

'Simple,' Lykanov replied. 'Stay out of sight. In Russia, we used to give elementary talks to KGB agents who suspected they were being tracked by satellite systems. The answer was always the same. Go underground and stay there. Or find buildings with tunnels connecting them. Anything. Just don't ever go into the open. So long as the targets are following that simple rule we will not find them.'

'Say they have to get to a particular building at a particular time?' asked Haverstone. 'Is that possible, without being detected?'

Lykanov shrugged. 'Any tunnels going into the building?'

'I don't believe so,' Haverstone replied.

'Then it is difficult for them. My guess is they will try to get relatively close, using the Underground system, then get a car, probably a taxi, to their destination. But at some point they will have to emerge and reveal themselves. That is to our advantage. If they were being smart they wouldn't go. It is too dangerous for them and they probably know that.'

Chung conferred briefly with Haverstone, before walking back across the floor to the bank of flickering screens where Lykanov was seated. 'I want the satellites configured so that by tomorrow morning they are checking every tube station in central London. At some point they will emerge. We need to find them and have time to stop them. Is that understood?'

Lykanov nodded. 'Understood,' he replied. It sounded like several hours of work. But an order was an order and he knew he had little choice but to obey. 'I will make sure it is done.'

'What are the vulnerabilities of the system?' asked Haverstone. He had walked closer to the bank of screens and was leaning down over one display.

'Vulnerabilitie ?' asked Lykanov. He was not sure what was meant by the question.

'It's weaknesses,' asked Haverstone, turning to face the Russian directly. 'Is there anything our targets can do to stop it working effectively?'

Lykanov laughed; at times he found it amusing to be working for people who had such a poor understanding of the technology they controlled. 'A satellite system does not have any vulnerabilities,' he replied. 'Unless these two kids can get themselves a little space rocket and go into orbit and start tearing up the machines with their bare hands, there is nothing they can do. You don't think they have access to a space rocket, do you?'

Haverstone smiled, a thin cold smile that spread

slowly across his lips, creasing up his face; he liked the idea that the system was invulnerable, not just to Harry and Julia, but to anyone. Invulnerable and under his control. 'What about hacking into our system?' he asked. 'Is there some way he could get to our computers?'

Lykanov shook his head once more and laughed again, louder this time. 'Hack into the system,' he snorted contemptuously. 'Impossible. I have used the same sort of security devices we designed back in Russia and as far as I know the Pentagon spent years trying to hack into it. They used the best programmers in the West, since, of course, if they could hack into the Russian satellites system they could disable the country's defences. But did they ever succeed? No. So if the Pentagon could not manage it over several years, I don't imagine these two, with no particular computer expertise, are going to have any luck. They might try, but they won't succeed.'

Haverstone smiled again; the thought of having a security system in place that even the Pentagon would not be able to crack was pleasing. It reminded him of the immense power he had assembled and which, within less than a dozen hours, would fall under his sole and absolute control. 'Do you think they will try?'

'They might,' said Lykanov with a shrug. 'But my guess is they will lie low for as long as possible, then make a run for it. They will trust to luck. It is the only thing they can do.'

Chung turned to Haverstone. 'Don't worry, sir,' he said calmly. 'You see, everything is under control. If we don't find them tonight then we will root them out tomorrow morning. It doesn't matter which. They will not be present at the meeting. Everything will work out exactly as planned.'

★

It was the first proper meal either of them had eaten for several days and it felt good. Indeed, Harry would later recollect it as one of the finest meals he had ever had; a plate of smoked salmon, followed by steak and chips, with a chocolate cake and coffee afterwards. He had never eaten at a branch of Garfunkel's before and had walked past them contemptuously many times, but on arriving at Terminal One that evening it seemed the perfect place to go. 'Nobody ever eats at Garfunkel's,' he joked to Julia. 'It's the one place in the world you can just about guarantee no one's going to spot you.'

They had talked about many things over dinner. At first they had been too hungry and too thirsty to say very much. Harry ordered a beer for himself, and a gin and tonic for Julia, plus a large bottle of mineral water. He felt hot and sticky in his clothes, and it occurred to him that he could at least go down to the concourse to buy a new pair of socks, perhaps even a fresh shirt. It would be a relief to change into some cleaner clothes and he imagined she would feel that way too; after all, Julia had been wearing the same dress now for three days and it was beginning to show.

They outlined what they had discovered so far and what remained to be done; the day had so far passed in such a blur of activity and tension that he had not had a chance to give her any more than the briefest details of the discoveries he had made on Strang's website. Nor had they had much time to discuss the information passed on to them by the man who signed himself 'the engineer'. 'At least we now know exactly what we're up against,' Julia had remarked, and Harry had conceded that was true. The power of their opponents was terrifying, but they had its measure and that was an advantage; once you knew the capabilities of your enemy you could start thinking about how to outwit him.

'What happens next?' asked Julia. She was sipping a cappuccino, her first proper coffee since her meeting in the café with Mitchell, a lifetime or two ago, and though it was not the finest she'd ever had, it tasted pretty good. The food and alcohol had revived her, and the coffee was already pepping her up; she wouldn't say she felt good about their situation, but at least she was beginning to feel better. That was progress.

'Next?' demanded Harry. He had not expected the question.

'After the meeting tomorrow,' she continued. 'Assuming, that is, that we make it to the meeting and that, once we're there, everything goes according to plan.'

'We'll get there,' said Harry. 'I'm certain of it.'

'And afterwards?' repeated Julia. 'What happens then?'

Harry shrugged. He had to confess he had not thought about it; his mind had been so focused on the immediate issue of their survival, and of Cassie's, that he had not for a moment considered what came next. What would happen after the next twelve hours he had no idea and, on reflection, it was disturbing to realise his future was so completely uncertain. 'Get back to our lives,' he replied with a faint smile. 'What else is there to do?'

He settled the bill in cash and together he and Julia slipped down the steps into the main hall of the terminal. Even though it was just after ten, it was still full of people, most of them dragging baggage from the tubes and searching for their check-in desks. Harry kept his eyes peeled as he walked through the terminal. A wariness and caution had descended upon him by now, and he briefly wondered how long it would be before he could turn a corner again without wondering what was waiting for him on the other side. Nervously he glanced

347

up at one of the many security cameras tracking the progress of the people around the terminal. He knew he was being watched electronically. *I just hope they don't have access to those cameras,* he thought to himself.

At the Heathrow branch of the Carphone Warehouse buying two new mobiles took just a matter of a few minutes. He filled in the forms, told the man at the desk he needed an instant connection and collected the brand-new Nokias. Both were paid for with cash he and Julia had taken from machines at the tube station they had passed through earlier in the day; those withdrawals might well be traced but it would not matter much, since they would long since have disappeared by the time the connection was made. He took the machines out of their boxes and tried calling Julia on her new number. The phone rang on her mobile just a couple of feet away. It was working fine. Next he slipped into a duty free shop and picked up a new Toshiba laptop, again with a built-in modem and with Internet software already installed. 'Okay,' he said to Julia. 'We have everything we need. I suggest we find a quiet place where we can get some coffee and start working.'

There was an adrenalin rush to the moment that Harry found he enjoyed. So long as he focused on the immediate task he found his mind was working okay; he was tired and, though he would not admit it to Julia, frightened as well. But so long as he stuck to the practical issues he felt confident he could cope. *Take the narrow view,* he told himself. *Avoid the big picture at all costs.*

They found a quiet spot in the corner of the airport branch of Burger King. Harry grabbed a couple of large coffees from the counter and brought them back to the table with a heap of sugar sachets; they both needed plenty of calories to pull them through the hours ahead. The place was crowded with people chewing their burgers and glancing up at the departure display on the screen in the corner. Escape, thought Harry. At a moment such as this it was tempting to flee, to put everything behind them, perhaps even to start again somewhere else. Dark thoughts briefly clouded his mind, obscuring his purpose. His life seemed to have turned into a mess, although why he was not sure. Something had gone badly wrong somewhere and one day he would put his finger on it. If it were not for Cassie, he realised, he would just get on the next plane and get out of here. Tomorrow, he sensed, he might not even have Cassie any more. Then there really would be nothing left to stay for. And he would be gone.

He took a long sip of coffee, drawing strength from the caffeine and sugar, and lowered his eyes to the two computers on the plastic table top. 'Let's start,' he said to Julia.

Both of them started carefully to attach the modems on to the laptops to the mobiles they had just bought and made a couple of calls to check if they were working. On his computer, Harry opened up a Netscape page and called up a website for the Spice Girls. He ignored the downloaded pictures and switched on to the e-mail function. 'For free pictures of Baby Spice naked, dial the bulletin board on 0044 171 211 2424 at 11.45 GMT on Friday, 21 March,' he tapped into the computer.

'You try the Jennifer Aniston home page,' Harry said, looking up at Julia with a broad grin. Julia located the web page and started tapping in a similar message.

Harry looked back down at his screen, called up a Microsoft web page and began to tap out another e-mail. 'For a free copy of the latest version of Windows, call the bulletin board on 00 44 171 211 2628,' he wrote.

He looked back up at Julia. 'You keep doing some

pop stars,' he said. 'I'll try some of the UFO websites, perhaps even the Diana conspiracy pages. Those nutters are good for thousands of calls.'

'Do you think this will work?' asked Julia. 'I mean, when he said if he were deaf he couldn't hear, can we be sure this was what he meant?'

Harry could detect a trace of nervousness in her voice and, although he was not certain, he felt she needed reassurance. 'Pretty sure,' he answered. 'Net types like nothing better than secret bulletin boards. Just so long as enough of them make the calls, it will work.'

Lykanov did not like the look of the ten men gathered in a circle at the far end of the bunker, a dozen yards or so away from his bank of screens and computers. He took a sip of the vodka he had persuaded Chung to bring for him, and eyed them closely. They were all at least six foot tall with broad shoulders and narrow eyes. Soldiers probably, he decided. Or former soldiers. He had seen their type before, in other countries, and had never liked them. Too much muscle and not enough brain, he decided. A bad combination. It would, he reflected, be a pleasure to see them defeated.

Chung was talking quietly to their leader, a former colonel called Bob Stamp, who had been retired out of the Army some years earlier, and who now ran a very private and upmarket firm called Security Decisions, based in one of the quieter suburbs of London. The firm never advertised and never attracted any publicity, but was known to the security officers of a few of the leading London-based corporations and banks as a reliable group of men who could always rustle up a squad of former soldiers for any situation that required high-level protection. There was a guarantee that absolutely nothing would be allowed to go wrong. They were well paid, and were both very discreet and very professional.

Chung knew of their existence and they had been hired once or twice before by Cable Media, although never for a mission as delicate as this one. He would have preferred not to get men such as these involved; it had long been a principle of his that nothing was a secret unless absolutely nobody knew about it. He liked to handle as many of the company's operations as he could himself; he trusted no one and it was only when he did something personally that he felt confident it would not leak. But this was an exception. His prey had proved remarkably resourceful and he had decided it was time to use the blunderbuss rather than the rapier. There was no way they could be allowed to make it to the meeting tomorrow.

The men were all dressed casually in jeans and sweaters, and they listened carefully as Chung spelt out their instructions for the next few hours. Each had been handed a set of pictures, a collection of colour and black-and-white shots of both Harry and Julia taken from different angles. The men studied the pictures, committing them to memory. Each of them felt certain he would recognise either person should he catch sight of them over the next twenty-four hours, even if they had disguised themselves. Each man had been trained to concentrate on the eyes and facial features when hunting down a target.

Chung pointed to a map he had displayed on the wall, showing an enlarged section of streets around the City and central London. He pointed to the head office of Harrington's Bank, located in a gleaming modern glass-and-steel building just off Cheapside. 'Our employers will be holding a vital meeting at this building at noon tomorrow,' he explained. 'I believe this pair will try to disrupt the meeting, with serious commercial consequences. It is vital that neither of them is allowed to attend.' That was as much explanation as was necessary, he decided. An advantage of Security Decisions, one which justified their massive fees, was their tact and discretion. They never asked questions about the reason for the tasks they were required to perform. All they were interested in were the technical details of executing the operation perfectly.

Chung drew a circle round the Harrington building with a felt pen, before returning to his audience, peering down at them with a narrow, intense gaze. 'Right now, we are not sure of their whereabouts,' he continued. 'But I have reason to believe they have been hiding on the tube system. They were last tracked to a location on the extension to the Jubilee Line, but have not been spotted since then.'

'Presumably they will try to get as close to the building as possible while staying underground,' said Stamp.

'I think that is probably correct,' agreed Chung. 'Tonight, I want as much of the Underground system as possible to be searched. We might be lucky, we might not. Obviously, it would be better to apprehend them before daylight. But if we don't, then it is vital we find them when they emerge in the morning.'

'We should have men monitoring the exits to all the stations in the vicinity of the building,' said Stamp.

'That is right,' concurred Chung. 'Every exit must be staffed, from daylight tomorrow. There is no way of knowing precisely when they will emerge. But when they do we must be ready for them.'

Harry glanced up at the departure board. The clock on the screen told him it was a few minutes before two in the morning and the schedule of flights was starting to thin out. Only a few irregular departures were listed before the rush started at six the next morning and the number of people around the terminal had dwindled;

some of the shops and bars were open, but only a few lost souls remained, wandering aimlessly from place to place. Below, Harry could see a number of bodies stretched out on the airport seats, trying to catch some sleep before it was time for their planes. He flicked the switch on his laptop, cutting the power, and folded down the screen. 'Enough,' he said, looking up at Julia. 'There's no point in complete overkill.'

'How many have you done?' she asked.

'About fifty,' replied Harry. 'And you?'

'The same,' she answered, stifling a yawn as she spoke.

Harry gazed briefly into her eyes. There were moments when he wondered what he was doing with her. She was beautiful, certainly, in a subtle, intriguing way; a woman with understated charm. Not even the last few days sleeping rough could disguise that. She was brave as well, as he had discovered. And he had little doubt that she cared for him; the small sideways glances she threw in his direction as they walked together told him that. But she was not Amelia, and he was not yet sure he was free enough of her memory to love Julia. Perhaps by tomorrow, if they made it through this ordeal together, he could start opening up another track to his life. 'We should get some sleep,' he suggested, moving his hand across the plastic table top to hold her arm. 'We can't hold out for ever on black coffee.'

'Follow me,' she said softly.

They collected their few belongings – the pair of laptops, the mobiles, some computer disks, all of them arranged in a series of plastic carrier bags – and walked down a flight of stairs into the main terminal building. A pair of policemen passed them, armed with machine-guns, and Harry averted his eyes, but the officers paid them no attention. Julia turned her head, as though she were looking for something, before taking Harry by the arm and leading him gently through the hallway.

When they reached the entrance to the Ladies, he stopped, ready to wait for her outside. 'Follow me,' she repeated, whispering in his ear.

Harry and she stepped inside. Her eyes ran the length of the room, checking it was empty. She walked a few paces and turned into a cubicle, leading Harry behind her. It was squashed inside, hardly enough room for both of them. Julia put her arms around his neck, dragging him close to her, and he could feel her breasts rising to meet his chest. 'Make love to me,' she whispered.

'Here?'

Julia looked up, meeting his eyes with hers. 'We might be dead by lunch-time,' she said, a small smile masking the truth behind her words. 'I don't want that to happen without having fucked you at least once.'

He could feel her hand sliding into his trousers, and the passion of the moment started to overwhelm him. Harry ran his hands down her back, feeling her skin respond to his touch, and loosened the buttons on her dress. He kissed her on the lips, moving his tongue down her neck, biting into her soft flesh. His hands slid down her body on to her legs, and he could feel her beginning to swivel against his fingers. Her breath was quickening. Julia leant against the thin wall, stifling the moans as her excitement rose. She took him between her fingers and guided him inside her. 'Oh, yes,' she muttered aloud.

Harry had no idea how long it lasted; minutes probably, though it seemed like an eternity. Their passion rose and subsided, briefly banishing everything that had been crowding his mind. For a short, delicious period there were just the two of them and nothing else; no pursuit, no meetings, no deadlines and no danger. Only the physical rawness of the present.

When it was over he held her tightly in his arms, hoping the moment could last and reluctant to step back into the world. 'Are you okay?' he asked.

She looked up, her brown eyes misted with sadness. 'I'm frightened,' she replied.

'I know you are,' he said, holding her closer. He paused, reflecting on what he should say next. 'Why are you doing this?' he asked. 'You could just have fled. There was no need for you to become this deeply involved.'

She shook her head slowly. 'I'm not sure any more,' she answered. 'How about you?'

Harry hesitated, uncertain how he should reply. 'Because they sacked the wrong guy,' he said. 'And because they hurt Cassie.'

For a moment, she rested her head against his chest. Harry ran his hands through her hair, his mind turning over the options in his head. There was not much point in delaying, he reflected. She had to know some time. 'I'm not going to the meeting tomorrow.'

Julia turned to face him. 'Why not?' she demanded. The affection in her eyes suddenly replaced by bewilderment and anger.

'Cassie,' Harry replied flatly. 'They are going to operate. I have to be there.'

26

Kim Chung checked the electronic time display on the side of the screen. It was now fifteen minutes after eleven, and there was no sign of his prey. They were due at the meeting at midday and the satellites had been trained on central London and the City for hours, but so far there had been no trace. He was worried about the rush-hour; between eight and nine o'clock, thousands of commuters poured out of the City tube stations and no matter how much computing power he threw into the system, he was not a hundred per cent confident Harry and Julia could not have slipped past his watchful electronic eyes among the crowds hurrying towards their offices. If he had been in their shoes, that is what he would have done: moved into the centre of a crowd and hoped for the best.

Checking the monitors, however, he could see the flood had subsided to a trickle. Should they attempt to come through now, there was no doubt the satellites would capture them. The information would be up on the screen within a minute, and the group of men readied for the pursuit would close in on them fast.

At his side, Lykanov was controlling the machinery. Next to him there was a bank of ten phones. Each of the ten men gathered last night had been posted to an Underground station in the vicinity of the Harrington headquarters. The previous night had been devoted to a search of the tube system; each man had gone out alone to walk the length of a different part of it, but by daybreak they had come up with nothing. 'It seems we have no idea where they might be,' Stamp had said just before dawn.

Chung had directed the men to abandon the search and to take up their positions near the tube stations. Two more were hired to stand outside the hospital where the child was still resting; there was a good probability Harry might have to visit his daughter. Another couple had been placed in the streets surrounding the headquarters. Nothing was being left to chance. He put a call through to Stamp. 'Any sign?' he asked crisply.

'Nothing,' replied Stamp. 'Do you have any leads?'

'No,' answered Chung. 'But they must be coming through soon, otherwise they will never make the meeting.'

'I'll tell all the men to be on heavy alert for the next half-hour,' said Stamp. 'Don't worry, I don't see how they can get through.'

Malcolm Fielding was feeling tense and wary as he contemplated the hour or two ahead. He had been involved in some tough negotiations before, where billions had been at stake, but he had seen nothing quite like this. Three things worried him. The call from Lamb for security to be on hand for the meeting. The request from a senior person from the SFO that he be permitted to attend as an observer. And the fact that Lamb had been too scared to meet at the office, or even to use the phone himself. Worst of all, he realised, he had no idea what was going on. Apart from knowing that it involved

Cable Media, and was deadly serious, he was completely bereft of information. 'Is the crisis room ready?' he asked one of his assistants.

The answer was yes. It had been ready since this morning; the coffee was made and the briefing papers were laid out along the table, one set for each delegate from the banks entitled to attend. Security had been informed and five extra guards had been posted in a room next door, just in case they were needed. Arrangements had been made for Lamb to be admitted as soon as he arrived. Even the public relations department had been briefed. They had been told nothing of consequence, of course. Only that even though it was a Friday, none of them was to take a long lunch, nor were they to think about getting home early for the weekend. It could well be a busy afternoon.

Fielding glanced down at his watch. It was half past eleven now. In less than thirty minutes he would discover how much of his story Lamb could prove. And how the forces ranged against him would react.

Richard Gregson looked down at the trading floor. It had been a quiet morning. With the crucial meeting to decide on the proposal to swap Cable Media's debts into equity less than an hour away, trading in the market had more or less ground to a halt. Everyone involved had, by now, taken their positions. There was nothing left for them to do, apart from wait on the outcome of the deal and discover whether they had made or lost a fortune. He had already spent the morning checking through the numbers. His firm had bought so much of Cable Media's debt that it was now the leading creditor of the company. In any reconstruction, his would have to be the decisive voice. Plenty of banks still had loans outstanding to the company. But they would have to listen to what he had to say and, he knew, when it came to a vote they would have to follow his instructions.

Across the trading floor the dealers were loitering idly. A few of them were completing trades in other minor positions, but most of them had been working on Cable Media alone for the past few weeks and that market was now virtually dead. Some were reading tabloids, others were playing games on their screens, a couple were downloading porn from the Internet and a few were just chatting among themselves. On Monday, Gregson decided, he would have to find them something else to do. There was nothing more financially dangerous than a bored trader.

He took a swig from his can of Coke and snapped open his mobile phone, putting a call through to Haverstone. 'Everything ready?' he asked, the tone of his voice moving down to a low grumble.

'I believe so,' said Haverstone.

'Any sign of our two young friends?'

'Not yet.'

Gregson was sure he could detect just the faintest sign of nervousness in the man's voice; a crack in its tone that betrayed his uncertainty. 'Think they'll make it?'

'Absolutely not.' Haverstone sounded more confident. 'Men have been stationed everywhere. I feel sure there is no way through.'

'Better not be,' said Gregson. 'Everything is in place now. Those two are the only thing standing between us and success.' He snapped the phone shut and placed it in his jacket pocket. It was twenty to twelve, he noted. Time to hop into the waiting car and start the ten-minute drive over to Fielding's office. No point in being late.

Three miles away, on the fringes of the West End, Samuel Haverstone closed his mobile, put it down carefully on the seat next to him and nodded to his

359

driver to steer the Daimler away from the kerb. He looked behind him to the Cable Media headquarters and watched as the building faded from view. I leave as a manager, he thought to himself. I shall return this afternoon as an owner.

No one would know, of course. Not initially, at least. That would be too dangerous. But he and Gregson, through a network of offshore companies, would control the majority of the equity in the company. No more would he need to listen to inconsequential advice from outside. He would not have to worry about what the shareholders thought. Nothing could curb his ambitions now. There would be no one to answer to. Nobody but himself. Best of all, he reflected, I shall control the satellites and the power they confer. All the knowledge in the world will be within my grasp.

Gregson, in due course, could be dealt with. The details were not important. That could wait for another day. For the moment, it was just enough to take control and to know the greatest concentration of information anywhere in the world could be bent absolutely to his will. Haverstone glanced down at his watch. A quarter to twelve. In an hour or so it would he his. The greatest prize anyone could imagine.

Bob Stamp stood alone, outside the main exit from Monument station. This was the closest stop to the Harrington's headquarters and, he figured, the one their target was most likely to use. He had decided he would monitor it himself. There was no point in emerging into daylight, then giving yourself a long journey across town. Might as well get as close as possible, then make a quick dash for it. Basic training, he reflected. Always try to get inside the mind of your opponent, try to think as he would and decide what you would do in his situation. Then intercept him. Simple really.

He pulled the collar of his coat up around his neck, feeling the weight of his equipment inside the thick parka. Nothing particularly special. He had sent each of his men out with a mobile so they could stay in touch. Each had a pair of handcuffs, which could be useful if there was trouble, particularly when you were dealing with two people, and each had an electric cattle prod, the type farmers used for steering their animals into the pen. It was his weapon of choice for city-centre manhunts; the prod was completely silent and the voltage it delivered was enough to bring even a strong, tall man swiftly to the ground, from where he could be disabled with ease. No guns. Stamp did not recommend them, not unless the opponent was likely to be armed. Not in the town centre. The sound of gunfire always created a panic, which made it easier for the target to escape. And there were a lot of nasty questions to be answered afterwards. Stamp did not need that kind of trouble. Not unless his fees justified it.

He checked his watch. A quarter to twelve. Time was getting tight now, he realised. He had been standing here for almost five hours, rooted to the spot, practically immobile. A beggar had hassled him three times over the course of the morning, getting on his nerves enough to be shown a quick flash of the cattle prod to frighten him away. Otherwise it had been a dull morning, spent scanning the faces of the commuters as they emerged from the escalator, ready for another day in the office. Poor buggers, Stamp reflected as he watched them trudge into the gloomy streets. A bloody awful way for anyone to make a living.

The mobile emitted a couple of beeps and Stamp flipped it open, careful to keep his eyes peeled on the exit as he did so. 'Any sign yet?' asked Chung.

'Nope,' replied Stamp crisply. 'What are you getting?'

'No trace,' said Chung. 'Unless they have given up it has to be any moment now. Keep your eyes open.'

Julia glanced at her watch anxiously, then looked down at her bags to make sure she had everything with her. A quarter to twelve. Once more she ran through the sequence of events in her mind. There was another seven minutes to go before she could make her move. And, if she was to survive, the plan would have to operate like clockwork.

She could feel her heart beating faster as she watched the seconds tick away and felt the train draw closer to her destination. Not much longer, she told herself. Be strong.

At first she had been furious with Harry. Had he been intending to abandon her all along? Or was it only after he had heard the threats from the man in the tunnel? When she had calmed down enough to listen to his explanation, she realised that he had had no choice. Cassie's situation had started to deteriorate and the doctors were forced to operate. Julia could only imagine how desperately worried he must be. He had to be with her, no matter what the cost.

Still, she would have preferred that he were here at her side. They had started this together and they should finish it together. Whether she had the strength to see it through by herself she had no way of knowing. She could only hope so. Once more, Julia glanced at her watch. Eleven minutes to twelve. She could see the light of the station approaching. Get the sequence right, she told herself, and pray that Harry can deliver on his promises. They would only get one shot at this.

John Mitchell stepped into the lobby of Harrington's Bank and strode up to the front desk. The receptionist took his name and checked her list. She asked for some identification and glanced only cursorily at the SFO swipe card he showed her. Fine, she said, not looking up again. The meeting is on the ninth floor, next to the chief executive's office. Take the lift. Someone will meet you.

He rode the lift with a sense of anticipation. He had not told anyone he was planning to attend this meeting today, but he had taken the precaution of a discreet word with one of the officers he knew well at the City of London police. Keep a few men handy at midday, he'd told him. In the vicinity of Harrington's. And be sure to keep your men alert for any strange disturbances in the area surrounding the building. No, he'd said in response to the question, he could not be sure what was going to happen. It might be nothing. Just keep some men ready in case they're needed.

Indeed, he reflected to himself, he could not really be sure if anything was going to happen. Not even that Harry and Julia were going to make it to the meeting and, if they did, whether they could deliver anything of substance. It might be that they would just embarrass themselves, and him, with a series of wild and unproven allegations.

He had done what he could to help them. Honour dictated that. But now they were on their own and would have to decide their own fates. If things did not work out for them that was just too bad. There was nothing to be gained by putting himself on the line.

Fielding met him at the lift and shook his hand warmly as Mitchell stepped out into the lobby. 'I just wanted a quick word before the meeting begins,' he said.

From the lines creasing the man's brow, Mitchell could tell he was worried. Fair enough, he decided, I'm worried as well. It had the makings of a tense day for everyone. 'I have met with Mr Lamb and heard of his companion,' Fielding continued. 'I suspect you may have had some contact with them as well.'

Mitchell nodded. There was no point in denying it now. 'Yes.'

'Is there any truth in the allegations they are making?' Fielding asked anxiously.

Mitchell paused. 'Some, I suspect,' he answered. 'I think it relates back to an insider dealing case the SFO was working on some weeks ago. The case was dropped for all sorts of strange reasons.'

'So they are not completely crazy?'

'Not crazy, no,' said Mitchell firmly. 'Wrong, perhaps, but not crazy.'

'Do you think they can prove their case?'

'To be perfectly honest, I'm not even sure if they can make it to the meeting.' Mitchell could see the man's shoulders slump as he listened to the words; that had not been the answer he was looking for.

Harry folded the laptop, listening to the case close with a satisfying thud. Okay, he told himself. Everything is going according to plan. Mitchell's instructions had been easy to follow. Five minutes and this thing will be ready to roll. Up above he could see the light of the station and beneath him he could feel the train's brakes scratching against the tracks. I'll be there in another minute.

He felt sick with nerves about leaving Julia alone, yet he knew there had been no other choice. That their enemies would stake out the hospital there could be no doubt. They were aware that Cassie was there and that sooner or later he would have to come and get her. It might as well be now. Just so long as Julia could hold herself together. It was a lot to ask after all she had been through.

They had, he believed, thought of everything. The mechanisms were all in place. It was just a question now of waiting to see if they would work; whether, as the engineer had put it, his enemies could be made both deaf and blind. If nothing else, thought Harry, we will at least have turned this into a more equal contest.

Joe Nathan had never seen anything like it. For fifteen years, now, he had been monitoring the flow of calls from an office in the British Telecom building in Newgate Street, just off Holborn Circus, checking that nothing was amiss with the system. Before him there was a bank of computer screens, regulating traffic and providing constant, twenty-four-hours-a-day surveillance of the calls around the country. Usually, nothing happened. Indeed, in the last fifteen years he could recall less than half a dozen incidents where anything had even come close to happening; the last was when one of the tabloid newspapers printed its bingo numbers incorrectly, and was flooded with calls from readers who thought they had scooped the jackpot.

Right now he could scarcely believe his eyes. 'What the fuck is going on?' he said to one of his assistants.

His colleague was also peering nervously at the screen. 'If this keeps up, the system is going to crash,' he said.

'Crash,' repeated Nathan, as much to himself as anyone else. 'That's impossible. It just can't happen. This is one of the biggest exchanges in the world.'

Each electronic exchange within the BT network was designed to handle a different number of calls, depending on the expected flow of traffic. Relatively sleepy exchanges in rural areas were built to cope with a couple of thousand calls a minute; anything more would be a waste of money. High-density city-centre exchanges were far more powerful and the West End exchange, covering most of the central London office blocks and government departments, was one of the most powerful of them all. It was capable of handling fifty thousand calls a minute, more than twice the peak level ever recorded in the area. There were only ten thousand phones served by the exchange, so unless each person received five calls at the same time there was no way it could run out of capacity.

At this moment, according to the screen an inch from Nathan's nose, the exchange was receiving forty-eight thousand calls. A couple of thousand more and the system would seize up completely.

'What happens when it goes over fifty thousand?' asked the assistant, a fresh-faced young trainee who genuinely didn't know.

'The shit hits the fan, that's what,' answered Nathan angrily. 'The system just can't cope with that kind of traffic. It shuts down, to prevent the circuits getting overloaded and blowing.'

The assistant looked puzzled. 'Doesn't that mean nobody in the area can make or receive any calls?'

The youngster was starting to get on Nathan's nerves. 'Of course they can't make any bloody calls. Or receive any. It means everyone's buggered. Find out where those calls are coming from.'

The assistant started tapping away on his screen, drawing up a display of calls coming into the West End area. 'There are thousands of them,' he said. 'Mainly coming in from modems all around the world. Most of them aren't getting through so they just start automatically re-dialling.'

Nathan sighed. 'I've always fucking hated computers.'

Chung held the receiver in his hand, briefly puzzled by the maddening continuous hum on the line. He put it down and tried dialling again. Nothing. He brought it closer to his ear, but soon drew it away again, irritated by the low buzzing noise. He could not even get a dialling tone. He cast a vicious look in the direction of Lykanov. 'What the fuck is wrong with the phones?' he spat.

Lykanov pressed the receiver to his ear. 'No dialling tone,' he said with a dismissive shrug.

Chung tried the rest of the instruments in front of him, picking them up one after another. None of them appeared to be working. He moved quickly across the room, grabbing a couple of the receivers on Lykanov's desk and pressing them to his ear. The same low, continuous beep. Not a single dialling tone from any of them. 'All the fucking phones are dead,' he said.

Lykanov shrugged; the prey had obviously followed perfectly his instructions about overloading the exchanges. 'A problem with the system, perhaps,' he said nonchalantly. 'It might just be a coincidence. In Russia the phones were always going dead, even the military lines.'

'Only fools believe in coincidences,' Chung barked.

The loss of the phones worried him and he could feel a trace of perspiration starting to trickle down his spine; without contact with any of his agents on the ground he would have no way of knowing how the chase was developing; nor would he be able to issue fresh instructions to Stamp and his men. The prey might even have a chance of escaping.

Chung leant close into the screen, peering down at a set of satellite images of tube exits. 'At least we can still see what is happening,' he snarled. 'I don't like the feel of this at all. Let's just hope nothing goes wrong with the satellites.'

Julia took a moment to try to settle her nerves. It's time. The doors on the train slid open and she stepped out on to the platform. Opposite she could see a set of plastic chairs and a vending machine. She walked a couple of yards and placed the simple black plastic holdall they had purchased earlier that morning underneath the chairs. She knelt to listen. The clock they had bought at Heathrow was the noisiest they could find and it was doing its job. She permitted herself a brief smile as she registered the sound of ticking through the material. This, she reflected, had been one of her better ideas.

Standing up, she began to stride purposefully along the platform. Where was a policeman when you needed one? she cursed to herself. She checked the area, saw nothing and slipped through a tunnel on to the next platform before she caught sight of the familiar black uniform that distinguished the British Transport Police. 'Officer,' she started, not finding it hard to sound nervous. 'I saw a man place a bag under the seats on the next platform. It looked pretty suspicious.'

'Where abouts, madam?' the policeman asked. From the expression on his face, Julia could tell he was not particularly concerned; there were, after all, several bomb hoaxes on the Underground every day at the moment and none of them turned out to be serious. This was probably just one more false alarm.

Anxiously, she led the officer through to the next platform, pointing to the bag stuffed beneath the plastic seats. The officer knelt and Julia could hardly help smiling when she saw the expression on the man's face as he detected the loud ticking sound.

The policeman had never actually seen a bomb before, nor had he ever heard one, and he could not say for sure whether they ticked in real life. But he was not about to take any chances. 'I think you'd better leave the station, madam,' he said to Julia. 'I'll have to clear the area.'

Julia turned away, walking purposefully down the platform. Above her head she could hear the announcer

368

coming through on the tannoy: 'Passengers are requested to depart the station immediately because of a security alert. This station is being evacuated. Please leave the station in an orderly fashion.'

The announcement was repeated in a slow loop, echoing endlessly around the tunnels. All about her, Julia could see people beginning to surge towards the escalator. Some appeared irritated; no doubt the victims of many previous bomb hoaxes. Others looked frightened, a few even started running. Within less than a minute, hundreds of people were jostling and shoving their way on to the escalator.

She glanced down at her watch, chewing her thumb as she did so. The crowd started to surge past her. Another thirty seconds or so, she told herself. Then it should be real chaos.

The chauffeur drew the silver-grey Daimler up to the kerb, bringing it to a stop on a double-yellow line outside the headquarters of Harrington's Bank. He stepped out and walked round the car to open the door. Samuel Haverstone ignored him as he climbed out. He looked up and down the street. To one side of the doorway there were a camera crew and a reporter from one of the newer financial cable channels, who looked briefly in his direction before returning to setting up their equipment. A couple of print journalists, probably from the wire services, were standing next to them, holding notebooks and cigarettes, and drinking coffee from styrofoam cups. Haverstone had already instructed his public relations people to be here later; he would get them to work out some suitable statement for the papers.

'Are you ready to rock'n'roll?' said Gregson, standing next to him, his hands in his pockets.

Haverstone smiled. This was, he reflected, his

moment of triumph, the pinnacle he had been climbing towards for several years. He should, he told himself, take time to savour the occasion; let the event play out in slow motion, the better to enjoy each nuance. There would only be one chance like this and he should relish every second. 'Absolutely,' he replied confidently. 'And you?'

'Ready to kick ass,' said Gregson with a grin. 'There's nothing I enjoy better than ripping off bankers. Has your man dealt with our two young friends yet?'

'I don't know,' said Haverstone, concern flickering across his face. 'I tried to call Chung a moment ago, but the phone didn't seem to be working.'

'Try him again,' barked Gregson. 'I don't want those two fuckheads messing up our day.'

Haverstone flicked open his mobile and pressed the button for the pre-programmed number. 'That number is currently unobtainable. Please try later,' intoned the irritatingly chirpy mechanised Vodafone voice. 'Strange,' said Haverstone. 'The phones still aren't working.'

Gregson looked across at the man. 'I sure as hell hope everything else is.'

'It will be,' said Haverstone with a smug smile. 'Nothing can go wrong now. We are too close.'

The escalator seemed to take for ever to reach the ground and Harry checked his watch nervously. Another minute or so and he could break cover. Ten to twelve. That should give him just sufficient leeway, if he moved quickly enough, to make it down to the hospital. He should be there in time. A few people were milling in the lobby of the station. Harry stepped off the escalator and glanced out to the street. He couldn't risk it yet.

To his right, he could see a couple of people angrily jabbing their fingers against the call boxes. 'What seems to be the problem, mate?' he asked one of the men, making his voice as casual as possible.

'Bloody phone boxes,' the man replied. 'Five of them here, and none of them working.'

'Typical,' said Harry with a shrug, edging closer to the street.

Well, he thought to himself. At least that bit of the plan is up and running. The rest is down to me and Julia.

Only the burning orange tip of Lykanov's cigarette was visible in the darkened room.

He had just lit the thing, and was on to his third drag, sitting back in the chair, wondering why there was no sign of their targets on the screens, when the lights had gone. The room was plunged instantly into complete and total blackness. Apart from the faint glow of the cigarette, absolutely nothing else was visible.

Lykanov sat forward suddenly in his chair, waving his cigarette around, hoping to generate enough light to see his keyboard and control panels. It was virtually impossible. The bunker was entirely sealed. Without electricity there was no light at all. You might as well be blind, he thought to himself, a smile touching his lips. They had followed his instructions well, he decided.

To his left, he saw the flicker of a flame. Chung had opened his lighter, holding it aloft and casting a dim glow on to a few feet surrounding him. Through the murky air, Lykanov could just about make out the face of the Korean and it was not a pleasant sight. His jaw had slackened into an expression of dismay and bewilderment, and his eyes were scanning the screens in front of them. For a brief moment, they had transmitted a pale light, as the white dots in their centres faded from view. Now there was nothing. The screens were silent, inert and entirely black.

'What the fuck is going on?' asked Chung angrily.

Lykanov knew, but preferred to remain silent. Chung could observe, on the surface, what was happening, but the deeper reasons would be a mystery to him. Nothing had prepared him for this moment and he realised in a flash that despite the hundreds of millions poured into assembling the most sophisticated information system on the planet they were now, both literally and metaphorically, completely in the dark. 'The power has gone,' Lykanov answered solidly. 'First the phones went and now this.'

'What about the back-up generator?' Chung said sharply, his voice stiffening as he spoke.

'What back-up generator?' asked Lykanov.

'The back-up!' bellowed Chung. 'How do we connect it?'

Lykanov shrugged. 'Nobody told me about a back-up,' he said. 'My job was just to work the systems, not to control the electricity.'

'Fuck that,' shouted Chung, close to exasperation. 'I know. What do we do now?'

Lykanov turned to look at the man, though he doubted he'd be able to see him through the darkness. 'When we are blind we cannot see and when we are deaf we cannot hear,' he said. He stubbed out his cigarette in the ashtray and immediately lit another. 'Without power, this equipment is useless. We can see nothing, we can hear nothing. Everything we have assembled might as well not be here for all the good it will do us now.'

'What about the satellites?' asked Chung. 'Aren't the satellites still working?'

'Oh, sure, the satellites are still working,' said Lykanov almost light-headedly. He was starting to see the humour of the situation, to appreciate the wit and ingenuity of his opponents and the precision with which they had carried out the plan. 'They will still be up there, still spying. I'm sure our targets will be in clear view. But we aren't going to see any of it, because without power we have no way of accessing them.'

Chung's fist crashed down on the desk, the force of the impact sending a keyboard flying a few inches into the air. 'There must be something we can do,' he screamed.

Like get out of here, reflected Lykanov. He had, he realised, a million dollars already tucked away in an offshore bank account. Not as much as he had expected, but enough all the same. He would be okay. The others would have to look after themselves. It was not likely to be his problem for much longer.

'Comrade,' he said to Chung with a fatalistic smile. 'There is nothing else we can do.'

Julia couldn't wait any longer. Riding up the escalator, amid a busy and noisy crowd, she looked at her watch. She was going to have to leave the station at any minute.

Suddenly the escalator ground to a halt. The panic underground worsened: people, plunged mysteriously into utter darkness, automatically assumed the black-out was linked to the bomb warning and decided this was not a scare but the real thing. A few screams could be heard and at least one person, convinced they had heard an explosion, began to cry. The noise was incredible, as people started shouting to one another, pushing and shoving, clearing others out of their path. Julia grabbed her bag tight to her chest and pushed herself forward through the crowd. She felt a surge of elation rush through her – they had done it. The National Grid was out – but for how long? She could not be sure how much time she would have.

She tried to shove her way to the top of the escalator, the surge of the crowd literally lifting her off her feet. Up above, she could see glimmers of daylight. She drew her hands up to her face, hiding as much of it as possible. When you see the exit, move as fast as you can, but don't run, she told herself. That will only draw their attention.

Only a few yards away, Bob Stamp was overwhelmed by the tide of humanity rushing past him. He tried to stand his ground, staying rooted to the spot, hoping to nail his targets. He did not believe for a moment there was a bomb downstairs, just a very clever opponent hoping to make a quick escape. He held his own for almost a minute against the rush of people surging past him, until a particularly violent skinhead told him to get the fuck out of the way, pushing him to the ground. A policeman helped him to his feet. 'You can't stay here, sir. You will have to leave the station.'

'I am staying,' he protested.

The policeman grabbed him roughly by the arm. 'You'll have to move along, sir,' he said. 'You are obstructing the exit.'

Outside, in the daylight, a vast crowd seemed to have assembled; people who had escaped were milling around, trying to find out what was going on. Others were attempting to get on to the tube, the two groups meeting in the middle, jousting with each other, trying to make their way through the confused crowd. Stamp's eyes searched feverishly as he tried to locate his targets, but there was no sign of them. The buildings all around seemed to have darkened and along the streets the cars were queuing up and honking as the traffic lights switched themselves off. Around the City, total chaos had started to descend.

27

Harry was already getting the measure of the madness he had just unleashed upon the city. He swerved violently as he crossed the road, dodging a taxi that had climbed up the kerb as it tried to inch its way forward through a queue of stationary vehicles. Within minutes of the power shutting down the cars had started to clog into a solid, immobile block of angry, snarling traffic. Horns were hooting everywhere and people were beginning to climb out of their cars, shouting at one another, hoping to see what was happening; most of them had already tried their radios, but were puzzled to find none of the London stations seemed to be broadcasting any more.

'Why don't you look where you're bloody going, mate,' shouted the taxi driver.

'Why don't you drive to the bloody zoo, then,' said Harry, before hurrying on. 'You might feel more at home.'

'Fuck off out of it, you cunt,' snapped the driver.

There was, Harry had to confess, a certain lightness in his step as he moved swiftly towards the hospital. Like most Londoners, he had spent too much of his life simmering in slow-moving traffic and to have spiralled the roads into total chaos so quickly was a rare piece of urban vandalism. Almost something to be treasured.

He spotted the hospital up ahead, a white brick building, the only new object along that stretch of the Fulham Road. From the windows, he could see a few lights shining. My guess was right, he thought; the hospital has an emergency generator and Cassie will not have been affected by the black-out. Just so long as the engineer does not have a back-up power supply I should be all right. They won't have seen me coming.

A crowd had gathered on the street surrounding the hospital. All the office buildings, shops, bars and restaurants had been plunged into darkness for several minutes and their people had come outside. Harry even recognised some of the girls from the gym up the road, in their smart red uniforms, standing in a small group. Unobtrusively, he slipped into the crowd and started to edge his way towards the entrance.

Julia looked around anxiously, her eyes blinking slightly in the first daylight she had been exposed to in what seemed like a lifetime. Her senses were heightened and she was not prepared for the angry scenes she found surrounding her. Crowds of people surged towards the station, inquiring furiously of the few policemen and guards why it was shut. They collided with the phalanx streaming in the other direction. Between them, Julia tried to push her way out into the street.

Up ahead, the lights on the rows of grand office buildings linking the streets of the City had gone out. Anxious-looking workers were gathering on the pavement, demanding to know what had happened. A few were taking the chance of a quick smoke, most were just gossiping with their colleagues. In front of them the road was snarled with dangerously blocked traffic.

Julia glanced down at her watch. Five minutes to

twelve. Using her elbows she started to shove her way through the multitude. There was not much time and she had not figured into her calculations the chaos that would descend on the street once the power went down. The journey would be harder than she had imagined.

Around her she could catch snippets of conversation; talk mostly of what might have caused the shut-down. She heard something about an IRA bomb and how the station was closed; another voice talked about eco-terrorists; yet another about the Thames flooding. If only they knew, she thought to herself.

She looked up. In the distance she could just make out the headquarters of Harrington's Bank. Another quarter of a mile at most. Leaning into the crowds, she fought her way gradually up the street, no longer caring how many people she shoved and jostled along the way. Plenty of elbows pushed back and she wondered how many bruises she had collected. At first, she hardly noticed the man tugging at her arm. With a flick, she brushed him aside, but he would not let go. It was only when she turned to face him and noticed the cold, calm expression on his face that she began to realise what was happening. For a moment she froze, unsure how to respond.

Well, thought Bob Stamp to himself, this is a rare stroke of luck. About time too. Everything else this morning has been a bloody disaster.

Chung stepped out of the back entrance of the Cable Media headquarters and into the bright, crisp sunshine of the street. His eyes blinked, taking time to adjust to the light, and several seconds passed before he could focus clearly.

He looked up and down, noting the chaos across the roads as the traffic shuddered to a halt. Policemen were doing their best to keep the cars flowing, but with the traffic lights all down it was a thankless task. Vehicles were jammed up against one another, their horns honking. Gridlock was taking over.

'Bastards,' Chung muttered under his breath. He had no doubt now that Harry and Julia were responsible for the failure of the phones and the power. How they had done it he had no idea, although he felt sure he would work it out in time.

With the satellites and phones working he would have found them and destroyed them. Without them, he was blind and helpless. There was nothing he could do. They had their freedom. It was probably too late to stop them now. But he, of course, also had his freedom and there was still damage he could wreak.

He walked swiftly through the crowded streets towards the grey Lexus, parked one block away from the headquarters building. To the Chelsea and Westminster Hospital, he reckoned, was about a three-mile drive. Normally he could make it there, he figured, in less than ten minutes. Today, of course, with the traffic all over the place, there was no telling how long it might take. But he would be there soon enough. Who knows, he pondered, with the lights down I might even make it in less time than usual.

The little girl was the only card he had left to play and he planned to use her well.

Malcolm Fielding coughed slightly to bring the meeting to order. Seated around the long table in the crisis room were representatives of all the main banks involved in the deal, a dozen people in all. To his side he had a pair of his own advisers, both legal and financial, on hand to cope with any tricky situations that might arise. In front, the bankers were stretched out in two flanks along the side of the table. At the far end, he could see Haverstone, surrounded by his own advisers. To his right sat Gregson, completely alone, with a thin smirk playing upon his face.

In the corner, partially obscured from his view, he could see John Mitchell who, at that very moment, was peering out of the window, looking down on the cars and trucks clogging the streets below. The instructions he had given them must have worked, he noted with relief. They would have a chance now.

All the eyes in the room turned to face Fielding. It was, according to his watch – although not to the clock on the wall, which had stopped some minutes ago – twelve precisely. Time to begin.

The loss of power had momentarily fazed everyone. Fielding had still been in his office when the lights went out and the bankers had already been gathering in the crisis room. He had cursed briefly, shouting to the security people to find out what was happening. They too were confused, but within a couple of minutes had established that it was a power cut affecting most of central London. It was nothing to do with the bank and, for the moment apparently, there was nothing they could do about it. The police were saying there had been some kind of terrorist alert and the power should be up and running again soon. 'Apologies for the power, gentlemen,' Fielding announced to the room. 'Perhaps we should wait until we have the lights on again.'

A delay, any delay, would have suited Fielding fine. He had no idea where Lamb was, or when he might appear. If, indeed, he appeared at all. And without that knowledge he was not sure he wanted to start the meeting; its outcome, he knew, depended crucially on his presence, and on how convincing the case was.

'Sunlight suits me just fine,' spat Gregson, pointing up to the tall glass windows stretching along the length of the room. 'I can see perfectly clearly.'

'All the same, it might be better to wait,' said Fielding nervously.

'We are busy men,' snapped Gregson. 'If there's business to be done here, let's do it.'

Judging by their expressions, Fielding reckoned he did not have the sympathy of the bankers present; so far as most of them were concerned, this was a done deal. Gregson had most of the votes, if not the majority, and the financial proposals on the table were the best that were likely to be available in the circumstances. The debts outstanding from Cable Media were only a small proportion of their global portfolios and none of their head offices particularly needed a powerful media company as an opponent. If the deal was going to be done, most of them figured it was best to get on with it and get out of here. There was nothing to be gained by hanging around.

Fielding glanced at his watch. It was now five past twelve and he could not delay much longer. He looked down the table towards Haverstone. 'I suggest the chairman of Cable Media talks us through their proposals, then we can proceed to a vote,' he said.

Haverstone looked around the room, paying particular attention to the closed door. It was now six minutes past twelve and still there was no sign of them. He wished he could contact Chung; reassurance that neither of them was going to make it to the meeting would be useful. But it seemed unlikely now. Presumably they had been dealt with.

He looked up to address the room. Keep this short and sweet, he told himself. Move to the vote as soon as possible. A serene confidence started to take hold of him; the phones might not be working, but it was obvious that Chung had located his targets and disposed of them. Nothing would stop him now. The game was over and he had won. 'I believe the proposals we have put before you are in the best interests of the company, the shareholders and the creditors,' he began.

Julia could feel her arm being twisted and the man at her side pushing her towards the ground. 'Down you go, young lady,' snarled Stamp, his voice marked by a raw military sense of authority.

The pain searing through her arm was intense; a ripple that started in her wrist and spread achingly through her back and her neck. His grip was strong and forceful and she knew it would be impossible to shake him free. She did not have the strength. Her eyes started to descend towards street level as she sunk to her knees. 'Let me go, you fucking bastard,' she shrieked.

The words rang out, piercing through the crowded street. As their echo resounded in her ears, even Julia was surprised by the force she had put into them. She could see several heads up above her, starting to turn and look in her direction.

The back of a hand moved downwards, slapping her across the mouth. The force of the blow took Julia by surprise and she could feel a stinging pain, followed by the taste of a trickle of blood seeping into her jaw. Her mouth was numb and for the moment she was not capable of speaking.

She saw the man withdraw a small baton-shaped object from his pocket and begin to examine what appeared to be a switch. Stamp had not wanted to use the cattle prod, certainly not in a public place. No doubt there would be awkward questions to be answered, perhaps even a few weeks inside. Still, he reflected, there was little choice. The woman had to be silenced and for the fee he was being paid for this morning's work he could handle a little trouble. 'What's your game, mate?' said a man, standing close to Stamp.

He looked to be about six foot fall, with short cropped

hair, and well-built; a motor-cycle courier, perhaps, or an athletic office worker, Stamp decided. It made no difference. He had chosen the wrong moment to play the knight coming to the rescue of a fallen damsel. With one sharp movement of his right hand he slammed the cattle prod into the man's stomach. A look of surprise lit up his face, an instinctive reaction to the high-voltage electrical charge running up through his chest and into his brain. He collapsed, stunned, on to his knees, falling to the ground. His right hand was still attached to the prod and as he fell over, his grip on the object tightened.

Two more men walked towards Stamp. 'Look what he done to Terry,' said the first. His colleague nodded and started rolling up the sleeves on his jacket. 'Shit,' muttered Stamp out loud. He could feel a blow connecting with his stomach, but it glanced aside from his hardened muscles. He had been trained to brush off much stronger men and he reckoned he could deal with these two idiots in a couple of minutes.

The trouble was, he didn't have a couple of minutes.

He could see the woman rising to her feet from the pavement and edging away, hiding behind the two young men.

Julia glanced up. It was just a few hundred yards to her destination. Spitting blood from her mouth on to the ground, she began to run.

Harry looked towards the hospital, judging the distance to his destination. Three or four hundred yards, perhaps. Not far. But someone would no doubt be waiting for him close to the entrance. It was unlikely – no, impossible – that he could make his way inside without being spotted. His enemies would capture him and that would do Cassie no good at all.

He could feel the sweat forming on his brow and the rapid beats of his heart as he contemplated the next few minutes. Time to make my move, he told himself. Steel yourself. If anything happened to her, you would never forgive yourself.

The pavement felt cold as he fell to the ground, clutching his chest, allowing a low wail to escape from his lips and contorting his face in agony. He lay there, his body writhing in pain, for what seemed an eternity but was in reality no more than twenty or thirty seconds, before a woman from one of the empty darkened shops came to ask him if he was okay. 'My heart,' Harry croaked. 'I need a doctor, now.'

'He's having a heart attack,' the woman shouted to her colleague. 'Run down to the hospital and get some help.'

From the pavement, Harry could see the woman's legs disappear down the street, moving swiftly towards the hospital. Above, the first one was running her hand across his brow, wiping away the sweat. With her fingers she began to loosen his tie and unbutton his shirt collar.

He lay still and silent for several minutes, while the woman watched over him anxiously. A small crowd had gathered by now and she had explained his condition. Several people were exchanging different ideas on heart attacks, but nobody had a clear idea what should be done. In the distance he could see two paramedics, dressed in starched green overalls and pushing a trolley, rushing down the street. The woman stepped back as they approached, clearly relieved to be handing over responsibility for the stricken man.

'I think he's had a heart attack,' she said.

Harry contorted his face some more, holding on to his chest, trying to mimic agony. A paramedic lifted him from the ground, while the other took his feet and together they started placing him on the hospital trolley. 'Just breathe as normally as possible,' the paramedic told him firmly. 'We'll have you with a doctor in a couple of minutes. It's only a few hundred yards.'

The sensation of being wheeled down the street, covered in a green regulation NHS blanket, was a strange one. Plenty of people glanced in his direction, their curiosity pricked, and most of them fell silent as he passed. Up above, Harry could see the entrance to the hospital approaching. He turned, still clutching his chest, lying on the trolley with his face down, one hand moving up towards his head. With the other he pulled the blanket up as far as it would go. By the time he reached the hospital entrance, most people watching would have assumed he was already dead.

Just another casualty on his way to the mortuary, thought Harry as the wheels of the trolley slipped inside the building. They must be coming in here all the time.

Julia ran, stumbling towards the doorway, her legs picking up speed as the grand entrance hall of Harrington's Bank drew closer, her breath tearing out of her in gasps. She could see a camera crew and a small group of journalists by the door, drinking coffee from styrofoam cups and talking to each other. They paid no attention to her. Still, she was relieved to see the cameras were switched on; nobody was going to try and attack her again and risk having it all captured on film.

She stopped for a few seconds to draw breath, once through the revolving doors, and made her way up to the desk. The receptionist recognised the name at once. She had been instructed by security to wave her straight through. 'Ninth floor,' she said, raising an eyebrow. 'Someone will be waiting for you. The lifts aren't working because of the power cut so I'm afraid you'll have to walk.'

Julia might have laughed if she could have got enough air into her lungs. She turned and saw herself in the mirror in the lobby. Her hair was matted and

384

uncombed, and her dress appeared distinctly grubby. She had managed to take a shower in the Ladies at the airport, her first in days, but sweat had been pouring from her body while she had been running and there was a smudge of blood across her mouth where the man had hit her. I don't think I'm going to make much of an impression, she reflected.

A kind of rough elation surged through her veins as she began climbing the stairs towards the ninth floor. This was a moment she had been preparing for. She had run through it in her mind a thousand times, picturing it from different angles and various points of view, replaying it again and again like a much-loved record. The details were never clear. She was not sure how or in what circumstances this moment would arrive. But the ending was always crystal sharp; a look of humiliation and shame on the faces of men who knew they were guilty and that they had been trapped.

You are as ready as you will ever be, she told herself. Just try to do your best.

Chung moved stealthily through the corridors. Nobody paid much attention to him. That was one of the things he liked about hospitals; you could move through them with ease, passing from one section to another, without anyone asking you why you were there, or what you were doing. He could just be a visitor. Or a concerned parent. No one would know and no one would think to ask.

He was unsure whether to check the children's ward or intensive care first. It did not much matter, he decided. When he had spoken to Stamp's two men placed at the doors, he had been assured that they had not seen Harry Lamb enter the building. He figured he had plenty of time to play with.

He checked the children's ward first, treading

carefully across the floor, anxious not to disturb anyone, nor to draw any attention to himself. There must have been thirty or so children there, strung out in their beds, some of them awake, a few playing with their toys, others either asleep or unconscious. Chung was not sure if he would recognise her. He had an early satellite photo to work from, but it was blurred and indistinct. She was blonde, about three, with a slightly chubby face, but that could apply to a lot of little girls. Two of the children in the ward were blonde and in the right age group. Chung checked the boards at the foot of their beds, but neither of them was his target. He would have to carry on looking.

The intensive care ward, several corridors away, was easier to search. The bulk of the people were old, many of them very old, and they played no part in his calculations. He glanced along the ward, then checked the private rooms. None of the occupants fitted the description he was looking for. 'Do you know where I can find Cassandra Lamb?' he asked a passing nurse. 'A small blonde girl.'

'And you are?' asked the nurse briefly.

'Her godfather,' replied Chung softly. 'Her father could not be here today.'

The nurse consulted a set of papers she was carrying, before looking back up at Chung. 'She is being operated on at the moment,' she said. 'Theatre eight. You can wait in the room down the corridor.'

A smart young flunkey in a neat pin-striped suit was waiting by the staircase, pacing the corridor nervously, staring at his watch. He eyed Julia cautiously as she walked through the doors, looking behind her to see if there was someone else. 'I thought there were two of you,' he said hurriedly.

'Just me,' replied Julia firmly. 'Shall we go?'

He accompanied her down the corridor, hesitating slightly outside the crisis room before opening the door and steering Julia inside. Fielding stood up, walking across to meet her, taking her arm and looking up at the flunkey, a question in his eyes. 'I think I know who you are,' he said. 'But where's Lamb?'

'There has been a change of plan,' replied Julia softly. 'Harry will be here as soon as he can. I know as much as he does. I think I can handle this.'

She began to cast her eyes around the room. In the far corner, she noticed Mitchell, who nodded towards her and smiled, a smile that seemed to communicate genuine relief. She saw Gregson, scribbling something furiously on a notepad; he glanced sideways, his eyes cold and malicious, before looking back down at the table.

Then she saw Haverstone. The man was still midway through his presentation, sitting calm and immaculate, reeling out fine-sounding words about protecting the interests of everyone with a stake in the corporation. His eyes locked on to Julia and for a brief moment he froze, his expression and words solidified, his face entirely immobile. A silence hung over the room. Julia looked back, determined not to blink, not to be outstared. Haverstone fumbled slightly, looking across at Gregson. The American turned away, towards Julia, his expression darkening by the minute. Haverstone recollected himself, smiled a thin smile and looked back at his audience. 'As I was saying,' he continued. 'These proposals represent the best possible solution to the financial situation the company finds itself in.'

Julia took a seat at the back of the room, behind Fielding. Haverstone was still speaking and for now she would just listen, awaiting her time to address the audience. She scanned the faces once again. The row of a dozen bankers had clearly sensed something was amiss. They could tell from Haverstone's reaction to her arrival that this was someone he was familiar with and whom he did not wish to see. A couple cast disapproving looks in her direction, their noses wrinkling at the sight of such an unkempt and messy-looking character. Others were intrigued by her arrival. Although they could not tell what, something was clearly about to happen. Perhaps, more than one of them thought to himself, this meeting would not be so predictable after all.

A strange cast of men to appeal to, thought Julia, as she eyed the two rows of suited dummies. Not people for whom sympathy usually came naturally. Nor were they people in whose calculations justice normally played much part. They were bottom-line men; characters used to assessing everything in terms of profit and loss. Okay, she decided, play them at their own game. Use language they understand. They might not have much time to sympathise with me, but they would be quick to understand if the potential profit from supporting Haverstone were outweighed by the loss of face involved in ignoring the evidence I am about to place before them.

She had one important factor on her side, she realised. None of them was a man who would be reluctant to throw an obvious loser overboard. Loyalty was not a creed any of them was familiar with. That was to her advantage.

Haverstone wound up his speech. He had recovered some of his composure and ended confidently, putting the best gloss on his proposals that he could. He rested his hands on the table to indicate he had finished. A look of anger in his eyes told Julia he was not anticipating what was about to happen next with much pleasure. Fielding had already started walking across the room.

As he approached Mitchell, he leant over and whispered in his ear: 'Can I trust her?'

Mitchell nodded. 'I would,' he replied.

Fielding hesitated for a moment. It was, he knew, a terrible risk he was about to take. He had little idea who this woman was, or what she was about to say. He was on the point of stopping her from speaking, when, from the corner of his eye, he caught sight of Haverstone and for a brief second thought he could see through the man; his arms were neatly folded across his chest and a look of serene, implacable pomposity had descended upon his face, as if he actually believed what he had been saying for the past twenty minutes. When men start to believe themselves, they are truly dangerous, he decided. Let her speak.

'Before we move to the question and a vote,' announced Fielding, turning to address the floor, 'I would like us to listen to an alternative view of these proposals from Miss Porter.'

Julia felt a twinge of nerves as the words were pronounced; my moment has arrived, she told herself. Make the most of it. You will only get one chance.

'I don't give a fuck what she has to say,' spat Gregson. 'Let's move to a vote.'

Fielding leant forwards, resting his elbows on the table. 'You may not care, Mr Gregson, but some of the rest of us are very interested.'

'I object,' continued Gregson. 'Why don't we get the doorman in to give his opinions? Nobody can speak at this meeting unless they represent the views of one of the banks involved in the deal. You know that and if you let her speak you can expect to find yourself in court.' Gregson sat back in his chair, a smug smile on his face. He noted a couple of approving nods around the table.

Julia could feel her confidence drain away from within. Perhaps Gregson was right, she thought. It was a technicality, but it could prevent her from speaking. And all of this would have been for nothing.

'True, but I believe Miss Porter is speaking on behalf of a Mr Lamb who works for me,' said Fielding gently. 'He is an employee of Harrington's Bank. Has been for many years.'

Gregson looked up. 'No he isn't. You sacked him.'

'Possibly,' drawled Fielding slowly. 'But on the usual terms of six months' gardening leave, during which he remains on the payroll and so counts as an employee of this bank. She speaks with my authority.'

Gregson sat back in his chair, glancing down at the floor, avoiding eye contact with anyone around the table. The other bankers merely nodded knowingly; Fielding, they knew, was technically correct and none of them felt minded to challenge the wishes of the chairman of the committee. That was not how the game was played.

Fielding walked back towards the head of the table, leaning down. 'Are you ready?' he asked in a low voice, his face grave.

'I think so,' replied Julia, aware that her voice was fractured and nervous.

Fielding turned back towards the table. 'Miss Porter will have the floor for a few minutes,' he announced. 'I suggest we listen to what she has to say.'

Harry lay immobile on the trolley for what seemed an eternity, but was probably no more than a couple of minutes. The nurse had been quite sharp with him and he figured it would not be long before he was discovered. What might happen then he had no idea and no desire to find out.

After the paramedics had rushed him through the hospital lobby they had taken him straight to the emergency casualty section, shouting to one of the staff that he had suffered a heart attack. A nurse had immediately appeared at his side, reaching down to feel his chest and holding his wrist in her hand. Within about thirty seconds the look of anxiety on her face had been deflated. 'Your heartbeat is pretty fast, but you'll live,' she said. 'Just wait here and we'll have a doctor with you in a few minutes.'

Once they know you're not about to conk out, they lose interest, thought Harry to himself. A doctor would probably be able to tell in an instant that there was nothing wrong with his heart and would throw him straight out. He peered up from the trolley, waiting for his moment. Finally, the nurses all seemed to have vanished and he was surrounded only by a collection of sick and sorry-looking patients. Slowly, he clambered from the trolley, glad to have his feet back on the ground. Looking around him once again to check he had not been seen, he walked casually out of the room and down one of the corridors.

Time to find Cassie, he told himself. Her operation might well be over by now.

Julia could feel the blood pumping furiously through her veins as she stood up and approached the desk. She tried to straighten her dress and ran her fingers through her hair, but she knew it did almost nothing to improve her appearance. Kick right in, she told herself. This is no time for half-measures. It's do or die. You have rehearsed this already. Stick to your guns and don't let them deflect you.

'I guess this is a long story, but it starts from a very simple point,' she began, shifting slightly from one foot to the other as she spoke. 'That this deal is not so much a financial reconstruction of Cable Media as a massive heist. A fraud, perpetrated on you, the lenders, by two of the men in this room, Richard Gregson and Samuel Haverstone.'

Well, Julia thought to herself, if nothing else I've grabbed their attention. A couple of the bankers were looking towards her, their mouths slack-jawed. Others were turning to Haverstone who, impressively, had cast his face in stone and was sitting impassively, tapping his signet ring furiously on the table top.

'It begins from the point that Cable Media is not in a financial crisis at all. It has been spending too much money, mainly on its satellite systems, for reasons I will get to in a minute. But the situation has been made to appear much worse than it is. The company deliberately pushed itself into a crisis in order to provoke this reconstruction. Why? Because through Richard Gregson's firm the debt is being bought on the cheap. Once this deal goes through the owners of that debt find it has been converted into equity and the two men who have been buying the debt end up controlling the company for a fraction of its real worth.'

Julia paused. She had their attention now; none of them was looking at Haverstone. They were staring in her direction, bound up in the drama of the moment, wondering where she was heading. To the proof, she decided. Without hard evidence they would soon lose interest.

'The plot has been simple but the execution complex,' she continued. 'The satellite system has been expensive to build not just because it is a sophisticated piece of technology, but because it has other purposes from those advertised. It's not just there to broadcast TV channels and to run telecoms systems. It is also a massive spying system, using military technology for civilian and criminal ends. The company is using the satellites, deliberately and precisely, to spy on people. In particular, on people like you.'

Julia took a sip of Fielding's glass of water. 'The Serious Fraud Office has been investigating a massive insider dealing ring, one which racked up profits of more than a billion pounds, by trading ahead of corporate take-overs,' she continued. 'The data was collected by using the satellite system and by eavesdropping on telephone conversations, to create perfect information on everything that was happening in the City.'

Julia let the sentence hang in the air, partly for effect, partly to collect her thoughts. She looked directly towards the far end of the table, noting the whispered conversation between Gregson and Haverstone. Face them down, she told herself. 'The money made from that operation is controlled by Richard Gregson and Samuel Haverstone. They have been using it to buy up the debt of Cable Media which, if this proposed deal is allowed to go through, will give them effective control of the company. In effect they are stealing it.'

'This is slander,' interrupted Haverstone. 'Nothing but slander.' His face was red; the blood was pumping furiously through his veins by now and his skin was flushed with anger. 'You, madam,' he continued, looking at Julia, 'can expect to find yourself in court. And you,' he added, his finger swivelling towards Fielding, 'can expect to be sued as well for permitting these outrageous allegations to be made. I demand an apology.'

Julia strode down the room, moving closer to Haverstone, and she noticed the man back away as she approached him. 'You have my apologies for being here, sure, and for inconveniencing you with a small blast of reality,' she said, her tone rising as she spoke. 'You have my apologies for blinding your thugs so that they couldn't kill us before we made it to this meeting. And I trust I have your apologies for trying to kill me and Harry Lamb, and for putting his daughter in hospital.'

'This is ridiculous,' spluttered Haverstone. 'It is unendurable that I should have to listen to it.'

'I suggest it is intolerable that you have been cocooned in power for so long that you have been flattered and deceived into thinking you can get away with anything,' snapped Julia. She turned on her heels, forcing herself to take a breath to calm down, to regain control. 'You asked for proof,' she continued. 'Fair enough. I have with me a set of accounting records that I think will bear out what I've been saying.'

Julia walked to the back of the room and retrieved one of the two bags she had carried with her. She unzipped the holdall and took out a sheaf of papers they had photocopied while they were spending the night at the airport – a flow of funds diagrams, showing how the money collected by the insider dealing ring had been transferred into a series of offshore companies owned by Gregson and Haverstone, transferred back to London and poured into buying up the debt of Cable Media via Gregson's firm.

She had saved two sets of documents for Gregson and Haverstone and now approached them slowly and laid the sheaves of paper in front of them carefully and with deliberate precision. Both men tried to look disdainful, but at the same time they were anxious to see what was contained within the papers.

'Have you tried calling your hired gun?' asked Julia, with what she knew was a smirk. Haverstone did not reply, but his face betrayed his curiosity. 'Because I think you'll find he's been disconnected,' she added.

28

The return of the electricity took Lykanov by surprise. He had been sitting alone for the past ten minutes, enjoying the darkness, keeping track of his surroundings only by the pale orange light of his Marlboro. The screen and the computers had been on for so long now that he was almost glad they had been switched off. He was tired of their incessant glow, and of the constant demands made upon him. You can probably buy loyalty, he thought to himself. But not with the currency they were offering. He would, he decided, be glad to see the back of them.

He looked idly down at his screen. The satellites had been running all through the morning, as he knew they would have. They had indeed traced their target. A flashing icon on the side of his computer was telling him an identification had been made, more than half an hour ago now. A punch on the keyboard showed him Julia had been identified leaving the tube station and making her way through the chaotic streets towards the headquarters of the bank. She was last seen stepping inside. Another set of pictures was of Harry in the streets surrounding the hospital; the last one displayed him on the ground clutching his chest. So they made it,

Lykanov thought to himself. Good for them. They were worthy opponents.

He scrolled forward. Chung had not said where he was going. After a fit of fury, during which Lykanov had briefly feared for his own safety, he had merely slumped back in his chair, cigar smoke surrounding his face, remaining silent. Then he had risen and departed, without uttering a word. Lykanov doubted he would ever see him again, but had not felt minded to say goodbye.

One of the satellites was trained on the hospital, programmed to observe the place around the clock. Lykanov punched a couple of commands into the computer. For the satellite to locate Chung's car and come up with a location took almost three minutes. When the target appeared on the screen, the car having been identified while sitting in traffic, it was not hard to work out the destination. There could only be one place he was going.

Lykanov stretched and walked towards the phones that had been ringing for the last few minutes. He selected one that was briefly silent and put a call through to Fulham police station. An attack was taking place, he told the officer on duty, on a small girl called Cassandra Lamb at the Chelsea and Westminster Hospital. They must send some officers as soon as possible.

The game is up, he told himself. There is no point in playing any more – at least, not for the same side. Carefully, he replaced the phone, stubbed out his cigarette and walked to the back of the room. He took his coat from the stands, pulling it over his shoulders and glanced briefly through the dim and sparse bunker. I have spent enough time underground, he told himself. My wallet is full and my conscience is clear. It is time to leave.

Julia paced the centre of the room, watching while

dozens of eyes scanned through the documents laid out on the table; from their expressions, she could tell they were consuming the information feverishly, but were not yet sure what to make of it. It was so far beyond their usual experiences that they were, for the moment, bewildered, waiting for someone to give them a lead. Right now, they were not sure what they were meant to believe. Except that this deal was not going to be resolved quickly, certainly not today. The minutes appeared to tick by slowly, painfully and agonisingly slowly, while a silence hung over the room.

'What the fuck is this all about?' asked Gregson eventually, his voice shattering the uneasy quiet. 'Call this proof? I've never seen such an unconvincing pile of dangerous speculation. Who are we going to believe here? The word of one of the most respected businessmen in the world today, or some jumped-up slut with a personal grudge, who can't even find the time to wash her face.' He stared directly at Julia while he pondered the next line. 'You want to fuck with me, honey, you are going to need bigger tits than those.'

Gregson was leaning back as he talked, pushing his chair away from the table, speaking in his most authoritative voice. Macho bluster, thought Julia at once. Ridiculous and banal. Just what she would expect from the man: an appeal to the natural deference to seniority and to the tribal instincts of self-preservation, which came naturally to senior bankers. And personally very insulting. 'You dispute my analysis?' she asked calmly.

'Sure I fucking dispute it,' replied Gregson. 'I've seen ten-dollar whores fake it more convincingly. This is nothing but a bunch of speculation. You haven't got one hard fact here. Who says these offshore accounts exist? Who says these companies exist? Who says this money has gone this place or that place? Who says these fucking

satellites exist, or that they can do what you fucking sa
they can do? Who says this is anything more than
fantasy?' He paused, looking directly at Julia. 'Who say
this isn't just a set-up by one of the company's com
petitors? Who says you aren't being paid, and hand
somely, to destroy this company? From my experienc
I'd say you were a pretty mercenary character. After all
it's your boyfriend who's been trading this debt for th
past few months.'

'To collect information, Mr Gregson,' said Juli
coldly. 'Nothing more, nothing less.'

She glanced around the room; the point had struc
home and, though Julia knew she was right, it had
muddied the water, the audience was now less sure tha
they should side with her. Gregson's intervention wa
swaying them and it would only take a few votes to giv
him the majority he needed.

'Whatever,' snarled Gregson. 'I say we ask Sam her
whether he agrees or disagrees with these allegation
and if not, I suggest we move right on to a vote. This i
all very provocative stuff, but it has nothing to do wit
what we've been called here to decide.'

Fielding looked down the table at Haverstone. 'Wha
do you have to say?' he asked softly.

Haverstone collected himself, straightening his back
wiping away a trace of moisture from his brow, an
turned his eyes coldly on the men seated around th
table. 'I deny every one of these allegations,' he sai
firmly. 'There is not a word of truth in any of it.'

Fielding looked at Julia. 'What about you, Mis
Porter?'

'You have my word,' insisted Haverstone, his cheek
puffing up as he spoke. 'I would have thought tha
would be good enough.'

Fielding smiled. 'I still think we should hear th
response,' he said softly.

Julia stood still for a moment, folding her arms across her chest. Haverstone's denial was impressive, delivered with perfect composure and authority. But it was also dumb; a direct lie to the committee would start to count against him soon. 'I wonder,' she asked, 'whether the committee would rather hear from another executive at Cable Media?'

'The operation has been a success,' said the doctor to the man who had introduced himself as Cassie's god-father. 'She's a strong kid. She'll need a few days' rest, but she's going to be just fine.'

A white-robed porter was already wheeling the anaes-thetised child through the corridor, back in the direction of the intensive care ward. Chung looked down, noting the bald patch on the top of her scalp and the stitches where the surgeon had operated. His lips spread in a thin, cold smile. 'You have been so kind,' he said slowly.

'She should be awake quite shortly. She might feel a little bruised, but otherwise she should be okay.'

'May I stay with her for a little while?' asked Chung. 'I am not sure she ought to be alone when she wakes up and her father is unfortunately detained this afternoon.'

The doctor looked disapproving; what could possibly detain her father from being here while his daughter was being operated on? she thought to herself. Some people hardly deserve to have children. 'It's against regulations, really,' she said hesitatingly. 'But check with the matron on the ward. It should be all right.'

Chung followed the trolley through the corridor, keeping a couple of paces behind as it was wheeled through the hospital. The porter stopped outside one of the intensive care rooms, lifting Cassie in his arms and transferring her gently to the bed. Chung stood at the window and watched while a nurse came into the room and started arranging Cassie in the cot, pulling the sheets over her small body. The nurse checked her pulse, before folding her hands beneath the sheets. She turned to leave. Chung tapped her on the arm. 'The matron said I might sit with her for a few minutes.'

The nurse looked up at him and smiled. 'I suppose so, but be quiet,' she said. She turned to look at Cassie before glancing back at Chung. 'She's a lovely little girl isn't she?'

'The best.' Chung's smile was reassuring. 'Thank you very much.' He stepped quietly into the room. They were alone now, just the two of them. He looked down at the small sleeping body, her head turned slightly on the pillow, her eyes closed. A shame, really, he thought to himself. But I must do what is necessary.

He looked out of the window, checking the corridor. To one end a couple of porters were chatting, but otherwise no one was around. Nobody will see or hear a thing; I can complete this task and be out of here within a few minutes. An anaesthetised victim was the perfect prey, he reflected. She wouldn't even squeal when the blow struck. She wouldn't feel a thing.

He turned from the window, standing by the bed, looking down, noting the slow rise and fall of her chest as she slept. His hand slipped inside his jacket pocket. The knife sprang to life, glistening under the stark light of the room. He ran his finger along its edge, enjoying its sharp ferocity. He glanced back up to the corridor. There was no sign of her father. No matter, he told himself. Once he had the girl, the father would be his. To control as he liked.

'Hold it right there,' shouted a voice.

Chung looked up. Two uniformed policemen were standing in the doorway, one moving quickly towards him. His eyes darted over the scene. Outside he could see two more policemen, both in black jackets and carrying heavy guns slung across their chests. To the back he could see Harry arriving from the distance, running, his jacket trailing behind him, his face red and haggard, his breath failing.

He looked down. One lunge was all it would take. The blade started to move in his fist, but his hand was shaking. It moved down, slower than he would have liked, catching the policeman on the arm as he hurtled towards him. Blood spurted from the wound, dripping on to the white bedsheets.

Chung fell, knocked over by the bulk of the policeman landing on top of him. His head began to spin as his neck was twisted back. A searing pain ran down his spine as the second policeman twisted his arms savagely behind him. From somewhere he could hear a dull, straining sound, as one of his shoulder muscles was torn. He opened his eyes slowly, in time to see two guns point at his chest and a pair of handcuffs being whipped out of the policeman's jacket. He felt the snap of cold steel against his wrists and through the doorway he could see Harry's feet rush into the room. If the policeman had not been holding him so tightly he would have recoiled as he watched the black shoe slamming fiercely into his chest.

'You cunt,' muttered Harry out loud. There was just time for one kick; an instinctive and emotional reaction that Harry would later feel good about. He turned from the man on the floor and looked towards the bed, gasping as he saw the wet, crimson stains on the sheets. He tugged the bedclothes away, looking down at Cassie, pulling away her night-gown, inspecting her for wounds. As he saw there were none, he hugged her tightly to his chest. 'Thank God,' he whispered, wiping a mixture of tears and sweat away from his cheeks. He laid Cassie back down on the bed gently and pulled up the sheet over her body. Her breathing and pulse seemed normal. She looked fine.

Behind him, the policeman had already lifted Chung to his feet and had started leading him out of the room. Harry watched him leave. He was bruised and his head was down, staring blankly at the floor, yet he could recognise him all the same: it was the man they had heard in the tunnel, taunting them into submission; the man who had tried to murder both him and his daughter. 'Looks like you picked on the wrong guy,' said Harry, looking up at Chung, a glint of triumph in his eyes.

Chung turned away. 'Perhaps,' he said softly, noting the sour taste of his own blood at the back of his throat. 'But you would have died a coward, like all the rest.'

Harry thought for a moment, but remained silent. There was nothing more to say.

The moment she mentioned that she had evidence from another Cable Media executive Julia could tell she had recaptured their attention. The initiative now lay with her. Even Gregson looked startled, leaning forward suddenly on the table, and Haverstone was casting an anxious glance in the direction of the window.

'Another executive?' asked Fielding.

'Sure,' answered Julia slowly. 'An informant of impeccable credentials. In fact, the chairman of the company.'

A slow smile spread over Haverstone's face, knowing and calculating. 'But I am the chairman of the company,' he insisted.

Julia smiled. 'Forgive me,' she said, the confidence starting to return to her voice. 'A slip of the tongue. I meant to say the former chairman of the company.'

'The former chairman is dead.' Haverstone's firm tone was slowly turning into a whine.

'As you of all people would know.' Julia turned towards her audience. 'Sir Ian Strang is dead, as many of you will be aware. Fortunately, he left a message on a website before he died, which I believe is most illuminating.'

Already, she had started opening up the laptop she had brought with her. She plugged in the mobile and started putting through a connection to the Internet. Sitting down, she tapped the keyboard, finding the site he wanted. There was a hush within the room, a sense of anticipation. The bankers placed their elbows on the table, resting their faces in their hands, as they leant forward, straining to get a better view of the twelve-inch laptop screen. At the back of the room, Haverstone was clicking his finger-nails nervously on the table top. Gregson was casting suspicious glances in the direction of Mitchell who, by now, had a notebook on his lap and was scribbling.

Julia stood back as the screen flickered gradually to life, turning first red then blue, as the pixels adjusted to the commands feeding down the modem. The video software sprang into action and the image of an old man, grey and wrinkled, came gradually into focus. Julia clicked 'play' on the mouse and turned the volume on the loudspeaker up to maximum.

'Anyone viewing this will be watching a dead man, so thanks in advance for any tributes or commiserations that may have come my way after my demise,' started the video. 'I have set a long time delay on this site, with the help of some of the Cable Media technical boys, and I plan to erase it if by any chance I survive the next few days, which somehow I doubt. They say dead men tell no tales, but I guess this is the exception.'

Julia bent over the machine, adjusting the focus and zooming the frame, so that just the face of Sir Ian was visible on the screen. The lines on his face and the tiredness in his eyes were stark and unmissable, as his lips ground out the words. 'I was chairman of Cable

Media for just about six months, following the merger of the company I ran, with Samuel Haverstone's telecoms business. At the time it struck me as a good deal, although it was made under pressure from Haverstone's team. As the months passed, my suspicions about Haverstone grew deeper and deeper. He seemed to me a man obsessed by the power and reach of modern communications technology. He wanted – no, let's say wants – to own everything. For Haverstone it was nothing to do with business. It was about power and it was about control.

'Enough generalisations. Over the last months of my time at the company I became increasingly suspicious about the money we were spending, both on the new satellites we were building, but also on the telecoms systems. It seemed far more than any of the estimates I had seen for the amounts this sort of technology should cost. I started poking around the accounts department and talking to the technical boys, the way a chairman should. Haverstone didn't like it and told me to back off. Relations between us worsened, so much so that in the last weeks of my life we were not even speaking to each other.

'I see why, now. In the last few days I have discovered why we were spending so much money and why Haverstone wanted to keep so much of the technology secret. It turned out that our telecoms systems included complex software that allowed the company to monitor and listen to pretty much any conversation that flowed through the systems. I discovered Haverstone has been doing that for years, although advances in software technology, particularly in the area of voice recognition, have enabled him to do it a lot better in the last couple of years. But that is not all. I also found out that the satellites we are building, as well as being able to broadcast TV channels and transmit phone conversations, have been furnished with cameras. Haverstone has been buying in the equipment from around the world, some from Russia, some from China, some from Japan and America. There is plenty on the market if you know where to look and have enough money. These are, in effect, spy satellites, the first to be built and controlled in civilian rather than military hands.'

Julia glanced around the room; she had seen this speech a couple of times now and was already familiar with it. But this was the first time she had seen its effect on another audience and she scanned the faces searching for their reaction. She could tell from the rapt and silent expressions that every word was being listened to with mounting horror. There was little chance, she decided, of Haverstone escaping now.

'I don't quite know why Haverstone wants this technology or what he plans to do with it. I do know, however, that what he is doing is wrong and that he has to be stopped. I went to see him and I told him that I planned to have him removed as chief executive of the company. To say he lost his temper would be an understatement. Haverstone is a vain and boastful man, basically a voyeur and a bully with a bad power fixation, and he did not take well to the idea. To cut a long and nasty story short, he told me he would do anything to keep control of Cable Media. If that included killing me, so be it. I must say, I believed him.

'I am an old man, I've had a good innings and I don't care too much what happens to me. But I do care what happens to my company and about making sure Haverstone is stopped. In the course of my investigations I discovered it would be dangerous to go either to the government or the police. Over the course of years of eavesdropping on telephone conversations and now with the satellites, Haverstone has built up an incredible library of dirt on everyone of any importance.

He knows all their secrets and does not hesitate to use them to make sure they carry out his will. Remember, this is a man who, through his control of the right technology, knows the truth about just about everyone and the truth is often not a very pleasant thing. He has done a deal with elements in the security services that would allow them access to the satellites in return for protection. In effect, he has made himself, or thinks he has, above the law. He no longer worries what rules he breaks. They mean nothing to him.

'I have decided that the best way to defeat him is to use my influence in the City to get enough of the shareholders together to vote him off the board. Haverstone is just a manager; he controls the company, but he does not own it.'

Julia glanced down the table towards Haverstone. The man was leaning forward, watching the screen, some twenty feet away, with fascination and dread. His face was drained and pale, but at the same time transfixed; there was no way he could drag himself away from the story that was unfolding before him.

'I have so far told nobody what I know. My plan is to flee, to go somewhere secret and to gather enough support among the shareholders to get rid of Haverstone once and for all. If anyone is watching then it is, of course, because I have failed, or because his henchmen have got to me first. Either way, it will be up to others to make sure Haverstone is stopped. My hope is that this testimonial will in some small way contribute towards preventing him advancing any further.'

There was a slight nod in the direction of the camera, almost jaunty, then the video started to crackle. It faded, disappeared from view, leaving only a silence in its wake. A silence that hung stiffly over the room. Nobody budged, but several pairs of eyes moved slowly down the table, fixing their gaze upon Haverstone.

Harry was cradling Cassie in his arm, running his hand across her brow. The doctors had assured him she had pulled through the operation fine, there was nothing he need worry about. She required rest and to recuperate for a few weeks to rebuild her strength, but she should make a full recovery. He believed them, he supposed, but he wanted to see it in her eyes; to have her smile and laugh again, the way she had always done before. He would have to wait for the anaesthetic to wear off before he could know for sure he had her back again. The doctors wanted her left to rest, he knew.

He looked at his watch. It was already getting close to one and Julia would have been in the meeting for almost an hour now. He had told her he would be there as soon as possible. He made a decision.

Leaving Cassie under police guard, ten minutes later Harry climbed into a waiting squad car. He hoped he would make it there in time. Much as he hated to leave his daughter, he knew he had to be at the meeting. Cassie would be safe enough now and he would return to her as quickly as possible.

The car pulled up at the kerb outside the Harrington headquarters sooner than Harry had thought possible. He thanked the policeman and, stepping out into the street, swept past the small group of bored-looking reporters and presented himself at reception. 'Harry Lamb,' he said hurriedly, 'I'm expected at a meeting.'

The lady at the desk nodded. 'Ninth floor,' she said, handing him a pass. 'You can take the lift.'

It took several minutes for Haverstone to regain his composure, but when he did so the transformation was sudden and complete. His head had been bowed as he watched the video of Sir Ian Strang, as though he could not bear to look, and he seemed to shrink, as though he were gradually being deflated. But then his head rose and his eyes swivelled along the boardroom table, fixing a cool glare on each man in turn. Finally they rested on Julia and for a moment she could taste the venom in his soul. 'You have proved nothing of consequence, young lady,' he said coldly.

At first Julia could not believe her ears. Nothing. The word rattled through her head. Surely she had demonstrated what Cable Media had been doing, on his orders, and why he had to be stopped. 'I think I've proved you are a liar and a criminal,' she said firmly.

Haverstone's head shook slowly and an amused smile started to play upon his lips. 'Your insults mean nothing to me, nor do the wild allegations of a dead old man,' he replied, his left hand waving through the air. 'Even if Sir Ian were right, show me the law that says I have done anything illegal.' He stood up and walked across to the window, gazing down on the street below. 'Any of you may feel free to join me,' he said, turning back to his audience. 'Unless of course you want this lady to accuse you of committing a crime. After all, what is the difference between looking down from a window and peering down from space?' He paused, returning to his seat. 'Nothing except distance. The company is guilty of no crime. I suggest we move straight to a vote.'

'Too fucking right,' interrupted Gregson. 'Let's vote right now and get this shit out of the way. Unless a crime has been alleged, there is no basis for delaying a decision.'

Julia was left momentarily dumbfounded; her head was spinning and no words would form in her mouth. I have fired all my missiles, she thought to herself. There is no ammunition left. Surely, they can't believe they can get away with this. Yet, as she surveyed the faces around the room she could tell they were looking undecided. Unless she could think of something else she couldn't be sure of winning this battle.

'How about murder? Would this committee accept that as a crime?'

Julia spun on her heels, recognising Harry's voice instantly. He was standing in the doorway and she knew she had never been more pleased to see him.

Taking his place at the head of the table, he cast a long sweeping glance around the room. 'There's more, if you want to see it,' he said.

'Go ahead,' replied Fielding firmly. 'I believe we need to see everything.'

Harry walked swiftly down the room, passing the silent bankers, stopping a couple of feet from where Haverstone was sitting. He leant forward, resting his hands on the table, bending down to the man, so that his mouth was just an inch away from his ear. He was so close he could smell the sweat and fear on his skin. 'You are not the only person in the world with a taste for hidden cameras,' he said coldly. 'Now watch this.'

Harry turned on his heel, walking back to the laptop. He took the mouse in his left palm and moved forward to a different section of the same site, keying in a password and pressing play. 'Sir Ian, it appears, had been talking to some of the technicians,' he announced, addressing the gathering, his tone calm and confident. 'He took along with him, when he fled, a small automatic video camera, which he hid on one of the beams of the building he was staying in. The camera was hooked up to a modem, which transmitted the images on to the same website where he had stored his message. It was lucky he did so, because the camera was destroyed in the fire. But the film of what happened was already stored away on a computer and that of course was unharmed.

The video started rolling. It was poorly captured footage, black-and-white and grainy, made worse by being transmitted over the Internet, but the pictures were still visible. The camera had been located high up and had a wide-angled lens, allowing it to picture most of the room, but curving the space it was viewing and turning it into a kind of sphere. A fire burning in the grate could be spotted, alongside two figures, one old, one young, one male and one female.

Julia leant forward. This was the first time she had seen this, and she was both appalled and grimly fascinated by the scene that was about to unfold. Her hand gripped Harry's, holding it tight, and she could feel moisture on his palms. She was aware he had seen this footage before, yet knew it must be hard for him to witness it again. The film sped forward. The old man was clearly Sir Ian. He could be seen standing up and opening the door to an oriental man, his face captured in rough but clear detail by the camera. A conversation was taking place, but no words could be heard. The film recorded only pictures, not sound.

The room was still as the bankers watched the small, grainy figures move around one another. Several members of the audience turned away as the oriental man bludgeoned Sir Ian to the floor, then deliberately killed the young woman. Few could escape the sight of the old man being beaten to death. They looked on as the man doused the room with alcohol, carefully setting it alight. They could see the flames start to rage, turning the two bodies to charcoal, then reaching higher. As the beam holding the camera came crashing down, the transmission stopped and the screen returned to a pale, translucent blue.

'The oriental man you just saw kill Sir Ian was this morning arrested by the police on a charge of attempted murder of my daughter,' said Harry, his tone hardening as he spoke. 'He works for Samuel Haverstone. Is that enough?'

'Is that everything, Mr Lamb?' asked Fielding.

Harry nodded, rubbing his face with his hands. He felt drained and exhausted, and he had nothing left to say. If that was not enough, then he could not imagine what else might be needed.

'As far as I am concerned,' Fielding continued, 'it is impossible for this deal to be allowed to proceed in these circumstances. Or for the current management to be permitted to remain in place. I propose the banks call in their loans immediately and start taking steps today to install new management at Cable Media. Does anyone disagree?'

There was no sign of disagreement around the table. The collection of bankers were still shell-shocked by the scenes they had just witnessed. A few raised their hands to vote the proposal through, the others just nodded. 'Shall I put you down as an abstention, Mr Gregson?' asked Fielding.

'Put me down as whatever you fucking like,' snarled Gregson, turning away.

Fielding looked up at Mitchell, standing towards the back of the room. 'I think you should take over now,' he said. 'Our work is done.'

Mitchell moved forward to the table. Harry and Julia had done their job well, he had already decided. It might take months for the case to be knocked into the kind of shape where it could be presented in court, but there was only one thing to be done now. The evidence was so strong it could not be dropped, no matter how many political favours the pair of them might be owed.

He looked down at Haverstone; the arrogance and swagger of his demeanour had departed, his stature already diminished. 'I am arresting you on charges of conspiracy to murder,' Mitchell said calmly. 'A police car will be waiting outside. You will need to be taken in for questioning. You may, of course, contact a lawyer.' He then turned towards Gregson, whose head was now

411

slumped in his hands, his elbows resting on the table. 'And I am also arresting you on conspiracy to murder and suspected fraud. There will probably be other charges as well. It may take some time to work out how many laws you have broken.'

Both men appeared shattered, broken spirits, leaning forward in their chairs, neither saying a word, or looking at each other. Haverstone's tie was loose and his face red. He did not want to face anyone and kept his eyes firmly rooted to the ground. Slowly he rose to his feet and the men seated around the table could see that his legs were trembling.

Four policemen had already been summoned to the room by Mitchell. They walked carefully towards Haverstone, taking him by the arms and leading him firmly towards the door. 'I'm glad we finally had this chance to meet,' said Harry, a smile lighting up his face, as he passed by.

Haverstone looked up, but there was nothing Harry could see in his eyes; they were blank, unrecognisable shells, emptied of everything except a hollow, relentless fear. There is nothing else I need to say to him, Harry decided. Our debts are paid in full.

Another pair of policemen rested their hands on Gregson's shoulders, demanding that he stand. He did so reluctantly, his shoulders sagging and the usual swagger in his eyes replaced by a look of bitter, ugly regret. Slowly, he began walking towards the door. 'I guess you really are a loose cannon,' he said to Harry.

Harry shrugged and smiled. 'If you wanted to play softball, you should have gone to the park,' he said, watching as Gregson was led away.

By his side, Julia slipped an arm round his shoulder. 'I think this means we won,' she said, her voice glimmering with relief.

Harry tugged her closer to his chest. 'Thanks to you,' he said.

'Is Cassie okay?'

'I think so, but I need to get back to her,' said Harry.

Slowly Cassie's eyes opened, one eyelid first, flickering, unaccustomed to the light, then the other, both eyes wide now, sleepy yet sparkling, looking around the room. 'Daddy,' she said excitedly.

Harry leant forward and kissed her lips. 'I'm here, princess,' he replied.

'Is Daddy okay?' she asked.

'Daddy's just fine,' he answered, slipping his arm tightly round Julia's waist and holding her close to his side.

'And Teddy?' she asked. 'Is Teddy okay?'

Harry smiled. 'Teddy's doing all right,' he said. 'He told me he missed you. He's looking forward to seeing you come home again.'

Cassie lifted her finger and started poking her father's nose, giggling as she did so. 'And what has Daddy been doing?'

Harry could not help laughing, a deep laugh of relief that echoed through the hospital ward. He pulled Julia closer to him and ran his fingers through Cassie's hair. 'Not much, princess,' he said with a slow shake of his head. 'Daddy has not been doing very much at all.'

Epilogue

The clatter of her feet running along the bare wooden floorboards lifted his heart. Harry shut the door behind him and knelt down, opening his arms wide. A smile crossed his lips as Cassie threw herself enthusiastically into his embrace. He held her tight, hugging her to his chest. The last year, ever since she had been home from the hospital, had been special; the knowledge of how close he had been to losing her had made every moment together precious. 'How are you, princess?' he asked.

She turned away, sucking her thumb, before swivelling to look at him. 'Pretty good,' she said. 'How's Daddy?'

'He's okay,' said Harry. 'Seldom better.'

'I've been baking a cake,' said Cassie. She reached up for the edge of Harry's jacket and began tugging. 'Come see,' she added.

Harry took off his coat, hanging it on a peg in the hallway, and followed Cassie through to the kitchen. There was quite a mess on the table; a collection of wooden spoons and trays, flours and packets of chocolate. 'Hello, darling,' he said, taking Julia in his arms and kissing her gently on the lips. 'Cassie tells me she's been baking.'

'She's been helping,' said Julia, pointing at the mess on the table.

Harry cast his copy of the *Evening Standard* on the table.

Julia could not help noticing the headline printed in thick black 72-point type. 'CABLE MEDIA BOSS SENTENCED', it read.

She picked up the paper and started reading. Samuel Haverstone had been convicted some weeks ago, after a trial that had lasted more than two months, in which both she and Harry had been called upon to testify. The charges were conspiracy to murder and fraud, and he had been found guilty on both charges. Richard Gregson had been tried alongside him, on the same charges, and he too had been found guilty. Kim Chung had been charged separately on multiple charges of murder and attempted murder, found guilty and sentenced to life imprisonment. He hanged himself in his cell less than a week after the verdict was delivered.

Her eyes scanned the story. There had been a delay of several weeks between conviction and sentencing, while various pleas of mitigation were entered by a group of highly paid lawyers. According to the newspaper, both men had received sentences of twenty-five years. The picture showed them being led away from the courtroom in handcuffs and bundled into the back of a police van. Haverstone's head was bowed, his eyes lowered, his look sheepish and afraid. Gregson's head was held high, making the most of a last show of defiance before he was led away into the van. 'It's what they deserve,' said Julia, looking up at Harry.

'At least,' he answered, his voice calm and even, yet somehow distracted.

To herself, she wondered if it would be over for him now. The last year had been among the happiest of her life. She had left the SFO and returned to her job at the consultancy; the secondment was not yet over, but it seemed pointless to carry on. Once that was done, she and Harry had taken a week away together, travelling through the French countryside, enjoying each other's company properly for the first time, though Julia, if she were being honest, might have preferred that Cassie had not come along on the trip. They had dated for a few months, seeing each other several evenings a week. Six months ago she had moved in. She loved Harry and Cassie, and she liked playing mother to the first, and wife to her father. And yet, as the trial dragged on and Harry was called to give evidence, the events of the last year seemed to weigh upon him. Although he was usually resilient and cheerful, at moments he was distant and cold, as if he could not quite forget what had happened to them.

Perhaps, now that it was finally over, that the last act had been played, he would be able to put it behind him. 'How did they take it in the office?' she asked.

'Everyone was fascinated, as you can imagine,' said Harry.

It was a few weeks after the final meeting, while Harry was still relaxing and wondering what he should do with his life, that he had had a call from Malcolm Fielding. The Harrington chief had taken him out to dinner, to thank him, so he said, for all the work he had done for the bank. All the people, he assured him, who had been involved in the insider dealing ring at Croxley, Palmer had been sacked; Trimble, he felt confident to say would never work in the City again, although there was unlikely to be enough evidence to press any charges against him. That was all in the past now, Fielding told him. The real purpose of the dinner was to offer him a job as part of the team appointed by the bank to run Cable Media. After all, Fielding pointed out, few people knew the business better.

The offer had been too good for Harry to resist; the dark irony of his becoming one of the few people in charge of running Haverstone's domain was too delicious and the prospect of dismantling his empire too tempting to pass up. He knew Haverstone would read about it in his prison cell and that was exquisite revenge.

'They all thought it was a fair sentence,' Harry continued. 'We watched it live on TV and some off us had a book running on how long he would get.'

'Still no mention of the engineer?' asked Julia.

Harry shook his head. Plenty of things had come to light at the trial. There had been no mention of the support given to Haverstone in the plans by the security services; they, predictably, had run for deep cover as soon as the scandal broke and the prosecutors had not wished to raise their involvement. Nor had there been any mention of the man from whom Haverstone had purchased his surveillance expertise; he had vanished into thin air and had not been heard from since. 'Nothing,' he replied. 'Just as well. That guy, whoever he was, deserves some kind of break.'

'Perhaps we'll hear from him one day,' said Julia.

Harry smiled. 'Somehow I doubt it.'

From the sitting room, Julia could hear the sound of the CD player, the noise drifting through the house. She hugged him again, as the lyrics and the music seemed to curl around them and her brown eyes looked up to meet his. 'It's just you, me and Cassie now. Nothing else matters.'

Gently, Harry ran a finger through her hair, gazing into her eyes. As they shut, he kissed both eyelids softly. 'You're right,' he said. 'And, after all, we won.'

Also by Matthew Lynn

INSECURITY

Jack Borrodin has a new job. He thinks he is just one step away from a seat on the board of one of the country's largest pharmaceutical companies.

Tara Ling has a new job. An expert in leprosy, she has been hired by Jack's company to work on creating a vaccine against a deadly new virus.

Outwardly a respectable conglomerate, the closer to its core Jack and Tara get, the more rotten it appears. Framed for crimes they did not commit, Jack and Tara have two weeks to strike back at the company that deceived them. Unless the company strikes them down first

'Insecurity does to high finance what Jurassic Park did to extinct species. Lynn has created a near-perfect thriller...he wraps a big idea inside an all-action plot' *Sunday Express*

'A rattling yam in the best traditions of the classic thriller... an excellent debut' *The Times*

Also available in paperback

SCALPEL
Paul Carson

A killer is stalking the corridors of Dublin's Central Maternity Hospital.

A young laboratory assistant is found brutally murdered at her bench. The only clue is a blood-stained scalpel. The police investigation, led by DS Kate Hamilton, is blocked by a wall of silence from hospital staff, desperate to protect their reputations. DS Hamilton suspects the murderer is among them. As she closes in on the killer, she little realises that the hunter has become the hunted.

In the same week, the new-born baby of one of Ireland's top industrialists is kidnapped, a baby born at the Central Maternity Hospital only days before.

Will Hamilton uncover the killer before he gets to his next victim?

Will the police find the baby before it's too late?

Every patient's nightmare is about to come true.

'As bad a baddie as Hannibal Lecter...a fast pace and an energetic storyline' *Irish Times*

'Thoroughly enjoyable... Paul Carson is a name to watch.' *Dublin Evening Herald*

'An undeniably compelling chiller' *GQ*

ROGUE ELEMENT

Terence Strong

The Sunday Times Top Ten bestseller

For twenty dangerous years he has worked undercover for Britain's Security Service. Then MI5 asks one favour too many, an act of personal betrayal. When he refuses, he sees his world collapse as he finds himself accused of a high-profile murder he did not commit. Yet the evidence against him is overwhelming.

Only his former comrade-in-arms believes his innocence. The SAS tracker finds himself on the trail of the most deadly adversary of all. A rogue element within the secret state.

With a crusading defence lawyer, who is as renowned for her fiery temperament as her good looks, he takes on the police, government and legal system in a harrowing attempt to prove his friend's innocence. Yet before justice can run its course, they will unearth dark secrets and a prophecy that is moving inexorably towards its devastating fulfilment.

'Remarkable' *Sunday Times*

'An extremely good topical thriller' *JackHiggins*

'The storylines are skilfully intermingled - the writing is fluid, the action furious and the political premise entertaining' Peter Millar, *The Times*

THE HOUSE OF WOMEN
Alison Taylor

Lonely, ageing and chronically ill, Ned Jones is found dead on a sweltering summer afternoon in his rooms. The doctor is unable to certify cause of death, and Detective Chief Inspector Michael McKenna and his team become involved as a matter of routine. But the post-mortem findings cast new light on what at first seemed a natural death.

Frustrated by personal and professional dilemmas, McKenna returns time and again to the house where Ned lodged, home of a distant relative, Edith Harris. But fragile, neurotic Edith, addicted to tranquillizers, and her three daughters - Phoebe, swaddled with puppy fat, driven remorselessly by her acute intelligence; Mina, nineteen, beautiful and blank-faced; and Annie, the eldest and an unmarried mother - spring one surprise after another on McKenna.

In search of Ned's killer, McKenna visits the sad remnants of the family, isolated in a decaying mountain farm, and comes into repeated contact with the unpleasant Professor Williams, whose place in Edith's life is far from clear. Slowly, McKenna begins to unravel a story of scholarship and greed, deceit and twisted loyalties, where the sins of the past, as well as the present, are avenged on innocent and guilty alike.

'Careful, complex, intelligent...unusually for a detective story, it is the characterisation and the writing, even more than the plot, that hold the attention' *Guardian*

'A gripping read if not a comfortable one - the new Alison Taylor... could put her up there with the likes of Ruth Rendell and Minette Walters' Mike Ripley, *Books*

With her third novel, *The House of Women*, Alison Taylor confirms her place among the new stars of British crimewriting' Susanna Yager, *Sunday Telegraph*